Pippa Roscoe lives in N makes daily promises to ~~~~ she'll leave the computer to take a long walk in the countryside. She can't remember a time when she wasn't dreaming about handsome heroes and innocent heroines. Totally her mother's fault, of course—she gave Pippa her first romance to read at the age of seven! She is inconceivably happy that she gets to share those daydreams with you. Follow her on Twitter @PippaRoscoe.

Tara Pammi can't remember a moment when she wasn't lost in a book—especially a romance, which was much more exciting than a mathematics textbook at school. Years later, Tara's wild imagination and love for the written word revealed what she really wanted to do. Now she pairs alpha males who think they know everything with strong women who knock that theory *and* them off their feet!

TAMING THE BIG BAD BILLIONAIRE

PIPPA ROSCOE

THE FLAW IN HIS MARRIAGE PLAN

TARA PAMMI

MILLS & BOON

First Published in Great Britain 2020
by Mills & Boon, an imprint of HarperCollins*Publishers*
1 London Bridge Street, London, SE1 9GF

Taming the Big Bad Billionaire © 2020 by Pippa Roscoe

The Flaw in His Marriage Plan © 2020 by Tara Pammi

ISBN: 978-0-263-27820-0

MIX
Paper from
responsible sources
FSC **FSC® C007454**
www.fsc.org

This book is produced from independently certified FSC™ paper
to ensure responsible forest management.
For more information visit www.harpercollins.co.uk/green.

Printed and bound in Spain
by CPI, Barcelona

TAMING THE BIG BAD BILLIONAIRE

PIPPA ROSCOE

For anyone who ever got goosebumps when they heard...
'Are you sitting comfortably? Then I shall begin.'

CHAPTER ONE

'Always stay on the path,' her grandmother had said. 'For bad things lurk in the woods...dark things, monsters and wolves.'

But Little Red Riding Hood didn't listen to her grandmother because she didn't believe in fairy tales. Deep down, she knew that the most dangerous stories were the ones we told ourselves.

The Truth About Little Red Riding Hood
—Roz Fayrer

IT WAS THE smell of coffee, as strong and bitter as his quest for vengeance, that usually heralded the beginning of Roman Black's day, not damp earth and tree bark. It was the richly carpeted floors of his office that he usually stalked at this hour of the morning, not the crunch of twigs and leaves.

The noise felt overly loud, as if the attempt to be stealthy had made him clumsy. But if there was one thing Roman Black was not, it was clumsy. Every thought, every move, every action had always held one purpose for Roman, and one purpose only. And finally, after years, the end goal was now within his grasp.

Ahead of him Dorcas, the dog he had acquired for

the express purpose of his visit here to the Occitaine region of France, loped with huge, graceful strides, occasionally stopping to cast a curious glance at its new owner, or to ferret out some invisible treasure at the base of a large tree.

Twelve hours ago, Roman had received the vital information that revealed his quarry had left a party on the outskirts of Moscow and returned to France to visit an ailing relative. Nine hours ago, he had arrived in France himself and took up residence in a small villa barely three miles from here. Seven hours ago he'd been interviewing for a canine companion at the local dog shelter—for what was more predatory than a single man alone in the woods? Let alone a man of Roman's imposing stature.

No. He had planned for this. He had worked out every possible variable. He needed to look, at the very least, non-threatening. Admittedly, he had thought to find something small and fluffy, perfect to lull his prey into a false sense of security. But Dorcas had been sitting there in the grey concrete cubicle, watching, as if she had known from the very beginning that he would come to get her. And whilst an Irish wolfhound was neither small nor fluffy, one look at her and Roman had not been able to stand the thought of such a glorious creature trapped in a cage. If he had been a more self-aware man, if, perhaps, he had had anything on his mind other than vengeance, he might have understood his decision better.

But as Roman stalked through the trees on his first reconnaissance of the woods where he knew he would find his prey—maybe tomorrow or the day after—he allowed himself to imagine the moment that victory would be his. That finally, after almost twenty years, he would make the old bastard pay for what he had done.

It was a sweet feeling, almost euphoric, rushing through his mind. Sublime in the sense that everything he'd ever wanted was nearly his, yet could easily be taken away at any moment. And it was while he was lost in that delicious imagining that Roman first laid eyes on his prey.

He stopped short. His breath stolen from his lungs.

For there she was, walking through the forest at this ungodly hour of the morning as if she'd just stepped out of the pages of his mother's favourite fairy tale. His eyes snagged on the black ball gown visible through the opening of a scarlet velvet cloak. The hood had fallen back to reveal the creamy swanlike curve of her neck, framed by tendrils of blonde hair that had escaped a complicated plaited knot. She was exquisitely beautiful. He'd known that, of course, from the photographs and extensive research he'd had his people compile. But nothing had prepared him for the effect of seeing her in person.

His swift gaze crossed her features back and forth, hunting for a blemish or flaw, but none were detectable beneath the overall impression of perfection. His pulse thrummed as he took in high cheekbones that perfectly framed an oval-shaped face, high arched brows that gave as much space as possible to large cornflower-blue eyes. Desire wound through him, as unwelcome as it was fierce, and he cursed this unexpected weakness within himself. The delicate arms holding the cloak against her waist looked almost vulnerable and for a moment he debated whether to stop, to turn back. But he knew he wouldn't.

She looked impossibly innocent—no sign of the hard edges that he had been forced to develop by her age of twenty-two years. How that had been achieved under the guidance of such a monster as Vladimir Kolikov he simply couldn't fathom, and as such cast it aside as an impossibility. Her beauty, her apparent innocence, was simply fancy dressing around one thing and one thing only.

The key to his revenge.

Exhaustion had settled deep into her bones and Ella barely knew where her feet were stepping. But years of summers spent walking the forest that bordered her grandmother's cottage had left the path indelibly inked on her mind and body. Her grandmother. Ella's heart ached, worry and grief twisting in her chest like a living thing. She had been at a party in Moscow when she'd received the phone call informing her that her grandmother had been found unconscious at the bottom of the stairs in her cottage and taken to hospital. Ella's mind had gone instantly blank and if it hadn't been for her guardian she didn't know what she would have done. He'd arranged for a car to retrieve her from the birthday party of the British Ambassador to Russia, a private jet to fly her to an airfield just outside of Limoux, and another car to take her to the hospital.

If any of the hospital staff had thought it odd that she had arrived dressed in a ball gown and velvet cloak, none had said as such. The doctor had explained that her grandmother had suffered a broken hip and fractured shoulder from the fall but the knock to her head had been what had worried him the most. Strange medical terminology, stretching her usually quite good hold on the French language, had made her want to shake the man and demand he tell her that her grandmother was going to be okay. But after nearly thirteen hours in the hospital, Claudette hadn't yet regained consciousness and the medical staff had ushered Ella out of the building to get some rest. And to change. Because if she'd looked dishevelled when she'd first arrived, Lord knew what she looked like now.

When she'd asked the taxi to stop on the other side of the woods, she'd given no thought to her clothing. Instead she'd wanted to make her way to her grandmother's cottage on the path that felt achingly familiar and yet strange and unknowable at this time in the morning. But the hems of the cloak and dress had dragged along the floor, soaking up the damp earth, making them impossibly heavy. As the material caught on twigs and thorns, Ella felt as if she were battling something physical, not just emotional, on her journey back to her grandmother's.

She pulled up short, wanting to wrench the damn thing from her shoulders, wanting to wail and shout and cry all at once. She forced herself to breathe in a long, slow breath, in and out. She had almost recovered when she heard the snap of a twig. The hairs on the skin of her arms rose in the early morning air, sending tingles and shivers down her back. Casting a glance around her, Ella's gaze snagged on something in the dense foliage and she took half a step towards the bush before she saw the gleam of yellow eyes staring at her. Before she could run, the beast crashed out of the tree cover and loped towards her in an alarmingly lazy gait that covered the distance between them in seconds and, just as it was about to pounce, she closed her eyes and—

'Dorcas, sit!'

Prising her eyes open, she watched as the massive beast careened to a halt barely a foot from Ella and sat on its hind legs, tongue lolling out of its mouth and a look of almost indescribable happiness at having found something for its master spread across its wolfish features.

An almost hysterical laugh of relief bubbled in her chest, until it caught there the moment she saw the beast's owner making his way towards her.

He was over six feet fall, more lean and lithe than broad, his every step almost graceful as he wove his way through the trees. Ella's heart thudded in her chest the moment he locked eyes with her, trapping her gaze as easily as the breath in her lungs. Longish dark hair swept carelessly around his head and hung down towards a low brow that appeared almost forbidding. Assessing eyes, squinting slightly against the pale morning sun, were a shocking shade of light blue, almost yellow, as if he shared some kinship with the animal which sat at her feet. Lips that were neither thick nor too thin made her wonder whether they would feel as perfect as they appeared to her... The fanciful thought momentarily startled her before she hungrily ate up what else she could see of him. The sharp edges of his cheekbones and jawline were strong and proud, and Ella's eyes tripped down to where the collar of his grey linen shirt peeked above a deep rich blue pullover, revealing a glimpse of the hollow that she inexplicably wanted to press her thumb to.

Ella's heart pounded in her chest. Never had a man had such an effect on her before. And never had her mind betrayed her with the errant thought that rang through her entire being.

This man is going to break my heart.

The shock and sheer ridiculousness of the thought made her shake her head, causing the figure to stop in his tracks. Ella used the brief respite to breathe. Despite his imposing stature, she couldn't sense any form of threat coming from him.

'I'm sorry about Dorcas—she gets excited when we meet other people.'

At this, the beast—*Dorcas*—decided its master's command had been lifted and she unfolded her giant frame and came close enough to nudge Ella's hand with her nose. As Ella absentmindedly stroked the huge hound, it took a moment for her tired mind to understand the source of her confusion because, although she understood him completely, she couldn't quite understand why he'd spoken in Russian.

Interpreting her confusion, the man pressed on. *'Je suis désolé, vous m'avez surpris.'*

He smiled apologetically, as if this strange encounter were his fault and not hers for walking through the woods at some awful hour of the morning dressed in... dressed in... Oh, God! Ella almost groaned, but turned it into a rueful laugh.

'Perhaps we could continue in English, if you speak it. It's been a...long day.'

'It is only six o'clock in the morning, so I must assume a *very* long day.' He looked her over and she suddenly realised that he could quite easily misinterpret the reason for her appearance, which made her think of all the reasons she *was* in the woods in a ball gown and red velvet cape after spending twelve hours by her grandmother's bedside.

The forest's dew had soaked into the cloak and, more than its heaviness, she now felt cold. Cold and hungry and tired. But as she began to shiver she realised that it was not from the damp or the temperature, but the effect of being this man's sole focus.

'Where are you going?' he asked gently, as if not wanting to scare her further.

'My grandmother's house. It's just up the path and not far.'

She braced herself as Dorcas leaned into her, almost at waist height.

'Dorcas!' the man almost growled at his dog in warning, yet the dog only answered with a playful yip before collapsing in a heap at Ella's feet and showing her belly as if to say, *Here. Rub here.*

'Stop flirting, Dorcas,' came her owner's somewhat exasperated response as he tucked the lead he'd been holding into the pocket of his wax jacket.

Ella couldn't help but smile at the interaction and it felt almost strange and unfamiliar on features that had felt so weighed down by worry and stress. She bent down to rub the massive beast at her feet and laughed as she realised that Dorcas had trapped her cloak beneath her and effectively pinned her in place. But in truth she felt more trapped by the steady gaze of the man whose name she still did not know.

'Out past your curfew?' he asked.

'I… I was at a party in Moscow when I got a phone call to say that my grandmother had been taken to hospital.'

His frown deepened and for a heartbeat Ella wondered what he might look like when not frowning. She could sense a barrage of questions building between them but he asked the most important.

'Is she okay?'

'I don't know,' she replied honestly, catching a moment of concern in his stunning eyes before something fell over them, closing off whatever she might have seen there.

'Are *you*?' he asked. Incapable of answering that question, of putting words to whatever it was she was currently feeling, she shook her head. 'We're going that way if you would like the company?' the beast's owner pressed on.

Dorcas elegantly leapt from the forest floor as if punctuating her master's query with excitement and joy, bringing yet another unfamiliar smile to Ella's features.

'Yes, that would be nice,' she replied truthfully, and suddenly she felt she might buckle under the exhaustion she'd held at bay for the last twelve hours.

'Roman,' he said, holding out his hand.

'Ella,' she replied and felt a jolt of electricity snap through her body from where her hand met his. He laid his other hand on top as if holding hers in place when she would have pulled away and, rather than feeling uncertain or awkward, she simply felt…safe.

The short journey to her grandmother's cottage passed almost in silence and Ella found herself unusually at peace in Roman's company.

They came to the edge of the forest and followed a dirt track leading towards the little chocolate box cottage that Ella loved so much. Her hand naturally went out to caress the small stone pillars either side of the short driveway, as she did every single time she came here. Almost on autopilot, she went to the large, worn wooden door and pushed it open—her grandmother never having once locked the entrance to her home. She led her strange procession of Roman and Dorcas into the house, and stopped the moment she saw the foot of the stairs where her grandmother had fallen and lain for hours before being found.

A shiver cut through her body and she had to fight hard against the urge to cry in front of a stranger who did not feel like a stranger.

The cottage was cast in darkness, the thin light in the centre of the front room doing little to dispel the early morning shadows, and she stood, blankly staring ahead until she realised that she was looking straight at Roman who, once again, seemed greatly concerned about her.

He nodded to himself once, as if coming to a decision, and turned towards the fireplace and set about building a fire from the logs and kindling beside it. All the while she stood there as if capable of no more. She certainly felt that way.

Once the fire was crackling and snapping, beautiful flames dancing and reaching towards the open damper, he came towards her and stood so close that she had to lift her head up to see his face. Some wicked sense within her wanted to lean into him. Wanted him to take her in his arms. As if sensing her thoughts, he lifted his hands.

'May I?'

She wasn't sure what he was asking for but nodded her permission anyway. She feared for a moment that she would give this stranger anything. A numbness had settled about her and she felt detached from the world about her but deeply present for the man in front of her.

His hands came together to release the clasp holding the cloak about her shoulders, and gently pushed it back and placed it aside. She shivered at the brief contact of his hands against her skin, the low neckline of her dress leaving her vulnerable to his touch. Her pulse kicked up and goose bumps prickled her skin as he guided her to the sofa opposite the fire and placed a warm cashmere blanket around her shoulders.

'Is there anyone I can call for you?'

'No.'

He seemed displeased by this answer, as if outraged by the thought of her being alone. Leaving her in the living area, he disappeared from sight and she heard the sounds of a kettle being boiled, cups and spoons being rattled and the fridge opening and closing.

When he returned to her, she marvelled at the lack of fear she felt as he loomed over her. No, most definitely not fear, but a strange yearning even she could recognise was outrageously inappropriate. Inexplicably, she wanted to reach for him, to steal some of the strength she could almost feel emanating from him.

In spite of the darkness of the cottage, Ella saw the molten heat in his eyes, felt it warm her more than any fire or flame. Heard the sharp intake of his breath, and watched with a sense of shame as he stepped back from her. Her cheeks burnt and she turned her head aside, hoping that she hadn't betrayed herself, as a curl of confused humiliation swept through her.

'I should go.'

This drew her gaze back to his, now completely shadowed by the shafts of shade in the cottage.

'How can I thank you?'

'We can figure that out next time.'

'Next time?' Ella repeated, hating that she sounded so hopeful.

'The next time we meet in the woods.'

It was two days before she saw any sign of Roman again. Two days in which her grandmother regained consciousness and underwent operations and procedures to heal her hip and the shoulder fracture resulting from the fall.

When her grandmother had first woken, she had mistaken Ella for her mother, Adeline. It had only been for a few moments, but the bittersweet cut to her heart had been deep. Her grandmother was Ella's only connection to her French mother and she hoarded any fragments Claudette had ever told her. Ella's childhood summers had been spent wandering the woods and delving deeper into the stories that her grandmother would tell of the handsome American tycoon Nathaniel Riding and the sweet innocent Adeline Ardoin who had met, fallen in love and married within months. She knew her grandmother had been heartbroken when they had relocated to Russia for Nathaniel's business and even more lost when Adeline had passed away, and Ella had been reluctant to break the spell that had returned Claudette's daughter to her, almost sixteen years after her death.

But her grandmother's sharp mind had quickly orientated itself and, with a single tear slowly tumbling down her softly lined features, Claudette Ardoin had shaken her head and apologised for being an old fool. After several meetings with doctors and medical personnel, it was clear that Claudette would be staying in hospital for at least two weeks and was highly unlikely to be able to return to the cottage and her independence that she valued so much.

It was the awful practicalities, the decisions to be made, the almost upsetting specifics of moving her grandmother into a care home that left Ella feeling a little shaken and unsettled. And with startling clarity she realised the magnitude of what her guardian had done for her as a child.

When her parents had been killed in a helicopter accident, Ella had been only five. Even all those years ago, Claudette had not been able to take her in and care for her, due to her age and minimal income, and Ella had been given over to Vladimir Kolikov, her father's business partner and closest friend. So the daughter of an American father—an only son whose parents had both died far too young—and a French mother went to live in Russia with a man who might have been a bit isolated and cold, but was more than ready and willing to give her a home, to care for her and make decisions for her. Vladimir was not the easiest of men, but Ella felt an affection there and as a child had split her time between boarding school in Switzerland, summers in France and winters in Russia.

As she prepared to leave the cottage to return to the hospital, she wondered at meeting Roman—who she had thought of a lot in the last two days. At the peculiarity of meeting a Russian in the deepest part of the South of France. Perhaps that was why she felt there was something slightly similar between her guardian and her rescuer, as she had come to think of him.

And once again she felt the painful blush of embarrassment sting her cheeks. Roman must have thought her completely incompetent. A woman who allowed a stranger into her home, watched in silence as he built a fire, made sure there was food in the fridge and went so far as to set out the makings of a cup of tea. A woman who wanted…things she should not, she concluded to herself as she grabbed her bag and opened the front door.

It was then that she saw the small parcel on the top of the steps. Casting a glance out into the woods, she saw nothing but swathes of trees with windswept leaves, enticingly cool shadowed pathways and long stretches of bluebells.

Returning her attention to the lavender-coloured tissue paper bound with brown string, she picked it up and saw a small cream tag with small, neat writing in English.

To replace what was lost.

Frowning, she picked the bow of the string apart and carefully unwrapped the package in case it might have somehow come by accident to the wrong house. The paper parted to reveal a swathe of burgundy, the softest cashmere she had ever touched. She drew out the present and marvelled at the floor-length hooded cape, by far superior to the one that had been all but destroyed by her journey through the woods two days ago.

It was exquisite and could only have come from one person. Her fingers ran down the stunning material and she was overwhelmed by the gift. Felt a heady combination of joy, surprise and excitement that Roman had thought of her and given her such a gift. Wearing it, she knew, would make her feel beautiful…but also strangely guilty. A guilty pleasure that was only surpassed by the hope that she would see him again. Soon.

* * *

Roman reluctantly turned away from the sight of Ella on the doorstep to her grandmother's cottage. Even as everything in him wanted to consume whatever sight of her he could, he ruthlessly thrust aside his base desires in favour of his true intention. He felt every inch the predator he had been forced to become to reach his desired goal. It was imprinted on his soul—it had shaped him, directed him for so many years and now vengeance was within his grasp.

He had been shocked by her innocence. Truly. Expecting to find Vladimir's ward hardened, sharp with angles by her time spent with such an evil man, instead he'd wondered at the untouched quality of her. She had, two days ago, seemed like a fairy-tale creature. It had made him forget his purpose. As if she had some magical power that had made him almost forget everything. He'd not missed how she had looked at him in the cottage. When the cashmere cloak had half slipped from her shoulder, revealing the curve of pale skin, he'd struggled with the urge to draw her near. He hadn't missed the way her pupils had dilated, casting her inky blue eyes in an unfathomable dark hue that spoke of desire and want.

Nor had he missed the blush of embarrassment as if she did not know what she was wanting. And it had been that which had broken the spell.

Her beauty was undeniable and he acknowledged, reluctantly, the small part of him that wished perhaps that things were different. But they were not. He had set about this path the moment Vladimir had signed his mother's death warrant eighteen years ago.

Searing pain gripped him hard and fast, taking him

by surprise and shocking him with its intensity. A thick, heavy grief-laden nausea swirled in his gut as if he felt that terrible blow for the first time. The horrifying blankness that had descended once he'd felt the bewildering impossibility of moving forward, of surviving without the one person in his life who had anchored him, who had loved him. It had crashed over him like a wave he hadn't already surfed. Roman struggled to breathe and forced the pressure in his chest to morph from grief to fury in a years-old practised technique.

Fury at the memory of his grandfather refusing the pleas of a thirteen-year-old boy, begging for help, for finances that would pay for the medical treatment his mother so desperately needed. Vladimir had slammed the door on him. And the consequences had been devastating.

Now Kolikov would know that same feeling. Roman wanted Vladimir to beg and plead as he had once done. Ella Riding was the *only* way he could take revenge against his grandfather. And he would take it by any means necessary.

CHAPTER TWO

There are many forms of disguise, some in cloth-
ing, some in nature, but the most dangerous of all
are those that have the thread of truth stitched
through them, making it even harder to pull truth
from fiction.

    The Truth About Little Red Riding Hood
                                    —Roz Fayrer

EVER SINCE SHE had come to France, time had seemed to
lose all meaning for Ella. Hours spent with her grandmother passed in a second—as if knowing it was running out, time raced headlong towards an impossible
finish line. Yet mere moments spent with Roman
seemed to draw out deliciously as if he held as much
command over the grains of sand in an hourglass as he
did over her body and senses.

But, more than that, in the last month he had become
her confidant, her support. She had spoken to Vladimir
on the phone, but his lack of interest in her maternal
grandmother had left her feeling strangely awkward and
isolated. Despite the initial fear for her health, the procedures and operations had gone incredibly well. But
that relief had been short-lived as Ella suddenly found

herself the only person who could, and had to, make decisions about care homes and closing up Claudette's long-lived life in the cottage.

Ella would have found it all too much to bear had it not been for Roman. He had listened to her fears, helped her talk through the visiting of various homes, advised her on how to approach her grandmother with the best on offer. Her grandmother's pension didn't cover anywhere near the amount needed and Ella had been forced to ask Vladimir for an advance on her trust fund from her parents. At the age of twenty-two, she was three years away from full access to it and the monthly stipend that had seemed more than enough simply wouldn't stretch to the beautiful care home she had found for Claudette. Only an hour away from Toulouse, it might have seemed like an extravagance—as suggested by Vladimir, who couldn't understand why 'the old crone' couldn't be left to public health care—but Ella simply couldn't wrench her grandmother away from the looming view of the Pyrenees that she had seen every morning since birth.

Ella had been surprised when Roman had happily put aside his business interests in the area to focus almost all his fierce attention on supporting her. Never before had she experienced such a thing and if she had been concerned with how quickly and how fast her dependence on him had come into her life she thrust it aside. Daily walks with Roman and Dorcas had kept her sane and forced her out of the cottage she would have sunk into and never left. Those walks had turned into evening meals where Roman would pepper her with questions about her life in seductive tones and with enticing smiles.

'So, tell me. What was little Ella Riding like?'

She spent hours sharing tales of her boarding school life, her hopes for the future, plans that she had only begun to discuss with her friend Célia. The business they wanted to develop by linking powerful industries and rich investors with charities across the globe. The home that Ella wanted one day. Roman had listened, smiling and laughing, and encouraging her fantasies of what it would look like, how many rooms, bathrooms, and how much land she would like. He had seemed to sense how important it was to her when she had tried to convey how difficult it had been growing up and feeling as if she'd never had a home of her own—her time shared between her boarding school, university, her guardian's estate in Russia and her grandmother's cottage here in France. All of which were welcoming and wonderful, but never truly hers and hers alone.

Once her grandmother had begun to rally, she and Roman began to wander further afield than the woods surrounding the cottage. It was only when she had arrived at the small airfield where a private jet waited to whisk them away to Paris for the evening that Ella realised that Roman was more than just a man of means, but someone really quite incredibly wealthy.

She was no stranger to money and had always lived with the knowledge that at the age of twenty-five she would inherit a vast trust fund from her parents. But, until that time, anything she needed had always had to be approved by her guardian or come from the somewhat conservative monthly allowance he had provided for her from that trust fund. And ever since completing her degree, ever since her return to France, Ella had begun to strain a little at the leash, envying Roman his complete freedom and control over his own destiny.

But as they had flown to Paris in Roman's private plane, as they had sat in the exquisite restaurant encased within the Eiffel Tower, a landmark Roman had mocked her for not visiting before, she had realised that for all that she had shared of herself, she knew very little about the tall, impossibly handsome man who made her heart soar and her pulse race.

'So, Roman Black. Who are you really?'

He'd explained in broad terms and simple descriptions that he hadn't always been wealthy, and that he had had to fight to get everything he now had. Her heart had burned with sympathy as he'd roughly told her of his mother's death when he was thirteen, and they had shared a sense of that impossible to describe feeling that descended when everything you thought you knew changed in a heartbeat. Ella might have been only five when her parents had died, but she knew what it was like to have the rug pulled from beneath your feet, to lose that precious mooring—the absolute conviction that your parents were there and would always love and care for you.

She had been impressed by the man who had managed to turn everything around against all possible hope and grow into a kind and generous, patient man who she couldn't help but build dreams around. So she could be forgiven, perhaps, for failing to realise that, once again, Roman had turned the conversation back to her before it became too focused on himself.

Trips to Paris were soon followed by visits to London and Stockholm, never too far from an easy return to her grandmother should anything have gone awry.

But it never did and soon Ella had begun to relax into this strange new world at which Roman was the centre.

Only her friend Célia had provided words of caution—fearing that perhaps it was all a little too soon, too much. *'What do you know about him?'* she had asked over the phone. *'Enough,'* had been Ella's determined reply.

She knew how Roman made her feel, she knew how Roman had made her want. Want more, not only for herself, but for him too. And her untried and untested heart blossomed beneath his every attention. Her feelings were even more assured once Roman had met Claudette, causing Ella to believe that, had her grandmother been several decades younger, she too would have fallen under his spell.

Claudette's joy that Ella might have found the same fairy-tale romance as her daughter once had with Nathaniel Riding only served to signpost to Ella that she was indeed on the right path. That of happiness and true love. In some small way, it touched Ella that she was echoing her mother's life. That, like Adeline, she had met and fallen in love with the man of her dreams. It made her feel connected to both her mother and the past in a way that she couldn't have imagined only a month before.

So when, only a week ago, Roman had revealed that he was needed back in Russia within a fortnight, Ella's heart had beat and pulsed with a pre-emptive agony and she had vainly struggled to hide the tears that had unexpectedly gathered.

He had swept aside one with the pad of his thumb and pressed the sweetest kiss against her lips. A kiss that had built a storm of need and passion within her as if, so desperate to cling to him, to keep him with her, she would have given him anything. She *wanted* to give him *everything*.

However, Roman had been steadfast on this one thing. A deeply traditional man, he believed that only her husband should have that right, and his declaration had served only to make him seem even more perfect in her eyes, no matter how much she wanted to dissuade him of his conviction.

That night, when he had left, she had been bereft. It was as if that simple declaration of what could be between them, but wasn't, had made her consumed with the desire to be his wife. It invaded her thoughts and heart with an insidiousness that Ella, in her naivety, believed was nothing less than true love.

So that when they had next met, when he had whisked her away to a candlelit dinner in a chateau overlooking the dips and swells of the rolling hillside, peppered with small terracotta towns and church towers and sprawling vineyards, she had seen nothing but the look of love in his eyes as he haltingly, almost hesitantly, admitted that he knew it was soon, knew it was quick, but he couldn't remain quiet any longer. That he wanted her to be his wife, his love, his companion. She had almost interrupted his proposal with an agreement so ready, so earnest he had smiled and produced the most beautiful ring she had ever seen.

The art deco ring—a ruby encased in diamonds, set on dual silver bands which were, in turn, covered in more diamonds—looked as if it had come from her deepest fantasies. Roman had explained that ever since their first meeting in the woods he had imagined her in red. And it had touched Ella deeply that he too must have felt all that she had, from the first moment they had met.

But still his departure from France loomed over them. It was only when she shared her joyful news with Claudette that Ella saw and felt her every desire was achievable. Her grandmother's insistence that she be freed from her caregiver duties gave Ella hope. But it also made her want to give something back in return. She knew in that moment that nothing less than having her grandmother present on her wedding day would make her the happiest bride in the world. Hoping beyond all hope that Roman would agree, she hesitantly broached her request to marry before he needed to return to Russia. His agreement was immediate and assured. But he had a request of his own—one that touched her very soul. Knowing how important her guardian was to her, he wished to return to Moscow on the eve of their nuptials and pay respect to the man who had given her so much.

So overwhelmed that he would consider her wants and needs, the small smattering of people she classed as family, soon to be stretched to include one more, Ella didn't give much thought to what would happen next. Roman had already given her so much that she placed her trust and her future in his hands. A future he seemed to consider a little more than herself, for he presented her with a prenup, insisting her future and her father's inheritance was and would always be hers, protected by the agreement he wanted her to sign, despite the fact she would willingly have not. It was as if he had thought of everything, and in those thoughts had put her first and foremost. And to a young woman who had always felt as if she owed a debt, to either her guardian or grandmother, it was everything.

And as she stood before the closed wooden door of the church she chose not to focus on the fact she hadn't called Célia to tell her of the wedding, nor that her closest friend wasn't even there. Ella felt strongly that Célia wouldn't have understood, hadn't even when she'd tried before to tell her how much Roman meant to her. Instead, Ella chose to defiantly remain in this little bubble world that she had created for herself and Roman.

Her pulse picked up as she cast one final glance in the floor-length mirror discreetly tucked away behind a pillar. She ran a hand down the smooth oyster-coloured silk dress that fitted her perfectly, simple but delicate silver and pearl beading detailing the plunging neckline between her small breasts and the fabric sweeping over slightly flared hips down to her ankles.

Ella hadn't noticed the split in the skirts until she'd first tried it on and walked towards the reflection in the mirror of her grandmother's cottage. Never before had she worn such a thing, but she couldn't shake the feeling that somehow a fairy godmother was looking over her. But it wasn't a character from some long-ago-written fairy tale but her mother who had kept the beautiful gown for her daughter to wear one day. And Ella believed it was yet another sign as she stood in her mother's wedding dress, about to marry the man of her dreams.

Everything was proceeding as planned. Better than Roman could have ever hoped, in fact. In the last month he had played his part well. And if somewhere deep within his soul his conscience thrashed, he ruthlessly thrust it aside, focusing instead on the end goal.

But strangely, as he stood at the top of the aisle of the small church with domed ceilings and faded frescos, as he smiled at Claudette, who already had a handkerchief pressed to the corners of her eyes, in the pews with only two others—neighbours who had known Ella since she was a child—acting as witnesses, he felt unease stirring in his chest.

Roman had no intention of making this marriage *real*. He was a monster, but not so much of one that he would take her innocence. He was sure that Vladimir would agree to his demands and the marriage would be annulled almost as quickly as it would take for Ella to say, *I do*. But, in spite of that mental assurance to himself, the small ceremony felt…more real than anything had for a long time.

A small whine from the floor drew his attention to Dorcas. The priest had been a little dubious about the prospect of having an animal in attendance, but Ella had insisted. Roman was half convinced that she loved the dog as much as she appeared to have fallen in love with her fiancé. Thinking of himself in the third person in relation to Ella had been almost the only way to isolate himself from her effect.

It had been Ella's fiancé who had whisked her away to Paris. Ella's fiancé who had listened to her hopes and dreams and Ella's fiancé who had believed very strongly in the sanctity of marriage. For if it had been Roman himself, he would have devoured her completely on that very first day and ruined the only bargaining chip he had with Vladimir.

Roman had always marvelled at the value placed

on a woman's innocence. Yet in the month that he had worked hard to preserve Ella's, for her own sake as much as his, he had begun to understand the fascination and had happily consigned his frustrated desire for her as the price he had to pay for his vengeance.

Dorcas whined again from where she sat by his feet, and stared up at him as if questioning whether he knew what he was doing. He frowned at the dog, a dominant warning growl threatening to rumble in his throat, and finally she turned her attention back to the church door as if knowing Ella stood on the other side.

And Roman couldn't help but be curious as to what those doors would reveal when they parted, excusing the sense of all-consuming anticipation as mild interest rather than the raging beast of desire. He had offered to arrange for her to go to Paris in search of a wedding dress, but she had smiled and simply stated that she had it *'covered'*.

Simple. On the surface that was what Ella seemed to be, but over the last few weeks he had realised that she was nothing of the sort. In an odd way, getting to know her had been like watching someone grow into themselves. Evolve, develop, try and test things out, ideas and hopes and dreams. All the things he had never been able to do himself, after being thrust into adulthood at the age of thirteen when his mother had died. The hardships and devastation of the following years as he had been moved from foster home to foster home, working any part-time job he could, saving every single penny for the university education he knew he would need if he was ever to get himself to a rich enough position to be able to get his revenge. Determination as much as

a shockingly intense intellect had been all he'd needed
to succeed.

That and an almost preternatural ability to identify
what it was that a person most wanted in this world.

At school, his stature and intellect had seemed to
entice weak-minded bullies who sought to either befriend or remove a possible threat to their power. But
Roman had never entertained their games, nor had he
existed within any specific circle—instead staying on
the fringes, a lone wolf, ready and able to befriend or
berate as suited his own personal needs. For he had
learned at a young age that true power was about dependence and manipulation. Getting someone to willingly hand over what it was he wanted was far more
valuable than coercion.

And as he grew older, through university and the following years building up a personal empire that made
him one of the richest men in the western hemisphere,
he had used that skill very well indeed. He had amassed
a vast property empire, including a number of highly
sought after and deeply exclusive nightclubs, but his
true skill lay in brokering hugely successful business
deals for others…at an eye-wateringly high price of
course. His telephone contact list boasted several roy-
als and world leaders on speed dial, more than a few
oligarchs, and one or two more nefarious characters.

But, in spite of this, his one goal was Kolikov Holdings. It was his mother's birthright, had her own father
not cast her aside the moment she had failed to give in
to his wishes and marry Nathaniel Riding. Instead, she
had fallen in love with a weak-minded carpenter who
had been bought off by Vladimir the moment he had
discovered Tatiana's unmarried pregnancy. As she had

refused to give in to her father's demands and terminate her child, Vladimir had severed all ties to his daughter and grandchild, emotional and financial. And Roman would make sure that he would pay for his actions.

The way he had felt when he had first realised that Ella had replaced his mother's position had been as if his heart were gripped in a steel vice. In fact, it had been as the door had slammed on his face when he had begged and pleaded with Vladimir to provide the necessary finances to fund his mother's treatment that he had first laid eyes on her. A little blonde girl of five years, hair curling around chubby cheeks and little fists grabbing for toys, the like of which Roman had never seen before in his life. He had ducked behind the bushes that lined his grandfather's estate in Moscow and watched in rage as this little girl played happily with all the things that he and his mother had been denied. It had not taken much investigation to discover the story of the daughter who had been presented to Vladimir as his ward, nor had it taken long to realise that she was presently enjoying a life that should have been his mother's.

And while he acknowledged that he could not place the blame for this at her feet, over the next few years he realised that Ella had become the apple of his grandfather's eye. The one and only object of sentiment the old man seemed to possess, aside from his precious Kolikov Holdings. And while the bastard had shored up any and all attempts to breach the impenetrable walls around his company, Roman had marvelled at how the man had somehow managed to leave his ward so utterly vulnerable in this world.

Vladimir had seemed to delight in showing off the exquisitely beautiful trophy child at the Russian Debutante ball in London, or presenting her at some high-profile gala across the globe, and every picture, every newspaper article only twisted the knife deeper and confirmed his conviction that she was the only way to truly get what he wanted: Vladimir to hand over control of the company that should be Roman's by right. Vladimir to pass ownership to the man he'd called a worthless bastard, good for nothing more than begging for scraps from a man who would rather cut his own nose off than acknowledge Roman's legitimacy. And once Roman had control of that company he would tear it apart piece by piece right in front of Kolikov.

The creak of the large wooden door at the bottom of the church drew Roman's thoughts back to the present. There she was. The key to his revenge. He was sure that it was that knowledge that made his heart leap in his chest—not the stunning sight of the lamb about to be sacrificed on the altar of his revenge.

Ella was dressed in an oyster silk dress, simple lines clinging to a figure most women would have paid thousands of euros to achieve. The low V of the dress moulded to Ella's perfect frame and his heart beat a powerful tattoo that he was too stunned to fight. Something primal roared within him. Need and want a heady combination that burned through his veins and his soul. But he'd sold his soul long ago and couldn't turn back now—no matter how much he might want to.

He felt his pupils widen as if trying to take as much in of the image of Ella before him. As if trying desperately to consume every single detail of this moment. And, for some inexplicable reason, he felt as if it would be his last. Because after this moment, after they said *I do*, it would all change. Because the moment she discovered the truth she would hate him with every fibre of her being, and he would deserve it.

In some twisted way, his inner voice lashed at those thoughts in self-defence.

Better she finds out now what Vladimir is like. What I am like. Because her innocence, her naivety, won't get her far in this life.

Just like it hadn't for him or his mother.

But as the words of the priest washed over him, joining them as husband and wife, as the music played to signal the end of the service and he was directed to kiss his bride, Roman lost all thought of revenge, of the separate person who had married Ella Riding, of his promise to leave her untouched. Instead he focused on the soft lips parting beneath his—the gentle, sweet sweep of Ella's tongue as she opened for him, as she enticed him further into her depths. He lost his head and drew her to him, heedless of the gentle laughter of the few others in the small church, and wished that it could be different.

Reluctantly he pulled back, because it wasn't different, and he wasn't. The only gift he could give her on her wedding day would be to leave her unsullied by his touch. Even if it nearly killed him.

CHAPTER THREE

*She had stalked his woods and haunted his
dreams. She had strayed from the path...and now
she was his, to do with as he wished.*
        The Truth About Little Red Riding Hood
                —Roz Fayrer

MARRIED. SHE WAS MARRIED. Ella pressed her fingers
to her lips, still thrumming from the kiss that had
sealed her fate. There had been kisses between them
before—of course there had—but nothing compared
to the searing passion she'd felt almost consuming her
the moment he'd claimed her before the priest and
God. Ever since, her body had been in a constant state
of awareness, soaring between hot and cold, both of
which produced goose bumps across her skin, prickles
of need and want. Heat coiled low within her and nothing would satiate it. Certainly not the hooded glances
she felt from Roman when he thought she was not
looking.

Barely two hours ago, she had bid her grandmother
adieu and been whisked away in Roman's private jet
and now they were en route to Belarus. It seemed impossible to her that she had taken the reverse of this

same journey only five weeks ago. Then she had been filled with fear for her grandmother, feeling impossibly lonely and helpless. Yet now her grandmother was safe and happy, and she was about to embark on a new life with a man who filled her days with joy and made her feel...strong? Capable? Even as she thought it, she shushed a very Célia-sounding voice chiding that she shouldn't need a man to make her feel those things.

'Can I get you anything?' asked the perfectly presented male attendant.

She smiled and shook her head, half fearful that she would blurt out that she needed no more than what she now had in her life. All that was left to do before she could truly begin was for Roman to meet Vladimir, and then... She frowned. They hadn't actually discussed where they would go after that meeting. She'd been so focused on actually getting to the wedding, thoughts and discussions of what would happen next had seemed almost impossible.

Now, sitting on the plane, she realised it was almost silly not to know where she was going. And it both excited her and made her a little uncomfortable. She had placed all of her trust in Roman. He would look after her, she knew it. But as she cast a glance at her husband, who had spent a large portion of the flight so far consumed by whatever he was reading on his tablet, that unease began to grow.

He was unusually quiet, and Dorcas seemed to pick up on this too as she padded between them, back and forth across the aisle of the small cabin. Dorcas hmphed down into a shape the size of a giant boulder at her feet and Ella didn't have the heart to be worried about her dress. The warmth and physical contact was a balm to her heightened senses.

She caressed the wiry tendrils beneath Dorcas's jaw and large yellow eyes stared up at her as if in concern. Strangely, she found herself reassuring the animal as much as herself with gently whispered words so as not to disturb Roman's concentration.

'Is everything okay?' she finally ventured after another half an hour of silence.

'Da.'

It was strange hearing Roman speak Russian. Even though Ella was fluent, they had always reverted to English. But from the moment they'd stepped onto the plane, all of Roman's directions to the pilot and the staff had been in Russian, even the few sentences he had shared with her. As if he had forgotten the way things had been between them for the last month.

'Are you nervous?' she asked, hoping that might be the reason for the strange mood that had descended over her husband.

At this, he finally put aside his phone and looked at her with some confusion. 'Why would I be nervous?'

'About meeting my guardian. I know your businesses are in a different area, but Kolikov is a fairly well-known name and I'm aware that he has…a reputation.'

Roman smiled—a smile that Ella had not seen from him before. *Predatory.* The word ran through her mind before she could stop it.

'No. In fact, I am relishing it.'

His response did nothing to appease the concern rising within her breast and suddenly she longed to call Célia. To tell her about her marriage, to hear words of reassurance that Ella couldn't be sure would be forthcoming. Her mind became unaccountably blank, as if choosing to think of nothing rather than the fears that were brewing.

In a limousine, they travelled stretches of tarmac drawing them away from the small private airfield outside of Moscow towards Vladimir's estate. Roman's usually single-minded focus was fractured. As much as he tried to force his thoughts to his goal, he couldn't rid himself of the awareness of his bride. He could sense her withdrawal—one of his own making. He knew that his curt answers and almost brutal brooding had affected her.

It both was and wasn't intentional, for he no longer needed the pretence of the doting husband. He had what he wanted—the key to his revenge. Now he just had to turn the key in the lock. Everything in his life since the age of thirteen had been about this moment. Every dark thing he'd ever done, educational achievement, business deal, his sole focus had been leading to this point.

He'd identified Ella as the only thing that Vladimir cared about other than his company. He'd watched from afar, seeing how Ella was showered with everything that his mother had not been. Suddenly he felt a surge of resentment towards her, knowing that to be unfair. It wasn't her fault, but she was connected to that man's world—her ignorance was no excuse. But, if Vladimir gave him everything he wanted, then perhaps she might escape with as little hurt as possible.

If Vladimir gave him the company that was his by right, to do with as he wished, to destroy in front of the very man whose sole focus had excluded his daughter, then Roman would retreat from Ella's life—leaving her untouched and their wedding annulled. She might never even know the true depth of his actions.

But only if Vladimir had even an ounce of sentiment towards the girl. Roman hoped he did. For her sake.

Roman found it strange that he recognised the roads leading towards the estate. As if everything about that day, all those years ago, had been indelibly printed on his soul. The way the sun had beat down on him for every single one of the twenty minutes it had taken him to walk from where the bus had stopped. The way his chest had ached from leaving his mother behind and spending the precious little time they had left on his quest. The way his rough clothes had felt against his skin. The way that hope had bloomed in his chest as he felt convinced that the old man would repent, would save his mother.

The slice of devastation, humiliation and agony that had torn through him as the door had been slammed in his face was still fresh. As was the bitterness and anger he'd seen in the old man's eyes, the resentment. That was the night Roman had been truly born.

As they passed through wrought-iron gates Roman remembered Ella asking him on the plane if everything was okay. Now he mentally answered that it was *more* than okay. That it was perfect.

As they drew to a stop, Ella almost excitedly launched herself out of the limousine. She had decided that once they got this meeting out of the way, everything would go back to how it had been before. That the man she had fallen in love with would return to her, and she would never see this dark, brooding wolfish figure again. Dorcas loped along beside her and if Konstantin—her guardian's housekeeper—thought anything strange about the presence of the animal he was too well trained to say.

Kissing the gruff man on the cheek, she blindly grasped Roman's hand and hurried into the mansion before she could see Konstantin's dark look at the man she had married. As always when she entered the sprawling entrance hall, she was stunned by the marble flooring and sweeping spiral staircase in the corner, the grandeur nothing like what little she remembered of her one-time childhood home with her parents. Releasing Roman's hand, she gave in to the desire for her childhood ritual of spinning in a circle in the centre of the hall. It had started as a way to stop from buckling beneath the awe of it all, the unfamiliarity of it, and Ella suddenly found she needed it now. A self-conscious giggle rose up in her chest at her own silliness as she drew to a halt, expecting to see Roman's soft indulgent, understanding smile that she had grown to depend upon. But instead he was looking about him as if disappointed.

'He is in a meeting, miss, and asked that you wait for him in the living room.'

Thrusting aside her fears, Ella instead reached once again for Roman's hand and drew him towards the room indicated by Konstantin. She chose to cling to the threads of her own happiness. A happiness she hadn't realised was missing from her life before Roman. She'd been going through the motions at school and university, Ella had realised. The roughly sketched-out company she'd been talking to Célia about just a way to pass the time. But now Ella was about to start a new chapter in her life. As a woman. As a wife. As someone in her own right. All this joy she desperately clung to, ignoring the fact that Roman's hand had slipped from hers.

She turned to find him pouring himself a drink from the small bar area and felt oddly disquieted by the way he seemed to feel so at home in a room she had never really liked. As if it was his. As if he had the right. It was such a contrast to the almost humble man she had come to know. The arrogance somehow made her feel embarrassed on his behalf as Konstantin took in the same action with something like disdain.

'Would you care for a drink?' The simple request had come from her guardian's housekeeper, not her husband, making it almost impossible for Ella to ignore that something was wrong. Very wrong.

'I think that would be a good idea,' came a gravelly voice behind her. 'I have a feeling she's going to need it.'

She turned to find her guardian looming in the shadows cast from the doorway to the hall. The smile on her lips wavered at Vladimir's proclamation. Even though he was nearing eighty, her guardian had always stood tall and proud. Stocky rather than softly rounded, and always shockingly dark-featured compared to her pale skin and blonde hair from her mother's side. He had always seemed formidable to her but now, here, he felt almost menacing.

'So this is the man you have married?' he demanded as he stepped into the room. The Russian words were harsh against her heart in comparison to the month spent with the softer, warmer French of her grandmother.

'Yes,' she said, looking back at her husband, hoping to have him stand by her side, but feeling an unbreachable distance between them across the room. 'Please let me introduce Roman Black. My husband.'

'Black?' queried her guardian. 'Not a surname I'm familiar with.'

Vladimir's gaze bored into Roman's unrelentingly. And Ella wondered why the man who had charmed her, who had eased her grandmother's concerns aside with smooth words and confidences, was not now attempting to do the same with her guardian. Instead, he appeared as if carved from stone, holding fast against the battering winds being thrown in his direction by Vladimir Kolikov.

It was as if the temperature in the room had dropped, a hostility she had never before felt covering her skin in goose bumps.

'I would like a moment with your new husband, Ella.'

The dismissal was perhaps not unusual, but most unexpected. She was about to protest, but one quick glare from Vladimir cut the words before they could form. Roman had yet to take his eyes from her guardian and Ella felt as if she were at sea, being pushed and pulled by invisible currents that she let carry her from the room.

But she refused to be so easily dismissed and instead paused in the hallway, leaving the door ever so slightly ajar.

'You said you would be back.'

Ella frowned from where she stood, hidden in the shadows beside the door. Roman knew her guardian?

'I did,' Roman replied, his voice almost unrecognisable.

'And you have married my ward.'

'I have.'

'To what end?'

'That is entirely dependent on you, Kolikov.'

Ella struggled to understand what was going on. The words she could hear as easily as if had she been in the room, but the meaning? It was completely lost on her. The shifting sand beneath her feet made her feel nauseous as she struggled to wrap her head around the conversation taking place through the door. Her heart beat fiercely against the invisible threat that hovered above her like a sword.

'Why Black?'

'What?'

'The name. Why Black?'

'It was the colour my heart turned when you kicked me off your property. It was the depth of the darkness my heart became when she died.'

'I see you are just as fanciful as that girl.'

'That girl was your *daughter*!' Roman raged and in that moment an overwhelming force of horror struck Ella hard and fast. Roman was Vladimir's grandson?

'She stopped being my daughter the day she chose you over me,' the old man spat.

'Well, now this is *your* choice. *Your* reckoning.'

'Really? Pray tell.'

'I have what you value most in this world. I wouldn't say love, because clearly you are not capable of such a thing. Or perhaps that is reserved only for your company. Either way, now you must choose. You can hand over control and ownership of Kolikov Holdings and I will let her go. The marriage will be annulled. Or—' Roman paused, as if ensuring he had the man's complete attention '—I will leave Ella Riding ruined and destitute, just like my mother was.'

Ella's legs buckled as she pressed a hand to her mouth to stifle the moan that threatened to escape her lips. It had all been lies? Every touch, every kiss, every word... Her heart severed from its moorings, cut through with a knife so sharp she felt flayed. Her husband was threatening to ruin her. The man she had fallen in love with, the man she had naively entrusted her future to. Bile rose in the back of her throat as she see-sawed between feeling devastating betrayal and hoping against hope that her guardian would come to her rescue. Would somehow defeat the beast that she had unwittingly married.

Later she would wonder whether she should have gone, fled the estate then. But if she had she would never have known. Never have realised the true depths of the two men who had been supposed to love her the most, but had revealed themselves to have betrayed her in the greatest of ways.

Roman stood before his foe, using the old man's silence to take in the changes in his grandfather over the last eighteen years. He searched Vladimir's face, hating the strange similarities between him and his mother. Between Vladimir and himself.

An almost dizzying sense of satisfaction roared through him as he finally held Vladimir in the palm of his hand. And the urge to squeeze, to destroy, to remove the man from the face of this earth was overwhelming. Until Vladimir laughed.

'So cocky. So arrogant. And so convinced that you have everything *you* want. But you are wrong. All these years I knew that you would want your revenge. I saw it in your eyes that day. And if you hadn't been the bastard son of my disowned daughter I might have even respected you for it, recognised you as part of my own flesh and blood.'

Roman worked hard to keep his face impassive. Unease stirred in his breast for the first time as he began to feel the steel traps close around him—but, like all prey, still vainly hoping that he was wrong.

'Did you know that your mother was to be married to Nathaniel Riding? That all I ever wanted was to secure our business partnership with an unbreakable bond of family? When instead *she* chose that carpenter it nearly destroyed the business, ruining everything that I had worked for years to achieve. Nathaniel soon got over the disappointment, but I did not. Imagine—my own daughter being my near undoing. So when I realised what a beautiful creature Ella would become, I knew that I had the perfect bait…for you. The innocent, naïve young woman who would tempt you into playing your hand. And I safeguarded that innocence. That naivety. Giving her everything she would need to be the perfect focus of your attention. All I ever wanted was the joining of the two families. Mine and the Ridings'. And you have delivered it to me on a plate.

'You want the company? It's all yours. After all, you've achieved what I could never have done. You have proved the lengths you will go to, the very depths, and that is what makes you worthy. Finally, I see myself in you. That is why you deserve it.'

The rattling cackle that left the old man's lips nearly destroyed him. Everything he'd ever wanted disappeared in a heartbeat—vengeance turned to ash on his tongue as Roman realised that all this time, all these years he'd thought himself better, quicker, smarter, and he'd done everything Vladimir had expected of him and more.

Roman felt a helpless fury ricochet through his body, every nerve, every cell vibrating with the power of it. Refusing to give the bastard the satisfaction of seeing it, Roman stalked from the room, the sound of laughter chasing at his heels.

He slammed the door behind him and turned, coming face to face with his bride. A bride who had clearly overheard every word.

Ella had stayed for one reason and one reason only. The vain hope that when she looked into her husband's eyes she would see some kind of explanation. Some kind of reason or justification for taking the threads of her life and pulling them apart. Over the course of the conversation she had put together enough meaning, enough understanding of the need for vengeance, and the horrifying game the two men had played over the years. But still—beating deep within her—was the hope that in spite of it all there was some trace of the man she had married. Yet in his eyes she saw nothing but anger and hatred, resentment and fury. Those emotions suddenly detonated within her, forging her own rage in a flame burst that threatened to consume her.

She slapped him. Hard and fast across his cheek, before stumbling half-blindly past Dorcas, who seemed torn between her master and her new mistress, past Konstantin, whose longstanding self-containment seemed sorely tested, and into the back of the limousine.

When the driver asked her where to, all she could reply was Paris. After a beat, the man put the car into gear and whisked her away, saying nothing to the command to cross several countries in the middle of the night.

As the estate grew small in the distance Ella vowed that she would never let herself be so cruelly used by these two men ever again. She would not let this destroy her. She would find a way. A way to cut them from her life, a way to secure her own freedom. And she would never, ever believe in fairy tales ever again.

CHAPTER FOUR

*It was wrong of the wolf to have underestimated
Little Red Riding Hood. An oversight on his part
and one that would change everything he thought
he knew.*

The Truth About Little Red Riding Hood
—Roz Fayrer

IT HAD BEEN eight months since Ella had set foot in Russia
and though it felt as if everything in her life had changed,
the landscape around her hadn't. She stood in the gardens of Vladimir's estate in Rublevka on the outskirts of
Moscow, nestled amongst the houses of various celebri-
ties and the Russian elite. Snow lay thickly on the ground
even this far into March, covering the sprawling garden
in a strange white blanket, but her waterproof knee-high
boots prevented the frigid dampness from reaching her.
All the lights were on in the grand neoclassical building
behind her, casting a false warmth on the bleak horizon.
But only she and one other remained. Konstantin would
stay on for another month, closing down Vladimir's vast
and deeply secretive estate, his pension well accounted
for in the terms of Kolikov's will.

Her guardian's life goal of uniting the two families

locked within his once vast empire complete, Vladimir had finally succumbed to pneumonia and passed away seven days before. And she didn't know how to feel. How to feel about a man who had used her as bait, but had also protected and nurtured her, allowed her certain freedoms and withheld others. While there had been legal conversations conveyed through her and Vladimir's lawyers the moment she'd realised that her marriage had triggered her trust fund, only one phone call had actually passed between them.

She had expected explanations or apologies, but she'd been mistaken. Again. She had felt so horribly mistaken about everything. As if every single aspect of her life had been a lie. But Vladimir's assurance during that last conversation that he had protected her interests, her trust fund and her future with Kolikov Holdings hadn't been a lie. Because while he had made good on his word to hand over control and ownership of the company he and her father had set up more than thirty years ago to Roman, Vladimir had had one last card to play. He had given her ten per cent of his shares—bringing the total, inclusive of the ones she had gained upon access to her trust fund, to twenty-five, automatically making her a shareholder on the board. Automatically handing her a voice, a bargaining chip, against the man she'd once thought of as her husband.

A man who hadn't even bothered turning up to Vladimir's funeral. Throughout the entire service her body had been on fire with nervous energy, drenched in ice-cold sweat one second and ferocious heat the next, hatred and disgust turning nauseous sweeps in her stomach. For every single minute of it, her concentration had been fractured with the expectation that Roman would appear, as if summoned by a call that even he couldn't refuse. But refuse he had. And she hadn't been the only one surprised by Roman's absence.

Various business associates Ella remembered from her childhood had come, seemingly not to pay their dubious respects to a man who had ruled with an iron fist, but instead wanting to see the fabled prodigal grandson return, each wanting to know what her husband's plans were for the company.

Ever since Célia had discovered Ella sobbing over a laptop open to a search about her husband—something she'd had neither the thought nor inclination to do during their time in France—she'd determinedly avoided any and all thoughts about Roman, Vladimir and that damned business. Célia's reassurances that Ella had been both too busy and too worried about her grandmother did nothing to protect her from her own self-disgust at the shocking naivety with which she'd met and married a stranger.

A stranger who was reportedly not only uniquely ruthless in business—a fact she now well knew—but also thoroughly disreputable between the sheets. At first she had been shocked by the contrast of the almost idyllically respectful man she had married—the one who had wanted to preserve her innocence—and the notorious playboy he was proclaimed by the world's press. It was then that she realised the true extent of his deception. That he really had only wanted one thing from her. Access to Vladimir.

And somehow that had hurt so much, so acutely that it had stolen her breath and stopped her tears.

Strangely, she had found no sympathy with her former guardian. Because there too she had done her research. The man had disowned his daughter, cutting her off both financially and emotionally, for not wanting to marry Nathaniel.

Ella shivered again at the actions of two men hell-bent on destroying each other…and her in the process. And now? All she wanted was to be free. From this, from him. From the memories of her own stupidity.

And worse, the hopes and dreams that had died that day. The ones that she had not realised she'd even had before Roman had conjured them from her like a magician. A childhood yearning for the things she had lost. And then he'd taken them away—the loss as real as if they had been solid things and not just the thin veils of heartfelt fantasies. And no matter how much she might want to erase her marriage to Roman, she knew she'd never be able to erase the mark he'd left on her heart.

And once again, as if a flame had touched the detonating cord of her anger, she was furious. Furious that Roman hadn't come to the funeral today. Hadn't bothered even to respond to the lawyers she had sent after him for a simple signature on the divorce papers she had had drawn up almost the moment she had been back in Célia's little Parisian apartment. So this was how it was to be then. The hunted would become the hunter. Ella embraced her resentment and relished the thought of tracking Roman down. It was *he* who would soon know the feeling of regret. Because she was no longer the innocent he had claimed her to have been. No. Now she was a force to be reckoned with.

Roman took a conservative mouthful of ice-cold *zubrowka*, despite wanting to down the lot in one go. He knew himself well and, loath as he was to admit it, tonight—the day his grandfather went into the cold, hard ground—would be a trigger and he wanted his wits about him. He could feel it crackling in the air about him, as if a finger from the past had pressed against the back of his neck and burned an ice-cool trail down his spine.

As much as he'd wanted to see Vladimir laid to what he hoped would be *un*rest, a greater part of him didn't want to see his wife. For somehow throughout the last eight months he had stopped viewing Ella's fiancé as some separate part of himself and embraced the person chained, legally and bodily, to her as her husband.

Because Roman was unable to forget that kiss. It was, he'd decided, the moment the disguise had evaporated. It hadn't been Ella's fiancé who had stolen that impassioned, impulsive moment. No. It had been Roman himself. He'd wanted more. He *still* wanted more. He was not such a Neanderthal that he put the constant state of his frustration down to the fact he hadn't spent time in a woman's bed for nearly ten months now. He knew he could have had his pick ever since leaving Kolikov's estate. But he hadn't. It had struck him with a painful irony that some of Ella's fiancé had rubbed off on him, and all the talk of the sanctity of marriage had somehow bled into him.

And it was that which was most threatening to him. That he had begun to believe his own lies. Begun to meld parts of the fiancé to parts of himself. In truth, it wasn't just marital faithfulness that had wrapped around his conscience, but some unfathomable desire for something beyond revenge and vengeance. Some unnerving yearning for something he'd long thought himself not only incapable of, but utterly immune to. A craving that scratched at him from the inside, rolled around his chest, one that took effort to beat back down.

In its place he sought the safer familiarity of anger, the need for revenge, but even that had been infected, ruined by the near gut-churning agony of realising that he had never really got his vengeance. Roman's death-bed promise to his mother had gone unfulfilled and he hated himself for it, whilst hating Vladimir more. But the one overriding question he couldn't help voicing to himself in the deepest, darkest nights was whether Ella had known. Whether she had been playing him too. He knew it wouldn't be answered until he looked her in the eye. Which was—as he repeatedly told himself—the only reason he had so far refused to sign the divorce papers her lawyers insisted on peppering him with.

As he took another controlled sip of his drink, in the back office of his nightclub in Moscow, Dorcas shifted by his feet. He'd not been able to rid himself of the beast. She had persistently followed him wherever he'd gone, seemingly not put out by either the noises of his clubs nor the strangely isolated life he'd returned to. And he'd come to enjoy the discomfort of the board members of Kolikov Holdings when they realised Dorcas would be attending his business meetings. It did great work in putting them on the back foot.

She had appeared to mope, somewhat disconcertingly for the first few months, roaming the rooms and halls as if looking for Ella. But she had finally settled into some long-term sulk that was appeased only by food or a good ear rub.

His mind returned to the question of Ella's involvement in his grandfather's plans. He appreciated the irony of doubting the truth of her intentions, despite the sheer villainy of his own. But with more than a few months' distance, the assurance of her innocence had begun to fade. Because surely no one raised by Vladimir Kolikov could have ever been that innocent.

As he scanned the security feeds of the club in his back office, he paused, frowned and returned to the previous screen, his fingers tightening around the small cut-glass tumbler.

Ella Riding. His salvation or damnation, for her to decide.

She looked up at the waistcoated barman, who appeared oddly like an old-world Victorian with the most improbable handlebar moustache. She'd not known what to expect from Roman's figurehead bar. Perhaps something a little more…seedy? A den of iniquity? Writhing, scantily clad women whose skin glowed beneath harsh red lighting even.

But certainly not this, with Art Deco stained glass designs across the ceiling and behind the bar, backlit and throwing soft yellows, greens and blues across a space full of dark wooden booths designed for privacy. The lighting somehow made the bar feel out of time—it could have been one in the afternoon rather than the morning, each of the customers seemingly ready to begin their night's festivities rather than coming to the end of it.

It was, she ruefully acknowledged, beautiful. She ordered a single glass of ice-cold vodka from the barman who, much to her satisfaction, couldn't seem to take his eyes off her. She had dressed purposefully for her task here. And while she would never usually wear such a thing, the skin-tight scarlet dress, slashed down almost to her waist, was having the desired effect. Because Ella had realised the need for disguise since she had married Roman Black. And now she would wield it as well as he once had.

Konstantin, still proving his complete and utter efficiency, had located Roman at this bar, at this very moment. And while Ella knew that she could ask, or even look, for her husband, another thing she had learned was that it was more important for the prey to come to the hunter. As *she* once had.

And her husband would come to her. She knew it as well as she knew her own mind. She'd done her research, and she'd planned and prepared this time. No longer would she wait to be used by others. She would be the one in control.

As she took a sip of her vodka, her eyes connected with a man openly staring at her with an invitation that needed no words. He was tall, attractive, but utterly uninteresting to her. Just as she was considering whether it would suit her purpose to appear to entertain such an invitation, the hair at her nape raised and the skin on her arms pebbled with goose bumps. She felt a bank of heat at her back, the towering presence looming over her from behind and, if that hadn't been confirmation enough, the look on the other man's face dropped as his eyes glazed over, having taken in the presence over her shoulder, and he turned away quickly.

Her pulse flickered, and she hated the fact that Roman still held this sensual power over her. But not for long. Tonight she would get him to sign the divorce papers. Tonight she would finally be free.

'I hope you didn't wear that to the funeral. Otherwise they'd have been digging at least four more graves for the board members whose heart attacks you would have ensured.'

She silently cursed, having forgotten, or chosen to ignore, the effect his dark tones once had on her. Still refusing to turn, she placed the glass on the table before her and, head held high, steeled herself.

'From what I hear, that would have done you a favour. Tell me, is all well? Or is there something rotten in the state of Kolikov Holdings?'

'Sarcasm doesn't suit you.'

'Really? I'm surprised you think you know me well enough to say so.'

'How well do I know you? That is a very good question and one I've been wondering for quite some time now.'

Roman skirted the table, refusing to stare any longer at the backless dress revealing more of his wife than he'd ever seen. The distracting need to run a thumb, or tongue, down the length of her spine had nearly embarrassed him. Not that the view from the front was any better— his hungry eyes ate up the inches of smooth pale skin between the shocking red fabric of her dress at her chest.

Forcing his eyes to her face, he saw she was both the same and somehow changed. At first, he thought the signs subtle. The way she held herself before his unwavering gaze, the way she was dressed. But perhaps this was who she had been all along and he had been taken in as much as she.

Her hair was twisted up into a knot held high at the back of her head. Not even a stray tendril spoke to the softness of her that he had once relished. The coldness in her eyes did nothing to dampen his arousal, only inflame.

Worthy.

That was what he thought. She was now worthy of doing battle with him.

'What does it matter how well you knew me? You got what you wanted.'

'We both know I didn't. Not really.'

'And that is my fault?' she demanded, just an edge of heat to her words betraying the smooth, calm, icy exterior.

He didn't react, didn't move a muscle. He felt every inch the predator he knew she believed herself to be—and he relished it. This was what he had hoped lay beneath the soft innocence she'd presented to him before. This thread of steel, encasing a molten core of passion and heat.

'You have the audacity to try to blame me?' she said on a half laugh, as if incredulous. 'You made your bed, Roman. It would seem to be beneath your dignity to whine about it.'

Her easy dismissal roused his ire. 'You come to me in that dress and talk of beds, Ella? It would be remiss of me not to warn you against such a thing.'

'Still looking out for my innocence, husband?'

Choosing not to answer her question, he pressed on. 'Did you know?'

'Know what?' She was playing with him. He could tell she understood what he wanted to know.

'What Vladimir was up to. Did you know?'

There was part of Ella—a very large part—that wanted to say yes. Wanted him at least to believe that she had been more in control in that month in France than she had been in reality. Wanted him to think she'd had the upper hand all this time. But she couldn't. She didn't want to be part of this cycle of hatred. It made her feel dirty and disgusted.

'I didn't even know what *you* were up to. How on earth was I supposed to know what my guardian was planning?' She saw his gaze narrow, searching her features, her disgust and resentment plain and clear. 'Would it make it easier for you? If I had been? Would that somehow excuse the horrifying lengths you went to achieve your revenge?'

Only because she had been studying his face as fiercely as he studied hers did she think that just this once she had struck home. That she might have been right. But she refused to credit Roman with enough conscience for that.

'Well, I didn't. Up until that night, I'd only known my guardian as the man who rescued me, gave me a home, education, security—'

'All the things he should have given his own daughter.'

'Is that why? Why you took your vengeance out on me? Because in some way you thought I had stolen what was rightfully your mother's?' She needed to know. It was the one burning question that cut through her like a knife. The fear that somehow she *was* responsible for bringing his vengeance down on her too.

'I took my revenge *through* you because, for a moment, I forgot what a cold unfeeling bastard my grandfather was and thought that he might have actually valued you as opposed to using you as bait.'

He spat the words out at her and if he regretted them, she simply couldn't tell any more.

'So, I was inconsequential to you both in your double-edged plans for vengeance.'

'Inconsequential? Do you know what it was like? To turn up at that estate, to have to beg a man for whom money was no concern for the equivalent of a measly twenty thousand euros for medical treatment that would have saved his daughter's life?'

Ella had wanted to know, had wanted to understand, but this? This was horrifying to her. Growing up, she'd been aware that Vladimir had once had a daughter and had believed the silence surrounding her had something to do with the grief he'd felt. She'd even been touched by the idea that they had been brought together by loss. Him somehow replacing her parents, and her Vladimir's lost child. And when she'd learned that he'd cut her off she'd been horrified. But to think that he'd held within his power the chance to save his own child and said no? It seemed almost impossible. Nausea mixed with the ice-cold vodka in her stomach, curdling, turning and twisting in her thoughts.

Now it was Roman's turn to exhale a bitter laugh. 'Why am I not surprised? Of course your loving guardian wouldn't have admitted that he'd had the chance to save his daughter's life and chosen not to.'

Rallying as quickly as possible, she pressed on. 'I am not responsible for the actions of a man who took those actions before I was even at school.' But guilt? Yes. She did feel guilty for all that she'd been given and all that his mother had been denied. And somewhere deep down she also felt heartbroken for the child who had been denied, the young boy she could see simmering beneath the surface of this dark façade her husband had come to wear, a boy who would have begged and pleaded for help to save his mother.

* * *

Despite her flatly delivered refusal, he could see the truth shining in her eyes. His wife was not such a great actress after all, and had clearly been as much in the dark as he about Vladimir's plans to dangle her like bait. Nor could he fail to see the open wound he had poked and prodded with the reminder of just how badly she had been used by Vladimir.

'Why are you here?' he demanded, seeking a reason to avoid the reminder that he had inflicted his own damage upon her. 'Because I doubt it was to rehash the past.' Instead he focused on words that would bring back his worthy opponent. 'You turn up on the night of my grandfather's funeral dressed like sin and my only conclusion can be that you want something—but I think it would be remiss of me to assume.'

'It would. I want a divorce.'

He'd known it was coming. Had been ignoring emails and letters sent to his office by her team of lawyers for some time now. Yet inexplicably he wanted to prolong this moment.

'And what if I suddenly find I don't want a divorce from my delicious wife?'

'Then you'd better rethink your intentions. Because I have nothing left to lose.' Her simple declaration sliced into his skin, the accusation hitting his usually impenetrable heart infallibly. 'You, however, have a great deal to lose.' He felt everything in him rear up at the warning. This wife of his should not be underestimated and suddenly he found himself enjoying this new version of her. This determined and confident woman was much more intriguing than the guileless young woman from France.

'So,' she pressed on, 'if you choose not to grant the

annulment you taunted Vladimir with, then I will make myself deeply inconvenient for you.'

He scoffed. 'How do you think you could do that?'

'As someone with twenty-five per cent of the shares of Kolikov Holdings, left to me by my father's trust fund, and now by Vladimir, a number that automatically makes me a shareholding partner rather than a silent one, I think I could become quite a problem for you.'

Shock cut through him like a knife. A physical reaction that wasn't missed by his newly determined wife and, much to his chagrin, she laughed, the cool sound scraping over suddenly sensitive nerves. That bastard. His grandfather had not only fooled him, tricked him, but, further than that, he'd had the last laugh.

'You might have got the company name,' she said, 'you might have got the CEO's position, but did you think Vladimir would make it that easy? Did you think *I* would make it that easy after what you did to me? If I were of a mind I could start by renewing my friendship with the members of the board. Is Burian still trying to brew his own beer? He would always try and get Vladimir to drink the stuff. And what about Evgeni and Illarion? Are they still trying to compete with each other over who can out-gift the other at Christmastime? Such dear men and so *very* kind to me growing up.'

Roman struggled to laugh off her warning. 'I don't think you know those men as well as you think you do. Each and every one of them would sell their grandmother for a greater payout.'

'That might be the case. But this company isn't the only thing you care about, is it? After all, your reputation is one of the things that makes men quake in their boots. How do you think they would feel to see you brought low by your wife?'

'And just how do you think you might achieve such a thing?'

'As my own reputation means so very little to me, I would be more than happy to create such a scandal that you would see my face everywhere you went, every newspaper, every online article—I would make sure that the world knew that the Great Wolf's wife was bringing him to his knees.'

She was joking. Surely.

'Imagine—the wife of the world's greatest seducer looking elsewhere for her pleasure. What would that do to your precious reputation?'

'You're an innocent, you wouldn't even know how,' he declared.

He watched in horrified fascination as his wife turned her gaze from his to some poor dolt at the neighbouring table. Roman hadn't spared a glance at him, but the other man had obviously not done the same for Ella—who now focused her entire being on him. A quirked eyebrow and delicious curve of red-painted lips brought a blush to the man's cheeks. Before he took in Roman's scowling features, put his drink down and made his way to a safe distance on the other side of the room.

Ella turned back to Roman, the look in her eyes unadulterated victory.

'My virtue is meaningless, my innocence destroyed. You saw to that. You like to think that you're the big bad wolf, but I was raised by the biggest, baddest wolf of them all. You taught me revenge and vengeance and I might just find that I enjoy it.'

CHAPTER FIVE

*And the wolf smiled. For Red Riding Hood had
knocked upon the door and in a heartbeat he
would bid her enter. And once he had her where
he wanted her...there would be no turning back.*
    The Truth About Little Red Riding Hood
        —Roz Fayrer

SOMETHING INFERNAL ROARED within him. Hot, hard and
angry. He was angry that she would try to seduce another in front of him, and also angry on her behalf. She
had no idea what kind of power she wielded. Especially
looking like that. He hadn't lied when he'd said she
looked like sin. All the images crashing through his
mind taunted him with what he could not have. Writhing in his mind as if on silk bed sheets.

The sheer naivety of trying to get at him, at his reputation by sleeping with another man, infuriated him. Not
that for one moment he believed that she'd actually go
through with it. But Ella's fiancé had fought hard with
Roman not to give in to his baser desires and take her
time and time again in France. All those opportunities
he'd turned back from in order not to ruin her innocence and here she was, just wanting to throw it away?

He rounded the table, grasped her elbow and practically dragged her through the bar towards the bank of discreet lifts at the back.

'That wasn't seduction, that was an open invitation.'

'Where are we going?'

'Somewhere private to have this conversation. A place where the patrons of my establishment won't be subjected to a crude opening of the bedroom door which would have left you both unsatisfied and grieving for the loss of your innocence.'

With the swipe of his key card the lift doors opened and, despite the urge to practically throw her into the small space, he released her elbow and gestured for her to enter before him.

She did so, surprisingly without argument, and he stepped in to face her. 'Seduction is about power,' he said, looming over her, yet also trying desperately not to make physical contact, not to touch a millimetre of the deliciously small form practically vibrating with the same ferocious energy he felt building within him. 'The giving and taking of it, subtly shifting between the seducer and the seduced. I do not think you are ready for that.'

'I am not the girl I once was,' she said. He gave her credit for managing to keep the tremors of her body from her voice.

'And I am not the man you married.'

'So, who are you then?' she demanded.

'The man who is trying to show you that, should you choose to go down that path, you would only get yourself into more trouble than you are in now.'

The lift arrived and the doors parted to reveal his penthouse apartment. But Ella saw none of the incred-

ible views of Moscow from the expansive floor-to-ceil-
ing windows that took up the entire length and width of
the side wall. She saw nothing of the expensively dec-
orated room, the fireplace and sprawling leather sofa
that could have easily seated six people. Instead, the
sheer dismissal of Roman's reaction to her threat had
fired outrage within her breast. An outrage that contained a hint of the hurt that her husband had refused to
touch her, that the Great Wolf, as the newspapers had
reported him to be, the *'errant seducer',* had chosen to
leave her innocent.

And that wall of heat, that fire within her wanted it
all to burn. Every last shred of a connection between
her and this man.

'Oh, how very kind of you to look after my innocence now. After you took everything I knew and tore
it down.'

'Everything you knew? Really? You met and married a man within five weeks. I did not force you into it.'

His words taunted her, scratched at wounds not yet
healed. 'You lied to me.'

'It was a kindness. I didn't have the luxury of lies
growing up.'

'A kindness?'

'Yes. Would you rather I'd kidnapped you and forced
you?'

She wanted to growl, to scream her rage. 'You present two equally awful options and ask me which is
better?'

'I did not blackmail you, nor abuse your body. Your
innocence is no defence against your own actions, and
ignorance is no excuse.'

'Who are you trying to convince? Me or yourself?' she demanded.

'Don't you think it is better to know the truth about Vladimir? He used you as bait for me. Does that not outrage you?'

'You think it worse to be used by him than you?'

'Yes. Trust in that. If not me, then there would have been worse options out there.'

'You think there is worse out there than what you did to me?' Ella said, unable to wrap her head around the fact that her husband clearly thought himself a saviour of sorts.

'Yes. Believe it or not, there are. Ones who wouldn't have stopped themselves from taking everything you had on offer, including your innocence and much more.'

'Don't you dare paint yourself in some heroic light, rescuing me from a fate worse than you.'

'I didn't come after your money or your body.'

'I hate you,' she growled, finally letting loose all the pent-up energy and hurt accrued over the last eight months.

'Good. Now you might just understand a fraction of what I felt for my grandfather.'

Roman turned away in frustration, stalking towards the window and passing a hand through his hair rather than reaching for her and shaking her as he wanted to do—shake some sense into the woman his wife had become. But he hadn't brought her to his apartment to talk about the past. No. Now he was working towards damage limitation for her and himself. He had to persuade her from her ridiculous plan. Had to show her the dangerous fire she was playing with.

Spinning back to her, he pressed on. 'Tell me. What would you do once you found the unsuspecting key to your revenge against me, Ella? Would you be able to do what I did? Would you be able to seduce? To bend another to your will?'

He snared her with his gaze and took slow deliberate steps towards her, the unconsciously lithe movements catching her attention and widening her eyes.

'Because true seduction involves the chase.' This he could do. This he could give her. A final lesson to teach her the error of her plans. 'It's about timing. When to make your move. Not when you are ready, but when *they* are.'

As if conjuring the very thing he wanted to warn her against, he watched as her body turned to him, in tune with his every movement, and cursed both her and himself to hell and damnation.

'It is the appreciation of what your prey is feeling,' he said as her eyes flared as much as his own arousal, no longer able to ignore the way that his body had reacted to hers. The way her nipples had pebbled beneath the tight confines of her dress, the way her breath hitched, caught in her throat, as if equally under the sensual spell he was weaving between them.

'The heady sense of anticipation when they know what's coming and no longer fight it but actively want it. When every nerve, every cell of their body is on fire with need, with desire, an intensity that becomes almost undeniable. It's the moment when your prey is most alive, ready and willing to succumb to their own desire.'

He was bare inches from her now, no longer sure who was the seducer or the seduced, his breath just as ragged as her own.

* * *

'You talk of seduction and power as if you didn't already know that you had all the power all along?' Ella threw at the man mere inches from her, crowding her in the most delicious of ways. She hated what her body wanted, the yearning that almost choked her. The need. Her only defence ineptly thrown barbs at a man who seemed more well versed in the cravings of her own body than herself.

'Really? And what if I gave you all the power now? What would you take from me? How would you exact your revenge? Is it a signature you want or is there something else?'

Her mind stopped. Short-circuited. Instead, it threw up images of her deepest, darkest dreams from the last eight months. Fantasies of a wedding night that had never been, ones that she could barely admit to herself even though she'd woken up morning after morning hot and exhausted, aching with an unsatisfied need. A need that only one man could truly satisfy.

'Is that why you're really here? Do you know as much as I that we have unfinished business?' he demanded, his words surprisingly soft, gentle almost, seductive.

'Says the man who reportedly *saved* my innocence,' she bit out angrily.

He leaned into her then, closing the small space between them, dipping his head to whisper in her ear. 'Says the woman who would give it away to have her revenge.'

He pulled back, his eyes raking over her body as if looking for something, some kind of sign—something she feared that her body would betray. Had perhaps already betrayed.

'What if I said that you could take your vengeance out on *me*? Right here, right now?' Once again, her husband was pulling the rug from beneath her. Turning her words and intentions against her. Because suddenly she wanted that more than anything. She barely had the time to wonder if she had been fooling herself all along. If she had, in fact, come here with that one purpose.

'What if I gave you one night—*just this night*—to take whatever it is you want? Because, Ella, I would lay myself prostrate on that funeral pyre and die a happy man.'

The raw admittance, guttural and dark with desire, completely undid her. A strange heady sense of vulnerability, the image of her husband willingly giving her whatever she desired for this one night, fired a heat deep within her until she ached, a sob of need rising within her chest threatening to escape.

'And I am supposed to believe a word that comes out of your mouth?' Her last line of defence, half begging and half pleading, for what outcome, she no longer knew.

'Then don't believe my words… Believe this.'

His lips claimed hers with an almost primal need. These were not the same gentle sweet-tasting lies pressed against her lips she remembered. This was raw, unadulterated desire. Seeking, demanding, expecting.

She gasped as her mouth opened to his, desperately seeking oxygen that only served to feed the fire within her. The fire of need and want and so much more. Yes, she admitted to herself, this was what she had wanted.

Ever since she had first seen him, Ella had sensed this about him, had desired and coveted it. All her imaginings of how she would feel, what it would be like, paled in comparison as his arms swept around her, his hands trailing fire across her body, over her breasts and clutching at her hips, drawing her into him, against him, against his arousal. Showing her his own need for her.

'This is what you do to me, Ella. Does that please you?'

Ella could not speak, could barely think to respond, but her body knew. She groaned into his kiss, the shocking sound of her own desire undeniable. Her hands flew to his chest, her mind warring with her heart as she fisted the cotton of his shirt, claiming and owning her own need for him in a way that shocked her.

While his tongue plundered her mouth, rendering her senseless to anything but the raw passion he was building within her, his hands teased up the taut hemline of her skirt a few inches, his fingers reaching beneath to mould her thighs and backside with his palms. Her passionate cries were nothing compared to the growl of raw want that vibrated across her skin.

Drawing back, he spun her in his arms and pressed her against the wall of the room, her arms coming up to brace against the strangely soothing cool panel. His body leaned against her from behind and he pressed open-mouthed kisses to her neck, nudging her head to one side to give himself better access to the sensitive area behind her ear. Held like this, she felt completely surrounded, crowded but deliciously so, desperate for more, for something she couldn't quite explain.

His hand clutched the nape of her neck briefly, strongly, a display of his power, there and gone in a moment, as he pressed the pad of his thumb to the top of her spine and traced the outline to where the material of her dress barely covered the curve of her hips.

She arched into the touch, pressing her breast into his other hand, and nearly cried out as he ran a knuckle over her hardened nipple.

His hands covered her, worshipped her, slipping beneath the material that barely covered her breast and causing her to lean back against him, against the hard ridge of his arousal. Her head drew back to rest against his shoulder, her breathing harsh and her cries of pleasure falling about them, discarded in the air.

'So glorious. So magnificent...' Roman's words were a continuation of the seduction his body was performing.

His hand swept around her neck, cupping her chin in his palm, and she couldn't help but bend into it, taking his finger into her mouth where his tongue had been, sucking on him, consuming him in any way she could.

She felt him tremble behind her, the action sending fierce satisfaction through her to have this man as weak with need as she was. And then he turned her in his arms once again, to face him, a raised eyebrow taking in that power she felt, appreciating her own power, encouraging it even. The harsh slash of red across his cheeks speaking of his arousal, the ferocity of his gaze speaking of his need.

'Will you let me give you this, Ella? For just this one night?'

She knew what he was asking. That, no matter how much of a villain she had painted him in her mind, he would not give what she would not willingly take.

And she did want to take it. She wanted to take him. All of him.

'This will be the end of your thoughts and plans of revenge. I will grant you the divorce you wish for.'

Something deep within her rent apart. She knew, with more certainty than she had ever thought he'd loved her, that this was not a condition but a gift of sorts upon parting. It was this that would symbolise the removal of Roman from her life. Not a signature on a piece of paper, but one indelibly written on her body.

'Yes.'

As if the leash had been loosened on the last threads of his restraint, Roman claimed her once again. His lips crashed against hers, his tongue, glorying in its freedom, pressed into the warm wet heat of her mouth.

If he'd known what she would be like beneath his touch, his kiss, he would not have been able to leave her untouched previously. Every inch of him was drenched with a need he'd never before experienced. He sought not to disguise the way his body trembled but to relish it as he realised that it fed her own desire, her own want. He had not lied when he'd promised to prostrate himself before her. Nor had he lied when he'd proclaimed he'd die a happy man.

His hands went to where his fingers had tripped over the zip as he'd caressed her body, pulling at the tab at the side of the dress and sliding it downward.

She stood before his gaze, unwavering. Only the pulse beating erratically at her throat, her cornflower-blue eyes almost black with desire, the flush across her cheeks speaking of how desperately she was clinging to her own control. And, bastard that he was, he wanted it gone, he wanted her completely at the mercy of her own desire. For if this was to be it, if this was to be their one and only night together before he signed the divorce papers severing their connection, he would give her everything she'd ever wanted in the way that her fiancé had never been able to.

'Take it off,' he commanded.

He saw the flash of defiance spark in her eyes, saw her internal war as she battled with his demand, battled with what she wanted and what she thought she should want.

He hadn't lied when he'd told her that seduction was the giving and taking of power. And if Ella had even an ounce of an idea of how much power she wielded in that moment she would have used it to destroy him completely.

Her hands swept up to the straps on her shoulders and brushed aside the scarlet material. His gaze locked on to the acres of smooth pale skin it revealed as it fell from her body and she kicked it aside with feet still encased in the highest of red leather heels. Her perfect breasts were bare to him, nipples taut and deliciously teasing, as she breathed in deeply beneath his gaze. Her narrow waist flared at her hips, where the smallest of thongs remained to hide the last vestiges of her modesty.

Red. He would always see her in red. And suddenly the memory of the red cape he had bought to replace the one damaged on their first meeting flashed into his mind. But now was not the time for thoughts or fantasies of the past. Now was the time for taking.

He stalked towards her in one powerful stride and halted the moment she placed a hand between them, stopping him in his tracks.

'Now you,' she commanded with the power he thought she did not realise she could wield.

He inhaled quickly, sharply, impossibly aroused by her self-possession.

His hands went to the tie around his neck and levered it free, pulling at the silk and casting it aside carelessly. The more she watched, the more her gaze consumed his actions, the more want and desire raged within him. Slowly and deliberately he freed the buttons of his shirt one by one, pulling the cotton from his chest and toeing off his shoes.

When his hands grasped the buckle of his belt, he almost halted his actions, torturously delaying the moment, testing the limits of his self-control. For, no matter how self-possessed Ella appeared to be, he could not forget that she was innocent. That this would be her first time. But he would make sure that this night would be everything he could never give her in the cold light of day. Or any day from here on in. Because this was the last time he would see his wife.

A wife who, for all his protestations, he *had* manipulated, *had* coerced into doing his bidding. Well, now he would willingly do hers.

He drew aside the leather belt with a snap, slipping it through the loops holding it in place and tossing it aside. As he drew down the fastenings of his trousers, Ella turned away, once again halting his progress in an instant.

'If you have changed your mind—?'

'No,' she said, bringing her gaze back to his.

'Then see. See what you do to me,' he demanded as he removed his trousers and boxers in one sweep and stood before her, more naked even than she. Bearing every caress of her gaze, proud and powerful beneath it. 'I am yours to do with as you wish,' he said. 'You wanted your revenge, you wanted the loss of the innocence you claim to no longer have. You threatened to take some unworthy other. But I am here. The heart of your vengeance and most definitely worthy of it. So take me.'

As if he had given her permission to feel, to want, to have…she closed the distance between them and claimed his lips with hers. To be on the receiving end of such a kiss nearly undid him. Instead of wrapping her arms around him as he had expected, her hands went to his thighs, her nails digging in deliciously to the hardened corded muscle before they swept around to his backside, moulding, pressing, gripping and he allowed her to feast on him.

His hands reached for her hips, pulling her against him, the skin to skin full body contact stoking an already out of control fire between them. But while she took her pleasure from him, he wanted more. To give more. Picking her up, he marvelled at the slight weight of her in his arms. As she wrapped her legs around his waist, he maintained the kiss as he walked them through his apartment to the bedroom beyond.

With one arm still wrapped around her, holding her to him, he gently laid her back across his bed and took just one moment to capture the image, burying it deep within him, knowing that, as much as he might deny it, he would remember it for the rest of his life.

Pressing a trail of open-mouthed kisses from her neck to her navel, his hands traced down her sides and beneath her to her hips.

'Do you trust me?' he asked.

Her eyes locked with his. 'No.'

An ice-cold shard cut through him, deep.

'Do you trust me in *this*?' he roughly bit out, knowing that he would stop if he needed to, but battling and raging against it.

'Yes.'

'Turn over.'

As he smoothed a hand down the length of her spine, Ella practically curved into his touch, still unable to account for why having him pressed against her back made her feel safe, made her feel secure.

She hadn't lied to him. She might not trust him with her heart, but she did trust him with her body.

She felt kisses against her shoulders, a tongue against her skin sending shooting sparks to her nipples and between her legs. Her hands gripped the cotton sheets beside her and she wanted to both curl and unfurl into them at the same time. To protect herself against the onslaught of need he was creating and open herself up to it, to take it in, to relish nothing more than the passion that was burning between them. Her whole body ached with the desire for something intangible to her, throbbing and building, both wanting and fearing the dizzying incomprehensible need within her.

He gently pulled at her hips, her body moving, lifting to where he wanted her. She felt his hands part her legs slightly as she levered herself up on her hands and cried out in both shock and pleasure when she felt his tongue at her core.

The growl of his own pleasure made her wanton as he sucked on her, his tongue delving into her from behind, her heart almost stopping from sheer ecstasy. Her arms began to shake with need, her body overriding any sense or sensibility, pressing gently back against his mouth and when she would pull away his hand at her hip held her fast, refusing her the ability to hide from this, refusing to halt the insurmountable pleasure beating harder than her heart in her chest.

His hand stretched out across her body to grasp her own where it gripped the cotton sheets, the feel of his fingers intertwining with hers a touch that moved her deeply. An assurance that she had not known she needed.

He whispered in her ear, telling her in Russian that it was okay, that she could let go. But she didn't know what she should let go of, clinging instead to the precipice of some unfathomable, undefinable point. The hand at her hip released her and she felt his knuckle against the soft throbbing core, wringing even more pleasure from her. But when she felt his finger thrust into her she fell, blindly and willingly, over the edge, while his arms held her, turning her onto her back, enfolding her so that she never hit the floor.

Watching Ella come apart in his hands had been almost indescribable. Almost, because Roman couldn't halt the words taunting his mind—words like incredible, unimaginable, impossible—or the feeling of awe within his chest. But, more terrifying, was a feeling of humility—something he could afford to neither voice nor consider.

As Ella ran a shaking hand down the arm that held her, and further towards his hip and groin, his body flared beneath her touch, reigniting an almost painful want within him. But tonight wasn't about him—it was about her.

'What do you need?' he asked her.

'You.'

That simple declaration unfurled something infernal within him, a need of his own that he'd never before experienced. He reached to the bedside table and retrieved a condom, feeling her gaze scrape against his bare skin as he tore the foil casing. The weight of her eyes on him furthered his arousal as he rolled the latex over his length.

Her body, still damp from exertion, shifted beneath him, her legs unconsciously widening to make room for him. Only the slight hesitation in her eyes gave him pause.

'Will it hurt?'

Not as much as the vulnerability in your eyes hurts me now, he thought.

'Perhaps a little. For a moment. But I will do everything in my power to lessen it.'

She nodded, the uncertainty replaced with conviction and determination as desire overrode her concern. He picked up her hand, placing a kiss in the palm, a gesture he had never before given another woman. The smile on her lips cut him to the quick as her hand reached for his shoulder and drew him towards her with a kiss full of the trust she had offered him only for her body.

A kiss that quickly morphed into one of passion and need. Roman settled between her legs and gently, slowly entered her. He felt her muscles surround him, caught the hitch in her breath and stopped as she acclimatised to the feel of him within her. A slow exhale, slightly stuttered, burned him. He hated that he was causing her physical pain, piling it onto the emotional damage he knew he had caused.

All the hours of this evening he had seen her as worthy, never once really understanding that it was he who was not. Not worthy of the gift of her innocence, of her body. He braced his arms, looking down at her, watching as she began to settle into the feeling of him. Locking his gaze with hers, he saw nothing but wonder, awe—all open to him, offered to him. And, bastard that he was, he wanted to take it all.

He pressed further within her and she gasped, a pleasure-drenched sound that caught at his heart. Holding himself there, glorying in the feel of her around him, joined with her in a way he'd never imagined, he strained against the leash of his control. Even without moving he could sense her arousal beginning, reaching, spreading through her body into his. Her sighs turned into moans of pleasure, and still he had not moved. Feeling her body tighten around him, his own arousal teased and taunted by hers, was an indescribable pleasure he'd never before tasted. Beneath his stillness, Ella began to shift gently against him, drawing him into her own passion, seducing him towards his own orgasm, closer and closer, and still he had not moved.

Her moans became gentle cries, words no longer possible, simply the sounds of need and want passing between them. He held himself still as inexplicably he felt the roll of her orgasm build, enticing his own, both fearing and wanting the moment it would end.

His last thought, before everything came crashing down upon them, was that he had not moved. That they had both come together in a moment of stillness that changed everything.

The sound of the shower roused Ella back to consciousness. Sunlight streamed in from the uncovered windows, warming her skin in a way that felt inadequate to how she had felt throughout the night as time and time again they had reached for each other, losing themselves in a wanton sensual dream. A dream that she did not want to wake from. A dream that her body clearly hadn't as it throbbed with want and need anew.

She turned onto her back, relishing the stretch of muscles, the gentle ache from where Roman had been between her thighs. As she reached for the covers, seeking the soothing caress of the cotton against her heated skin, she took in the sight of his room—the windows, the long bank of cupboards on the opposite wall, the side table. And her heart stopped.

The envelope she had brought with her the night before, the one that had been nestled within her handbag, now lay on the side table, the paperwork levered open, a yellow tab pointing alarmingly to the space where no signature had previously been, but now was.

The sight of the divorce papers nearly robbed her of breath. And suddenly she needed to leave. Needed to get her things and go. Wanted to hide, not only from the papers but from what had happened last night. She hated the feeling that coursed over her skin, leaving goose bumps in its wake. She hated that she felt the need to hide…again. Roman had been right. She had set out to get her revenge and only given him his.

CHAPTER SIX

If there had been a moment when the wolf could have turned back, could have changed his mind and left Little Red Riding Hood to her own devices, it was long since gone. He'd had a taste of her now. There was no going back.
The Truth About Little Red Riding Hood
—Roz Fayrer

ROMAN HAD HEARD nothing from Ella for three months since he'd emerged from the shower, breath locked tight in his lungs, knowing that she had left his bed, his apartment. His life.

He'd made himself retrieve the papers from where he'd seen them in her handbag. He'd signed them even as his hand had shaken from the most powerful encounter he'd ever shared with a woman. Signed them as he'd promised he would. But perhaps that was why. Ella wasn't just any woman but his wife. Apparently she hadn't been the only one to succumb to the fantasy he'd woven about them on his path for revenge.

At least that was what he'd told himself that morning—that his unacknowledged hesitancy at the time had been down to sensual shock. But in the days and months since then, that moment had intruded on his thoughts. It was the pause—most likely imperceptible if anyone had been looking on—that taunted him. A heartbeat of a moment in which he'd seen a future, a whole lifetime of possibilities…

But each and every one of those possibilities required something from him that he was unable and unwilling to give. It had been a dangerous moment—poised on a precipice of temptation and damnation.

But he'd known then, and he knew now, that such a thing was impossible. Laughable even. As if he were or could ever be something other than what he was. The Great Wolf. The Lone Wolf.

And the sheer fact that it'd even given him pause was enough to put pen to paper, to punctuate his signature with a full stop that nearly broke through the page. But he could not deny that he'd begun to avoid his apartment. Avoid the memories of that one night as they gripped him from beyond the past into the present. A possessiveness he couldn't shake had taken hold and every day he searched for the signed divorce papers in his mail, every day he looked for emails from her lawyers that he'd previously ignored—anything to sever a connection he feared he might never achieve—but none came.

Dorcas had resumed her sulk, seemingly betrayed by the scent of her mistress but the absence of her presence, and happily heaped the blame at his feet. Perhaps Dorcas would have been better off with Ella. It was a thought he couldn't quite shake.

Nor could he seem to shake the almost constant state of arousal he was in. One night with his wife had not been enough to satiate the ragged beast within him, the one that prowled the edges of his mind as he had prowled the corners of his apartment in Moscow.

For three months since that night in Moscow, he'd barely been able to focus, to concentrate on what needed to be done for both his own business and the dismantling of Vladimir's. And it was three months too long as far as Roman was concerned. Which was why he was now standing outside an unassuming apartment block in Paris. Because, more than anything, he wanted to draw a line under it all.

His fist pounded on the door, perhaps a little too harshly, but he refused to keep himself in check. Instead, he relished the fury coursing through his veins. The fury that was directed solely at himself. He never should have allowed it to happen. He never would have, but she had turned up at his business, at his home, and he'd signed his own fate the moment he said, *'So take me.'*

The woman who answered the door might look like Ella but she was a completely different vision from the woman he'd last seen in his bed. She looked terrible, neither the woman he had married nor the woman he had slept with visible in the figure who stood before him, turning a horrible shade of pale.

'Are you—?'

Before he could get the sentence out of his mouth she rushed off, and Roman reeled at the sounds of her being sick in a bathroom he couldn't see.

He cursed and entered the apartment, expecting to see signs of a spectacular night out, but there were no empty bottles of wine, no signs of debauchery, only several varieties of herbal tea and what looked to be a raft of vitamins half opened on the counter.

Frowning, he took in the small, homely apartment, so different from the wide expanses of his own. Small feminine touches marked the huge difference between Ella's lifestyle and his own lone wolfish nature. His eyes pounced on the manila envelope, one he recognised from the morning of their last meeting. Had she signed them? Were there now two signatures on the paperwork?

Dorcas swept around him, pawing at the door which he presumed Ella had hidden herself behind. Ignoring the half whining dog, he turned back to the sound of the boiling kettle clicking itself off. Oddly tempted by the thought of pouring the hot water into the waiting cup, his eyes snagged on one of the many vitamin bottles and stopped.

Everything stopped.

His heart crashed in his chest as he grasped the bottle in his hand and drew it close for further inspection, for further confirmation he no longer needed. Pregnancy vitamins. White knuckles framed the name on the bottle. Ella Riding. And in that moment, he knew. He knew from the look in her eyes when she'd seen him standing at the door, before fleeing. He knew instantly that it was his. A baby. *Their* baby.

Ella took giant gulps of air from where she sat with her back against the bathroom door, her heart unaccountably in tune with the gentle whines from Dorcas scratching at the wood. She didn't even know how Roman had found her. She had been sharing the apartment with Célia for almost a year. Her name wasn't on the lease, but she didn't imagine that it would have taken much for Roman to uncover the relevant piece of information if he'd chosen to do so.

She'd thought she might have had more time. More time to figure out what to do, to figure out what it meant to her now that she was pregnant. Now that she couldn't have the divorce she'd wanted, that she couldn't have her freedom.

Because the moment she'd seen the little blue cross appear on the pregnancy test she'd known that she wouldn't, couldn't, keep Roman from her life, from their child's life. Not after what they had each experienced in their own childhoods. But that hadn't meant that she'd been able to reach out to him, to tell him about it. No. She admitted to herself now that she'd been a coward. And that just as surely as she'd taunted Roman about making his own bed, she would now have to lie in one of her own making.

Though she did not presume to know what Roman's reaction might be, she knew her own. She'd promised herself that she'd never be beholden to another's whims again and she'd meant it. But she also wanted to ensure that her child had the best chance in life for a happiness neither of its parents had so far achieved. She would do everything in her power to make sure that this child never felt an ounce of what she or Roman had. The cycle of vengeance had to end. And she could only hope that he would want that too.

Levering herself off the floor, she turned the handle on the door, only to find it immediately pressed inward by Dorcas's wet grey nose nudging the wood aside. She buried her head into Ella's hip and hand, her tail thrashing against the doorframe.

The small gesture of affection—the kind of physical comfort she hadn't known she'd needed—brought tears to her eyes but she wiped them away, knowing that she would need all her armour for the conversation that was to come.

She rounded the corner of the small living space of the apartment and stopped under the weight of Roman's intense gaze.

'Were you going to tell me?' he demanded.

'Yes.'

'When?'

She bit back a sigh, knowing that he had every right to ask such questions of her. 'If you look in the drawer to the left of the stove, you'll find a plane ticket to Russia booked for five days' time.'

'When did you find out?' His clipped words lashed at her, and she took every single one with her head held high.

'I guess about a month ago, but I wanted to make sure before I spoke to you.'

Roman looked towards the drawer she had indicated, but made no move to check the truth of her words. That he didn't touched her. Soothed her a little, fanning the dull flame of hope in her chest.

He poured the water from the kettle into the cup of tea she'd had waiting before he'd knocked on her door, before she had been ready for him, and set it on the counter top between them as if unwilling, yet, to risk any physical contact between them.

'Are you okay?' he asked finally, his focus laser-sharp as she nodded.

'Have you seen a doctor?'

She sighed her *yes* more than said it.

He nodded once. 'You will return to my side,' he

declared, inflaming the rage banked momentarily by their previous detente.

'Why?' she asked, genuinely curious.

'Does everything have to have a damn explanation?'

'Yes. In this case it does,' she replied, choosing to ignore the angry outburst. 'Because, really? There's very little between us aside from resentment and lies. And that is not something that I will inflict on my child.'

'So, you are keeping it?'

'Of course!' Ella's outraged declaration thrummed through the air between them, beating at him accusingly. 'You would ask me—?'

'No!' He couldn't even let her finish that sentence. The words, the thought that she would think him capable of such a thing, truly shocked him.

'Don't act all outraged. The lengths to which you have gone to get what you want are well documented by this point, don't you think?'

'Is that why you waited this long to tell me?' He had turned away despite his probing question, unable and unwilling to see the look on her face, to read the truth in her eyes.

'No. I waited this long to make sure my baby was safe.'

He heaved out a weighted breath which was half relief and half frustration. 'Our.'

'Our what?'

'Our baby, dammit.'

Roman cursed, already feeling a step behind, already feeling cut from his own child's life by her simple declaration, and it scalded him from the inside out. A child, the presence, the reality of which he simply couldn't wrap his head around. His hand flew to his hair, sweeping it back from his forehead, only just resisting the urge to grasp it in a fist and display his frustration for the quick gaze of his wife, consuming his reaction to this sudden news as if it were a test. One that he really feared he might fail.

He had never wanted children. Couldn't even fathom how it had happened because he knew they had used protection each and every time. But he also knew that protection failed, plans failed, and that nothing in Ella would have willingly bound herself to a monster such as him. And now he had somehow tied an irrefutable bond between him, her and…their child. An innocent child brought into his world, a world formed only from anger, vengeance, hurt.

He was going to be a father.

'What are you planning?' he asked, focusing his confusion on her rather than himself and the thoughts their child had conjured.

She sighed, delaying her response by taking a sip of the tea she cradled carefully within her hands. Refusing to let her hide from him, he stared her down, taking in all the emotions passing across her face. Emotions that echoed within him.

'I honestly don't know. I have a barely-off-the-ground business, half-signed divorce papers, no home of my own and a baby on the way.' As if by listing her current predicament had somehow brought it all to bear down upon her shoulders, she swayed a little where she stood and he cursed. He reached for her then, stopping a few inches from actually touching her and guided her towards the small sofa and chair set of the open-plan living area.

The moment she sat down Dorcas resumed her guard of his wife, placing her large head in Ella's lap and staring between them, adoringly and accusingly, depending on the focus of her gaze. He didn't have to see where Dorcas placed the blame. He felt it down to his toes.

'You are pregnant and will return to me,' he asserted, as if it were that simple. As if that would somehow make sense of everything that was swirling through his mind and heart.

'What will you threaten me with this time?' she asked, her words at odds with the almost numbness of her tone.

'I've never once threatened you. And you can say that I coerced you into marriage, but I sure as hell did not coerce you into bed.' The lack of emotion behind her words somehow ignited his own.

'No,' she agreed. 'I would never say that.' The pretty blush on any other woman could have been considered coquettish, but in Ella he knew it to be real. As real as the baby that they were to have. That she could still prevent him from having access to. And though Roman might never have wanted even the abstract idea of a child—now that Ella was carrying his heir, his flesh and blood joined with hers, it was as if something primal, something raw and ancient had gripped his heart and made him more sure of this one thing than he'd ever been in his life. That he needed his wife and child with him. So, he would do, say whatever it was that Ella needed him to say in order to secure that.

'You lost your parents at a young age. And I do not for one moment dismiss the tragedy of that,' he insisted vehemently. 'But my…*father* chose to take money instead of staying with my mother. He left her pregnant and alone. Knowing this, knowing that he chose her father over her and her child, it devastated my mother.'

Through his words, Ella heard and felt the echoes of pain that such a thing would have, in fact *had*, inflicted on Roman as a child. A pain that still held such a grip he had distanced himself from the effect of his father's actions.

'And you?'

'Any finer feelings on the matter I have long since dealt with.'

'Please don't. Please don't fob me off. I need to understand, to know what raising our child together means to you,' she begged.

He exhaled harshly through thin lips, as if desperately fighting his own self-preservation instincts against giving her what she wanted. She could tell that this was a vulnerability that he didn't reveal to many, if at all. But, from the look in his eyes, she sensed that he understood her need to know.

'I grew up as the illegitimate son of a single mother. And, yes, there are many, many others who grow up exactly the same way. But it was different for my mother. She lost too much, sacrificed too much for me...' He trailed off, shaking his head. 'She blamed herself,' he continued through gritted teeth. '*I* blamed myself, until I was old enough to understand the selfishness of my father's actions. Growing up, my mother did everything she could to make sure that I was loved enough. She worked three jobs to keep a roof over our heads, to keep food in the fridge, and it was just us against the world. So when she got ill...'

'It was just you,' Ella concluded for him. And in that moment she realised why Roman had been so good at helping her with her grandmother. Why he had known and seemed to understand what she needed even before she'd realised it for herself. 'And you were thirteen?' she asked, pulling other details from their time together in France, adding it to what she knew had happened after Roman had gone to see Vladimir, and her heart ached for him. Ached not only for his loss and the cruel actions of his grandfather, but for what it had caused him to become, how it had forged the path his life had taken.

'I was eleven when my mother first became ill. Tatiana had always been small, which was why she'd been such a wonderful dancer. Small but powerful,' he added with a sad smile Ella was sure was purely unconscious.

'What kind of dancer?' Ella asked the man lost to memories of his childhood.

'Ballet. Before she met my father and Vladimir disowned her, Tatiana was the principal ballerina at the Utonchennyy Ballet Company.'

Ella's shock must have shown on her face because Roman looked up and smiled, proud of his mother's incredible achievement. A pride that was both contagious and shocking. Shocking because, for just a moment, she caught a glimpse of the fiancé who had courted her, who had—at the time—appeared proud of *her*.

'But after Vladimir and her lover abandoned her she was alone, Ella. She had no one and no help. She worked herself to the bone and it didn't seem to matter how much she did, or how much she tried to love me, she never felt it was enough.

'So hear me now, Ella. My child will know me. They will bear my name and they will want for nothing in this world. They will never have to beg for anything, from *either* parent.'

That vehemence in his tone she understood. The need to protect she felt beat strongly within her own heart. Her own loss, melding with his, made her determined to find a way for them both through this. But she'd meant what she'd said when she'd proclaimed herself no longer naïve. And that forced the next words to her lips.

'I have some conditions.' He caught her gaze and gestured for her to proceed. 'I need to know who you are. I married out of deceit—I will not continue that way. Neither will I blindly sign my life and my child's life away to a man who has broken every single piece of trust I had. You cannot lie to me again.'

He nodded.

'I mean it, Roman. I will not live like that.'

'I understand.'

'And I also need to know that you are done with your plans of revenge. Which means that I need to know that you're not taking down the company.' She wavered on the edge of a precipice, half hoping and half fearing that he would agree. But she needed him to understand. 'That company might have been Vladimir's, but it was just as much my father's. It is a part of our child's history.'

'A history that you would own? How on earth do you plan to explain that to our child?' he demanded, anger vibrating within his words. 'That company was more important to Vladimir than his own daughter and even you. How can you want anything to do with it?'

Everything he'd ever done, every single achievement, every single motivation, goal and broken thing within him, had been about bringing the destruction of Vladimir's company and now she wanted him to keep it? His heart rent in two, half denying her request and half ready to do whatever she wanted.

'It is the only thing I have left of my father. A father I barely remember. And, like you, that is not something I want my child to experience. So I would very much like you to agree to my conditions. But know this—if, at the end of the next five months I don't want to be in a relationship with you, then you will buy my shares from me, give me a divorce and let me go.'

'Why would I buy your shares?'

'Because if I don't want to be married to you, then I don't want any kind of relationship with you, professional or personal.'

'And the child?'

'You will grant me sole custody.'

He nearly laughed. A choking bitter laugh that caught in his throat and burned. Because, no matter what she thought, in this moment he had no intention of letting either her or their child go. And if she thought he'd let his plans for Vladimir's company go, then she was sorely mistaken about the kind of man he was. Nothing would stop him from either goal, not her conditions, and certainly not her feeble attempt to coerce him into breaking the promise he'd made to his mother on her deathbed. The promise to dismantle every single piece of that damned company.

But Roman also knew that simply giving in to her demands would appear too easy—and although he had once thought his wife naïve and innocent, she was most definitely not stupid.

'If you have conditions, then so do I. If I travel for work, then I want you with me.'

'And if I travel for work? I have a fledging business that will require a lot of international travel.'

'What is this business?'

'Do you need to know?'

'In so much as you seem to need to know about most of my reasoning.'

'It's the one I told you about before,' she said, not having to explain what 'before' meant to either of them. Before they were married, before Ella had become pregnant. *Before* he had revealed his true self.

'You've done it?'

'Yes. Well…started to,' and Roman couldn't help but respond to the spark of pride and excitement in Ella's eyes. He recognised it, had seen it in his mother's eyes when she would sometimes dance for him, beneath the stars in the night sky. 'Célia is at the offices now—they're being set up as we speak,' Ella pressed on, drawing him back from memories of the past. 'So I will need to be in Paris.'

'And I will need to be in Moscow,' he growled, chafing against the demand in her tone.

He watched as Ella valiantly struggled with her own anger. The flame of it lit her eyes and flushed her cheeks and for a moment he was back in that bed three months before and gripped by the arousal that had plagued him ever since, in spite of the shocking revelation that had seemed to change his life in an instant. In spite of the mental decree he had placed on himself never to touch Ella in such a way again. Possessiveness cut him to the quick. Her body, cradling the life they had created, was somehow even more appealing to him, and he felt every inch the beast he knew himself to be. He wanted her with a fierceness that stunned him. The need to taste her on his tongue, to feel her beneath his hands and body was now almost painful.

'If we can't figure even this out, then what kind of hope do we have?'

Her words drew him out of the sensual haze he found himself in and he forced his mind to broach the practicalities of the situation.

'Do you have any clients yet?'

'We're in the process of—'

'That's a no,' he concluded, perhaps more harshly than necessary. 'While I have not one, but two businesses based in Russia.'

'I appreciate that but, of the two of us, who will be least exhausted by travelling between the two places? I can barely even make it to the shops.'

'Should you even be working then?'

'Do not even suggest that this pregnancy would undermine—'

'Not what I meant, Ella,' he cut in before her ire could reach its full strength. 'Fine. I'll relocate to France, but we can't stay in your friend's apartment. I will need to return to Russia to wrap up a few things, but I'll be back with a list of properties we will visit.'

'I am perfectly happy to start looking myself.'

He ignored her as he pressed on to the one thought he simply couldn't rid himself of.

'And my one last condition is that you will share my bed.'

'Oh, please,' she scoffed, but the sound was only half able to disguise the true response he could see flaring in her eyes, in the way she hid from his gaze, in the way that her pulse kicked at the edges of her jawline.

'Ella, you demanded that I not lie to you. And yet

you would try to lie to me in this?' he demanded. 'I would perhaps forgive you your inexperience that night, and the fact you have no comparison, so let me tell you. What we shared that night was unique.' Her gaze snapped up to his, as if she was shocked by his words. A shock that he felt every single time he thought of it, of being surrounded by her, of her body tightening around his, simply by their joining.

'And if you are demanding that you know me, if you want to see the truth of me, then you must have it all.'

At least, he promised himself, until the insane attraction that blazed through him the night they'd conceived their child was spent, was rid from his system. But until then he intended to indulge every possible moment he could have of it.

His words shocked Ella. The vague ideas she'd had of them sharing a living space but being able to retreat to their own privacy of an evening disappearing in the haze of smoke created by his demand. Because she had wondered whether that night had been…*normal*—it had been impossibly wondrous to her but perhaps it might have been almost habitual to him. But his words, the sincerity ringing in his eyes, the intensity as he somehow managed to bring forth her own intoxicating attraction and desire for him, they soothed as much as they aroused, linking them both on a level field of need and want. One that she'd craved and battled since leaving his bed.

'You agree?' he demanded from her silence.

She nodded, unable to speak past the sensual web he'd woven around her with a few simple words and a heated glance. But, despite the arrow of desire hitting a mark deep within her chest, she agreed because she desperately wanted to make this work. Their child was innocent and she wanted more for it than what they had had, more than the constant repetition of a cycle of vengeance that had brought them here.

She watched as he stood up from the sofa, his tall frame unfolding and stalking, with a lithe grace he must have inherited from his mother, towards the kitchenette. She frowned as he took the manila envelope in his hands and slid out the paperwork that contained only one signature.

Casting aside the envelope, he turned to Ella and slowly, and most definitely deliberately, tore the papers in two.

And all Ella could do was hope upon hope that he wouldn't do the same with her heart.

CHAPTER SEVEN

*'Cast your clothes into the fire, Red Riding Hood,
for there is no need for them any more, said the
wolf. Neither clothes nor lies will separate us. I
will be all that you could ever need.'*
The Truth About Little Red Riding Hood
—Roz Fayrer

AS ROMAN MANOEUVRED the sleek car that had been waiting for him on the tarmac of the private airstrip just outside of Toulouse around the small winding roads that sadly did not take up enough of his concentration he wanted to curse. Ever since Ella had demanded that he give up his plans to dismantle Vladimir's business it had thrown everything into disarray. For what felt like his entire life he'd had but one goal. Even his grandfather's death hadn't prevented him from wanting to ensure that the company that had meant more to Vladimir than his own daughter was wiped from the face of the planet.

But now? He was going to be a father. A husband. A *true* husband.

He'd meant what he'd said to Ella. He would do anything to protect—to keep—his child. But a lifetime's pursuit of vengeance didn't stop on a dime. Nor did a lifetime of being a lone wolf. Which was why he was in the middle of this latest argument with his wife.

'You just bought it?' she demanded from the passenger seat beside him. 'Without giving me the opportunity of seeing it, of making my own decision?'

She was working herself into quite a state and he couldn't really see what the problem was.

'What if *I'd* just gone out and bought a house?'

'Then we'd simply have two houses which we could either keep or sell. And, either way, it's moot because you didn't go out and buy a house.'

'No, *you* did. Without me knowing.'

'Ella, if you don't like it then we'll sell it. It's not a big thing.'

'It's a house. Of course it's a big thing! It's completely wasteful.'

'You haven't even seen it yet.'

This was why he preferred being alone. There was no one to question, to interrogate, second-guess or disagree with his decisions. He simply did what he wanted. It had been that way ever since he had escaped the clutches of his fourth foster home at the age of sixteen. None of the foster parents had been able to deal with a determinedly independent child who refused to listen to their rules. Even worse had been their attempts to break through the armour he had created around his heart. Nor had they been able to tackle a mind so quick and so intelligent they could barely keep up with his train of thought.

Looking back, he'd almost preferred the last couple, who had made their intentions clear. They didn't want to see or hear from him, only to accept the maintenance cheque they'd collected at the end of each month. It was certainly better than the first couple, who had *seemed* to want him and professed to take him into their hearts, but had persistently turned a blind eye to the fact their natural son had hated him with such a passion that Roman had been lucky to only suffer a bloody nose and black eye.

If it hadn't been for one of his teachers, sensing the fierce intelligence hidden behind a fair amount of bluster and anger—Roman ruefully admitted to himself—he might never have found his way into the invaluable scholarship programme that had led him to America. Ilyasov had been the first person, aside from his mother, who had seemed to genuinely want nothing from him. Because while his grandfather had *seemed* to want nothing from him, Roman knew that he had been the stick Vladimir had used to beat his daughter.

And the moment Roman had realised that he'd understood true power. True desire. To be able to identify or, better, *create* that which someone felt they wanted most in the world and to be the provider of that want… that was true control.

And while Roman hadn't been able or desirous of creating such a want in his wife, not yet at least, he knew from his time spent as her fiancé—the other *him*—what she wanted from a home. At the time he'd entertained it without really realising that it had struck a chord in him. It was as if she had focused her future as much on her imaginary house as he had on his path of vengeance. And as much as she might protest, he knew, with a certainty that had driven him to pay almost twice the asking price, that she would love the house he had found for her. For them. A them that would, in six months' time, include a small baby. A tiny, living, breathing part of him, of Ella, who would only have them to protect it, to put it first. A tiny baby whose equally tiny fist had already grasped his heart in its clutches.

Ella knew she was being unreasonable…to a point. She would love to have excused it as hormones from the pregnancy, but she knew she couldn't. Neither could she fault Roman's efficiency. Within three weeks he had apparently wrapped up enough of his business to take the time to find a property for them to share. And what had she done? Buried herself in her fledgling business. Choosing to ignore the way Roman and her future with him seemed to loom over her. Instead attempting to reach out to more international business contacts who might want to offset some of their income and guilt by aligning with the charities that Célia had already brought to the table.

It might have struck her as a little strange that Célia, who seemed to positively shrink at the prospect of interacting with billionaires and businesspeople, was happy to reveal her inner core of strength and persuasiveness with the other half of their intent. Célia seemed to know everything and anything about the international charities she drew to their company, and planned to entwine them with Ella's contacts, which was why the Venn diagram symbol on their business cards worked so well.

But in the short time since she'd last seen Roman, all Ella had been able to do was get Ivan Mozorov vaguely interested in a potential meeting. And she hated that her husband's apparent efficiency seemed to make her feel…inadequate. As if she was failing. Had already failed.

She'd gone to his club the night of the funeral to

ensure her freedom and only succeeded in tying herself to Roman in the most fundamental of ways. And as much as she'd hoped for a different future for them both, the fact that she was being driven to see a house he had already bought, already planned for them to share, proved to her that once again Roman was doing things without her knowledge. That, no matter what he said, he hadn't changed at all. And the fierce wave of uncertainty caused by that realisation made her feel awkward and a little panicky. And guilty. Most awfully guilty, because she hated herself for the fact that all she'd wanted was to be free and now she felt trapped by him.

Roman guided the car down a dirt track in between sprawling, undulating fields. On one side an industrious farmer was hard at work slicing down the wheat, leaving tracks behind him that reminded Ella oddly of Van Gogh's paintings. On the other side dark green cloud-like trees gathered between brief glimpses of a small terracotta-coloured town in the distance sitting against the pale outline of the looming Pyrenees.

It was the sight of the mountains slashed against the horizon, as if painted in watercolours, that poked and prodded at her memory. Of before. Before she'd known the truth of him. And once again Ella felt the loss of that man. Her fiancé. The one she had trusted implicitly before he'd revealed himself to be false. The one who had drawn from her unconscious the very things that she had wanted most. A child, a husband, a family. She was then struck with the painful irony that she now, in fact, had those things.

But she had not wanted them this way. Not with this man and not under these circumstances.

Resentment roared within her, but was it really her

husband that was directed towards or her own naivety? She honestly couldn't say any more.

Ella was about to launch into another verbal attack when they rounded an old stone wall and slowed before a set of wrought-iron gates. Even Dorcas poked her head up from the back seat, as if knowing that something of great interest lay beyond. The gates slowly inched open, as if purposely teasing the car's occupants before revealing the treasures that lay ahead.

The gravel driveway flicked up stones and crunched beneath the wheels of the car and she felt, with some not so small satisfaction, Roman flinch each time his precious paintwork came under attack. Then she caught sight of the sprawling converted farmhouse that sat at the top of the driveway.

And in the same way she had taken one look at the man to whom she was married and known that he would break her heart, she knew, *knew*, that this beautiful creamy-stoned estate was everything she'd ever wanted. Everything she'd once told Roman she wanted.

And for some inexplicable reason that made her want to cry.

Dorcas whined in the back seat of the car as if sensing the conclusion of their journey, scratching against the leather and causing Roman to wince again. *Good dog*, she mentally praised her as she blinked away the gathering tears pressing against her eyelids.

Ella looked up at the two-storey building stretching across and beyond the top of the driveway. Several outbuildings loomed in the distance, drawing her gaze beyond the estate, down a sloping bank of grass and across to the forest, where sunlight glinted against a copper dome she couldn't quite fathom.

'It is the gazebo down by the spring-fed lake that borders the property lines.'

The gentle tones of a French-accented female drew Ella's gaze back to the property with a snap. Expecting to meet the stranger's eyes, Ella frowned as she took in the immaculately dressed woman who apparently had directed her statement to the man who would naturally have known what his money had bought.

'Dominique Delvaux,' she said with a feline smile, directed at her husband. 'I am the estate's *guardienne*.'

Ella just about managed to restrain the growl she felt vibrating within her throat. Dorcas, apparently, had no such self-control as a low warning rumbled from the beast in spite of the look of disdain the beautiful French-woman cast in the dog's direction.

Ella looked down at her clothes, creased and crumpled and slightly damp from the journey, despite the powerful air-conditioning that had at first sent shivers across her skin. At the time, Ella had allowed herself that small lie, pretending her body's reaction had nothing to do with the impossibly handsome man beside her.

A handsome man whose charms were apparently not wasted on the *guardienne*. Ella had dressed for comfort, where Ms Delvaux seemed to have dressed for a fashion show. And now, as she looked at the other woman, she felt the slightly tight press of the waistband of her linen trousers and wished that she had listened to Cé-lia's suggestion that she think about purchasing a new wardrobe for her slowly developing bump.

She followed her husband as the *guardienne* beckoned them into the building and the enticing cool interior of the hallway. A small table by the entrance held a jug of water with cucumber, mint and ice, the white linen tablecloth beneath soaking up the condensation forming on the glass. Ms Delvaux filled two glasses and Ella nearly smiled as decorum finally won out over desire and the other woman offered her a glass before her husband.

'*Merci,*' Ella said overly graciously, while taking the glass with one hand and gently pressing her other to her abdomen, unnecessarily soothing the almost indistinguishable shape beginning to form there. The *guardienne*'s eyes snapped back and forth between Ella's hand and face and Ella practically preened under the dawning realisation she could read in the other woman's face.

Message received and understood, Ms Delvaux retreated into professionalism and began to outline the impressive attributes of the house.

'The main building dates from the seventeenth century, when it was the heart of a growing estate. The charmingly renovated façade reveals large and light interiors. As you can see, the dramatic ninety square metre reception hall has a grand fireplace—as does the master suite on the floor above at the other end of the house. It is one of seven bedrooms and the restoration brought about an additional two bathrooms, bringing the number to five. Below you'll find a garage and a generous wine cellar...'

Ella let the woman's voice recede into the background as she drifted off into the large living area she could see on the left, Dorcas nuzzling her hand and keeping her company while her husband and the *guardienne* remained behind in the '*dramatic ninety square metre reception hall*'. It *was* impressive, but it made her only think of Vladimir's hall, the one she had spun in the night that Roman had revealed his deceit.

But all thoughts of that night fled under the beautiful streams of light filtering in from the windows as she took in the soothing cream tones of the living area, centred around an incredible fireplace that she thought she might actually be able to stand within. Two sprawling sofas stood sentinel either side of it and the terracotta stone flooring beckoned her further into the large room. Rounding a corner, she came to a stunning open-plan kitchen, connected by beautiful aged oak beams running across the ceiling, giving the space a warmth and cosiness despite its size. Utility rooms sprang off to the side, her eyes eating up every inch of the incredible space.

She looked to Roman, sensing the heat of his gaze. The smug look of satisfaction across his features at having recognised that she'd fallen in love with the house took the wind out of her sails somewhat.

Ella approached the staircase and moved through the rooms slowly, as if scared that she'd miss something or move too quickly, in case it would all disappear. It was everything she'd ever wanted. There was enough to remind her of her grandmother's cottage, a homeliness and simplicity that could only be afforded by extreme wealth. A wealth that her husband had brought to bear against her. Or for her? She simply couldn't tell any more.

She felt overwhelmed, confused and strangely hurt by the fact that he'd found a home that was almost straight out of the fantasies she'd discussed during their engagement. Because she was desperately trying to see Roman as two different men—the fantasy she had fallen for and the man who had destroyed all that she had known. But this blurred the lines—this confused her because it meant that she could not keep them separate. She loved the house immediately and her heart ached. Because it meant that she would have to admit that he knew her. He knew her well enough to give her this house—her dream house. But, more importantly, *she* didn't know *him* at all.

Roman dismissed the overly attentive *guardienne* and, as he waited for Ella to return from inspecting the rooms upstairs, he stood in the living room, trying to imagine what his life would look like in a month's time, a year's time, five years' time even. Would there be a child's toys scattered about this room? Would there be the subtle touches of Ella on the walls and in the rooms as she placed her own mark upon the house? And what traces would there be of him? Would there, his inner voice questioned, be *any* trace of him?

His thoughts were cut off as he heard the click of Ella's heels coming down the staircase. And suddenly he didn't want to look, didn't want to know what she thought of the house he had conjured from the descriptions she had given him during their engagement. Because if he had got it wrong...

But when he turned he saw neither love nor disappointment. No. His wife surprised him yet again with her anger.

'What is wrong?' he demanded, his voice rough and guttural, resisting the urge to run his hands through his hair in frustration. He had been so sure of it. So sure of her.

'Nothing,' she said bitterly, causing him to frown. 'Absolutely nothing is wrong with it. You've apparently thought of everything.'

'And that is a bad thing?'

She glared at him mulishly. And suddenly he wanted nothing more than to kiss away that anger, to use it, to bend it to his will. But he couldn't. Because she was his wife and she deserved more than that. Even if she was glaring at him with a strange combination of anger, resentment and hurt. The former he could handle, the latter not so much. Because he was beginning to think that even a lifetime's worth of compensation wouldn't atone for his sins. Sins he was apparently still committing, though he couldn't quite fathom what this one could have been.

'Words,' he bit out.

'What?'

'You're going to have to use them to tell me what I've done wrong this time.'

She scowled again and Dorcas chose wisely to vacate the room. For there was a storm brewing, one of quite spectacular proportions if he wasn't mistaken. One he felt echoing in his own chest for release.

'I...' she said as she paced the length of the room and then turned on her heel. 'You...' she said, trying again, as if she were afraid of what would be released if she lifted the lid on the ferocity of what she was clearly struggling with.

'Ella,' he warned. 'If you try to keep all that in—'

'I don't think you want to know. Truly,' she ground out.

'I know how damaging anger can be. How it can scorch you from the inside out and twist every last good thing in you and make you dark, make you...vengeful.' And suddenly it was the most important thing to him. He wanted, *needed*, to hear whatever it was she had to say, because it was killing him to see the beautiful, innocent, joyful young woman so tormented.

'It's perfect. It's absolutely everything I ever wanted. Everything that I never knew I wanted until I met a man in the woods and he offered me a future I had yet to realise I desperately sought.'

She turned away from him, trying to hide the overwhelming ache that beat in her chest. An ache borne from the past, into the present and a future she now feared she'd never have. But Roman was right, she did need to find the words to explain…to release this overwhelming *hurt*.

'I was young when I lost my parents. Five. Too young to articulate what I was feeling, too young to understand Vladimir when he tried to explain that my parents were never coming back. That I'd be living with him now. Too young to understand why everything hurt and why I could not stop playing with the doll's house and the small wooden figures of two parents and a child. Why in my mind I had them eat dinner together every day. Why the mother and father used to tuck their child into bed each night and read her stories.

'As much as you might hate to hear it, Vladimir *did* look after me, but mostly he was focused on material needs. And then with my grandmother… Summers with her were magical. Truly. But she was an older woman— she had raised her child and had buried her. She loved me completely, but she wasn't exactly a suitable companion for a child. I spent more time in the woods alone, looking for fairies, hiding in the bushes, running after birds and the rabbits. I was…' Ella twisted her hands before her, unaccountably ashamed of admitting her loneliness as if it were a mark against her perfect grandmother. 'I was isolated. There were no children to play with, all of them already with school friends or away for their own summer holidays.'

And somewhere in those months, those long stretching summer days, she had formed an idea of her future. One that she now both had and didn't have. She turned back to Roman, who was watching her, his usually bright eyes a deeper stormy blue.

'When I met my fiancé in the woods he offered me everything I had always wanted. Companionship, someone to confide in, someone with whom I could have the very thing I'd always wanted, ever since it had been ripped away from me at the age of five. A home, a family.

'You, Roman. You offered me my fantasy and this? This is too close and yet so far from what I wanted.'

'Fantasies aren't real.'

'Like your fantasy of revenge?' she couldn't help but taunt. 'It's not the house, Roman. It's the fact that after all these years, all the things I wanted…it's so nearly there, but I can't help but feel that I'm going to be just as lonely as I once was in the woods. Just as lonely in this perfect house.'

She dared to cast a look at him then, hoping beyond hope that he'd reassure her, that he'd have words and compassion to make all her fears disappear. His whole body stilled—as if he were made of marble, as if he too realised how important his answer would be, what she was really asking him, the truth behind her words, the question.

'Ella,' he said, shaking his head, 'I don't want to make promises I cannot keep.' She huffed out a cynical breath, and he pushed on. 'There have clearly been enough of those between us. But you are pregnant with my child. You are my wife. You are not in this alone, not if you don't choose to be. When I am not in this house I will be at the other end of the phone any time, *any time* you need me. I'll fly back in a heartbeat if you desire it. And if you feel that my business in Russia takes me too much away from you then we will visit that if and when you choose. But Ella, that is not what is really upsetting you,' he stated with determined simplicity, the glints of gold in his eyes firing against the blue. As if he were made of the stuff. As if he had steeled himself for an answer he already knew.

She cursed and stalked from the room, paying no heed to the lithe graceful strides that caught up to her in a heartbeat, her exit halted by the hand at her wrist, spinning her back round to almost crash against the hard chest looming over her.

'No. It's not,' she said, finally owning up to the truth of what she really feared in that moment. 'It's you,' she said, punctuating the statement with a strike against his powerful chest. 'I don't trust you. You took away the only solid, stable things I had in my life. You took away a loving guardian and replaced him with a Machiavellian monster, uncaring, unfeeling and manipulative. You took away the man I wanted to spend the rest of my life with, a man I had fallen in love with, a man I shared my hopes and dreams for a future with. How on earth am I supposed to believe that you won't take this away from me now? How am I supposed to trust you?'

Roman wanted to argue with his wife's words, deny them as lies, but couldn't. She had been badly used by both Vladimir and himself. And while he'd tried to explain it to himself as just, as necessary for his pursuit of revenge, with the damage from his actions clear to see before him, he could no longer fight the awful truth of what he had done. That all the power and incredible self-possession he had seen the night they had conceived their child had been a thin layer of newly formed defence against the deeper devastation he had wrought on this extraordinary woman. He cursed himself to hell and back, lashing himself mentally with a thousand different painful thoughts. But this wasn't about him, not here and now. It was about Ella. And what she needed.

'I wanted to show you, with this house, that you can have whatever you want most in the world.'

'But that is the problem. You know what it is that I want because you got the truth out of me when we were engaged…and I did not do the same. You know me, but I don't know you. All I know is that you have taken decisions that I would want to have made myself away from me. You have…'

'Taken away your freedom.'

She nodded sadly as she bit into the lower lip he wanted for himself and then castigated himself once again for his inappropriate wayward thoughts.

'I am not used to having others to think of,' he admitted roughly. 'So much of my life has been lived under my own direction, my own decisions. But that will change. I do understand why you feel this way. And I know that I am the cause of it. But, if you let me, I will prove that you can trust me. I will not take those decisions away from you again. I promise you that.' He held her gaze with his, determined to allow her to see the truth, the honesty of his words, hoping beyond all hope that he could honour that promise.

'And you are right. I did see the truth of you before. Not just the innocence and naivety I once taunted you with, but the strength of a woman who cared deeply about her grandmother. So much so that she would put her own dreams on hold. A woman determined not to rely on the money provided by her guardian and father, who would not fritter it away on silly ephemeral comforts but create a business that would provide much needed support for charities throughout the globe. And even after events that would have cowed a great many other people, a woman who found her own strength and determination to ask for what she wanted, to demand what she was due. And that woman was incredible to me. Empowered and enthralling enough to make me beg her to take what she wanted from me and leave me wanting more. A woman who will make the most wonderful mother, caring, honest and with an integrity that leaves me ashamed,' he admitted.

'But you have to decide whether you can trust me. Because, if you don't, then you will never stop second-guessing me and it will drive you mad,' he concluded. Just like it had driven Roman almost mad in those first few months after his mother's death—wondering, questioning whether he could have done something—anything more to save her. He could not, and would not, allow Ella to live under such a damaging weight.

He produced the keys to the house from his pocket. 'This is the only set of keys to this house. The deeds are in your name and no one else's. It is yours. Completely. You can do with it what you will. Sell it, rent it, keep it.' He pressed the keys into her hands. 'I'll wait outside until you're ready to leave.'

* * *

Ella felt the loss of him from the house as something physical. The hurt, angry part of her cried that she would never be able to trust him. But the softer yearning part of her looked about a house almost made from her dreams and hoped. Roman was right. She had to stop. She had to draw a line under the past if they had any hope of the future.

As Roman had painted the picture of her as he had seen her, Ella had wavered, wanting to be all that he described. Hoping that he was speaking the truth and feeling something unfurl within her, reaching to be that person. Instead of using her fears against her, he had listened to them, comforted them and her. She looked around the room, seeing with hope what her future could be. And for the first time in a long time she felt strong enough to reach for it.

But within that strength was a deep knowledge, a belief. She might be able to trust her husband with this, but she would never trust him with her heart. Could never. Because that hurt would be too much to bear.

As she left the house she saw Roman sitting on the steps leading down to the driveway, Dorcas lifting her head from her master's touch in happy expectation. The tableau was oddly moving. Her dog, her husband, her home.

'So what else does our lovely new estate have to offer?' she asked him, the ache in her chest easing just a little as she saw the answering smile in his gaze.

CHAPTER EIGHT

And now every bite, every snarl, every gnashing of his teeth was about to be heaped on the wolf tenfold. For the one thing he had not learned yet was that you can never escape the actions of the past.
The Truth About Little Red Riding Hood
—Roz Fayrer

ELLA FINISHED THE phone call to Célia with a smile on her face, having gone over the details ahead of the meeting with Ivan Mozorov. In the last few weeks they'd found more interested parties and Ella could now sense the way their business would begin to take off. Célia had sent photos of the office in Paris that was a few days away from being not only fully functioning but very beautiful.

She and Roman had settled into a routine of sorts. Roman would spend the middle three days of the week in Russia, Monday and Friday commuting, and would stay in France with her at the weekend. And, despite what he'd said about sharing his bed, he hadn't enforced the decree, which had—at first—made Ella feel a sense of relief. But as the days wore on…she became dissatisfied. She rolled her shoulders at the thought of it, as if shaking off some inner sense of frustration. She couldn't help the feeling that she was waiting for the other shoe to drop, only it felt less like a shoe and more like the sword of Damocles.

Her body, thankfully having moved past the morning sickness stage, had begun to blossom. She'd never thought she'd enjoy pregnancy but at the moment she was relishing the new freedom in her body. Their child was now about the size of a pea pod, the doctor had explained, which had caused her to refer to her baby as Sweetpea. And each day she marvelled at the subtle changes happening, the new gentle curves of her body. A body that Roman seemed intent on ignoring for the most part.

It was as if now that Roman had given her the space to relax, to ease into the situation and the house, she couldn't escape him, her thoughts of him and the ecstasy of what they had shared that night. It made her feel…wanton, and slightly obsessed. She had begun to dress each day with Roman in mind, trying to tempt him into something he suddenly seemed to think was inappropriate.

When she wasn't lusting after her husband she was delighting in the house he had found for them. It was close enough to visit her grandmother and a short flight to Paris for when the offices were up and running. And although she had visited her grandmother several times, Ella found herself not quite wanting to leave the beautiful home.

There was simply too much to see and discover about this place. After breakfast in the morning she and Dorcas would roam the sprawling acreage down to the freshwater spring that wound across the border

of their lands and she couldn't have stopped Dorcas
diving into it for a moment because the pure joy in the
dog's eyes made her laugh, and soothed some of the
past hurts.

But her favourite part of the estate was the stone gazebo with the copper domed roof. Every day she reached
for the almost grey pillars, placing her hands against
the cool stone, wondering who might have done so in
the years before. She enjoyed imagining the different
women who might have stood there looking out over
the same view, generation after generation, feeling a
strange kinship with them.

She wondered what they might think of her choices
in the house, the few small personal touches she had
brought to the already incredible spaces. She had
claimed an office from one of the bedrooms, which
Roman had insisted on filling with state-of-the-art technology, eager to provide whatever material need she
could think of. But it had left the stark difference between the material and the emotional even clearer to
Ella. For while on paper everything Roman did was
perfect, was the epitome of the doting husband, it didn't
quite feel like *him*.

Ella left her office and made her way to the bedroom she had been using. Because that was how she
found herself thinking of it. A room that she was using
until she finally took up residence with her husband in
his room. She opened the wardrobe, scanning her eyes
over the new dresses she had bought, picking out the
one that she had chosen for tonight's meeting with Ivan
Mozorov in Paris. And her eye caught on the red cloak
her fiancé had bought just over a year ago.

And while Ella had been too fearful of shaking the

still fragile foundations of what they were building together, could not quite bring herself to question it, to question him, she couldn't help but wonder whether this might be the jolt they needed. The memory, reminder of what they had been, and hope for what they could be.

As the small private jet banked to the left to come in to land at the small private airfield just outside of Toulouse, Roman rubbed a hand over his face, trying to erase the exhaustion he was sure was now visible. It had to be, because he felt it in every single inch of his body.

Maintaining two fully functioning businesses was surprisingly difficult as, despite the efficient team he had brought into Kolikov Holdings to do a full audit, his grandfather's business had accrued a little more than its sterling reputation over the years. It had accrued debts. And the steel fortress around his heart tightened at the thought that the old bastard really had had the last laugh.

Roman wanted nothing more than to tear it to shreds, but the promise he'd made to Ella… It had him warring with an instinct that had been honed over nearly eighteen years, and a desire to be better, to do better, to give her what it was she wanted. And if that came at the cost of what *he* wanted? That was why he'd had two proposals drawn up by his team. One for liquidation and one for a complete overhaul.

But, he ruefully admitted to himself, it wasn't just that. His exhaustion stemmed mostly from the fact that he hadn't had a decent night's sleep for even one night in the estate he shared with Ella. Knowing that she was along the hall, knowing that he hadn't enforced the sleeping arrangements he'd crassly thrown at her in a fit of pique, was undoing him.

And when he wasn't thinking about the ecstasy that only his wife had brought him he was wondering what kind of father he would be. His own father had abandoned him, Vladimir had been a cruel, manipulative piece of work and the foster homes afterwards not much better. Until now, he'd embraced a solitary path, a ruthless pursuit of single-minded vengeance. What if he betrayed his child? What if he betrayed Ella? All these thoughts were sneaking in under the defences of a certainty that usually protected his conscience. The certainty that he was doing the right thing. Though he knew that generating two plans for two different futures was not *'doing the right thing'*. Not for Ella, anyway.

Slamming the door on the car that had brought him home, he closed the door on the fears he refused to expose to his wife. Dorcas was standing guard at the door, wagging her tail furiously but clearly knowing better than to pounce on him. Unaccountably, something in his chest eased to see the animal so happy at his arrival.

As he entered the hallway he ground to a halt at the sight of his wife, at the large mirror by the side table, putting in her earrings. It was such a simple gesture, so simply domestic, that it took him a moment to realise that she was dressed in a stunning creation that shone beneath the lights in the hall.

The bodice that encased her chest was made up of thousands of folds of pale pink chiffon, all meeting to twist in the centre of her breasts, drawing his hungry gaze to the perfection they hid. The cap sleeves, dotted with crystals, perched on her shoulders as if almost about to fall, illuminating the length of her collarbone and the beautiful curve of her neck. The material gathered beneath a band at her waist, and plunged to the floor in swathes of silk.

The beauty of his wife undid him completely, robbing him of speech or thought—at least any thought other than *mine*.

She turned to him then, head still bent, fiddling with an earring, and frowned. A look of hurt passed across her features, which she vainly tried to hide. Turning back to the mirror, she said, 'You have forgotten.'

Honestly, Roman would have replied that he'd forgotten his own name until he caught sight of the invitation on the table and something cold and hard gripped his gut.

'The ballet,' he said, his tone completely devoid of emotion.

'The meeting with Ivan Mozorov,' she clarified. 'Apparently he enjoys mixing pleasure with business, and has generously graced me with the period of the interval to make my pitch.' She turned back to him, having won the battle over her earring. 'It's okay,' she said, shaking her head in a way that clearly indicated it was anything but, 'you can stay—'

'I just need ten minutes,' Roman said, stalking past his wife and towards his room and the shower, desperate to wash off the cold sweat that had gathered at the nape of his neck.

Not for a minute did he think Ella had realised what she had done, what that would do to him. And, for the first time he could remember, that hurt.

His muscles ached as he climbed the staircase towards the bedroom. He pulled off his jacket and threw it on the bed, he struggled with the cufflinks at his wrists and toed off his shoes. All these things were done automatically and blindly. Because, in his mind's eye, he saw his mother staring at the small black and white television set in the small room they shared as she watched her old ballet company perform for the Russian president. He saw her round, wide unblinking eyes fill with a sheen of tears still yet to be shed. Even as a child, he'd heard her unspoken thoughts.

That could have been me. That should *have been me.*

His touch, his attempted hug, his words of love hadn't been enough to pull her from the trance-like way she had watched every second of the performance.

And that had been the one and only time he'd ever seen the ballet. Before tonight.

The Palais Garnier in Paris was breathtaking. The nineteenth-century opera house was a glory of pillars and arches, flanked by two magnificent golden statues proclaiming the beauty of the building. If Ella had been awed by the exterior of the building, the interior was almost too much. Stunning marble flooring reached to the dual arched staircases, at the bottom of which two female allegories held torches as if to guide the visitor onwards and upwards.

As they took their seats in the box that Célia had somehow arranged for her and her husband, Ella scanned the auditorium in the vain hope that she might be able to catch sight of Ivan before the interval. The hushed whispers of the audience rose up from below, inciting a low thrum of excitement within her—not just for the business meeting but because she had not been to the ballet for years.

How much had changed since she'd last seen a performance. Vladimir now gone from her life, she now married and about to be a mother herself. But Ella forced her mind back to the task at hand. She wasn't here for this performance, but one of her own. To secure their first client. It had meant so much to her that Roman hadn't cried off and had come with her. Although, casting a glance to where her husband sat, grim-faced and clench-jawed, she wondered if perhaps it would have been better if he had stayed behind.

Just as she worked up the courage to ask him if he was okay, the orchestra began their warm up and an expectant hush descended. The lights in the auditorium dimmed and soon Ella was lulled into the beautiful and heartbreaking story of *Giselle*.

By the time that the curtain came up for the interval Ella's heart ached and the tissue clutched in her hand was damp from the tears that she had swept away from sight. But she thrust all thoughts aside as she now had to focus on Ivan and her business.

Roman shook his head when she asked if he wanted to accompany her, his focus zeroed in on the empty stage. If she'd had more presence of mind, if she hadn't been so distracted by her own focus, she might have entreated him to explain, might have wondered what had happened to cast her husband in such a dark aura. But she hadn't and as she went in search of Ivan she instead only felt the thrill of the chase, the hope and expectation that she would secure her and Célia's first client.

'Come on, darling.'

It was his mother's voice, not Ella's, that Roman heard when she returned to him.

'Let's go.' Ella's clipped words cut through the memories that had shrouded him the moment he'd remembered where she'd wanted to go that evening. As if his mind had worked against him, had purposely chosen to forget that they were to attend the ballet.

He frowned, his mind taking a moment to catch up with what Ella had just stated.

'Go?'

'Yes. I… I want to go.'

'What happened with Ivan?' he asked as he stood up and was practically hauled from the box, out into the hallway mid-performance and out to the waiting car that would take them to the helicopter he'd arranged to fly them back home.

'Nothing.'

'Nothing?'

'Are you going to repeat everything I say?' she asked, the bitterness on her tongue nothing compared to the glittering tears he could see gathering in the corners of her eyes.

'But I've heard your pitch, it was faultless. He would have been mad to turn it down.'

'It wasn't a problem with the business plan,' she said, her head turned away from him as they slipped into the limousine.

'Then—'

'You.'

'What?' he asked, outraged.

'Ivan was deeply apologetic, but he simply wouldn't do business with the wife of the Great Wolf,' she concluded scathingly.

An almost savage fury roared within him—that he had been the cause of Ella's upset—and then he truly appreciated the irony within that thought. His mind quickly veered away from that to action, to purpose. Roman was more than willing and capable of tangling with anyone who would want to mess with him, but his wife? Oh, no. That would not stand.

'He will regret it,' Roman forced darkly through his teeth.

'Really? And what damage would that do to my business? You can't bully and cajole clients into working with me.'

'I will find someone for you,' he declared.

'No.'

'But—'

'I said no. I think you've done enough, don't you?'

Every single other question, suggestion or attempt to broach the shield around his wife was met with a withdrawn silence that cut him as deeply as the thought that he had been responsible for her failure.

By the time they had returned to the estate and he had watched Ella, all poise and elegance, retreat to her room, Roman felt as if he were fit to burst. Sleep would be impossible as fury had lined his veins like detonating cord and he needed to move, to walk off this energy that was almost sparking from his fingers.

Restlessness like he'd never known before spurred him out onto the sloping garden that led towards the stream and the forest. The darkness of the night shrouded him in a heady combination of past memories and present concerns. That he'd been the cause of Ella's failed business meeting ate at him, that the reputation he'd garnered in order to achieve his own ends with Vladimir had somehow directed Ella's future had caught him by the throat and the ache that formed there lodged into a solid, painful thing.

* * *

Ella hadn't been able to sleep. She'd tried, forcing herself to let go of the anger and frustration that had clouded her since being dismissed by Ivan. That it was not the business or the plan that he had objected to but the person she had married had infuriated her. Not for one moment had she placed the blame at Roman's door—but as she lay in bed she realised that was quite possibly what he thought.

No, she was furious that, once again, she had not been seen or valued in her own right, but as an attachment to someone else. A way to lash back at Roman for some prior reckoning that he had nothing to do with.

Only now, as flashes of the night before burst through her mind, did Ella realise that something had been wrong with Roman long before her business meeting with Ivan. Something she had failed to see at the time. Because the dark aura that had surrounded him belonged to neither her fiancé nor the man she seemed to have married. It was something strange and new and something she now desperately wanted to confront.

But his bed was empty, his room, the entire house, save for Dorcas, curled up on her bed in the corner of the landing. She had raised her head briefly as Ella had moved about the empty rooms and, apparently deciding that this was the business of humans, had promptly gone back to sleep.

Returning to the landing, Ella took in the view of the sloping garden, the forests, the copper domed gazebo glinting in the moonlight and the silver thread of the freshwater lake winding across the bottom of the garden like a slash upon the horizon. Although Ella hadn't seen a glimpse of him, she instinctively knew that he was out there. She ran back to her room and grabbed the first thing that came to hand—the red cloak—swept it around her shoulders and, with bare feet, slipped from the house and into the forest.

She found him sitting on the cold stone steps of the gazebo, staring out into the distance, where a strange fog had begun to roll in off the Pyrenees, creating an odd sense of foreboding. For a moment she held her breath, taking in the sight of him—shirtsleeves rolled back, tie loose and hanging down either side of his collar, as motionless as the stone he sat upon.

The fall of his slightly long hair had been swept back from his forehead, his nose proud and jawline determined, clenched, as if warding back some great bank of emotions. It had been the same way he'd looked as she had snuck glances at him through the ballet that evening.

She heard him sigh, an exhalation of something more than just oxygen, an acknowledgement of her presence. Without a word, she stepped forward from the soft springy grass that had been merely damp with dew onto the solid frigid stone, sending shivers through her feet and legs all the way up her spine. Ignoring it, she took a seat beside him, leaving the smallest space between their bodies.

For a moment they stayed like that, the silence vibrating with unspoken words, a conversation of bodies, adjusting to the presence of another.

'So, do you come here often?' she ventured, regretting the crass joke almost the moment the words had come out of her mouth.

'Yes,' he replied after a breath, surprising her with his honesty.

'Really?'

'Yes,' he said, smiling gently into the night.

'I didn't know.'

'I… I've always found it slightly difficult to sleep, but…'

'It's been worse here?'

He nodded. Ella opened her mouth to ask why, but Roman pressed on.

'When I was younger—before my mother…' He stopped, seeming to begin again in a different time and place. 'After Vladimir cut off my mother, and she could no longer dance because she was pregnant with me, she was hired as a cleaner by a rich family in Voskresensk. They were a decent enough family, from what I could tell. But they had this garden that bordered the river there. And sometimes—more often after she became ill—she would wake me in the middle of the night, and bring me out under the stars to dance.'

As if he had conjured her from his memories, Roman could have sworn that he saw her that night. Dressed in a white cotton shift, moving beneath the stars, twirling pirouettes, the gentle sweep of her arms as they reached, yearning, probing the night air, dancing to music that only she could hear, the gentle footfalls and sweeps creating their own rhythm. He had sat there for hours, over hundreds of nights, and it was not enough, would never be enough. He would swap his soul to be sitting there, shivering in the cold and not minding it one bit, because it was the only time he'd ever seen his mother truly happy. Truly free.

'She was an incredible dancer. She had been the principal at the Utonchennyy Ballet Company. And the last performance she had with them before Vladimir cut her from his life was *Giselle*.'

From the corner of his eye he saw Ella raise her hand to her mouth as if to stifle some expression he wasn't sure either one of them wanted to acknowledge.

'What was she like?' Ella ventured after a while using hushed tones as if not wanting to break the gossamer-thin web around them.

'Sad,' Roman admitted. 'She was sad a lot of the time. It was hard for her, the life of a cleaner so different from the luxury that she had grown up in. I could see, even as a child, the wrench that she felt at not being able to give me more. The struggles she had, working and raising a child on her own. But the nights when she would bring me out were…they were enough for me.'

'I'm sorry. So sorry. If I'd known, I would never have asked you to come with me.'

Roman didn't do her the injustice of dismissing her apology. 'I know.'

'I wish I could have seen her dance.'

He smiled. Somehow, no matter how their wedding had come about, he knew that his mother would have liked Ella. The kindness in her, the goodness. All the things that he was not. That he had forced out of his breast the moment he had laid his mother to rest. And, for the first time ever, he feared that while his mother might have liked Ella, she might not have liked what her son had become.

'She would have been proud of what you have achieved,' Ella said as if she had somehow sensed his inner thoughts.

'But would she have been proud of me?' he said, finally giving voice to his fear.

For a moment he thought she might not answer, might not be able to find any redeeming quality within her husband.

Then he felt her small hand slip beneath his arm, winding him towards her, and her head lay on his shoulder as she leaned into him.

'She would have been proud of the man determined to raise his child with its mother. Proud of the man determined to give his wife the home she'd always wanted. She would have been proud of the man who comforted his wife when she felt lost.'

'Even if that man was the cause of his wife's insecurity?'

Ella nestled her head deeper into his shoulder. 'And proud of the man who would change his ways to try to be better for his wife and child. Because that's all we can do. Try.' She paused, as if working up towards something Roman feared might hurt. Might cause an even greater ache in his chest. 'Earlier I said I was sorry for asking you to come to the ballet tonight. But I'm not,' she said, pulling back so that she could look at him, so that he could see the sincerity in her eyes. 'I'm not, because it brought us here. Because I now see a little of your mother.'

'I haven't thought about her dancing in years,' Roman admitted roughly.

'That is a shame. Because I want you to have those memories. I want you to talk about her, so that our child can know their grandmother. I don't have any real memories of my parents, only what Vladimir told me, and my grandmother told me. And I want you to be able to talk about Tatiana—share stories, anecdotes, memories that made you laugh and love, because that's what I want our child to be surrounded by.'

He looked at his wife for the first time, seeing her properly as she sat beside him, her cornflower-blue eyes large and round and her lips so red against the pale creamy skin lit by the stars, and he wanted to lose himself in her. Wanted to take what she was consciously or unconsciously offering. But he didn't feel as if he had that right. Didn't know if his touch, his kiss would be welcome after all the damage he had wrought. Not just the loss of a business deal, but long before then.

And as if she could sense his hesitation, sense the current of his thoughts, the need coursing through him like wildfire, as if all this time, all these weeks and months of frustration and want and desire, came crashing about them in this one moment, she pulled him to her and pressed her mouth against his in comfort, in her own need.

The passion she offered him, matched only by his own, set light to his thoughts, to the hold of the past and the uncertainty of the future. The moment her lips opened to him, her tongue drawing his deeper into their kiss, he was lost.

He spread the red cloak across the marble floor of the stone gazebo, the crimson pooling about her as he laid her back.

'This was what I saw when I bought this cloak,' he admitted, desire painting his voice dark. 'Removing it from you, revealing the beauty within.'

The thin cotton nightdress glowing in the starlight made her angelic and him unworthy. 'I should take you back to the house, to soft cotton sheets and soft deep mattresses. You deserve more than this.'

More than he could offer.

She looked at him then, large crystal-blue eyes wide and crimson mouth part opened on a breath. 'There is nowhere I'd rather be than here beneath the stars with you.'

In a second Roman had claimed her lips with his, and Ella felt an almost primal cry rise within her. A cry of loss, of longing, of comfort, of desperation. The sword that had hung above them for so long had dropped and severed the final barriers holding them both back as hands swept across bodies, tongues swept across teeth, lips across skin. She felt him draw up the cotton nightdress at her thighs, bunching it in his hands, both trapping her by the taut material and protecting her from him.

The peaks of her nipples pressing against the thin fabric refused to disguise her want and she no longer wanted to hide it. No longer wanted the power of her need to come from anger or resentment, or a yearning for the unknown. This time, she strove for something more. Because she knew that this night had cost them both and only their touch could offer comfort the way that words, yet, could not.

Her hands ran over his shirt, desperate to feel skin, wanting, needing more. As he pressed open-mouthed kisses against her neck, across her collarbone and further to between the V of her neck, she vainly struggled with the buttons on his shirt—the passion he wrought in her making her fingers clumsy and awkward.

His hands released her for the moment it took to haul the shirt over his head and discard it, as if equally impatient as she to be skin to skin, but instead of returning to the kiss he held himself back, hovering over her, as if consuming her with his gaze. There was something in it, something deep and dark, and she went to raise a hand of comfort to his hardened jaw. But he shook his head to warn her off.

'I… I don't even know if I can hope to be the man you should have by your side. You're making me want to, but…'

'You once asked me to trust you. And now I'm asking that of you. Trust me, because I know you can be. You *are*,' Ella said, feeling the truth of her words settling in her chest—a chest that ached for her husband, for the pain he had experienced, all that she could see he had sacrificed. A boy trying to avenge the death of his mother, a man trying to be better, do better. A man scared of opening himself up to what it was they were weaving between them.

He returned to their kiss as if he too understood the need to feel the purity of the connection they seemed only to share here, now.

Roman pushed up under her nightdress, his hands sliding over her thighs, the heat from his palms both soothing and torturous at the same time as each sweep moved closer and closer to where she wanted to feel him. She felt his fingers pull at the edges of her underwear, drawing them almost leisurely down her thighs and from her ankles.

Her fingers once again struggled with the belt on his trousers, only to find them thrust aside by Roman's efficient swift movements as he freed himself.

'Tell me you want this.' His words were more of a plea than a demand. 'Tell me you're as lost to this as I am. Tell me—'

'I do, I am, and right now I'd tell you anything you want to hear if you would—'

All words, all coherent thought was lost as he thrust into her, the delicious smooth glide of him within her taking her by surprise and propelling her towards an edge that she felt far too close to. Her hands flew to his hips as he entered her again and again, wringing pleasure from her that she feared would never be satisfied, would never be appeased. But she had been wrong. Because almost against her will the world came crashing down about her as everything within her rose to reach out to it. Her body, heart and soul pushed and pulled in a million different directions, yet all coming back to one place, one thing… Roman.

CHAPTER NINE

And for a brief moment Red Riding Hood was happy. She was proud of the relationship she'd forged with the wolf, proud of what she'd accomplished. But, as we all know, pride comes before a fall, and Red Riding Hood couldn't see the chasm before her. Only him. Only the wolf.
                    The Truth About Little Red Riding Hood
                                        —Roz Fayrer

ELLA HAD NEVER gone back to her room in the house. Since the night of the ballet she had shared his bed, waiting for him while he was away in Russia and delighting in him as he returned to her in France.

And each time he did, he marvelled that what had once been a small, almost imperceptible presence around her abdomen was now most definitely there and had required yet another shopping trip exclusively for maternity wear. Roman thought she might have only a few more weeks before being visibly pregnant, provided she wore very loose clothing. And part of him couldn't wait until the moment he could see it, the constant proof that his wife was carrying his child.

They'd had the second scan—the first for them both

together—and the scariest. But the tests came back clear and they had both heaved an emotional breath, reached for each other in that moment, seeking and finding support, and Roman felt another stone in the wall around his heart break loose.

But as the stones fell, fear came with it, slipping through the cracks. Insidious whispers and thoughts he fought valiantly to keep from his wife. His innocent wife, who had been punished enough for his actions. She had tried to keep her own disappointment at failing to secure the client from him, but he had not missed the worried phone calls to her business partner, Célia. That Ella sought to protect *him* from the responsibility of it ate at him. He might have lived his whole life walking his path of vengeance alone, but he no longer felt like the Great Wolf—a name he had once delighted in.

He had found himself a pack, and Dorcas had taken to fiercely protecting Ella, following her everywhere she went, resting her head on her lap when Ella would sit, almost as if guarding their child.

Her words from the night of the ballet performance had run through his head as if on a loop, in time with his breathing and heartbeat. Her assurance that he could be enough, that he could be more than he had been. For her. With her. It had been a seductive call and it had somehow morphed into being his want and need.

He realised he wanted to embrace all the things that he had hidden from for so long. That he wanted a future with her, not just because of their child, but because of her. In the days since he had spoken to her of his mother, other memories had surfaced. Fractured moments of his mother laughing, the feel of her hand on his cheek, the way she had swept back the hair from his forehead and placed a kiss there. For years he'd only remembered the sadness, and now he saw that his mother had given him so much more. And, rather than pushing the memories back down as he had as a young man—as he'd needed to—or quickly refocusing his mind on some damned pursuit of vengeance, he took the time to remember, to hold them up and inspect them, feel them and embrace them. And it had caused a painfully sweet yearning for the love he'd forgotten.

None of which would have happened without his wife's belief that there was something worth saving within him, something worth preserving there for their future. For their child's future. His mother had once made him feel like that and now Ella was making him feel the same way.

And he wanted, *needed*, to give her something back, but felt it had to be perfect, that he had to do everything in his power to give her what she so greatly deserved.

Which was why, he justified to himself, he had made the call. Loukas Liordis was a Greek billionaire with a bad-boy reputation to match. And Roman, after a particularly intense drinking session in his New York club three years before, knew Loukas needed to redeem that reputation. It was that which made him the perfect client for Ella and Célia. Loukas had agreed to keep his involvement a secret, more than happy if it would lead to the redemption of his reputation, and promised to find a way to reach out to Ella through official channels.

But as the days wore on, without any word from Ella about a surprise new business contact, Roman began to regret his impulsive decision.

Instinctively, he knew that Ella would see it as an act of deceit, of going behind her back in precisely the way she had forbidden. Even in his attempts to make things right, to do and be better, he was starting from an act of betrayal. He'd even begun to hope that Loukas would have forgotten, would somehow have changed his mind.

Until he heard the most unlikely scream of delight from his wife and cursed inwardly, because he knew. All his hopes had been in vain. Because whether Loukas revealed his involvement or not, he knew that Ella would find out. And she would never forgive him.

Better to ask forgiveness than permission, his inner voice whispered seductively, even though something in his chest cried foul.

Ella came running down the steps, pausing midway when she saw him in the grand hallway of their house in France. The pure joy shining from her eyes and lighting her features made his heart drop, even as a smile pulled at his lips.

'Can we go to Fiji?'

'What?' he replied, not quite expecting her request.

'Fiji—can we go? Célia can't, and I…we might have a client, and I've never been and it would be—'

'Of course,' he said, willing in that moment to give his wife anything…anything but the honesty she had made him swear to.

'Are you sure you don't mind? I know that you must be busy with Kolikov Holdings and your own business.'

With yet another whip lashing against his conscience, Roman smiled through the self-recrimination. 'When are we going?'

She looked uncertain for the first time. 'Tomorrow?'

He laughed at this, not at Ella's uncertainty but the speed with which his future could come crashing down upon him. The impending moment when his wife would realise that he would not, could not, be what she needed him to be. The moment she would realise that he was so irretrievably damaged by his past that he could not hope for his future.

'Of course, Ella. Whatever you wish.'

Because he could at least give her this. He could ensure her future was secure, even if his was not.

Viti Yalo was a private island in the South Pacific that only allowed seventy visitors at any one point. As the private jet approached the small landing strip Ella peered at glimpses of paradise through the small round window. Turquoise sea and slashes of white sand bordered lush green patches peppered with tiny brown rooftops and the little square tiles of infinity pools that seemed unnecessary when next to the beautiful South Pacific Ocean.

It was a patchwork quilt of the dreams of the rich and famous—and suddenly Ella felt neither rich enough nor famous enough to be here. But her husband descended the small steps of the aircraft, covered the short distance towards the sleek black limousine waiting for them and barely spared a glance for the uniformed driver holding the door open for him as if he did this kind of thing every day.

She marvelled at the inherent power and authority of her husband. Wished and wanted to borrow it for herself. Because despite the brave face she had worn since Ivan had turned them down Ella had begun to fear that, although he had given the reason as her husband, it was her business plan that was the problem. It was a fear she had kept to herself, not wanting to betray Célia's confidence any further.

She had been relieved when Roman had agreed to her request that they arrive two days prior to the meeting with Loukas Liordis, so that she could prepare the pitch and the specifics and details and all the other minutiae that was in all likelihood unnecessary. But she would be prepared this time. Not willing to let herself, her business or Célia down. And, in some small way, determined to prove herself to her husband too.

But all Ella's internal musings were cut short when they arrived at the one-storey dwelling where they were staying. At each corner of the main house sat triangular turrets of a sort, bamboo thatching topping the roof of the building that sat squat and wide, clinging to the edge of the ocean. Stone arches indicated several rooms with windows that looked out across the water, a small pathway at the side of the house leading towards a long stretch of white sandy beach, dotted with palm trees. A somewhat improbable glass-encased pool sat to the left of the house and the sweep of the bay ensured complete privacy from any other dwelling nearby.

'I've changed my mind,' she said, laughing at the look of concern—almost horror—that passed across Roman's features. 'I don't want to live in France any more. My grandmother will be fine. Let's just move here!' she cried in delight as she ran to the doorway of the house, desperate to see what treasures she could find inside.

Every single room had large windows revealing the incredible view of the ocean. The two rooms bracketing either end of the house simply opened out onto the elements. Large hurricane lamps swinging gently in the breeze hung from the ceiling and swayed before large sprawling round benches that could easily have been the most exquisite beds covered in cushions and draped in throws that had her imagining a sunset with her husband beside her and… She broke off that train of thought as her cheeks heated and her pulse began to thump.

It was a luxurious fantasy, magical in the sheer opulence of it all. In the central living area, on the table had been placed a large vase of gloriously bright crimson flowers, beautiful in their bloom. A bottle of champagne, glistening with condensation, sat in a bucket beside two glasses, and a bowl of chocolate-tipped strawberries nestled on ice cubes. And that barely even began the welcome package the island had left for them.

As she moved through every room she saw signs of small gifts and touches that made her feel like a princess. Rose petals on the floor of the most beautiful bedroom she'd ever seen, swathes of richly patterned silk wraps for her to keep with 'our compliments'. Local artisanal paintings hung on the pure white walls, adding splashes of colours Ella would never have imagined liking, spreading joy through her, covering over her fears and concerns about the upcoming meeting— and suddenly she wished they were there just for them.

Everywhere she looked, the hypnotic horizon of the ocean was displayed in the distance and she thought that she never wanted to leave.

Roman found her where she had dropped herself onto the plush sofa, gazing at her as if searching for approval. She smiled. 'I think I could lower myself to spend a few days here,' she said mockingly.

'Very gracious of you,' he replied and she loved the teasing tone in his voice, so different from the husband who had seemed pressed down under an invisible weight she couldn't fathom since the night at the ballet.

'We have reservations at the restaurant…' and Ella couldn't help but feel a little crestfallen at the idea of leaving this beautiful place, even in all likelihood for an equally beautiful place, but she didn't want to share this. Share Roman. She wanted to tuck herself into this magical bubble and never leave. 'But I'm sure we could ask them to bring the food here.'

It was startling how easily he could read her. She'd never thought herself that expressive, but Roman seemed to know, to sense what she was thinking— sometimes even before she did.

'This is going to be impossible,' she almost wailed, once again mockingly. 'How am I supposed to focus on a business proposal with all this…?' She gestured around her, searching for a word that would express even an ounce of the beauty she was staring at. But for once she wasn't looking at the ocean, or the rooms, or the beautiful things contained within. She was looking at her husband. A husband who did not seem hungry for food in that moment.

Roman couldn't, wouldn't, stop the smile lifting his lips at his wife's insincere complaints. He had wanted to give her this—to give her everything and more.

'First, we eat. And during our meal you can practise your pitch as much and as many times as you need. But after…that time is for us,' he promised.

'Nope. Don't need to. I know it by heart. Let's just skip to the "us" time,' she said, reaching for him, pulling him towards her.

He placed a kiss on her lips, chaste and sweeter for it, and pulled away. 'I am simply making sure that you go into the meeting feeling completely prepared,' he gently whispered, refusing to be responsible for any further damage to her career.

Her large round eyes, matching the colour of the turquoise sea behind her, flickered with understanding, seeming to sense his guilt, and she reluctantly agreed.

Over a first course of filo pastry wrapped scallops in a creamy leek sauce, finished with fresh figs, Ella outlined the strategies of placing Loukas's business with handpicked charities within Greece and across the globe. Through the second course of sous-vide lobster with a mango, avocado, red onion and lettuce salad, Ella described how she and Célia would ensure each event and investment would be carefully curated by them, all communication running through them in order to filter only information of the utmost importance to him directly, reducing the tax on his precious time. And over a dessert of gingerbread cannoli, kirsch mousse and cinnamon ice cream, she delivered the financial incentives for offsetting some of his extraordinary wealth against global tax breaks and outlined how the positive impact of the publicity garnered would be immeasurable.

By the time coffee was served, Roman was halfway to demanding she drop all and any interaction with Liordis and muscling in as her first client himself. He was impressed. The vague gathering of thoughts she'd had when they had first met in France had been honed, stripped back and fine-tuned to the point of excellence. Ivan had been a fool. A fool that he was pleased his wife had not succeeded with. Liordis, he was sure, would not make the same mistake.

'And now,' she demanded, placing her knife and fork together on the plate, 'can we please—pretty please— get to the "us" time?'

Yes, everything in Roman roared. Whatever she wanted, while she still wanted it, he would give.

Two days later Ella swept into the restaurant she and Roman had still not visited. She felt…powerful. Powerful and sensual and confident. The soft white linen shift reaching to her thighs and a deceptively comfortable pair of palazzo trousers in a beautiful rust colour were both elegant and practical. Because, Ella realised, this would be the last business meeting that she could have while still disguising her pregnancy.

She was not naïve—she knew that her pregnancy could affect the way some potential clients viewed her and her future involvement in any deal she would secure. But both she and Célia had already decided that they would not be the clientele they would wish to attract. Roman had reassured her that it was unlikely to worry Liordis and she trusted him. Nothing would dim the excitement she felt thrumming through her veins. It was almost an echo of the sensual delight her husband had driven her to on the two preceding evenings as they'd watched the sun descend over the South Pacific Ocean, as their cries of pleasure mingled with those of exotic birds and the unconscious rhythm of their bodies followed the gentle sweep of waves moving back and forth over the beach below.

Ella would not have needed the careful guidance of the head waiter to direct her to Loukas Liordis. The man sat at a table on the decking, separated from the rest of the customers inside the restaurant, who were unable or unwilling to prevent the curious glances they cast his way. Although there were a few other tables dotted around the sweeping decking, Ella knew that they would have the space entirely to themselves so that no one would be able to eavesdrop on their conversation. She had ensured as much.

She took the short walk winding between the other diners to look at the man she hoped would be her and Célia's first client. With his view secured on the horizon, she could take her fill. He was very attractive—Ella could see how he had earned his wicked reputation—and was even mildly surprised not to feel something within her pull towards his impressive aura. But a red ribbon had formed around her feelings for her husband, one that would never be severed by anyone other than Roman.

Even sitting, she could tell he was tall. Low brows lay heavily over deceptively slumberous eyes and the tawny hair, stylishly chaotic, almost roguish in its refusal to adhere to neatness, was a surprise to someone who expected to see darker features. His full lips drew into a large smile as he stood upon seeing her and graciously met her with a kiss to each cheek.

'Ella,' he said, and the informality of using her first name, the intimacy it invited, would probably have made another woman swoon. The heat of his hand at her arm and the smell of his cologne, all appealing, yet Ella found herself immune—as if her body craved only one touch, one scent, one person.

'Mr Liordis,' she replied.

'Loukas, please,' he said, charmingly, refusing to return to his seat until she had taken her own.

They ordered their drinks, his gaze not once wavering from her face as she requested a tonic water, as if he didn't need to look for confirmation of her situation. Although no expression passed over his features, she realised in an instant that it wouldn't do to underestimate this man, despite his lazy demeanour. Whether he realised her pregnancy or not, he had the grace not to allude to it.

'You are here with your husband?' he asked.

'Yes,' she said, unable to keep the smile from her face.

'Ah, then I will not keep you from him for long, for this place is a paradise for lovers.'

Loukas proceeded to explain that he'd been looking for a charity to put his energies into for some time, but had been hampered by his reputation. He was charming, self-deprecating, but with a fierce intelligence she recognised from her husband. She read between the lines and a little thread of excitement curled through her as she realised that he needed them as much as they needed him.

But, for all his practised charm, Ella found herself longing for the dark edges and plain speaking of her husband, figuring them somehow more real than the careless façade Loukas was presenting.

The meeting was going well. Really well. He had listened with a focus that simmered beneath the languorous gaze, had questioned a surprising amount of the finer details, yet Ella had risen to each one—and she could tell that he was impressed. Impressed and tempted. However, she could feel the 'but' on the horizon and she began to feel the first prickling of concern.

'This is a very strong business plan, Ella. Your anticipation of many of my concerns has been impressive, and I really would like to look into this further.'

'But?' she asked with a smile to take the sting out of her fear.

'But I do have one concern. I'm not quite sure yet that your company is financially viable enough to do what I need you to do for me.'

'I assure you that we are.'

He grimaced as he shook his head, clearly not convinced, but also clearly not refusing them outright. 'If you can show me that there is more capital, say between four or five million, then I would readily sign the papers. But without it...' He trailed off and shrugged apologetically.

As Ella's stomach dropped, her mind furiously spun, filtering through her private bank accounts, calling to mind Célia's own investments. There was one option, her only option. But would she take it?

'Would you be willing to give me two days?'

'Of course,' he replied. 'I do believe in your company and what you are offering and would very much relish the opportunity to work with you and your clients. Get in touch when you're ready and we'll talk.'

Roman had been pacing almost since the moment Ella had left to meet Liordis. Whether because of the effect he had had on her last client meeting or that he had come to see just how much this meant to Ella, this meeting had eclipsed even his own business interests in importance.

And while he had been the one to bring Loukas to the table, still as yet undiscovered by his wife, he had not been assured of the outcome. In what felt like a matter of minutes Ella returned, and he was shocked to find, when he checked his watch, that nearly two hours had gone by.

He realised immediately that something was wrong.

The way she looked not at him but at the horizon, her mind clearly whirring away rather than relishing the joy of success. It ate at him, and even the knowledge that he should wait until she was ready couldn't prevent the question falling from his lips.

'What happened?'

'He… Loukas does want to sign with us…'

'But?'

She let loose a gentle, not quite bitter half-laugh at something he couldn't fathom.

'He doesn't think we have the capital to do what we say we can.'

'He's wrong,' Roman declared with a finality that surprised them both.

'Maybe…maybe not. He made some suggestions that were surprisingly astute—'

'Given his reputation?'

'Yes. It would most definitely not do to underestimate him. But I can't deny that those suggestions might stretch us, given our current finances.'

'Yes, but trying to arrange for more capital could stretch you further,' Roman responded, quickly seeing to the heart of her concern.

'Maybe. But…' She turned to him then, her hands rolling over each other before her, an unusually insecure gesture from his wife. 'But if I were to sell you my shares in Kolikov Holdings—'

'No.' Roman's quick, determined response surprised them both.

'Roman,' she chided. 'Will you hear me out?'

'I don't need to.'

'Roman,' she tried again, and he realised that she just couldn't see it. Couldn't see how giving him her shares, how handing control over to him would tempt him. Would give him the power to take it all away. She would hand over the very thing that kept him on a leash. And instinctively he knew. He knew that should she lose that hold, should she lose the last bargaining chip she had with him, it would destroy everything. Because he would be unable to resist putting those shares to the very use that she would not want. No matter how much she had come to mean to him, no matter how much he wanted to be more…he simply wasn't capable of it. He couldn't change. He had needed to be a monster to fight Vladimir and he was still that same monster. His…feelings for her hadn't changed that. And if he did use the shares to achieve what he wanted, the cost to Ella would be devastating. Her pain and the shock of a second betrayal…it would be too much for her to bear.

'Firstly,' he tried, desperately and silently needing her to understand, 'I don't want you to overstretch your company at such an early stage in its development. At the moment you are risking a great deal. If I say yes, you would risk even more. And secondly, we haven't actually done a market share price, so I couldn't honestly say that you'd get a fair price.'

'I believe in what Célia and I are doing. I believe in this company and know, *know*, it will work. And I don't need a market price, I need a fair one. And I trust you to be fair. I don't need more. I just need enough. And I think five million is a fair and appropriate price. It's enough to inject some of it into the company and still have a cushion that allows for some wiggle room.'

'Please think about this.' He was almost begging. Never before had he felt that sense of a precipice before him.

'Roman, honestly, I don't need to. I know that this will work, I know that this is what I need. Please, would you buy the shares from me?'

And his earlier promise came back to haunt him. That he would give her anything she wanted, while she wanted it from him. Only this time, giving Ella what she wanted…would cost him everything.

Within two days the money had come through from the sale of her shares to Roman, Loukas had happily signed the paperwork, becoming their first client, and Ella was almost bursting with joy. She knew that she had put all of her eggs in one basket, but it was a basket that she and Roman shared. She was investing not only in herself, but them.

Roman was still out wrapping up things with the bank and Kolikov Holdings as Ella watched the sun begin its descent into the South Pacific Ocean. It felt so strange to have the night sky begin to glow about three hours earlier than France, adding to the feeling of a stolen moment outside of time. Ella shivered a little, remembering the last time she had felt like this—before her marriage to Roman. A time that she had felt just belonged to them.

But this was different, she told herself. This was their second chance. How it should have been all along. With a hand soothing over the gentle bump of her abdomen, Ella marvelled at just how much had changed since she had met him that day in the woods near her grandmother's cottage. In some ways, everything she had wanted back then had come to pass. Her marriage to Roman, her business, even their child, she acknowledged.

She might not have liked how they'd got here, but

she couldn't wish it away. Had it not been like that, she might never have got to know the real Roman. Neither the one who had appeared perfect nor the one who had appeared monstrous had been the man she had come to…had come to…

Love.

With a surety that shocked her, the knowledge raced along her veins, fizzing in her blood and lighting something like pure joy within her. She did love him. She loved the man who would do anything to protect their child, the man who had confessed the deep pain hidden beneath his quest for vengeance, the one who still slept lightly in the hope that his mother would one day come and wake him and dance for him in the moonlight. The man who brought her exquisite pleasure and the man who had given her the ability to secure the business she and Célia had worked so hard for.

Energy raced through her body and she wanted to move, to dance, to take this moment and embrace the sheer happiness of it, having reached such a low shortly after her marriage. She picked up her phone and found a song on her music list, one that would perfectly echo everything she feared she might never capture in words.

As the song began the notes swept around her, filling the space and echoing in her heart, asking that she feel love. And she did. Paying no heed to the thought that someone could come upon her, dancing around the beautiful living space, with the most incredible backdrop, Ella danced and danced and danced, an almost intoxicating high running through her veins.

She performed another twirl, the layers of her skirts spinning out from her waist, making her feel like a child again, which was perhaps why she didn't see Roman at first. Didn't see the look on his face that might have stopped her in her tracks had she not been so caught up in her joy.

Roman knew she hadn't seen him yet, and was thankful for it. Because it gave him time. Time to adjust to the fact that, as she spun round the room, he saw his mother. Ella's movements were not the elegant sweeps his mother had made beneath the night sky. Her arms didn't extend and reach out for something intangible, as if the gesture would never end, never stop reaching. Because, he realised, Ella believed she had already found what she was looking for.

The happiness and joy he could almost see vibrating on the air about her, as she moved in time with the song that taunted him, cut him off at the knees.

She turned to him then, eyes seas of sparkles that would rival the night sky, and he knew. He didn't want to, almost asked her not to say what she clearly wanted to say. But his words wouldn't come, while hers poured from her lips like raindrops.

'I'm so happy,' she said, almost strangely apologetic, or embarrassed. But those feelings were apparently put aside or pushed down as he watched her transform into someone assured, confident, someone owning her own sense of self. It was like watching a flower unfurl to bask in everything the sun could give.

'I couldn't have done it without you,' she said as she closed the distance between them. A distance that he wanted, needed, coward that he was. He wanted to explain that she was wrong. He wanted to ask her what she thought she might have been able to do had he not nearly destroyed her by seeking her as his tool for revenge. In a heartbeat, all the times he had seen her question herself because of him, doubt herself because of him, doubt those around her... Because of *him*, came to his mind.

'I love you,' she said. He didn't hear the words above the roaring in his ears but he saw them on her lips, felt them against his skin.

He kissed her then because he couldn't think of what to say, couldn't really begin to understand why her simple declaration could have scared him so much. But one thing he could imagine was the hurt and pain and devastation she would feel when she realised what he was about to do to Vladimir's company.

So he kissed her, stopping all words, all thoughts, all doubts and fears, as if this were the last time he would ever kiss his wife.

CHAPTER TEN

And the wolf gnashed his teeth and snarled, hissed and bit and growled. It was his nature. It was all he knew.

The Truth About Little Red Riding Hood
—Roz Fayrer

SHE HAD BEEN the root of her own downfall, Roman told himself as he marched through the offices of Kolikov Holdings in Moscow. The moment she had sold her shares to him, no matter how much she clearly felt that she had changed, had proved that she was just as innocent and naïve as she had been when he had met her over a year ago in France.

Yes, there was more there—a drive, a deeper complexity, a confidence and self-assurance that almost awed him. Almost. But she was still the same Ella who had agreed to marry a man after only one month of knowing him. And, like her, Roman was still the same as he had been when they had met. A man out for vengeance at any cost.

Ever since she'd let loose those three little words…

Too wrapped up in her thoughts and too busy since, Ella had absolutely no idea of the effect they'd had on Roman. They had haunted his dreams and sliced through his waking hours. The only other person to say such a thing to him had been cruelly torn from him without Roman being able to prevent it.

For so long he had been sure. Certain that his path of vengeance was just. For so long he had lived by the promise he'd made his mother on her deathbed. That Vladimir would be punished, that the company he'd loved more than his own child would be destroyed.

But Ella had made him want. Want things to be different, for *him* to be different. And he realised that for a few months he'd been living more of a lie than any he'd ever told. Because he'd lied to himself. Told himself that he could have things he didn't deserve. Could feel things that his closed off, damaged heart would never be capable of. That he could, in some impossible way, compensate for the truly awful things he had done to Ella.

And it had lasted until she'd asked him to buy her shares. Until she'd given him the final tool to complete the journey he had started almost eighteen years before. And he'd known. Known that he could not, would not refuse to use it.

Because if he put aside his plans now, if he changed his mind, then it would mean that every single thing he'd planned, done, right down to marrying Ella in the first place…it would have all been for nothing. And that was impossible. All the things he'd given up, all of the softer parts of him he'd sacrificed in order to exact revenge against Vladimir, all of the things that Ella deserved were gone.

Roman could not have, or *be,* both. He couldn't love her and not pay the price of his own actions. He couldn't love her and not acknowledge that he was more dangerous to his wife and child than any other threat they could face. So the only thing left to him was to burn it all down to the ground. Every last piece of Vladimir's company—and his marriage along with it.

Because that was the only way to protect Ella and their child, to ensure that his decisions and actions didn't hurt them beyond repair. To ensure that the damage done to his soul by so many years of vengeance didn't poison their innocence. The greatest act of love he could show either of them was to walk away.

He paused just outside the doorway to the boardroom, filled with the sycophantic men and women who had bolstered his grandfather's ego, who had come to represent all that had been inflicted on his mother. In that moment he felt hatred course through his veins. A hatred that *had* to be more powerful than anything else in him if he was to finally get what he'd wanted. A hatred he needed if he was to overcome the desire to turn back. To seek what he did not deserve. To throw himself at Ella's feet and beg for forgiveness. With gritted teeth, he hung on to his anger like a drowning man, walked through the doorway and came to a halt at the head of the table.

'Ladies and gentlemen, I have a proposition for you. One that you would be inconceivably stupid not to accept...'

Célia's laughter rained over Ella, who had not been able to stop smiling since Fiji. They had celebrated the success of securing their first client with a lovely long lunch—Célia sipping on champagne and Ella on ginger and elderflower *pressé*.

She leaned a shoulder against Célia's as they stood

at the large iron-work windows of their beautiful new office that looked out over Paris. The nineteenth-century building had needed extensive work to make it a space suitable for their needs, but Célia had risen to the challenge. Ella loved the exposed brickwork and open space of the central offices, settling beneath steel girders that gave it a heady sense of both history and modernity, melded in the way in which they both wanted their business to bring together charities and businesses in order to help those who most needed it.

'You've done such a great job here, Célia.'

'And you've done such a great job with the clients,' Célia replied, smiling and leaning back into Ella.

Ella couldn't, wouldn't, disguise the little squeal of delight, the little jump of joy, nor the smile when she caught Célia rolling her eyes.

'Are you sure you didn't have a drink at lunch?'

'Not a drop.'

'Then you're high on hormones and happy ever afters,' Célia almost groaned.

'I'm high on success,' Ella said, pulling on Célia's arm. 'After Loukas, I thought we might have some client interest, but three secured, and four more speculative?' Ella let out another childlike exclamation of glee before sweeping a hand over the now definitely visible bump beneath her loose shirt.

Célia's eyes caught the gesture, and Ella felt just a little bit of guilt. 'Are you sure you're going to be okay taking on the client-facing work while I'm…'

'On maternity leave?' Célia smiled. 'I will be. I *have* to be,' she concluded somewhat ruefully. Ella knew how much Célia disliked being the centre of attention, had witnessed more than once the panic that would descend over her shy friend.

'Please know that you can call me at any time.'

'Hmm, except when you're breastfeeding, changing nappies or gazing adoringly at your husband and child,' Célia joked then rolled her eyes again when Ella descended into another happy squeal. 'You're incorrigible! I still have to get the figures to the accountants by end of play today, and—'

'And, and, and. I know. Off you go. I'm just going to sit here for a moment and admire all the amazing work you've done getting the offices in such beautiful shape before I head back to Puycalvel.'

Ella sank into the swivel chair and swept back around to face the desk that looked out onto the offices, her heart leaping at the sight of Roman striding across the parquet flooring as if nothing else existed other than her. He was so focused that he clearly hadn't even seen Célia's awkwardly raised hand in greeting, but any slight Ella might have felt on her friend's behalf was buried under the happiness she felt at his unexpected visit.

She had risen and crossed the length of her new office by the time he had reached the doorway. She couldn't help but reach for the lapels on his jacket to pull him closer to her, smiling at the sense of decorum he had in her office space, while she had none. She went to kiss her husband, but he held back.

Finally looking at him closely, she could see signs of strain at the corners of his eyes and mouth, the clench of his jaw.

'Is everything okay?'

His reply was a slight inclination of his head—one that suggested, maybe not so much.

'Come. I have something to discuss.'

Frowning and knowing better than to push Roman until he was ready, she picked up her large cream leather handbag and followed him from the office.

He led her out onto the Parisian street, where a limousine was waiting and whisked them a short distance before stopping.

'Where are we—?'

As she exited the limousine, Roman holding the door to the vehicle open for her, she stepped out onto a street in front of Comte Croix, a three Michelin starred restaurant that reputedly took bookings half a year in advance. For a moment she was speechless—she had always wanted to come here—and Ella warned herself not to inform him of her recent lunch with Célia. Of course, now that she was eating for two, she determined to enjoy every single minute of the treat Roman had organised for her.

As they walked through the two majestic wrought-iron gates into the restaurant, Ella was distracted from her brooding husband for a moment by the incredible French-English classical style of the establishment. Louis XIV furniture greeted them as they passed large regency mirrors and the gold and grey colours of the room soothed nerves Ella didn't realise she had. It was only as they reached the main seating area that she realised they were the only people in the whole restaurant.

She looked up, confused, at Roman.

'We have the place to ourselves.'

She laid a hand on his arm as if to convey some sense of the awe that she was feeling in that moment, the sheer magnitude of his power and wealth on full display. If she thought it odd that he was the one who directed her to a table nestled within a sea of others, each covered in crisp white tablecloths and ready to serve no other customer, she didn't think on it too much. At that moment, she was staring up at her husband with moon-eyed love and couldn't help but laugh at the situation.

'I can't work out whether this is incredibly romantic or incredibly unnecessary,' she said, her stomach turning slightly under the still firm set of Roman's features.

'I have a few things I want to discuss,' he said, pulling two thick envelopes from the inside of his jacket and placing them before her on the table. He pushed one closer towards her with his forefinger. 'I need your signature on some documentation.'

Ella, trying to shake off the feeling that something was terribly wrong, retrieved the envelope and slipped out the paperwork.

'It is a trust fund for your child.'

As she scanned the documents, the sheer amount that Roman had secured in trust for their child shocked her enough not to realise the oddly chosen words from her husband.

'It secures that amount in place until their twenty-fifth birthday—or their marriage, whichever comes first. Until then, you will be the sole trustee.'

She came to the last page, where a yellow plastic tab pointed to a line next to the one Roman had already signed. The tab was oddly horrible and practical against the smooth beauty of the table and their surroundings. She couldn't quite tell why she was oddly resentful of its presence, but she was.

Roman produced a pen and passed it to her, the thick

silver barrel weighty in her small hand, but still warm from where it had sat nestled next to Roman's body inside his jacket.

As she signed the papers her hand shook just a little and Ella was unsure as to why.

Still, when she had finished, she placed the pen on the tablecloth. 'Done,' she said, struggling for a smile, struggling with a strange sense of something she couldn't quite grasp.

'And these,' he said, pushing the other envelope towards her in a similar fashion as before, as if the contents were somehow disdainful to him, 'are divorce papers.'

She had started to pull the papers from the envelope, started to scan the tight neat rows of printed words, with legal headings topping the pages, found the page with another horrible yellow tab pointing to where another signature from Roman had been scrawled, had almost put pen to paper, when his words finally registered and the thick sheaf dropped onto the table.

'What?' she demanded, shaking her head as if she could deny his words, deny the dawning realisation spreading through her body as if to protect her heart for as long as possible.

Roman leaned back in his chair, as if already wanting to remove himself as much from her presence as possible.

'Four hours ago the shareholders of Kolikov Holdings agreed to begin the liquidation process.'

'But—'

'You're not a shareholder any more.'

A sharp inhale was about all Ella could manage.

'Roman, is this some kind of joke? Because it's not funny.'

'It's no joke. And you're right, it's not funny.'

'I don't understand.'

'I could see that the moment you asked me not to destroy Vladimir's company. And then later again, when you wanted to sell me your shares, even though I asked you to reconsider.'

Roman knew then that he was surely going to hell. Everything in him fought, raged, snarled against the words coming from his mouth, words that would eternally sever his connection to this incredible woman and his child. *His child.* But he had to. If not for Ella's sake, then for the sake of that very same child.

Many months ago, Ella had voiced her desire, her need for freedom. And Roman had realised that it might just be the only thing he could give her. And in order to do that, in order to really ensure that she was in no doubt about the need to have that freedom, that distance, he would have to make her hate him more than she had ever done before.

'You saw it when…when I asked you not to destroy the company? But that was… That was months ago, Roman. Have you planned this the whole time?' she asked, her voice thick with the tears he could see about to fall from her cornflower-blue eyes.

'Yes,' he lied. 'The whole time,' he said, unable to bear the sight of his wife so distraught any more. Instead, he focused his gaze over her shoulder, but was unable to avoid the images of Ella dancing in Fiji, seeing her cry her pleasure the night they'd shared at the gazebo, seeing the way she had looked at him the night they had conceived their child, with wonder and awe and—even then—the beginnings of a foolish love.

'I was the one who called Loukas,' he said, knowing that this would lay bare the true darkness within him.

'You…what? I don't… I thought…'

'You thought wrong. I have known Liordis for nearly four years. Knew that he'd been looking for something that would redeem him in the eyes of the world. He was perfect for what I needed of him, and what you wanted of him.'

'And you got him to demand the money that I could only achieve by selling my shares.'

It was a statement. Not a question. And he was thankful for that, for it meant he didn't have to lie about that, he could simply let her assume the worst. And somehow, even though that was his intention, it hurt. It hurt that she could so easily believe that of him—and he realised that painful bitter irony of his hurt. Because that was precisely why he was doing this. Because, for all her declaration of love, of trust, she couldn't really love him or trust him. He had done far too much damage before they'd even had a chance at something more. He knew that. And far better for it to end now than later. Than after he had let down his guard, after he had allowed himself to fall…

He cut off that thought with a sharp slashing movement of his hand, which Ella seemed to interpret as confirmation of her supposition.

'Once you sold me your shares I was finally able to destroy Kolikov Holdings. And if there is any justice in this world then Vladimir is turning in his grave, knowing that I, not he, got the last laugh.'

'Laugh?' she demanded. '*Laugh?* You dare reduce my life and the life of our child to a *laugh*?'

She was shivering now, but with anger, with fury. And it incited his own.

'*Nyet.* No. No, I would not.'

'I loved you.'

'Then it can't have been that great a love if it is already gone.'

Nausea swelled in her stomach, her hand sweeping to soothe, to calm the erratic kicks she could feel there as if even their child was reeling with horror at her husband's…her… *Roman's* actions.

She thought then that she might have seen him flinch, might have seen the tightening of his jaw and an echo of the pain that she felt rising within her, but knew she was wrong. Because this man…wasn't capable of such a feeling. Gone was her fiancé, who had indulged her every whim, gone was the husband who had confessed his pain, his hopes for the future, his passion and, she had once thought, a bourgeoning love, in his touches and kisses. This man was new—he had neither the smooth charm of the former nor the hot anger and heated passion of the latter. This was someone cold to her. Someone almost dead to her.

Her soft heart cried foul, desperately torn by the hope that he was lying. That her husband had not utterly manipulated her once again. He had arranged the meeting with Loukas to make her hand over her shares? That was a blow too low. That all the while she had been hoping for the future and he had still been held in the past, where vengeance and the need for destruction were his only focus.

'What kind of monster are you?'

'The kind your grandmother warned you about. The

kind that would steal more than your innocence. A monster made in my grandfather's image. One who was only ever after the money I could get from Kolikov Holdings' liquidation—a small compensation for the life of my mother. One who would do whatever it took to get what I wanted. And who is letting you go now that I *have* what I want.'

Unaccountably, images from their time together rose in her mind. The first time she'd felt as if he were stalking her in the woods, the weight of the red cloak around her shoulders, the glimpse of him smiling at her joy in Fiji, the way he had looked at her when she had asked him to buy her shares, almost with fear, as if he didn't want her to do that. There was a fervour in him now that she had never seen before. An almost wild determination, as if he were trying to convince her of something too much. Too hard. Money? He'd said it was about money?

She shook her head, hating the way her thoughts, even now, seemed to want to find the good in him. Wanted to find the truth in the lie. Only there were so many lies and so many versions of the truth, she simply didn't know any more.

So, instead of trying to find a way through, she tried for a way out. A way out of the only conclusion Roman was forcing them towards.

'Look me in the eye and tell me this was just about the shares. That all this time,' she demanded, 'it was about destroying the company. When you told me I would have to return to your side. When you told me our child needed its father. When you told me about the loss of your mother. When you lost yourself in my body, when you slept beside me all night long for the first time in years.'

'Puycalvel is still yours,' he said, as if completely ignoring her. 'Everything you came to this marriage with is still yours and yours alone—'

'Apart from the damn shares—'

Apart from my heart.

'For which you were paid generously.'

And for a moment she almost thought he'd been talking about her heart too.

'Have your lawyer look over the paperwork. If you would like to negotiate anything further, I will consider it—'

'How gracious of you,' she hissed, the ire taking over her heart and mind now flowing fully in her veins.

'And you will have full custody—'

'I would *never* let my child near you,' she spat.

'*Da.* It is probably for the best.'

She rose jerkily to her feet and stared in confusion at the arm Roman had offered to steady her. Confusion and disdain. She flinched away from it, knocking back the chair, and blindly wound through the tables that now seemed like obstacles to her. Her eyes brimming with tears, some escaping, falling to the floor from her cheeks, felt sore and her heart ached in a way she had never felt before.

It was so much worse than before. So much. Because she had really loved him. She'd been sure of it. Of him. He had asked her to trust him and she had. She had given herself to him and now felt oddly disconnected from everything. Her feelings, her confidence, herself.

His betrayal slashed through her a thousand times as she passed through the iron gates of the restaurant and out onto the bright sunlit Parisian street, as if emerging from some dark horror. She caught the frown of the waiting driver, the stares of passers-by as they took in the sight of what must look like a hysterical woman on the verge of…on the verge of…

'Ella…'

She refused to turn to look at the man who had hurt her more than anyone else had ever done, she refused to see the stranger staring back at her with nothing more than cold dead eyes, uncaring and unfeeling. She didn't want to, couldn't, let that be the last thing she saw of him.

'Ella,' he said again, and she felt his hand on her arm, turning her back to him. She closed her eyes, hoping that the next words from his mouth would somehow contradict everything that had just happened. Would somehow explain what had just happened, and take it away. Beg for forgiveness, plead with her.

But when she opened her eyes, all she could see were the two envelopes in his other hand. He pressed them towards her as he looked over her head and told the driver to take her wherever she needed to go.

He finally turned his gaze on her, that cold, painful look in his eyes doing more to damage the fragile threads of any kind of hope in her heart, and said, 'It was all about the shares, the company, the money. All this time. From the very beginning to the very end, you were only a means to give me what I wanted.'

And as Ella fled from his grasp, into the back of the limousine, Roman realised that he had been wrong. He'd thought he'd known pain. He thought he'd survived the worst that life could throw at him. But he hadn't and he sure as hell didn't deserve to this time.

CHAPTER ELEVEN

Red Riding Hood had always thought her grand-mother's tales were to teach her the difference between a hero and a villain or good and evil. But, she wondered, what if the only difference came down to who it was that told the story?
The Truth About Little Red Riding Hood
—*Roz Fayrer*

LOOKING OUT FROM the patio, down the sloping green garden towards the silvery thread of the lake winding across the border of her land, Ella saw the copper dome of the gazebo glinting in the morning sun. Since returning from Paris five days ago, she hadn't been back there.

And she hated Roman for that. It had been her favourite place in the grounds of her home. He'd promised that it would always be hers. But it didn't feel that way. Everywhere she turned, she saw him. She smelled him on the sheets that she had washed twice now, but it hadn't worked. It was as if his scent clung to the very air she breathed, and she had been driven outside by the memories that crashed through her relentlessly.

Ella hated the way her mind seemed incapable of creating walls around her heart and mind, instead opening her to everything she had experienced over the last few months, and before. All the different variations of the man she had married competing and contradicting everything she thought she knew.

Dorcas lifted her head as a flock of swallows soared above them on their long migration towards South Africa before the winter months, but didn't move from where she had taken up her almost constant guardianship. One eye on Ella at all times, and the other on the door as if waiting for her master to return.

She was glad Roman had left Dorcas with her. She didn't think she could have been here alone. Célia had offered to come and stay, but Ella had said no. There was too much going on with the company and too much breaking in her heart. She didn't want her friend to see her like this. It was something she needed to bear alone. Because she had done this to herself. She had been *so* stupid.

And, of all the things, that was what turned her stomach, fired the ache in her heart. He had fooled her once and the shame had been his. But this second time? And just as those insidious thoughts crept into her mind, her baby kicked and turned, and kicked again. As if reminding her that she'd had her reasons. That she'd wanted, so, so much, to give their child a better chance. A chance for something more than they had each had. And that she would never regret. But then the pain that Roman had taken that away from them began again.

Her first instinct had been to sever ties with Liordis. She was still very much struggling with the desire to do it now. She hated to think that he had been in on it with Roman. That he had been part of her manipulation. That he had professed his interest in her business not because of what they could do, or how good they were, but because he too was using her for her husband's ends. That Roman's interference had infected the one part of her life she felt completely her own had been devastating.

Célia had tried to reassure her, to insist that she would follow whatever Ella wanted to do with regards to the Greek billionaire. Let him go, keep him, whatever Ella wanted. No matter the effect on their business. But, despite how Ella felt personally about the man, she couldn't deny the damage that would be done should they choose to sever ties with their first client.

Yet that didn't mean she was willing to let it go.

As she dialled the contact number for Loukas, she took a fortifying breath. She could still do this. She was still the co-founder of the business. She was still capable—even if she had made terrible mistakes in the past, it didn't mean she would carry on that way. No. Unlike the men in her life, she would refuse to make decisions about her business for personal reasons.

'*Naí?*'

'Mr Liordis? It's Ella Riding.'

'Mrs Black?'

She flinched and was glad he wasn't there to see it. Incensed that the man would dare to use her married name.

'Not for much longer.'

'Oh, I am sorry to hear that.'

She almost growled at the man's audacity. For surely he would have known the full extent of Roman's plans, once he had his hands on her shares. Ignoring the platitude, she pressed on. 'I have something I want to discuss with you.'

'All ears, *agápe mou.*'

'If we are to continue to do business together—'

'Wait… What?' Loukas's shocked voice interrupted.

'Let me finish, Mr Liordis,' she commanded. 'If we are to continue to do business together, then we need to place all our cards on the table.'

'Okay…' His voice was laden with suspicion.

'When we did our deal, I was not aware of your interaction with my husband.'

'I wouldn't call it an interaction as such,' he stated.

'No? Asking me to fund an extra five million euros was not an *"interaction as such"*?'

There was silence on the other end of the phone—at being caught out? she wondered.

'Look, Mrs… Ella, I'm not quite sure what's going on here, but the only thing your… Roman…asked me to do was to take a business meeting. It was very much for both my and your benefit. I was the one who needed to be assured of your financial viability. Beyond that one request to listen to your proposal, there was no other interaction, other than a rather drunken night in his club in New York three years ago. I promise you, I do not mix business with pleasure. So, whatever you *think* passed between us, you are mistaken.'

He seemed to give her the time to take that in, but whatever pause he had left her was not enough.

'Now, I would still like to continue to work together very much and will happily put this down to a misunderstanding. But if you plan to sever ties with me, then I need to know now. I have other things riding on this, and will not risk a single one of them.'

Part of Ella wanted to rail against the dark commanding tone she encountered now from a man who had been seen as more playboy than billionaire, but she couldn't. Because she was lost in her own confusion.

'No, Mr Liordis. That won't be necessary. My apologies.'

'Think nothing of it,' he said, his tone instantly turning back to his usual charm. 'I shall look forward to seeing you in two months at the first gala.'

Ella cancelled the call and the phone fell from slightly shaking hands. Liordis had no reason to lie. Well, that was not actually true. There had very much been a sense in his response that had strongly indicated how important their business deal was to him. But his surprise at the question about the money had seemed genuine.

More genuine in some ways than Roman had sounded when he had claimed it had all been about the money. Because Roman had never been obsessed with money and the keeping of it. No, instead, money seemed to be something he was barely even aware of.

She forced herself to think back to that day in the restaurant. The divorce papers. The trust fund. Now that had been an obscene amount of... Of...

She almost tripped over Dorcas, trying to get back into the kitchen where she had thrown both sets of papers the moment she had returned from Paris, not daring to look at them since.

She gave herself a paper cut trying to get into the envelope and pulled out the thick bundle, still with the sticky yellow tab affixed. Instead of turning to that page, she started with the first, scanning and flipping through the pages until somewhere about the fifth page she stopped.

Looking at the inconceivable number of millions on the page outlined by little black print, she didn't have to wonder long at where all that money must have come from. It could only have been the total amount of the sale of Kolikov Holdings, give or take an extra five million.

Her husband had lied to her. Again. She howled out loud in frustration. What on earth was he doing? Because if it wasn't about the money, if he had given it all in trust to their child, then what was it really about? He had pushed her away. Telling her the only thing that would make her leave. Now she remembered all the bits and pieces he'd shared with her about his childhood. The machinations of a truly awful grandparent, the insecurities of having foster parents who'd never really wanted him. Now she remembered how sincere he'd been about asking her to rethink the sale of her shares. He'd almost pleaded with her not to do it. Now she remembered how he had claimed to be a monster made in his grandfather's image. But he hadn't been. She'd seen him. The day he'd discovered he was going to be a father…the pain and desperation as he'd told her about his mother…the night he'd said that he could only hope to be the man she deserved to have by her side.

And she'd said, *'Trust me.'* She'd asked him to trust her to know that he *was* better. And she had been the one to break that trust. She had been the one, despite knowing that the man demanding a divorce didn't seem like her husband, didn't seem the man she'd fallen in love with, who had broken that trust.

Oh, God, she thought, a shaking hand to her mouth. For all her words of assurance, her apparent faith in him…she had believed the one lie he'd truly told her, the one that had fed her fears rather than her faith. And she'd done exactly what he'd expected her to do. Think the worst. To leave. Just like everyone else in his life had done.

* * *

Roman strode through the tables of the club in Russia, ignoring the slightly worried looks of his staff and oblivious to the gazes of his patrons. At first, after returning from Paris, he'd thought a numbness had descended, wrapping around him and protecting him. But then he'd realised. It wasn't numbness, but silence.

No more little tapping noises as Dorcas trotted behind him, her toes clipping along the hard wooden floors of his apartment. The little yips of joy or pleading whines, specifically designed to incite guilt or attention. No more warm weight on his thigh as she would lean into him. How on earth had a damned dog come to mean so much to the Great Wolf? he wondered ruefully.

And that had only been the beginning. Because as soon as he realised the absence of Dorcas, he knew it was masking the absence of *her*. Ella. His wife. Mother of his child. And suddenly he realised all the sounds that he would miss in the future. His child's first cry, first laugh, first word. He realised all the sounds he was already missing. His child's heartbeat. His wife's cry of pleasure, her gentle, teasing laugh, the sounds she made in her sleep unconsciously, the way her hand sounded as it swept towards him across the bedsheets.

All these noises that were consumed by the silence of his life. And even as a part of him wished he'd never met her, the other, the part of his heart still beating, still hoping, knew that he would be thankful for it for ever.

He knew what he'd done that day. Still held to the decision he'd made. Ella *was* better off without him. He had told her lies and she'd believed them. His mind taunted him with evil thoughts.

She never loved you. If she had, she wouldn't have

*believed you. She only ever loved the fiancé, the man
you were not.*

And he felt he deserved every single one of them.
Because that questioning, that self-doubt, wasn't that
what he'd done to her that first time? If he'd known what
it had been like for her he never would have taken her
innocence, never would have allowed her back into his
life. Because this? This was pure hell.

So he took his punishment, knowing that he fully
deserved it. Every single sharp twist of the knife, he
would take a million times over because he had done
worse to her.

And that was why, no matter how much he wanted to
go to her, to beg her to take him back, to beg to spend
each and every day seeking to make up for his awful
actions, to be better, to do better, he would not. Because
he would never be worthy of her.

He reached the corner of the bar, where a barman
jumped to attention, knowing without Roman even having to ask for the bottle of vodka he'd appeared almost
nightly to demand, before disappearing to his lair above
the club.

The bottle appeared on the counter top and Roman
swept it up and stalked towards the lift in the back corner
of the room. But in his mind he was not holding the slippery condensation-covered chilled bottle, but the warm,
slim crook of Ella's elbow, his palm heated despite the
cool feel of the glass. As he swept his key card over the
electronic plate he followed a ghost into the lift, unconsciously making space for the image of her with him.

Roman caught sight of the image of his reflection
in the mirrored surface, barely meeting his own gaze.
He grimly acknowledged that he looked like hell, the

dark sweeps under his eyes speaking to the fact that he'd not been able to sleep fully through the night since he'd left her bed and, in all likelihood, wouldn't ever again.

The only thing that soothed the ache was that he'd provided for them both—Ella and their child. They would never want for anything. Certainly not for a husband or father who wasn't good enough, who wasn't worthy enough.

Was that what his mind had kept hidden from itself? he wondered. All these years and all that determination for vengeance. Had it hidden…this? These feelings and this fear he'd never voiced before he'd met Ella. Never needing to account for his actions or his behaviour to anyone before now.

He cursed and, rather than waiting to cross the distance of his living area to find a glass, unscrewed the lid of the bottle of *zubrowka* and raised it to his lips, anticipating the taste of the ice-cool alcohol on his tongue. But, before he could take a sip, he stopped, his hand hovering before his mouth, holding the bottle but not moving.

Ella sat on his sofa, encased in the red cape he had bought her, and he wondered whether he had finally lost all sense. Because surely his twisted mind had conjured her from his thoughts and memories. Surely she was not sitting there, her beautiful shapely legs crossed, her hands placed in her lap, her level gaze one that could easily be mistaken for serenity.

But he knew, the moment he took a breath, that she was real because her scent had filled the air of his apartment. A delicious taste of something almost like orange blossom, mint and memories.

Everything in him became alert, the hair at his nape

raising slightly as his first fearful thought careened through him.

'The baby?'

'Is fine.'

He took a moment for her assurance to sink in, to smooth out the erratic pulse of his heart, but it didn't work. He was still fired with adrenaline as if under threat, as if the ground was shifting beneath his feet. She looked incredible. Everything he'd ever wanted, right there, within touching distance, and he couldn't. He just couldn't.

'Then we have nothing to discuss,' he growled as he stalked past her to the kitchenette. 'You can let yourself out.'

'I could. But I won't.'

He hoped to high heaven that she didn't see the way his fingers shook as he reached for the glass he would have easily forgone just moments earlier. He felt a growl rising in the back of his throat, the need to lash out and release some, if not all, of this pent-up fury he felt rising in his chest. The fury of pain, of hurt, of loss.

All of it he swallowed as he forced himself to turn around and look towards his…well…if she was here with the divorce papers then he couldn't really call her his wife any more. Landing on that explanation for her appearance here in his apartment, a cold fist so fierce it burned struck his heart. That was it. That was why. It could only ever be that.

'You could have sent the papers to my lawyers. This,' he said with a sweep of his arm and the bottle he still held, 'is unnecessary.'

'On the contrary. I find it deeply necessary.'

'If there is something you want to contest—?'

'And if I wanted to contest the whole thing?'

Roman reared back as if slapped. 'I don't…'

'It's not often that you are lost for words, Roman.'

He stared at her, unsure what she was saying, unsure as to what was happening.

'What game are you playing?' he demanded.

She cocked her head to one side. 'The one you apparently decided we were playing.'

'Would you stop speaking in riddles!'

That his anger apparently caused her only to smile was deeply unsettling.

'I think that might be the first real and honest reaction to this whole damn thing since you took me to the restaurant. A tad ironic, but real at least.'

Roman ground his teeth together so hard he thought he might have heard something crack. For here she was again. The beautiful, proud, determined fury that he had met here six months ago. The woman who had seduced as much as been seduced. The woman who had become the mother of his child and keeper of his heart.

'You want my anger? Then get out,' he roared, even more horrified that his fury seemed to have exactly the opposite effect on Ella.

'But how am I supposed to witness your anger if I am gone? No, Roman. Surely better for me to be here and witness you in your full monstrosity, no?'

He wanted to hurl the bottle he still held against the wall beside him, and the only thing staying his hand was that somehow the glass might shatter and catch her. And when everything in him was screaming out to protect her, to keep her from *him*, that he could not do.

'What are you doing here? What do you want from me?' he demanded.

'I want to know why you lied.'

'Good God, Ella, everything I've ever said to you has been a lie.'

'Not everything. But certainly all that you said in the restaurant.'

He couldn't look at her. He had done that day, but it had taken everything in him and he no longer had the energy to fight. He knew that if she looked too hard, thought too much, she'd realise the truth. And he had to protect her from that.

'You are fooling yourself. Once again. So naïve.' He forced the cruel words through thin lips.

'But no longer innocent?'

'Have I not hurt you enough? Have I not proved to you how depraved and damaged I am?'

'I will not lie and tell you that. Because there have been too many lies between us and you have hurt me. And I'd not use *depraved*—that was your word—but damaged? Yes, you have been damaged, but not broken and not irretrievably so. I…' She paused, and he couldn't not look at her, couldn't not face whatever it was that she would say next. 'I owe you an apology.'

'Hell, Ella. What are you—?'

'I asked you to trust me. I asked you to trust me to know that you could be better. Trust that I knew that about you. And I let you down. Because at the first sign, the first suggestion that you might not be, I walked… ran even, not looking back. Not looking back enough to see the truth.'

He was shaking then. He was racked by it, the trembling that had started in his heart, spreading out through his body, and he felt the press of hot wet heat against the back of his eyelids. He couldn't do this. He couldn't…

'I told you that I loved you and I left.'

She was killing him. Tearing him apart with her words. All the things he had never wanted to face, never wanted to know or feel.

'I will not take *full* responsibility for that, because you did have a hand in that. But, for my part, I am sorry.'

He wanted to rush to her, drop to his knees and beg her forgiveness. Beg her to take him back, promise to do whatever it would take to make it up to her. Tell her that…that…he loved her more than life itself. But he couldn't. Not yet.

'Ella, please.' Roman no longer knew what he was asking for. For her to stop, or never stop.

'Tell me the truth,' she demanded and he owed her that much.

'I thought—*think*—that you deserve more. That you are owed more. After all that I have done, under the guise of vengeance… I simply don't know how to be. When you asked me to buy your shares, you didn't know what you were doing. Didn't know that it would give me the only possible chance of having what I had spent a lifetime wanting. I felt, believed, that if you did love me then you wouldn't ever have asked me to give that up. Kolikov Holdings was the last tie to my past, to my grandfather, to my mother's death…and I wanted, *needed*, it to be gone and you placed, in my hands, the ability to do so—and demanded that I didn't.

'Do you understand, Ella? Do you see? The promise I made to my mother on her deathbed, it was a promise that kept me alive, made me get up in the morning, drove me beyond anything else in this world to succeed and achieve the impossible. You made me promise not to do it, and I couldn't live up to that. I couldn't because my mother came first. That promise came first.'

* * *

For the first time since she had made him make that promise Ella realised the cost of it. Tears rose to her eyes at the position she had put him in, unwittingly. In her mind, the destruction of Kolikov Holdings was simply the embodiment of his betrayal—of Vladimir's betrayal—of *her*. She hadn't really thought what it had meant to him, what it had symbolised to *him*.

'Why didn't you tell me this? Why didn't you try to explain?' she asked in a softer voice than the trembling she felt within her.

'And risk you leaving with my child?'

'A departure you specifically engineered only a few months later?' she couldn't help but interject.

'The few months it took me to realise just how much damage I could do to you. When I realised that I was too weak not to give in to the urge to destroy the last trace of Vladimir's hold on this world.'

Ella took a moment to think through his words, the pain and anguish clearly ringing within them. She had been so determined, so sure of her demand when she'd made it, she could see that she would have walked away. Her own pain and anger, the fierceness with which she'd thought she had been in the right.

Taking a breath, she made herself feel the intention of his words, to feel the truth of them.

'And now?' she asked.

'Now?' Roman seemed confused, as if in his mind there simply couldn't be a now.

'Yes. Now, how do you feel?'

'About Vladimir's company?' he asked.

'I don't care about the damn company and never want

to hear its name again,' she cried. 'I want to know how you feel about me.'

She looked at him, watching his features closely as if they could give her some kind of hint or hope to what she believed he felt. He crossed the room to come before her, dropped to his knees and took her hands in his. 'There is nothing in this world more important to me. I love you with every single beat of my heart.'

Her own heart leapt, her hands shaking within the press of his.

'I would give anything to take back all the hurt I inflicted upon you, all the times you felt doubt, or questioned yourself because of me. I have had only a week of that myself and...' He broke off, shaking his head. 'I am truly sorry for it. And if you give me the chance I will spend each and every single day trying to make up for it. I will never, ever speak an untruth to you again. I will never make you doubt me, my love for you or our child. I will do whatever it takes, Ella. Because I love you. There is so much of it, there is no room for anything else. Not thoughts of vengeance, not the need to destroy. Just love. And all of it for you and our family.'

She was startled to feel the pad of his thumb sweep aside a tear she hadn't realised was there.

She reached for him then and pulled him towards her, delighting in the feel of his kiss, sweetened by her tears of joy.

'I love you,' she said between presses of her lips against his. 'So, so much,' she said. And that was the last thing he allowed her to say before sweeping her into his bedroom, closing the door and showing her how beautiful their lovemaking could, and would, be for the rest of their lives.

EPILOGUE

*Cinderella, Snow White, Rapunzel...they each
found their handsome prince. But Red Riding
Hood found something so much more. She found
her mate, her wolf...her pack. And in doing so
she found herself.*

The Truth About Little Red Riding Hood
—Roz Fayrer

ELLA STOOD IN the doorway to her daughter's room in
Puycalvel watching the four-year-old spin slightly off-
centred circles in her little pink leotard and ballet shoes,
both of which were extremely cute but nothing compared to the full length pink, frothy, layered, sparkly
tutu that Roman had produced for her just hours before.

It was completely over the top but Tatiana loved it
and had refused to take it off, not even for bed, despite
the warnings that she might damage it.

'I'm going to be the greatest ballerina ever,' she proclaimed between spins, 'but not as great as Grandma,
because *no one* could be as good as Grandma.'

The sound of footsteps above on the staircase drew
Ella's attention towards her husband, who had their

second daughter in his arms as he made his way carefully down the steps. Not once had he ever betrayed his promise to keep her and their children safe, not once had he ever given her cause to feel anything but joy and love. Frustration sometimes and perhaps, even on occasion, a healthy dose of anger. But never sadness and never fear.

The moment his eyes found hers, the smile on his face brightened, his eyes widened with an awe she would never tire of as he took in her, once again, rounded form.

'We're going to have to stop at three, you know,' she warned in a voice still low from trying to settle her unruly daughter.

'Why?' he said, as if he would never tire of seeing her pregnant, of meeting the children they bore, of increasing the amount of love each time within their family. It seemed in almost never-ending supply.

'Because I want you to myself for a while,' she mock growled as he pressed a kiss to her cheek.

'You can have as much of me as you like, for however long you like. I am here, yours, always and for ever.'

'It's words like that that got me in this situation in the first place,' she moaned, her hands sweeping down around her bump. Their third child was due in a few months' time and neither parent could wait to meet the new addition to the family.

'I will keep saying them until they stop working,' her husband insisted.

'I want to see Auntie Célia and my cousins,' Tatiana announced, jumping up and down, despite the late hour.

'And we will, but tomorrow, sweetheart. Now, it's time for bed.'

'Nope. Not time for bed.'

'Yes, time for bed,' Roman chimed in, walking into his daughter's bedroom and sitting at the bottom of her bed. 'And you know what that means?'

'Story, story, story,' exclaimed Tatiana as Adeline clapped her hands together with as much co-ordination as an eighteen-month-old could manage.

'I believe it's your turn, wife,' Roman announced with a smile full of satisfaction and happiness. Ella believed that he loved this nightly routine almost more than the girls did.

'No, surely you're mistaken. It was my turn last night.'

'No, Maman, last night was *The Frog Prince*. It's your turn tonight.'

'And what story would you like to hear?'

'My favourite one, silly.'

Roman growled softly, and Tatiana looked apologetic enough for long enough, before reaching out a hand towards Ella to pull her on to the bed. Dorcas stalked over to her doggy bed in the corner of the room, seemingly content that she had successfully herded her entire family into one room.

As she sat down on the edge of the bed, next to her husband and children, Ella felt wrapped in a cocoon of unconditional love. Her family, all joyous, beautiful, beaming, happy and safe.

'Once upon a time, there was a sweet little maiden and whoever laid eyes upon her couldn't help but love her, nor help but remark on the beautiful red velvet cape her grandmother had given her...'

She looked at her husband and he didn't need to hear the words that cried through her heart straight to his. For Ella did believe in fairy tales now that they'd both found their happy-ever-after.

* * * * *

THE FLAW IN HIS
MARRIAGE PLAN

TARA PAMMI

CHAPTER ONE

"LET'S GET MARRIED, PRINCESS."

Vincenzo Cavalli adopted his usual composed expression but it didn't come easily this time. Shock made it hard for him to pretend as if he'd been planning to say those words all along. As if they hadn't erupted out of some place inside him that he didn't even know existed.

Alessandra Giovanni—top supermodel and the most beautiful woman he'd ever met, froze in the act of pushing her hair back from her face, her expression arrested.

It was as if a circuit in his brain had shorted, bypassing years of unwritten rules he'd always lived by. Every step in his life for the last two decades had been planned meticulously, building toward a future he'd pictured for himself as a young boy denied everything—love and basic security.

Every step dictated by his final goal—to take over Brunetti Finance International and nothing else. Every hour of every day he'd poured sweat and blood into pulling himself up from poverty to be able to claim his birthright one day.

Pursuing Alessandra Giovanni had initially been a part of that carefully crafted plan, as he'd discovered Alessandra was attached to all the Brunettis, especially the matriarch of the family, Greta Brunetti, who had thrown his mother and him out to starve.

Asking her to marry him—no. That was as much a surprise to him as it was to her.

But now that the words were out, he found he meant

them. And not because he was an honorable man who kept his word at all costs.

Honor had always been a luxury he couldn't afford—like shoes or three meals a day when he'd been growing up on the streets of Milan.

Honor had no place in his world.

No, this request was purely selfish. Maybe the first selfish, nonstrategic thing he'd done in a long time. In forever, actually.

It was irrational and illogical, but the shocked look in Alessandra's eyes, the quick flare of excitement she buried the next second, the flush of color dusting her cheeks as her chest rose and fell, the fast rush of blood in his own veins as he imagined facing the famed Brunettis with Alessandra at his side as his wife—he knew this was utterly right.

More than anything, he wanted Alex in his life.

The chemistry of their instant connection had taken him aback when he'd hunted her down to this perfect corner of Bali. Their mutual attraction a useful tool he hadn't counted on. But now that he had her, he wasn't going to give her up.

As to the fact of her being connected to the very family he'd been planning to destroy for so long, he was certain he could persuade her to see his point of view. Once he explained his reasons, Alessandra would take his side. She wasn't a blood relative of theirs. She would understand his need to topple them all. Her strong sense of right and wrong, her championing of causes around the world—it was an innate part of her nature, a quality that only added an extra dimension to his already magnetic attraction to her.

He raised the glass of champagne in his hand while never breaking eye contact with her.

Clad in a sky blue bikini that hugged her firm breasts like a lover's caressing hands, she looked voluptuously beautiful. As a supermodel who had worked for most of the large international design houses, he hadn't been surprised by her punishing fitness routine. But the natural energy of the woman as she geared up to take on the world and its myriad injustices… It still amazed him.

The blue of the infinity pool they were standing next to, in the grounds of her private villa, with the backdrop of Bali's lush hills and valleys surrounding it, couldn't equal the breathtaking quality of Alessandra's beauty. Hers was not simply the beauty of flawless skin or perfectly symmetrical features or curves most women would die for, though she possessed all those things.

It was her imperfections that delighted him, the quirks that made Alessandra Giovanni one of the most beautiful women in the world.

The gap between her front teeth, that fresh-faced girl-next-door quality, the awkward, self-deprecating sense of humor, her mad obsession with the world of boxing, her incredible verve for life, the audacious drive to fix all the injustices of the world…

On paper, she'd been too good to be true, stoking Vincenzo's curiosity into a wildfire.

In real life, she was magnificent, a force to be reckoned with, and he'd stood no chance against her from the second their eyes had met.

And then there was her air of wary vulnerability that innumerable magazines and countless photoshoots had never managed to accurately capture.

It stared back at him now out of bright brown eyes. The quality that had kept him awake the past few nights. Even with her warmth wrapped around him like a vine.

She's innocent, the small part of his conscience that he hadn't been able to silence kept piping up. *She might be hurt.*

Not when he was making her a part of his life, he told himself. Not by offering her something he'd never even considered in his entire life. Not if he carefully explained his reasons, not with her innate sense of right and wrong.

"Married?" she repeated, her tongue swiping over that plump lower lip that millions of women over the world tried to emulate with collagen. Her eyes widened in her gamine face. "Don't mess around with me, V," she said, with a little laugh at the end. A rough, rasping sound that never failed to arouse him.

A brave little effort to hide her emotions while the madly fluttering pulse at her neck betrayed her. Using that moniker she'd allocated him that first day when they'd met as though it was a kind of shield against him. Against her own feelings.

This was what he liked about being with Alessandra—she was an open book, somehow having retained a genuine quality in a cutthroat world.

He finished his drink and dived headlong into the pool, his heart thundering loudly in his chest. When he reached her, he pulled himself out of the water, and stood, her body flush with his. Her warm breath feathered over his cheekbones.

He pushed a tendril of hair away from her temple, his fingers, as always, itching to touch her. Hold her. Possess her. "You should know by now that I don't say things I don't mean, Princess," he said, pressing his mouth to her cheekbone. He filled his hands with the dips and valleys of her waist, the hitch in her breathing as he touched her pinging over his nerves.

"Yeah?"

"*Si, cara mia.* The last few weeks have been…" He frowned, trying to locate the elusive word. He'd never lost himself in the sensuality of a woman as he'd done with her. He'd never lost his mind over a woman like this, period.

"Wonderful. Fantastic. Amazing," she added in a breathless tone, a stark honesty in her voice that he was coming to count on more and more.

He laughed, the sound of it strange to his own ears. "All that. And I find…" He pulled her closer until their breaths melded. Until her arms locked around his neck. Until she sank her long fingers into his hair and pulled his head down. Until their hearts beat against each other in a harmony of need and want. "I'm not ready to let you go, *cara*. I don't think I'd ever want to. So why not make it official?"

She let out a gasp. He could feel her trembling against him. "It's crazy. These entire last few weeks have been completely crazy."

"Crazy bad?" he added, a ball of something he didn't want to name lodged in his chest. He'd never waited on an answer with such gut-twisting anticipation. All his adulthood, he'd manipulated things into working his way. He'd taken, instead of asking. Because he'd learned early on that it was the only way he could have things. Now he disliked the feeling vehemently. Once he had her, he would never subject himself to it ever again, he promised himself.

"No," she answered promptly. "Crazy good. Crazy fairytale-esque, almost. When I'm with you, I almost feel like the princess you call me. I…"

He waited. On a knife's edge.

"But then I've never been bowled over quite like I've been by you. I was just about ready to give up on men, in fact. And the world, even. When I was younger, I heard this story of a girl rescued by a prince. And you…"

"I'm no prince, Alessandra."

She sighed and burrowed her face into the warmth of his shoulder. Her teeth sank into his skin at the juncture of his neck. And his body reacted instantly, pressing against her soft belly. "It's been magical. And no, I don't want it to end. I don't want to go back to real life." Big eyes held his, penetrating in their intensity. "Only we don't know everything about each other yet."

"Is it enough to know that until I met you I'd never ever considered sharing my life with a woman, ever? Is it enough to know that the last few weeks have truly taken my life in a new direction? Is it enough to know that the future you confided in me you want is the one I want too?"

She looked up and all the hopes and dreams of the world seemed to be shining from her eyes. For an infinitesimal second, the intensity of that scared Vincenzo. Just for a second.

A wide smile turned her face into breathtaking beauty. "It is enough. Yes, V. Let's do this. Let's get hitched."

Any lingering doubts Vincenzo had about whether what he was doing was right or wrong got swallowed up by Alessandra's kiss. By the sweet taste of her lips, by the honest urgency of her desire as she pressed up against him, as she whispered she wanted him right then and there.

Vincenzo devoured her mouth, his hands reaching for her hips and buttocks. Within seconds, he'd pushed aside her bikini bottom and was inside of her, and that sense of belonging once again filled every inch of his limbs. A feeling of peace that he had never known enveloped him as she took his mouth in a sweet kiss.

And for a man who'd never shared his life with anyone, who'd already spent too many years on a certain strategic path, it felt like a benediction. An invitation to a future he hadn't known he could have.

The loud and persistent chirp-chirp of a cell phone somewhere woke Alex out of a dreamless sleep. She stretched her body and found the sweet soreness invade her limbs as a result of the passionate night before.

With a smile, she buried her face in the pillow next to hers. The empty pillow.

Of course, the man she'd married was a workaholic.

The sound came again. With a sigh, Alex got out of the bed and looked around. After several tries, she located the sleek cell phone in a drawer under a laptop.

And frowned. This wasn't V's usual cell phone.

The number on the screen amplified her confusion.

She knew that number. It was Massimo's.

Why was Massimo Brunetti calling Vincenzo? How would he even know him?

Ever since Greta Brunetti, the matriarch of the Brunetti dynasty, had welcomed Alex with open arms almost thirteen years ago as a teenager—after discovering her much-younger second husband had an illegitimate daughter from a previous fling—the Brunettis had become her adopted family, including Greta's grandsons, sired by the son from her first marriage. Despite being no blood relation to Alex, Leonardo and Massimo Brunetti had nevertheless embraced her, generously sharing their home and hearts with her.

But of course, Massimo was worried about her. They all were. Guilt assailed Alex as she thought of the last few weeks. She'd never planned to stay away from Milan for so long. She'd only meant to spend some time in Bali after her latest photoshoot getting her head on straight about her career, about where she wanted her life to go. She'd even turned her phone off, wanting a complete break from social media and endless phone calls.

Instead of focusing on her future, she'd met Vincenzo. And married him in secret.

And had postponed telling the Brunettis, because Massimo and Leo, and especially Greta, deserved better than to be told her momentous news in a voice message or via an impulsive text.

But now… Somehow, the technical genius that was Massimo had discovered that she was holed up with Vincenzo. How was that even possible? Why hadn't Vincenzo mentioned that he knew the Brunettis?

Alex finally hit Answer on the screen and scrunched her face. "Hey, Massimo."

"Alex, *cara*, is that you? What are you doing with Vincenzo Cavalli's phone?"

Alex bit her lip. Massimo sounded different. Something was wrong here. "Why are you calling his number, Massimo? How do you know him?"

A sense of urgency filled Massimo's voice. "Cara, listen to me. Vincenzo is…he's the one responsible for all the trouble we've been facing at Brunetti Finances. He's the one who launched the hacker attack on the cyber arm. He's the one who's been goading board members into getting rid of Leo. He's a…a very dangerous man, *bella*. He's been hitting us from all sides for almost a year now. Concerted attacks on all of us—me, Leo, Greta. He's even achieved ownership of Father's stock somehow."

All of us… Massimo, Leo, Greta.

And her? Was she some kind of target too?

Alex felt as if the ground was being stolen from under her. She sank to the bed, her knees shaking, her belly swooping in a series of never-ending somersaults. "Massimo, I don't understand. But why…how…"

"Leo's been trying to reach you for some time, *bella*, but you seem to have been incommunicado. We learned that this Cavalli was also in Bali, and we wanted to make sure you stayed clear of him. Finally, Natalie, who used to work for him, had the idea to call his old number to try and talk to him. We were running out of other options."

Alex was numb with shock and betrayal.

"*Cristo*, Alex! What are you doing with him? Why—?"

"I…if I organize a taxi out to the airport, can you get me out of here, Massimo?" Alex cut him off. God, she needed to get out of here. Now. Before Vincenzo came back. Before he charmed her again with his sweet words and addictive lovemaking.

"Of course. I'll… Alex, is everything okay?"

"Just…please, get me out of here. Now."

"Okay, *bella*. Just sit tight. Give me a few minutes to organize you a flight. Alex, whatever it is, Leo and I will fix it. We're here for you."

Alex ended the call before she started bawling on the phone. Before…

What had she done?

Why hadn't Vincenzo even mentioned the Brunettis? Why was he attacking them like this? There was no chance it could be a mistake. Massimo and Leo had been having troubles at the company for more than a year now. Even Alex had been peripherally aware of it.

And now the man she'd fallen for so hard, the man she'd married so quickly, far from being the romantic prince she'd thought him, was in truth the enemy.

But even hours later, as she flew home to Milan, without having even breathed a word to Vincenzo, Alex couldn't help wishing it was all a mistake.

That Vincenzo was not the man who had been wreaking destruction on her adopted family.

That he was not the man who remained a serious threat to Leonardo's CEO position on the BFI board.

That he was not the man who had been unerringly finding weak spots in one of the most powerful families in Milan and hitting them where it hurt the most.

CHAPTER TWO

VINCENZO STARED UP at the villa on the shores of Lake Como. The villa that had been the seat of the Brunettis' power for nearly two centuries.

He walked up the very marble steps where his mother had stood and begged Greta Brunetti to believe that her son, Vincenzo, was the old woman's grandson, sired by Silvio Brunetti.

Greta's own flesh and blood.

But two decades later, as he walked up the same steps again, there was no fear or doubt in him. Soon this would all be his. Power and confidence surged through him as he walked in through the huge archway into the lounge.

Of course, his sweet wife, Alessandra, had hastened his arrival by running away and hiding here. He didn't quite mind the acceleration in his plans though.

He enjoyed walking into the lounge to see them all assembled there—the matriarch, Greta Brunetti; her grandsons, Leonardo and Massimo Brunetti; their wives, Neha and Natalie, and, amidst them, sitting on the chaise longue, was Alessandra.

She looked up as he entered. And he found his pulse started racing, like a schoolboy's. Instead of the anger he had nurtured from the moment he'd returned to find her gone, he felt a pang of concern.

Her eyes were puffy and red rimmed. Light brown hair pulled into a messy bun that highlighted the sharp cut of her cheekbones. A loose sleeveless T-shirt and denim shorts with pink flip-flops completed her ensemble.

No makeup touched the flawlessly boned face, no designer clothes showcased her stunning beauty, and yet she looked like a million dollars.

Hurt shimmered in those eyes as she held his gaze without blinking. As if she meant to look straight into his heart. As if she was trying to search for a speck of honor within him.

But she would fail. There was no honor in him. None at all.

He swept his gaze over her entire length and found a little satisfaction in spotting the diamond still shimmering brilliantly on her left hand.

Mine, she's mine, he wanted to growl like a savage beast.

"Running away without a word, *Princess*? This marriage thing is new to both of us, *si*, but we clearly need some ground rules," he mocked, refusing to acknowledge the two men standing there like sentinels, guarding her.

Leonardo Brunetti, CEO of Brunetti Finances Inc. A financial conglomerate that was synonymous with prestige in the rarified circles of Milan, the man he intended to replace. And Massimo Brunetti, the brilliant, technical mind behind the highly successful cyber arm of BFI—Brunetti Cyber Services—and the man that had captured his past associate Natalie's heart.

Men who had everything that should have also been his.

Men he intended to take everything from.

"You think there's any ground to stand on after what you've done, V?"

If she'd yelled it at him, he would've felt much more in control of the situation. But the shaken whisper... He didn't quite know to handle it, to stop it from disarming him. "Come, *cara.* Whatever questions you have, I'll answer them in privacy."

"You had numerous chances to do it in privacy. To explain what the hell you've been doing to my family. To at least...hint to me that you've been turning their lives upside down. You lost all those chances. You lost..." She bit her lip, her chest rising and falling. A wet sheen coating her eyes. "Just tell us...why."

"Why what?" he said through gritted teeth. *Maledizione*, he shouldn't have waited to explain it all to her when he so badly needed her to understand his point of view.

"Why've you been targeting them?" Frustration raised her voice. "Why did you arrange for Natalie to take down BCS before she fell in love with Massimo? Why did you use Neha's bullying stepfather to spy for you? Why did you buy up BFI stock until you could square off against Leo for the position of CEO?"

"I thought all those actions were quite self-explanatory," he said smoothly.

Alessandra stood up and took a step forward, breaking away from the group. The subtle scent of her hit him, bringing with it such vivid sensations of entwined damp limbs and sinful pleasure. Of long, warm nights and warmer sheets and soft gasps. Of intoxicating smiles that chased away the web of loneliness he hadn't even realized he'd woven around himself.

He saw the pulse at her neck flutter rapidly but when he raised his gaze to hers, the sheer depth of dismay in her eyes was a stinging slap to his senses. The same eyes that had looked at him with such affection and desire...

"You think this is all a joke?"

He tucked his hands in his pockets to stop himself from reaching for her. "It is not a joke, Alessandra, least of all to me. If it's still not clear, then let me make it so.

"I have spent most of my life working toward this moment. Moving people and contracts and money like chess pieces just to arrive at this point.

"I intend to take over as the CEO of BFI. I intend to own the company outright. I intend to drive every Brunetti from the company until it's all mine. Only mine."

One lone tear drew a path over a sharply defined cheekbone. "Why?"

"I believe in taking what's mine. Especially when it's been denied me for so long. Especially…" He lost the fight against himself and reached out to catch the tear with his finger. Skin like silk beckoned a deeper touch, and he gave in to that too. Damn it, he'd never intended to hurt her.

He rubbed the line of her jaw with the pad of his thumb, marveling again at how much he wanted her to lean into his touch, how much he wanted her to take that last step and mold her glorious body against his. How much he wanted her to look at him as if he were her hero.

But he'd never aspired to be a hero in his life.

In fact, he was the furthest thing from being a hero. He didn't believe in self-sacrifice or putting someone else before him or in the happiness of others enriching his own.

No, he believed in taking, possessing, having. And keeping hold of what was his.

"Especially…when I've made a commitment to having it in my life in the first place," he finished slowly, his voice gone all deep and rumbly.

A quick intake of breath. A parting of those luscious lips. A quick rush of color into her cheeks. She swallowed and looked up. And for an infinitesimal moment, he knew she was as lost in him as he was in her. In the magic they created together. In the indescribable, illogical thing between them that had made him take such a big step.

That made him stand here explaining himself to her even after she'd run away from him without a word.

"Alessandra?" Greta broke in, puncturing the magic.

Alessandra laid those doe eyes on him. "You think BFI should be yours?"

"*Si.* Since it was Silvio Brunetti that seduced my mother with a hundred lies, got her pregnant and then discarded her like yesterday's trash.

"Since my mother was called a whore, and she and I were accused of being beggars and liars and kicked out into the street by the woman you consider a stepmother. Since I was denied all of this privilege growing up, I decided that I wouldn't be satisfied with just a small part of it now.

"I want to see every last Brunetti walk out of this house, their heads hanging in shame.

"I am going to take it all."

"That's…" Her eyes wide in her face, Alessandra looked like he had sucker punched her. Her tall body swayed where she stood. When he took a swift step toward her, she jerked away, her beautiful face contorted in shock. "Greta would never do something like that. She welcomed me with open arms when I came here to live with my father, her second husband. She's more than a stepmother to me. She loved me even more than…"

Whatever defense Alessandra wanted to offer on behalf of Greta died on her lips as she turned to face the older woman. A soft gasp escaped her mouth, her body bowing as if against a sudden, forceful gale.

Truth shone in the older woman's eyes, the only remainder of an encounter she'd probably never given another thought to. Whereas it had become the foundation of his life.

The dirty accusations. The supposed higher ground of privilege. The utter lack of sympathy.

The entire room filled with a vibrating sense of shock, all heads turning toward Greta with various degrees of accusation. Except Alessandra. Even in the face of the older woman's guilt plainly written on her face, Alessandra still looked disbelieving. She looked as if she were the one dealt the hardest blow. Something he hadn't accounted for and should have.

Even the legendary Brunetti brothers looked horrified, their gazes alternating between their grandmother and Vincenzo in a parody that he would've laughed at any other time. A string of colorful curses spewed from Massimo's mouth while Leo stared in numbed silence.

"We could do a DNA test, if you want to lend legitimacy to my taking over what should be mine," Vincenzo added dismissively. "I'd quite like to keep my mother's name though. There's a certain poetic justice in heading the prestigious BFI with her name, *si*?"

"We will take your word for it, Cavalli, though you're quite the spiteful bastard," Massimo said evenly.

"That's mighty grand of you since your father and grandmother denied my mother even that small decency," he couldn't help adding, the very thought of the blankness in his mother's eyes filling his throat with a corrosive taste he'd lived with for far too long.

"And me, V?" Alessandra said in a soft entreaty. "Where do I fit into this sordid tale?" For all it was asked in a tremulous voice, it reverberated around him as if it had been fired out of a gun.

His gut tightened, a cold, clammy feeling drenched his skin. A feeling he tried to battle and dominate into submission. He found he had no answer to give her right then.

At least, not one that wouldn't shatter the painful hope glimmering in her eyes.

Not one that he could articulate in so many words.

Not in front of all of them.

She nodded as if he'd given her a clear-cut answer. As if his silence didn't end up damning him after all. And then she fled.

Alex suppressed the tears that threatened with a deep breath and a big gulp of water. God, she'd cried enough over him in the last week.

She looked out of the French doors at the neatly maintained acreage around the villa. The greenhouse that Leo had had restored on the grounds. The ancient wine cellar that had been restructured and repurposed to serve as brilliant Massimo's state-of-the-art computer lab.

The pride and sense of history of this place was in their blood. It was their legacy. Their place in the world.

A place, and a sense of belonging, that Vincenzo had been cruelly denied. Along with his share of the legacy. She'd never forgotten the utter sense of inadequacy, the powerlessness when she'd discovered as a teenager that her mother's husband, Steve, the man she'd always thought was her father, actually wasn't—remembered the desperate need to belong somewhere, anywhere, completely.

She could imagine the pain and loss a little boy might feel being rejected by his family, the scars that would carry over to the man. But to destroy Leonardo and Massimo after all these years... She couldn't abide that. She couldn't.

"You have to stop running away from me, *cara mia*."

The deep, bass voice carried over to her on the soft breeze from the open doors, playing over her spine as if she were a set of piano keys and he the maestro.

She stayed with her face averted from him. Like a coward. No, a woman who knew her own weakness and was assembling her armor. But it was time to decide.

To look into the eyes of the man who'd seduced her so thoroughly that she'd lost all her hard-earned common sense and rushed straight to the altar with him.

"You left me no choice," she said. Even after she'd learned the truth, even on the long flight from Bali, even the past couple of days until Vincenzo caught up with her, there had been a small part of her that hoped that they'd all gotten it wrong. That the man she'd fallen for and married in secret wasn't the same man ruining the very people she loved.

"If I'd stayed in Bali, you'd have gotten the boxing match you've been asking for and I'd have beaten you to a pulp the way my mind's working right now."

His laughter enveloped her. Her spine stiffened, but she was no match for the frissons that husky sound created in her. Or the scent of him that twisted like a screw in her lower belly. Or the memory of the warmth of that tight body covering her like a favorite blanket.

The explosive chemistry between them had been instantaneous, all-consuming, mutual. And apparently, had no intention of abating even when her heart felt bruised inside her chest and her brain rebelled.

"Then maybe I'd have deserved it."

"You think it's that simple?" she said, turning around, frustration driving the words out of her. "That I yell at you, or scream at you, or pound that gorgeous face into mush and then we're even?"

Their eyes met across the room and held. That stillness she found fascinating about him descended again. He reminded her of a jungle cat—all restless energy and contained violence, preparing every single move for an attack.

A white shirt unbuttoned showed off the tanned V of his throat, with an enticing glimpse of curls at the bottom. Dark smudges under his eyes told their own tale—he was as much of a workaholic as her.

He looked a little rumpled after the long flight chasing her, coming after the fact that he'd been working straight for thirty-six hours when she'd left him. The gray of his eyes deepened—the only signal in all his stillness that betrayed him. That told her he'd been just as consumed by what was between them as she had.

Even now as she looked at him, there was no doubt what her foolish heart and her greedy body wanted.

More of what he'd made her feel. More of those warm,

lazy nights. More of the man who'd promised her she'd never be alone again.

More of him.

She cleared her throat, ashamed of how little control she had around him. "Natalie spent a lot of hours—at the risk of increasing wrath from Greta and Leo and even Massimo—trying to convince me that you're not the utter monster your actions prove. That long ago, you were the only protector she'd known against a cruel world. That she owes you a lot. At a time when there was nothing she could do for you in return."

His gaze became opaque, but Alex noted the stiffness of his shoulders. "Didn't she tell you that I did demand a price for all that I've done for her, in the end?"

"You're surprised she stuck up for you. Are you that much of a villain then?"

"I don't know if I'm a villain, *Princess*. But I'm definitely not a hero," he said, walking into the expansive room and completely owning it in a matter of seconds.

Greta had gone to great pains when Alessandra had moved in to create a welcoming space for a lost teen. Every inch of this room had been a haven to a girl whose own mother had broken her heart repeatedly.

"I thought Massimo had all the rights to Natalie's loyalty," he said so softly that she could barely make out the words.

"I'm sure they wish it was that simple, that one emotion for one person could trump or cancel out the emotion you feel for another. But it doesn't work like that, does it?"

His head jerked. She'd chinked that armor, she was sure.

But when he spoke, his voice was as cool as ever. "I will admit I do not have much experience with emotions and family and all the complex, twisted drama that comes with it, *si*? So, no, I've no idea how it works.

"But if Natalie's misguided loyalty toward me—she was

a fierce little thing even as a teen—paints me in a different light in your eyes, then I will thank her for it.

"Don't look for redeeming qualities in me that don't exist, *cara*. Don't forget either that I'm the same man you married recently."

The sheer arrogance of his statement swept through Alex like a wave threatening to drag her under. "You expect me to just shove everything you've done to them under the rug and carry on with you as though nothing has happened?"

"What if you learned that I had done all this—" his arms swept out to encompass the villa "—*to them*, for no other reason than that I was a cutthroat businessman who wanted to rule the finance center of Milan and BFI is automatically the first target?"

Afternoon sunlight gilded his face, caressing it with loving hands.

Her breath hitched in her lungs as she suddenly saw the resemblances she'd never seen before. The set of his eyes—so much like Massimo's, especially when he was smiling. The curling disdain Vincenzo's mouth so artfully expressed—exactly like Leo's when he was displeased.

So many small things hit her, causing her heart to stutter. Ramming her conscience again and again with the fact that he belonged here, in this place she'd called home. Weakening her anger. Confusing her hurt with too many emotions he far too easily evoked.

"That you can even think it could ever be that simple… shows how completely differently we're wired."

"Fine. How about we forget the whole cursed lot of them for a few minutes?" A little frustration slipped into his voice.

"You're the one who entangled me in this."

"Our marriage can stand outside of all this Brunetti drama, Alessandra."

"That's where you lose me, V. Maybe that's what comes

of playing with people's lives like you're conducting a chess game. Maybe you're incapable of seeing that to demand my loyalty while at the same time you're destroying them… is impossible. I can't see how we can possibly go forward from here… *Because you lied to me.*"

"Not a single time did I lie."

"Fine. If you want to split hairs, then you hid a great big truth from me.

"I'm *trying* to understand what you might have felt as that little boy, why you chose this path of revenge years ago. How much Greta's momentary thoughtlessness might have hurt—"

"I wouldn't refer to calling my mother a whore and a gold digger as a momentary thoughtlessness," he said, baring his teeth in a growl. "I grew up destitute, thanks to her. My mother had a mental breakdown she never recovered from. She lost her livelihood, and we were turned out onto the streets. It turned into early onset dementia."

Her heart thumped in her chest, the anguish in his eyes dissolving her righteous fury. Still, she had to try. "That *is not* Greta's fault."

"No? That my mother went untreated for so long, that she had a mental breakdown and that she didn't even have access to the minimum level of medical care is their fault. That she now lives needing round-the-clock nursing care is their fault." He reminded her of a wild animal, hurt and pouncing to attack. "That her disease spread so far and so fast that she doesn't even recognize me is totally their fault."

"She doesn't recognize you?" Alex whispered, her heart breaking for him. For herself too.

Because how was she to cross this divide caused by him holding on to his pain and fury for so long? How could she hope to turn him from this path of destruction when he was utterly determined to see Leo and Massimo as enemies, when his hatred had such strong foundations in his terrible childhood.

And if she stayed with him, knowing his plans for people she loved so deeply, what did that make her?

He shook his head, his jaw tight. "She thinks I'm still a ten-year-old boy. She's…frozen in that year."

"Why didn't you tell me any of this?"

"Because I don't want the pity I see in your eyes."

"Then what do you want from me?"

As she watched, half fascinated, half furious, he reined all that emotion back in. As easily as if he'd packed it away and locked it up. No, instead he channeled all that pain into hatred, into fury, into revenge. "The vows you made to me. The future we promised each other. That's what I want."

"I still can't believe Greta could've done something so—"

"Because you're buried under the weight of your obligations to them. You don't know their true colors—you're not tainted by the privilege and power that resides in their blood."

"And you think that means I can't love them just as much? When I found out Carlos was my biological father and came to live with him, Greta was already married to him and didn't even know I existed. But she welcomed me with open arms, she made a home for me here, she was the rock in my life when he died. Leo and Massimo, they accepted me and treated me like a real member of their family. You can't imagine what they mean to me, Vincenzo."

"And yet you presume to understand my animosity toward them?"

The leap of anger in his eyes—so unusual, especially directed at her—gave Alex pause. She wanted to try and see this from his point of view, but he'd put her smack-dab in the middle of it.

She took a deep breath and chose her words carefully.

"You're right. It's nothing but lip service of me to say that I…understand what you went through. But you…you don't know what life was like for Leo and Massimo with your father, Silvio. They're innocent of any wrongdoing. They don't deserve to have their lives ripped apart like this.

"Your true culprit is Silvio Brunetti. Not them. But he's dead now."

He shrugged and the casual cruelty with which he did it with no pause to even consider her entreaty felt like a slap. "They bear the name I've hated all my life. Anyway, there are always casualties in war, *cara*. It's unavoidable."

Her heart sank. "Is that what this is, V? War?"

"*Si*. One I have waged for a long time. One I've invested everything into. I looked for weaknesses, sore spots, for years. I hit them with everything I had. And I don't intend—"

"Wait…" interrupted Alex, a cold finger raking its way down her spine. Pieces falling into place emerging in a picture that made her want to run away again.

Alessandra Giovanni: Supermodel. Style Icon. Businesswoman. Philanthropist. Adopted Daughter of the Powerful Brunettis of Milan.

She remembered the headline now.

That feature had been released in a magazine no more than a few days before she'd flown to Bali for yet another photoshoot.

Where the mysterious, gorgeous, gray-eyed Italian businessman had showed up.

Their accidental meeting when she'd visited the ruins of an old temple…

Their shared love of ancient architecture…

The three hours he'd waited the next day while she finished her shoot, as if there was no other place on earth he'd rather be, those gorgeous eyes eating her alive.

The promise to show her sights she'd never see on a formal touristy visit...

Their first kiss under the most magnificent waterfall...

The questions about her charity, about the business she planned to launch, about all the things near and dear to her... The way he'd left her wanting more after that first night of intimacy on the balcony of her villa... The fairytale proposal and the marriage vows he'd recited in that deep voice...

Had any of it been real?

Nausea threatened to flood her mouth. "Did you come to Bali specifically looking for me? To see if you could use me in this *war* of yours?"

He didn't precisely flinch but she knew him. Knew every small shift and jerk of his beautiful face.

"Answer me, Vincenzo," she screamed, the question bursting out of her on a wave of fury and unspeakable hurt.

"*Si.* I did come looking for you. Alessandra—"

"Because that article quoted Greta as saying, 'Alessandra is the one I love the most in the world,' right?"

Again that dreadful, soul-crushing silence.

Despite her best efforts, tears broke out onto her cheeks, making her vision fuzzy. Distorting those clear-cut features. Twisting that sensuous mouth.

"I looked for weaknesses, sore spots. I hit them with everything I had."

It hadn't been enough that he'd come after BFI and BCS. Or that he'd somehow achieved ownership of Silvio Brunetti's shares in BFI. He'd had to hit them where it would hurt them personally too, hadn't he, especially Greta?

Everything had been premeditated. Planned. Perfectly executed.

And she'd fallen for him like a ton of bricks.

She turned and faced him, wiping her cheeks roughly. Hurt gave way to anger, to a fury unlike any she'd ever known. "So how do you see this whole thing playing out exactly? What is it that you expect of me while you wreak havoc through these people's lives? People I love, let me clarify."

"I expect you to do what you'd have done if you hadn't found out. To give our marriage a real chance. To spend the rest of your life with me. To keep the vows you made to me."

"Our marriage is nothing but a…farce."

"*No! I married you*, Alessandra. I promised to spend the rest of my life with you. It is not something I undertook lightly."

Alex searched his face, hoping to see a flicker of something that she could hang on to. That implacable gaze didn't soften. Slowly, his words sank in, bringing yet more questions.

"Why? Why did you marry me? Why not just seduce me and walk away? I made it so easy for you anyway. I begged you to take me to bed. I chased you for the entire week after you showed up in Bali. I…you could have just walked away after we slept together. You could have dumped me—told me I had been nothing but a toy to play with."

"I do not treat women like toys. That's a Brunetti specialty."

"Then why?"

"You're beautiful, you're smart, you're a treasure any man would love to possess. For a man who grew up with nothing, who would always remain a bastard, who built his empire by trampling all the people in his way, you're the real prize, Alessandra.

"I married you because for the first time in my life, I saw something I wanted outside of revenge and everything it stood for. Outside of a campaign that has consumed me for the last twenty-odd years.

"I married you because taking you for myself was the final icing on the cake. Because taking you from that old woman makes it all complete."

Alessandra nodded, her stomach falling. "I don't know what to say to a man who thinks he can take me from the woman who gave me a home, who thinks I'll support the total destruction of my family. Who thinks possessing me somehow…improves his standing in the world. I will not…"

God, she wasn't going to be used again in a battle between people she cared for.

She'd done that and had the scars to show for it.

She wasn't going to be anyone's weakness. Or anyone's weapon. "I'm not a prize. To be won. To be possessed. To be snatched from someone's hands. To be used as a weapon against someone else." Alex forced herself to meet his gaze. "I want you to leave. Leave this house. I can't deal with this now… Please, leave, V."

He stood there, unmoving, unaffected, like a bloody big boulder that not even a gale of wind could budge.

After what felt like an eternity, he nodded. And left.

Alex stood there at the window, her throat dry. Her chest empty.

Of course, he hadn't married her for herself.

She wasn't a princess and this wasn't a fairy tale where she could magically wave a wand or press a kiss to Vincenzo's mouth and her frog would transform into a prince.

"She's gone."

"What the hell does that mean?" Vincenzo barked the question at the carelessly lounging figure of Massimo Brunetti.

He tucked his hands into his pockets and stared down

at the two men relaxing in their chairs on the balcony on this unseasonably cold early June afternoon.

The drive up to the villa had been just as spectacular as it had been the first time around. He looked at it with the objective eye of a man who meant to cut it all up to pieces and scatter it into the wind.

But as much as he relished the idea of destroying the very symbol and stronghold of the Brunettis' centuries-long power and privilege, other concerns rode him harder right then.

Alessandra hadn't returned his calls in five days, forcing him to visit the ancestral home again.

His patience, always on thin ice these days, was spiraling into a monster of a temper after this latest stunt from his sweet wife.

Cristo, it had been the worst week of his professional and personal life.

Beginning with a huge crisis in the finance department of his company, followed by Alessandra jumping on a flight out of Bali to Milan without informing him. Then his own long flight to catch up to her, their ill-timed confrontation that had quickly spiraled out of control thanks to the Brunettis bringing her up-to-date with all his supposedly Machiavellian motivations, followed by an urgent call from the twenty-four nurses that looked after his mother demanding his immediate presence at his estate in Tuscany.

Which meant he'd been forced to leave Alessandra alone for too long, letting the doubts he'd seen in her eyes fester and harden. He had loathed giving her that time apart from him, especially when it was spent around the Brunettis, who were more than happy to fill her ears with poison against him.

But he'd had no choice but to go to his mother. Usually, he didn't mind dropping everything in his empire to look after her.

"You shouldn't have left her like that..." Leonardo offered in an almost polite voice, his expression thoughtful. "Not so soon after she found out your true colors. The least you could have done was let her rage at you, maybe even let her throw one of her powerful punches at you. Anything would have been better than to leave her alone to stew in your betrayal."

"I didn't betray her—" Vincenzo bit out and then calmed himself with a discipline that was hanging by its last thread.

He had not betrayed Alessandra. He had simply left out a chunk of truth that he'd hoped to explain in full later on. He'd hoped to appeal to her strong sense of justice and fair play. He'd totally miscalculated the depth of her attachment to this group of privileged, spoiled Brunettis. "I had obligations I had to meet. Now, how about you tell me where the hell she is?"

"We *don't know* where Alex is," Massimo said. "After you left, she locked herself in her room, and when Natalie went to check on her the next morning, she was gone."

"You expect me to believe Alessandra didn't ask you for help to hide from me? That you didn't happily join in this childish game to thwart me?"

"You're right," Leo added. Still no rancor in his voice. Only a mild curiosity. "We'd have happily joined in. You went after the one person who had nothing to do with all this. But you're forgetting that Alex has connections in high places, all over the world.

"There's no shortage of people that will happily help her out, to save her from an untenable situation.

"She's the most loyal person I know, even if the person getting it is questionable.

"Knowing how much you despise even our name, she'll twist herself around to not give you any more ammunition against us. She knew you'd demand to know where she is. Keeping it a secret is her way of protecting us."

"She fought with me like a lioness because she thinks she needs to protect you from me. And you didn't come to her aid?"

"You're not listening, Cavalli. Alex's long gone. No one here knows when she'll return or even if she will."

For the first time in a week, Vincenzo felt the sure ground under his feet shift. There was no gratification in Massimo's voice or Leonardo's gaze crowing over the fact that Alex had trumped him. Only worry for her. "She can't escape from her life. She has obligations, a global career," he protested.

"A career she's been slowly decoupling herself from. If you knew her at all, you'd have known she's been finishing up all her contracted work and not signing up to anything new," Massimo said. "*Cristo*, you really did a number on her at an already rough time, when she's been questioning everything about herself, her career, her life."

"What are you talking about?" Leo asked his brother the question that Vincenzo wanted to.

"She broke it off with that photographer boyfriend of hers—Javier Diaz—a few months ago. She plans to quit modeling altogether. I've been wondering why she'd marry a practical stranger after—"

"Alessandra and I have known each other for a few weeks," Vincenzo put in. But he was slowly losing ground. Losing his belief in her.

Had her vows to him meant nothing at all? Damn it, why hadn't she fought with him? Demanded an explanation? Given him the chance to convince her his motives were sound?

"It still makes you a stranger. But now I think I see it." Massimo's gaze bored into him. "You were a rebound from Javier. An escape. A temporary madness."

Vincenzo was more than tempted to knock the smirk

off the tech genius's face but it went against everything he believed in. "Watch your words, Massimo."

"Walk away, Cavalli." The younger man stood up. "It hasn't dawned on you yet, has it? Alex has gone. It's what she does when the pain gets too much for her."

Vincenzo had no retort. No words, even.

This wasn't the Alessandra he knew. The sophisticated and yet vulnerable minx that had demolished his self-control with one genuine smile. This was not the woman who'd seduced him by giving away pieces of herself. The woman that had distracted him from twenty years' worth of strategizing in a mere few weeks.

But then how much did he truly know Alessandra beyond the report a PI had provided him with, beyond the picture the media painted of her?

"I'm supposed to believe that this complicated woman... is the woman I married?"

"It doesn't matter whether you believe us or not. We've known Alex for a long time," Massimo pointed out, satisfaction pouring out of every word. "You betrayed her trust. Learning about how Greta treated you was a double betrayal for her to have to deal with. And if I know your convoluted, labyrinthine mind—and I'm beginning to—you had every intention of using her against us," he said with a shrewd gleam in his eyes that for Vincenzo was far too much like looking in the mirror. "And I'm guessing she knew that. But then Alessandra has always known her own weaknesses," he finished cryptically.

Vincenzo had had enough. "If this is her way of telling me to pick between her and my original intentions, then she—"

"If she'd thought she could convince you to abandon this crazy revenge you're bent upon—" Leonardo's dark gaze held the first stirrings of anger in it "—she wouldn't have left her own home in the middle of the night *without* telling even us, would she? Which means you did nothing to reassure her. Nothing to prove to her that she wasn't just another pawn in your game."

"My plans for the Brunettis have nothing to do with her."

"Then you truly do not understand what family means to Alex. What family means at all." Vincenzo looked away, despising even the hint of sympathy in Leo Brunetti's eyes. "Accept she's gone, Cavalli. And that she's not returning anytime soon."

Vincenzo tensed, reeling under the other man's words, fury and frustration building inside him. A future he hadn't wanted but had gotten used to looking forward to for the last few weeks was slipping through his fingers.

Was this the depth of Alessandra's commitment? To run away at the first sign of difficulty? To abandon their marriage because things had got tougher than she'd like?

Massimo gave him a pitying look. "I bet you anything she's gone running back into Javier's arms. Can't really blame her, can we, when her prince actually turned out to be a frog. And for all your scheming steel trap of a mind, I bet she won't be found until she wants to be."

CHAPTER THREE

Nine weeks later

THERE WAS GOING to be the devil to pay.

The very devil.

Alessandra stood near the bank of elevators, her feet rooted to the ground, staring across the vast white marbled lobby to the dark oak door that should bear the warning "Beware all you who enter here" or some such.

Everything in her wanted to run away from this. From *him*. But she was done running.

Her reflections in the metallic shine of the elevators—all six of them—had her second-guessing her direct arrival here at BFI's towers in Milan's financial district straight from the airport after her long flight from San Francisco.

She felt grungy in clothes that she'd worn for the last forty-eight hours. Her eyes felt permanently gritty from all the different time zones her body had had to endure in the past fortnight. But the one upside to her disheveled appearance was that no one had recognized her on either side of the Atlantic.

The last thing she'd had, after the initial hearing with the family court in the States and the subsequent meetings with her lawyers, was any energy left to charter a private jet to bring her over to Italy. And seeing that she'd already annoyed her agent; her two assistants, and Greta and Leo; Massimo—though at least he had sympathized with her actions and warned her she was just postponing the final reckoning—Javier; and the man sitting behind the oak door in front of her, she hadn't felt she could reach out to any of them and ask for a favor.

God, it felt like she'd been traveling forever, jumping from one painful situation to another, never stopping and thinking, never standing still.

Because if she did, if she stood in one place for more than a moment and allowed herself to look inward she'd have to listen to her heart. Her pathetic, bruised, still-foolish heart.

She'd have to face the fact that her mother was gone and the last time Alex had seen her, she'd said hateful words to her, that all the memories she had now were stilted, sterile meetings of the last few years. She'd have to swallow the bitterness she'd nursed when she'd realized her mother loved her little half brother, Charlie, far more than she'd ever loved her.

She'd have to face the fact that she had let that same, soul-sucking desperate need to be wanted, to be loved push her into a disastrous marriage with a man she didn't even truly know, that she'd given her heart to a man who didn't even understand what that meant.

The image of Charlie's small, scrunched-up face, determined to look strong in front of Alex as she'd said goodbye to him, rose in front of her eyes, and she pushed away all the fears that could shake her resolve to do the right thing for him. For all her estrangement with her mother, she had fallen in love with Charlie from the first moment she'd set eyes on him as a newborn baby seven years ago.

Whatever the nature of her complex relationship with her mother, whatever insecurities she'd felt for years, whatever bitterness she'd nursed after Charlie's birth, she had to put all that away now. This was not the time for guilt or grief or regrets.

This was the time to take action. To make sure Charlie wasn't lost in the shuffle of adults' mistakes like she'd been as a child.

She had to stop running. She had to be strong for that innocent boy. She had to face the one man she never wanted see again in her life.

In the nine weeks that she'd been hiding, the world had exploded with all kinds of speculation about the mysterious billionaire Vincenzo Cavalli, who headed up Cavalli Enterprises, a finance shark that had its fingers in myriad industrial sectors.

That he was battling with Leonardo Brunetti for the position of CEO of BFI, although they didn't know why.

That he was a mathematical genius who'd made his first billion on the stock market.

That he was ruthless when it came to his opposition.

All the things Alex had been blissfully unaware of when she'd said yes to his sudden proposal.

She still couldn't assimilate the man she'd known in Bali—tender, funny and kind—with the man who'd been raining hell on the Brunettis with not a hint of conscience. And now she had to beg him to cooperate with her after hiding from him for nine weeks.

No, she wasn't going to beg. She was going to demand that he do this for her. She couldn't show weakness in front of a man who didn't understand the meaning of family.

"Mrs. Cavalli?"

"Don't call me that," Alex snapped.

"I'm sorry. You look…quite unlike yourself," came the tentative response from one of the receptionists hovering behind the huge swathe of gleaming white marble designed to intimidate anyone who dared assume they could approach the mighty Vincenzo Cavalli.

But not her.

She squared her shoulders. "Yeah, it's me."

"Shall I get one of the Mr. Brunettis for you? They're

both in the building," a different woman asked, her perceptive eyes taking in Alex's state.

"No, thanks." Leo and Massimo, as powerful as they were, couldn't help her now. Only the devil she'd tangled with would do. "I was told on the ground floor that Mr. Cavalli has taken over this floor. Is that right?"

"Yes, he has. He's already made many changes—"

"Is he in there now?" Alex interrupted.

"Yes."

"Okay. Thanks, Miriam," she added, looking down at the shiny plaque sitting in front of the woman. "I'll just... Don't announce me."

The woman nodded, sympathy shining in her eyes.

Alex looked away. The chance to get a quick, quiet divorce had come and gone. Now she needed this marriage to work. And, oh God, Vincenzo was going to love that, wasn't he?

But only temporarily, she promised herself.

Whatever deal she made with Vincenzo, it only needed to last for as long as she needed him. After that, she would walk away forever. From his charming words, his penetrating eyes and him. Far away from him. From her own naive heart and its foolish hopes.

Vincenzo wondered if going so long without regular sleep was making him hallucinate. If his sanity was truly hanging by its last thread. Alessandra's continued absence—with not even a leaked rumor in the last nine weeks about where she was—had stripped away any semblance of civility from his demeanor.

Even his own team—people who'd been with him for more than a decade—were giving him a wide berth for fear of having their heads bitten off. He hated admitting it, but the ease with which Alessandra had walked out on their far-too-brief marriage rankled like a festering sore.

And still, he wasn't ready to give up. The creak of his door had him barking out a command to be left undisturbed.

His words stuck in his throat as the tall, lithe form of his runaway wife stood inside his office, her back plastered to the door, her white-knuckle fingers clutching the strap of her cross-body bag, neatly delineating the globes of her high breasts in a way he was sure she didn't realize.

"Hello, Vincenzo," she said, and then he knew she was real.

That soft, lilting voice, with its strange mix of American and Italian accents—he'd know it in his sleep. He'd had it whispered in his ear while he'd moved inside her body, finding refuge in it at long last, after never knowing it. Refuge that had been denied him for more years than he cared to count. Peace that he hadn't been able to afford however many millions he had made.

And then, just like a very vivid dream that you never wanted to wake up from, that refuge, that sense of peace had been snatched away from him.

No, she had snatched it away. At the first sign of trouble, she'd run. Very possibly straight into her ex's arms.

His heart thudded in his chest as he took her in, his blood rushing through his veins with a ferocious hunger along with a burning resentment for how easily she evoked his desire. But something was different about her.

This Alessandra looked nothing like the woman who'd worn her hurt in her eyes when she'd learned who he was, nothing like the advocate who'd argued passionately about the children she championed all over the world, or like the beautiful princess he'd taken to his bed for a night and decided to make his wife the next morning.

One night and he'd been lost. Enslaved as simply as if she'd woven a spell around him.

This woman looked as if she was barely held together at the edges.

Her clothes had seen better days. At first glance, she could be mistaken for a poor grad student with no time or energy for anything beyond academics.

Her hair was a glorious mess, a light brown halo around her face, the edges falling to those high breasts. Her skin had always been golden, but now she was tanned, as though she'd spent the whole of the last nine weeks outdoors.

Frolicking under the sun with her ex, perhaps, the insanely jealous part of him piped up.

But it was her eyes that transformed the panorama of her perfectly symmetrical face. They held a fire Vincenzo had never seen before.

Instead of guilt or shame or any of the other emotions he'd imagined he might see when she returned, pure challenge shone in her eyes. Her mouth, lauded for its pillowy pout, was set into a firm line. Now that he was over his shock, he recognized the energy, the determination pouring out of her very stance.

She didn't want to be here. But she was resolved to a particular action.

"Welcome back, Princess," he said, pushing his chair back, but without making a move to get up. He wasn't entirely sure his legs would hold him. His throat felt hoarse, his heart pounding away at a rate that threatened to send it bursting out of his chest. She'd been gone for weeks without a word, leaving him in a special kind of hellish limbo.

"Had enough of traipsing around the world with your ex?" he said, baring his teeth in a mockery of a smile.

She startled but recovered fast. Pushing away from the door, she ventured a few steps in. "That's the most ridiculous thing I've ever heard. I was nowhere near Javier."

The hotter the anger that flared inside him, the more Vincenzo forced himself into stillness. He'd be damned if he showed his fragmented self-control in front of a woman who'd run out on him at the first sign of trouble. "No? Both he and you conveniently disappeared at the same time for over two months. It's a logical conclusion."

She snorted, her nose scrunching with distaste. "You think I'd run away from one deceitful, dishonest man to another?"

Beneath the resentment still burning within, Vincenzo heard the truth in her indignation. He ran a hand through his hair, wondering at how far his jealousy had taken his thoughts. How much Alessandra's abandonment of their marriage had affected him.

How much he wanted the loyalty she gave so freely to the Brunettis.

"And yet, when I finally tracked him down on the phone, your ex wouldn't deny that you weren't with him."

She sighed. "That's because Javier, just like you, is a devious bastard. If he thought it would torment you, he'd say anything. He isn't particularly happy with me at the moment, like the rest of the world."

Vincenzo heard the weariness in her tone but it did nothing to assuage his own jagged emotions. Nothing to tell him that he was any different from that damned ex of hers. Nothing that would remove Massimo's taunting claim that Vincenzo had only been a rebound fling for her. "But he knew where you were, *si*?"

"Yes," she admitted, her gaze searching his face. "He got me in touch with a friend of his, a stud farm owner in Brazil." Something shifted in her expression. "But he wasn't with me at any point."

"And while you were having this extended temper tantrum on a stud farm in Brazil, did you wonder about what it might look like to me? Nine weeks, Alessandra, you were gone for nine weeks with no word. Not even a bloody text."

"You knew I was safe within a week of me leaving. I told Massimo to inform you."

Vincenzo caught up to her in two long strides, frustration mounting. Almost as tall as him, Alessandra looked straight at him, chin lifting, shoulders squaring. Readying herself for a battle. *Dio mio*, where was that seductively sweet, uncomplicated woman that had beguiled him in Bali? "I'm your husband. Being informed secondhand, especially by that taunting creep Massimo, that you're quite safe in some hole that you've crawled into is not acceptable."

The slender set of her shoulders tightened. "What did you want from me, V? A call telling you that I was questioning everything you said and did with me, that I couldn't even bear to look at myself in the mirror because I'd made such a fool of myself, or that the thought of being near you while you happily destroyed Massimo and Leo made me physically nauseous?

"I needed to get away. From you. From Greta. From all of it."

"And?"

"And what? What's with the interrogation? How can you not see that all the promises we made to each other mean nothing when the foundation itself is cracked?"

The last bit of his temper frayed and his voice pitched dangerously low. "And if it's broken, you simply walk away, instead of fixing it?"

Still, she didn't back down. "Not if it's completely shattered, like my trust in you."

Tears and hurt were preferable to this version of Alessandra that looked at him with stony defiance and distrust. "I guess Massimo is right.

"The Alessandra that's lauded in the papers, that captures millions of hearts with her take-charge attitude is a

sham. The Alessandra that said she'd always dreamed of
having a big family is a lie.

"The woman I married is in fact an impulsive brat who
runs when things don't go her way.

"Whose promises means nothing.

"Who clearly thinks marriage is only fun and sex and
romantic escapades. Who's so immature that she can't even
stand and communicate with the man she'd promised to
spend the rest of her life with."

CHAPTER FOUR

IMPULSIVE. IMMATURE.

Words she'd heard before. Words she'd buried deep. Her mother, Alyssa, had used them far too many times in the conversations they'd had over the years. When Alex refused to take any kind of step toward healing their relationship.

From Vincenzo, the accusations rang true and stung deep. But it was the flash of disappointment in his eyes before he buried it under a thick veil of resentment that she couldn't ignore. It didn't help that she was already feeling fragile after attending her mother's and stepfather's funerals.

She'd expected Vincenzo's anger, had been warned by Massimo of the cold burn of it getting worse with each passing day. She'd chalked it up to an arrogant, ruthless man not getting his own way, probably for the first time in his life.

Away from his commanding presence, awash in her own hurt, it had been easy to forget that he had certain expectations of her, that her learning of his true identity and actions toward the Brunettis made no difference to him, to how he felt about their marriage.

"Running away from problems only makes them worse, piccola." Her biological father's wise words when she'd begged to come and live with him after yet another fight with her mother. But in the end, Carlos had indulged her wish, and as a result, the ocean of distance between her and Alyssa had become permanent.

Had she done the same this time too? What did she owe a man who had trapped her in a web of lies?

And yet, he'd gained nothing so far by marrying her.

"I married you because for the first time in my life I saw something I wanted outside of revenge."

Heat flamed her cheeks, but she refused to look away as if she was in the wrong. "If I apologize for my actions, it won't be truthful," she finally offered. "You left me feeling like I had no other choice than to go."

"And now, *bella*?" He leaned against his massive desk, throwing those long legs out in front of him. Pulling her starved senses to the sheer masculinity of him. As though she were a magnet and he was her true north. "Have you found one? Is that why you've deigned to return?"

With him standing no more than two feet from her, Alex weakened and let herself drink him in.

Take in the magnificent presence of the man she'd allowed into her heart.

Power and arrogance shimmered around him, a second skin. An armor he was using to keep her out now. But he hadn't done it in Bali. He had let her in. He had been a different man. Or was that just her naive belief in a fairy tale that didn't exist?

And how had she not seen the similarities between him and Leo and Massimo? The cut of his features, the very way he held himself slightly separate from the crowd, the affection she'd heard in his voice when he'd spoken of his mother—he was so much like his half brothers. So much a Brunetti through and through.

But she knew instinctively he would hate that comparison. The confidence in his speech, the commanding power of his look—it had been hard-won for Vincenzo and would be so much harder to shed too.

Deep smudges darkened his electric gray eyes, gilded by long lashes that should have made him look almost feminine. But the aquiline nose, with no fewer than two dents marring its aristocratic lineage, and the strong chin saved him from that. While his thinly sculpted upper lip hinted at the contempt she'd foolishly never seen before today, the lush lower lip spoke of the sensuality he hid beneath that ruthless mask.

She shivered slightly, even though his office was set to a comfortable ambient temperature.

The gray shirt revealed a teasing V of olive skin, skin Alex had kissed and petted to her heart's content. Her palm tingled in desperation for that contact again—to be able to slide her hand over his warm skin stretched taut over sculpted muscles. She'd thought it so romantic that she, with her always cold toes and fingers, had found a man who could warm her up just by holding her.

But even that reminder of her naive dreams couldn't stop her mind from imagining the slide of her hand moving farther down his defined chest to the thick slabs of his abdominal muscles, down to the solid strength of his thighs and then back up…

"Alessandra!"

Lost in the splendor that was the man she'd thought she had fallen headlong in love with, Alex said huskily, "Have I found what?"

He closed and opened his eyes, his patience apparently paper-thin. "What prompted you to come back? Did Greta promise to save you from the big, bad wolf? Did Leo and Massimo tell you they would protect you from the devious man you'd entangled yourself with?"

"I don't need anyone to fight my battles," Alex snapped, a fresh thread of anger thankfully drowning out the lust that was useless right now, that would only distract her from what she needed to do. "I have found myself in a situation where I… I—"

"You what?"

"I need you," she said, going for defiance but it ended up being an entreaty.

As if she'd woven a magic spell into the air, the very chemistry of the room changed. Like that first moment on Bali when their eyes had met, a real connection arced between them.

A pure electric charge that had nothing to do with revenge and all its twisted consequences. The luminous gray of his eyes flared into something dangerously feral and her pulse spiked.

God, was she really getting a thrill because she could still provoke this reaction from him? When would her stupid heart and her foolish body learn that he wasn't hers? That for all the pleasure he'd woven with his skillful caresses, he'd had an ultimate goal all the while?

"You need me for what, *bella*? I made the mistake of trusting you blindly once. I will not do it again."

The sheer arrogance of the words broke their connection. Alex laughed. "It's like you stole the very words from my script." She shook her head. If his gaze wasn't already drilling holes in her skin, she'd have smacked herself on the head. God, she needed him, yes, but for a good reason.

Not to dissolve into an overheated puddle at his feet.

"I need the appearance of this marriage," she announced clearly this time, tilting her chin up, holding his gaze. "That's why I returned."

His gaze irate, his jaw tight, he just stared at her.

"My mother and stepfather—" she swallowed the lump in her throat "—died in an accident two weeks ago." She didn't wait for him to offer a sentiment. If he showed any sympathy or touched her, her grief would come bursting out and she'd lose control of herself. And this situation. Never again was she going to depend on him. "I flew here straight from the funeral in San Francisco.

"My stepfather left a huge fortune to my half brother,

Charlie. He's only seven and already his paternal uncles are fighting over who gets to take control of him. Just so they can control his fortune."

She blinked and turned away for a moment, trying to hold back the threat of tears.

"I'm sorry you've been dealing with such horrific news," he said, his voice coming close behind her. The scent of him was a tempting invitation, offering the illusion of an escape from her worries. "You didn't have to take it on alone, Alessandra."

The tenderness in his voice beckoned her, and it took all her strength to not fall into his embrace. To not let herself drown in grief. To not let his strong arms hold her through this pain.

She turned back to face him. "I kinda had to," she said vehemently, rejecting whatever comfort he was offering. "I've always dealt with life alone."

His mouth opened and closed, frustration etched onto his features. Long fingers pushed through his hair, sudden energy brimming from his demeanor. "Alessandra, I miscalculated how much what I—"

"I want to take custody of him," she said, cutting off his words. It was too late for apologies anyway. "I want to raise Charlie. I want to give him the kind of loving family life he deserves, the security I always yearned for as a child.

"Knowing how my stepfather's brothers are already fighting over him, as if he were a piece of meat, I can't give him up to them. I refuse to."

She looked up at him to realize she had his full attention. Thankful that he hadn't interrupted her again, she went on. "I've spoken to a firm of family lawyers that comes highly recommended. I've been informed in no uncertain terms that it's extremely unlikely I'd get custody of him with my current 'lifestyle.'

"I'm single, as far as anyone else knows. I travel around

the world with no stability or roots. I've been in the media spotlight a lot of late, creating controversy, and my breakup with Javier was messy and all over the news. In short, Charlie's uncles plan to use every morsel ever printed against me, even the smallest things I did ten years ago, to prove me an unfit guardian for him.

"So that's where you come in," she finished.

"Where?" His voice was whip sharp, his gaze cutting to her with a withering contempt that should've reduced her to a heap of smoking ash. "All I've heard so far is that you came back to me only because you were forced to do so. That something terribly tragic had to happen to make you show up here today. That your wedding vows still mean less than nothing to you.

"So where *exactly* do I come into this situation, *bella*. Spell it out for me."

Her behavior, so neatly summarized in his stinging words, made shame burn in her chest. But she buried it deep. She was never again going to project what she wanted to see in his eyes, what she wanted him to feel for her onto him. Never again.

"I'd already made a decision to quit modeling even before this happened. I plan to prove that I can be a steady, secure presence in Charlie's life, however long it takes. I plan to take the battle for custody to the courts and win it.

"It's just a matter of finishing up existing contracts, setting up a permanent residence somewhere and settling down to a less chaotic lifestyle. With my husband, so that I can prove to the courts that there's a stable, two-parent home waiting for Charlie."

"Is that all?" he said dryly.

"Yes, that is all," she snapped, fatigue finally taking over. "And since I already have a husband handy, I thought I should just use him to help my case."

"As opposed to?"

"As opposed to getting rid of the current one and shopping for a new one. What else?" she retorted, rolling her eyes. Her head was beginning to pound from all the lack of sleep, her body in a state of near exhaustion. "This is not a joke."

"Should I truly take you at your word this time, *bella*? Is that what I should have demanded—an extra clarification that it was not a joke when you made your vows to me?"

Alex refused to indulge the guilt that burrowed into the most private recesses of her heart. Or the hope that it had somehow hurt him when she'd left. God, the last thing she needed was to look for any supposed feelings for her. "You owe me this, V."

He raised a brow, arrogance dripping from the gesture. "Owe you, Princess?"

"Yes. You married me without telling me the whole truth. You appear to have conveniently forgotten all the mistakes you've made and blame me for the disturbing farce that is our marriage. You misrepresented yourself to me and I want reparation. This has to be it."

"I told you before. I'm saying it again. Our marriage is not a farce to me."

"I'm not asking you for a happily-ever-after, V." She cut him off, that tough mask in place again. "That's kind of lost its shine for me.

"I'm asking, since we're inconveniently tied together legally already, if you'll help me secure the happiness of a small boy who's just lost his parents and has been thrust into a battle between greedy adults who care only about the bottom line.

"If you were really once that boy who fought against overwhelming odds to survive, you will understand that a child's well-being is at stake here."

* * *

After the almost soap-opera-ish drama that had been his life recently, Vincenzo hadn't thought he'd ever be shocked again. But the fire that burned in Alessandra's eyes, the fighting stance of her body as she faced him, achieved that effect quite thoroughly.

This was the woman he'd lost his head over.

Vulnerable yet fierce.

Fragile and yet with a steely core.

In her, he'd seen a woman that would get behind him. A woman who'd have fought against all the injustices that had been done him. A woman who'd understand his life-long fight, his ambition, his need to even out the scales. A woman—his *wife*—whom he'd thought would take his side against people who were not even her blood relations.

But he refused to be taken in by her again. Refused to let his heart rule over the little sense his head spouted. Refused to forget that, for all her determination now, she'd walked out on him, on their marriage, without even a word.

Worse, she wouldn't have returned if she hadn't been forced into it by a cruel twist of fate.

But for all his reservations, he couldn't remain untouched by the very real grief in her eyes, the guilt whenever she mentioned her mother, the hopelessness when she recounted how Charlie was being fought over.

All feelings he was too familiar with.

"Do you comprehend what an enormous responsibility you're taking on by seeking custody of Charlie?" he asked softly.

Her gaze jerked to meet his. "Yes." Calm. Steady.

"This is not an impulsive decision, is it? Because apparently you're the queen of impulsive behavior."

She fidgeted with the strap of her bag, bringing his gaze to her breasts, before weakly refuting, "That's not fair."

"I've gained a broader picture of you in the weeks you've

been hiding, *cara*. Apparently, you have a history of making major, life-changing decisions on a whim."

A stiffness imbued her movements as she approached his desk and poured herself a glass of water. "I've no idea what you're talking about."

"Signing up to a modeling career—just because you knew your mother would disapprove.

"Walking out on a two-million-dollar contract with a cosmetics company because you discovered that their practices were not entirely ethical. Hiding from the fallout of that in Bali, which was when I found you. Then there's your decision to quit modeling altogether—for reasons unknown.

"And finally, marrying me on the rebound…because you got dumped by your ex," he said, giving voice to the thing that had bothered him the most.

Her almond-shaped eyes widened. "Javier again?"

"Oh no, this is all according to Massimo. He's been quite voluble in your absence, volunteering information about you at regular intervals. Exacting his own version of revenge on me, I'd say."

"Revenge?"

"He knew how…angry I was by your middle-of-the-night flight. So he dealt me a few punches and got some laughs out of it." Massimo, Vincenzo had realized in the past few weeks, found him endlessly fascinating, as if he were a puzzle the tech genius was determined to solve.

It was damned hard to hate a man who kept dropping down into his office for little chats as if they were childhood friends. Or, God forbid, long-lost brothers. Not even on pain of death would Vincenzo admit, however, that he was just as curious about the cyber tech genius.

"So, is it true?"

"Is what true?" she asked.

Vincenzo had a feeling she was playing with him. And

yet he couldn't help gritting out the question that had been gouging a hole in him for nine excruciatingly long weeks. "Did you marry me on the rebound, Princess?"

The little minx fluttered her eyes at him, sweetly pretending to consider the question while his insides tightened into a knot. "You know, there might be some truth to that after all. How else can I explain the temporary madness that took hold of me in Bali? Javi and I...had such grand plans together and then it all fell apart so spectacularly. My relationship had failed. My career held no thrill any longer.

"I found myself hiding in Bali, devastated by everything that had shifted beneath my feet and then there you were... Prince Charming, running to my rescue.

"Except you're more like the slimy, cold-blooded frog than the prince."

His jaw tightened and Alex knew she'd landed a solid hit.

She straightened as he came to her, his voice deceptively soft when he spoke. "You've just been through a terrible loss. Grief and guilt should not be the motivators to involve yourself in a child's life. He's not something you can return to a shop when the fancy wears off."

The sudden change to this most serious of topics, and offering his sensible opinion stole the ground from underneath her. The complex facets to this man amazed her, and the surprises kept hitting her just when she thought she had the measure of him.

He smiled thinly. "You're shocked that a man like me— ruthless, cold, cruel even—can think of a child's well-being in this situation, can see beyond our petty differences, *si*?"

"No. Yes, I mean... I didn't think you'd be quite so rational about it." She shrugged. "It gives me hope that I'm not pushing Charlie from one horrible situation to another. Even if it is only temporary."

"You have considered that I might be a different but just as horrible situation for him then?"

"Of course I have. You lied to me. You've lost my trust. I thought long and hard over that before I came back to you today."

"And what did you conclude?"

"My first step is to get custody of Charlie. Once I achieve that goal, once this marriage becomes nothing but a liability to me, I'll—"

"You'll do away with me?" he said, a glint of wicked humor gleaming in his eyes.

Alex shrugged, a small smile playing around her own mouth. "Something like that, yes."

His gaze turned thoughtful, as he stood there caging her with his body. She could almost hear the gears turning in that Machiavellian mind of his. "*Bene*, I'll play along for the world. But I have a price for my cooperation."

"Of course you do." She glared at him. "It seems you're nothing if not predictable."

"You're asking me to take on an important role in the life of a child—"

"I'm not asking you to be a permanent parent to him—"

"Ah…how do you see this playing out, then?" he asked, parodying the question she'd asked of him. "We pretend to be an adoring couple, you get custody of your half brother and then you run off to some quiet corner of the world with him in tow, never to be seen again and forget all about your poor husband?"

There was no place in the world she could go to where she could outrun her feelings for him. "What's your price, V?" she demanded, facing him, refusing to back down even though everything inside her was building to an unbearably heightened sense of unwanted anticipation.

He tucked his finger under her chin and looked her straight in the eye. "The same as always, Alessandra."

"Spell it out for me."

"I've only ever wanted what was mine. No more, no less.

"I want the wife you promised me you'd be. I want the marriage that this was supposed to be. I want you to stand by my side while I achieve the goal I've worked toward all my life."

"Those promises were made based on false assumptions. You're not the man I thought you were. And nothing will make me betray Leo and Massimo."

Impatience glittered in his eyes. "You do them a disservice, *cara*. Leonardo and Massimo can look after themselves. Charlie can't. Why don't you focus your energies on him?"

"You make it sound so simple. As if everything sits in a different compartment—"

"You don't seem to grasp one crucial thing. Whether I had seen you in Bali or not, whether or not I had thrown all my own rules out the window and married you when I've never even had a girlfriend for more than two months, this was always going to be my path in life, Alessandra.

"I would still have done everything I could to ruin all that bears the name Brunetti."

"And I'll be damned before I let you use me against them," she threw back at him.

Vincenzo took her in, reluctant admiration and pride building up in his chest.

From the portrait Massimo had drawn of her, from her own actions in the last nine weeks, he'd wondered at the sanity of what he'd done. If he'd been taken in by her beauty and his lust. But now, he knew he'd made the right decision.

He wanted this Alessandra that fought for the people she loved in her life so ferociously. He wanted that loyalty all for himself.

And whether cruel or not, fate had given him another chance with her. Alessandra's resolve to do the right thing by her half brother was his chance, his opportunity to set things straight between them.

An opportunity to get her to spend time with him, to make her see his side of the story. To turn this temporary arrangement she'd suggested into the permanent marriage he still wanted.

"Fine, I'll give you what you're asking for. We will pretend to be a happy, blissfully in love couple for the world. I will help you win custody of Charlie. After a trial period of say three months."

"Trial period of what exactly?"

"Of you behaving yourself."

"Behaving myself? How dare you—"

"Hear me out, Alessandra. You say I've broken your trust? You have done exactly the same to me. Believe me, Princess, you're the first person I gave that to and you threw it back in my face without a single moment's doubt."

The thin thread of resentment in those words killed Alex's ready argument. Words fell away from her lips as she stared at him, a simple truth emerging from all of it.

Their marriage had meant something to him. Maybe not the same thing as it had to her. But something. And her walking out on it, on him, he saw as...what? Abandonment? A betrayal? Had this marriage, his vows, really been sacred to him?

"I won't… I can't let you bring a child into this thing between us without ensuring it is truly what you want. That you'll see all this through—these huge decisions and being a parent—without running away from it. For three months, don't make any more life-changing decisions. Deal with your grief over your mother's loss. Decide what you want to do with your career."

She hated that he was being the sensible one here. "There's nothing to deal with, V."

"You've just lost your mother, Princess. You—"

"I never really had my mother in the first place to lose her."

He reached for her hand but Alex instinctively jerked away from him. Because she didn't trust herself. Not with him.

He exhaled roughly. "Don't run away. Don't… Just stay still, with me. Show the world that you're settling down. Show me that you're committed to this arrangement over the next three months. And then we'll start the custody proceedings."

"But that's three months that Charlie's…"

"Visit with him in the meantime. Wrap up your other obligations. Three months is a small drop in the ocean when you consider the fact that you'll give him a stable home for the rest of his life."

"Three months is a long time to a child who's just lost everything, who's living with family members who see him as nothing but a meal ticket to a better life. You're doing this just to punish me. Because I walked out on you."

"No, Alessandra. I'm doing this to make sure we both know what we're getting into this time. To make sure we're not compounding the first mistake by bringing an innocent into this mess."

"Both you and I know how much damage could be done to a child by the smallest thoughtless action. We can't…" Her throat caught on the words. "I can't leave him there alone, unprotected."

"Fine, Princess," Vincenzo offered in a soothing tone. His brow furrowed into a thoughtful frown while he stared at her with that same intensity he brought to everything he did. "Did your mother have any friends that Charlie knows well?"

"Yes." Alex nodded.

"People you trust?"

"Yep. They have a little boy Charlie's age. I met them when I visited him for his last birthday party."

"You said you and your mother were estranged."

Alex shrugged. "Yes, we were. But that doesn't mean I was going to completely shut Charlie out of my life. I never missed a birthday of his, and as soon as he learned to read, I regularly sent him little cards and letters."

"I'll make some calls. Maybe we can arrange for him to stay with that family until the custody hearing is done. He can go to the same school as their son, keep the same routine and have familiar people around him while you and I figure this out."

Alex nodded, gratitude cutting away any words that could rise up and ruin this temporary détente. At least in this matter, her trust in him hadn't been misplaced. And he was right.

She'd run away from her problems in the past. More than once. But not anymore.

This time, she was going to face them, and him, head-on.

She was going to stay by his side and do everything she could to stop this destruction of the Brunettis that he was bent on, using every weapon available to her. But never again was she going to forget that there was a bone-deep ruthlessness inside him; never again was she going to foolishly believe that he was capable of love.

"I have a condition of my own too," she threw at him impulsively, the idea of three months living in close quarters with him seeming like a lifetime. A lifetime of intimacy, of awareness and desire, of shattered dreams and naive hopes.

"What?" he said smoothly, even as he uncoiled himself and sauntered toward her. It was like watching a predator emerge from stalking, ready to pounce.

She stood rooted in place, refusing to reveal how much his nearness affected her. How much the heat of his body called to her. "I'm not sleeping with you. This is not a real marriage. Not anymore."

"Ah… Massimo was right."

Her breath stuttered in her throat as he lifted his hand and gently pushed away a strand of her hair from her shoulder. "About what?"

"That I don't know you well at all. But even he doesn't know how cruel you can be, does he, Princess?"

Alex compulsively licked her lips just as his gaze zeroed in there. "It muddies everything for me. That's how you trapped me in the first place. You're too damned good in bed."

A wicked light came into his eyes, making them magnetic. "I think that's just the connection between us, *bella*. A connection that you're doing everything to run away from."

"Hot sex, however tempting, can't be the only bedrock of a marriage."

"Unfortunately for my body, I agree." He pursed his lips and leveled a thoughtful look at her. "Shall I suggest an amendment to your condition?"

"What?"

"We should each be allowed to try to seduce the other, *si*? If I try and you give in, you can't hold that against me."

"I won't give in. And I definitely don't want to seduce you."

He tilted his head to the side, his gaze holding hers captive. "Then there's no harm in the challenge then, is there?" She had somehow managed to nod when he bent his head and whispered in her ear. "I do wish you'd change your mind about seducing me, Princess."

Her heart raced, sensation zinging across her skin. "Why?"

"There's nothing more arousing, nothing sexier in the

world than a beautiful, powerhouse of a woman who goes after what she wants with a single-minded determination.

"In fact, I'd say that's how *you trapped me*, Princess." His lips never really grazed the sensitive skin beneath her ear, but Alex felt the touch nevertheless, like a searing burn. "Being so thoroughly wanted like that by you is an incredible high unlike any other in the entire world."

CHAPTER FIVE

ALESSANDRA HATED TO admit it, even during the most peaceful moments while she'd been hiding out in Bali, but there had been a kernel of doubt in her mind as to whether she'd done the right thing in deciding to quit modeling.

Show after high stakes frantic show for top designers around the world, running from city to city, country to country like a nomad, working close to eighty hours a week, with no time for a personal life or the deep commitments she'd wanted—the stress of it had taken its toll on her.

Of course, she'd partied in the beginning—partied hard with the heady freedom of a sixteen-year-old who'd found the world at her feet—but over the years the vacuous, often cutthroat glamor of it all had paled and she'd become more and more unhappy.

Photographers who'd once loved working with her had started calling her fractious, restless, the second she hadn't been performing to perfection. She'd been turning up late for fitting appointments, finding a myriad of excuses. Once she'd arrived late and covered in glitter and hair spray from a previous show, minutes before she was due to walk, the stress of running across the city during fashion week making her nauseous. Making her want to run away from the sea of frantic strangers surrounding her.

That particular evening, she'd confided in Javier that her heart just wasn't in it anymore.

The creep had mocked her. From there, their argument

had spiraled into a complete destruction of their relationship, the only place it had left to go. Only then had she realized she didn't want to be with Javier. He had become another crutch.

And then she'd learned the appalling facts about the working conditions of the cosmetics company she represented. Horrified, Alex had scathingly criticized the company in an interview and quit the contract on the spot.

It had been a hotheaded, more than reckless, move. Her agent had blasted her—she was gathering too much ill will in an industry where reputation meant everything. Even the warning hadn't been enough to make her care.

She'd had enough. So she had run off to Bali and ended up marrying the first man who'd shown an interest in her.

Seen like that, the picture of her that emerged didn't look good.

Now, while she stood like a mannequin with her arms stretched out, her face upturned for a makeup artist to dab highlighter onto her cheeks, Alex looked at her reflection in the mirror under the overhead lights and smiled.

Relief was a river gushing through her insides.

God, she was so done with this.

Only a few minutes to the show and backstage was packed with people, all to ensure a fabulous show. She was totally aware of the strange looks she'd been getting from all of them, ever since she'd arrived.

Gossip was the backbone of the fashion industry, and she'd no doubt her stunt with the cosmetics company, her subsequent absence for the last few months and her sudden reappearance now were the hot topics of discussion.

She felt free, as if a weight had been lifted, as she shrugged on a sheer, lacy, red cover-up and moved to join the line of models about to go on.

Someone sidled up to the producer, Isha, who was one of Alex's few friends in the industry, and a heated argument ensued. All heads turned to them as both women bent their head over a seating arrangement.

Alex sidled up to her friend in the wings and enveloped her in a side hug, being extra careful as to not smudge her makeup or even breathe the wrong way. "Everything okay?"

"Some big *bajillionaire* VIP has shown up, unannounced, at the last minute, and his team of assistants wants a front row seat for him, of course. Even the crazy genius that is Jean Benoit," she said, mentioning the designer whose collection they were showing off, "doesn't want to get on this man's wrong side. They're all turning themselves inside out figuring out where to put him.

"Apparently, he's here to see one of the models."

Alex felt a flutter of alarm in her chest. It had been a fortnight since Vincenzo and she had butted heads, then agreed to a plan. Since they both had super busy schedules, they'd barely seen each other since. It suited her just fine, even though she knew the logistics of their deal would come at her soon enough like a freight train.

Suddenly, Alex understood how a hunted animal felt. "Any idea who it is?"

Isha shook her head. "Focus on the show, Alex."

The flutter morphed into a full-blown panic attack. "Isha, just tell me."

"It's the same Italian businessman—the reclusive owner of that international brokerage firm who's been in the media spotlight the past week. It was leaked that he's related to the Brunettis of Milan, which is why he's been going after them. Apparently, he's the secret illegitimate son of the old coot, Silvio. His name's…"

"Vincenzo Cavalli," Alex added, her insides turning into spaghetti. Her heart thumped with a dizzying excitement, and it had nothing to do with the high she usually associated with doing a show.

Alex squared her shoulders and strutted out onto the catwalk, wondering how apt the song blaring out of the speakers was.

Something about bad girls living fast and burning out.

She had to be if she wanted to change the mind of the man sitting in the middle seat of the front row, eating her alive with those penetrating gray eyes.

Too late to back out now that she'd made a deal with the devil.

Vincenzo threw back the last bit of his whiskey and walked up the curving designer staircase onto the balcony that offered a bird's-eye view of the latest nonstop party central that was the nightclub he'd launched recently.

Seeing the final product tonight, when it had been the ruins of an old, abandoned train depot not long ago, filled him with an immense satisfaction.

The secret nightclub—not so secret anymore now that the high fashion crowd of Milan had discovered it—was bustling with people from the show. Hip-hop music blared through the loudspeakers, while bartenders delighted the crowds with colorful cocktails.

But even with purple strobe lights flashing on and off from crowd to crowd, he could still spot his dear little wife.

His gaze unerringly returned to Alessandra again and again, desperate to drink in the sight of her after two weeks of drought.

He'd always been a man who took risks. A man who played against the odds and won. Or else he wouldn't have been in a position to challenge the Brunetti brothers, who'd been born with every conceivable advantage.

His marriage had been a risk, just like this club had been, but not a strategic or financial risk like all the others. It had been a different kind. But in the end, it would pay out.

Alessandra fluttered through the party like a butterfly,

flitting from flower to flower. Her toned, curvaceous body that she maintained with an iron-willed discipline show-cased beautifully in the slinky black number that parted with a wide V-neck, displaying the sides of her breasts, and yet somehow remained tasteful, elegant. There was a slight ruffled hem that flirted around her upper thighs, again just about covering those round buttocks he'd cradled in his palms a few months ago.

No such contact was forthcoming anytime soon, he realized with a self-deprecating smile. He'd just have to be patient. He'd have to win Alessandra like he did everything else in life.

Knowing that the woman he'd married was an international supermodel that men fantasized over was one thing. Seeing it in person was another. It felt like every man here at the club had swarmed her.

"Everyone adores Alessandra."

Here was proof. And yet she'd chosen to marry him after knowing him only for a few short weeks.

"I'm not a prize, Vincenzo."

Her angry words reverberated inside his head, and he knew he was wrong for feeling this sense of pride whenever he saw her.

An atavistic response, uncharacteristic and unworthy of him. Mine, something inside him insisted. *Only mine.*

He frowned, as a particularly tenacious man followed her from group to group, an urgency to his swarthy features. A stocky Spaniard by the name of Javier Diaz, Vincenzo had no doubt.

He kept an eye on them, ready to lend help if needed, but she dismissed her ex with a scathing remark that had her eyes flashing sparks. That made Vincenzo smile despite the tension stiffening his shoulders.

Other than a brief tilt of her head in acknowledgment, she'd been avoiding Vincenzo all evening.

He let her.

She needed to decompress after the electrifying atmosphere of the show and the relentless demands it had placed on her, and he… He needed to get a better handle on his own emotions tonight before he approached her.

While he'd intended to give them both a breathing space and the energy to finish their immediate obligations before the media ruckus the announcement of their marriage would cause—two fashion shows and one photoshoot in Alessandra's case—and everything had gone to hell. Someone had leaked his relationship to the Brunettis to the press.

He'd had to cut his Beijing trip short to deal with the media circus and the crisis it had caused with the BFI board.

"Is it true that Silvio Brunetti seduced a hotel maid and you were the product?"

"Are you the illegitimate son of Silvio Brunetti?"

"What are your intentions for BFI?"

The Brunetti Bastard one trashy tabloid had called him, choosing to go with the lowest denominator.

Upon arriving at the HQ of BFI this morning, there had been further challenges to deal with. He wondered if it was Alessandra who'd leaked the news, causing him considerable damage.

The fallout with the two board members he'd had in his pocket, had set him back almost two months of careful negotiations. Considerable speculation had been raised as to how and why he'd started taking over the board of BFI. Exactly how he had gained ownership of Silvio Brunetti's stock.

He'd arrived at the fashion show, temper frayed, determined to confront the woman whose loyalty should've been to him. Only him.

Instead, seeing her strutting on the catwalk, challenge and confidence oozing from every pore, her body a finely honed machine, her eyes glowing with some inner zeal had completely undercut his anger.

Alessandra in that bloodred bikini top—some sort of studded corset that propped up her already high breasts—and a thong in the same color, with light brown high heels that almost blended into her skin, and all that golden-brown hair pulled back into a tight bun that sharpened her already flawless bone structure, was never going to leave his memory bank even if he lived to be a hundred.

Her red lipstick had made her pouty mouth a lesson in sensuality and sin.

The woman had far too much power over him, moving him from anger to laughter to desire as if he were a windup toy she could turn on and off at her leisure.

She looked up at that precise moment, the flashing purple lights lighting up her lithe body, her eyes shimmering with naked challenge.

Something inside him awakened with a growl.

Because this woman, who challenged him, who was making him work for her loyalty, whose surrender would be so delicious when he finally won it, she set his blood on fire. And he'd had enough of watching her from a distance, like those other besotted men. Enough of pussyfooting around her because of misplaced guilt about hurting her. Enough of trying to give her space and time to deal with her grief.

The world needed to know that she belonged to him. That she had thrown her lot in with him. The explosive news that Alessandra Giovanni had married the Brunetti Bastard should be enough to gain him back some of the ground he'd lost this past week.

It should have been all about damage control at this point. But the thought of winning his wife over fired his blood like nothing else.

Leaning his forearms on the wrought iron balustrade, Vincenzo held her gaze. And beckoned her upstairs with his index finger. Laughter broke out of him at the dawning effrontery in her expression, a fire in his veins as he imagined those beautiful brown eyes clouding over with passion when she eventually surrendered to him.

He was a man used to surrender, and he would accept nothing less from the woman he'd married.

Apparently, whatever reprieve she'd been offered over the last two weeks was finally over. Foolish of her to hope he'd disappear after the fashion show without seeking her out.

He stood on the balcony, looking down upon her, his gray gaze perusing her with such an intense possessiveness that she felt owned.

How dare he beckon her with a finger, as if she were his puppet!

And yet, here she was, answering his summons. Their encounters in Bali had hinted at a depth of emotion that she didn't see in most men.

Greta had really lost it with Alex, calling her a naive, besotted fool for not realizing his true nature. But she'd been so sure about him. If there was one thing she'd had exposure to from the ripe age of sixteen, it was men.

She'd been hit on, propositioned, come on to, even harassed, by everyone from a lowly lighting manager to a megarich designer, to a CEO of a multinational corporation.

Most men were either intimidated by the idea of all that she was and tried to overcompensate for it in various ways. Others—usually rich investment types—thought that all it took to impress her was a bigger fortune than hers and a bigger ego.

But Vincenzo hadn't fallen into either camp. He had been different from that very first moment.

There had been something very down-to-earth about him, an awareness of his place in the world and the power he could wield. Respect that he offered her immediately for the basic reason that she was another human being, a sense of reserve that she'd been itching to topple from the first time he'd walked her to her villa and then walked away without presuming anything.

She hadn't been wrong about the fact that here was a man who felt deeply about things. Who had more emotional bandwidth than anyone she'd ever been involved with.

Only all that emotion had been deliberately channeled, for years and years, in a bitter quest for revenge, to destroy the people she loved most. And she meant to sway him from that path...

No wonder Leo had thought she was in over her head. Massimo had simply smiled, winked and asked her to load herself up with dynamite for she was trying to move a mountain.

She took the final step and immediately regretted leaving the safety of the crowd behind. The space beyond him was expansive but cut away from the prying eyes of others. Too much privacy. Too many secluded corners with dark leather couches that could swallow up a newly married couple who hadn't touched each other in months.

"You're not my lord and master," she said tartly. Drumming up her defenses.

"And yet here you are."

"I didn't think this was the time to engage in that particular battle."

"Ah...so you do know your limits."

"What limits?"

"You know you've pushed me far enough already, *si*?" he asked huskily, stepping from the shadows into the light. "Do you want to sit?"

"No, I don't. I wouldn't like to sit." She lowered her voice, realizing he'd moved even closer. The lemony scent of him swept through her, evoking a piercing shaft of need. "I like standing. In fact, I haven't done enough of it today. I—"

"We don't have to do anything you don't want to do, Alessandra," he said, his baritone voice going all deep and low and smoky, just the way it did when he was aroused. When he wrapped those skillful hands around her. When he moved inside of her.

But there was something else too.

Pulling in a deep breath, she finally let herself look at him. The dark leather jacket he'd worn to the show had been discarded. His gunmetal gray dress shirt was unbuttoned and uncuffed, giving her a glimpse of the chest hair that had the most incredible effect when rubbed against her own naked skin...

A lazy smile split his mouth, crinkling at the edges of his eyes, shooting straight through to her heart. The damned man was laughing at her.

"You look quite flushed, *cara mia.* Maybe a cold drink will help."

She did feel overheated, even the soft lace of her dress feeling far too tight. She clenched her hands around the cool metal of the balcony. "I'm fine. Stop being so..."

So irresistible. So knee-meltingly gorgeous. So blatantly masculine.

"So what?"

"So...solicitous. As if—" She shook her head far too forcefully, and her hair tumbled down from the loose knot she'd put it in, the brown clip clinking against the cool marble floor. Swearing, she bent down, but he got there first. "Thanks," she said, extending her hand, but he pulled away.

"Leave it like that."

"I don't want to—" she pulled the heavy weight away from her neck "—and it's too—"

"The entire world gets to see you strut down the catwalk in a bikini that's been designed to fire up every red-blooded man's fantasies, *bella*, and that's fine with me." His gaze took in the thrust of her breasts as she held up the swathe of her hair, the pulse hammering away at her throat, the swipe of her tongue against her trembling lower lip. His eyes met hers with a naked hunger that was a balm to her wounded ego. "But do not deny me my fantasies, Alessandra.

"All I've wanted for the past two weeks is to see you sprawled on my bed, that hair spread out on my pillow, but clearly that's not going to happen anytime soon, no? This is the least you can do to keep your poor husband going. Even as you thrust a knife into my back, Princess."

The feral possessiveness of his voice was like a thunderbolt filling her veins with an electric sizzle. "A knife into your back?" she said, her words breathy, distracted.

"You *have* been a bad girl, *bella*. Helping out the defenseless Brunetti men."

The edge to his words made Alex frown. "I don't know what you're talking about."

He tilted his head, considering her thoughtfully. "You're going to persuade me that it wasn't you who leaked my dirty beginnings to the tabloids? That dented my reputation in the financial circles of Milan?"

She stared at him, aghast. "The last thing I'd do now is lie to you. I think there's been enough of that between us already, don't you?"

"You're magnificent even when you attack me, Princess."

"You're gorgeous even when you're being Machiavellian, V."

He laughed and those crinkles appeared again. And it was damned impossible to hold herself at arm's length when she badly wanted to melt into his broad frame and beg him to walk away from all this.

To put their relationship first. To put their future first. To put *her* first.

"I didn't leak it, V. Whether you believe me or not is up to you. You might not think twice about hurting people but that's not how I operate. Especially when I can understand how painful it must have been to be that innocent child.

"I've thrown my lot in with you. At least for the near future."

He held her gaze in the flickering light for a long while and finally nodded. "Then it has to have been your lovely stepmother, Greta."

"That's an unfair jump. You're determined to see them all as your enemies."

"Who else benefits by it?" he pointed out. "I'll admit that it was a clever move on her part, that it set me back quite a bit."

"What? How?"

"I lost the support of two members of the BFI board who'd been ready to throw their vote behind me instead of Leo. Stock prices for Cavalli Enterprises have been plummeting ever since the news hit the papers.

"*The Brunetti Bastard* has quite the ring to it, *si*? A clever little moniker."

"Of course it's not," Alex replied, the latent bitterness in his words shaking her up. That his plans had been set back gave her no satisfaction in the face of his hurt. But… "Has it made any difference, V?" she couldn't help asking.

His head jerked up. "Difference to what?"

"To see yourself from a different perspective.

"Face what you've done, what you're doing publicly, going against ethical businessmen like Leo and Massimo, against a revered institution like BFI that they've rebuilt into something of value.

"Shouldn't it at least make you pause and reconsider what you—"

"You think I care what the world's perception of me is? Or that I've been only half-awake for the past two decades while I planned and plotted against them using every weakness I could find to further my cause? You think I can stop now, after all these years?"

She blinked, feeling as if she'd been dropped onto the concrete floor of reality with a bruising thud. But she refused to look away. Refused to back down. "If I can stop running from my life, then you can—"

"Enough, Alessandra! Let it be."

He looked away from her into the crowd. "You didn't last long before you broke our agreement, did you?"

She frowned. "Our agreement, which you just dictated by the way, was that I don't make impulsive, life-altering decisions in the next three months. Standing mutely by your side while you take down people I care about is... Well, let's just say that will never be me. Honestly, it's not like I have any ammunition against you. All I have are words."

"I'm glad you think that," he said, with a self-deprecation that had her jerking her head up. "You were...brilliant, glowing on the stage today. I can see why the fashion world is bemoaning you leaving the industry."

"My modeling career grounded me when I was directionless, true. But I'm done with it." She cleared her throat when he looked up. "It was an impulsive decision initially, I admit. I was disgusted by the working conditions that the cosmetic company was using. But it was just the catalyst I needed.

"I was tired of the constant grind, the relentless probing into my private life...the loneliness behind the bright lights was consuming me."

"What about that one?" He tilted his head toward the dance floor.

Alex didn't have to look down to see who he meant. For a minute, she dallied with the idea of embellishing her relationship with Javi just to save her pride. Just to make Vincenzo feel a little unsure of where he stood with her.

Wanted to see the flash of jealousy she'd seen that day when he'd asked if he was a rebound for her.

She discarded the idea in the next. Lies and deception had never been her thing.

"Things hadn't been right between us for a long time. When I told him that I was considering walking away from it all, he revealed his true colors. His use for me was going to be considerably reduced once I stepped out of the lime-light."

She shrugged, even though a part of her still hurt. It had been a long time since she'd indulged in the fantasy that Javi and she shared some big, romantic love, but to learn that for him all her value lay in her modeling career was still a bitter pill to swallow. Just like discovering that she'd only been a duty to her mother—a necessary punishment for the sin she'd committed in having an extramarital fling with Alex's father.

"He's still sniffing around you."

"I was spectacular today, like you said. So Javi's wondering if he let me go too soon."

"After that fight, you dumped him instantly and high-tailed it to Bali, *si*?"

"Something like that, yes. But on that occasion my impulse was absolutely right. Realizing that I'm at the tail end of this career now, that retirement is truly what I want at this point in my life…that gave me that extra sparkle on the stage tonight.

"I'm going to finish at the top. No regrets. No looking back as I start the next chapter of my life."

"You sound determined," he said quietly.

"Enough to convince you that I mean this?"

"Si." He straightened from the lazy pose and every cell in her stood up to attention. "Maybe I can suggest the first paragraph in the new chapter? It's time to reveal the little secret of our marital status to the world, don't you think?"

"I guess."

"What better venue than now? Tonight?"

"Okay, yeah," she said, casting a look around the huge, packed nightclub.

It hadn't gone unnoticed that he'd summoned her and she'd answered the arrogant summons. One look at their body language would be more than enough for anyone to see that their interest in each other was anything but platonic. "Most big media outlets have someone down there. What were you thinking? A statement as we walk out?"

After what felt like an eternity, he covered the short distance between them, his arrogant stare taking on an edge of something else. Another step and their thighs grazed just a little.

Alex shivered, every inch of her body, desperate for contact, bowing toward him. His fingers landed on her temple, pushing the mass of her hair from her face. And then he cupped the back of her neck gently. Giving her a chance to step away. "I was thinking a kiss, right here. Stir up some interest before we announce the pertinent facts."

Music hammered around them. The intimate contact, after the drought of so many months, felt like a spark of fire in her body. She was going to say yes. She knew it. He knew it. The hungry denizens of the press were just a reason they were both using. Except she didn't want to be the one who gave in too easily. Who blinked first.

She ran her fingers through her hair and fluttered her lashes at him. "You're doing this to punish me for walking out on you." She pouted, knowing that the particular red she was wearing tonight made her mouth look like a tart strawberry.

"I didn't realize kissing me was such a punishment, *bella.*"

She bent her mouth closer to his ear. "It isn't. In fact, there's very few things in life I enjoy more. And you know that. That's the punishment. To be reminded of how helpless I am to this…thing between us even when I don't trust you."

A vein pulsed in his temple. "All I want is to kiss my wife after months of going to bed alone, wishing she was there to welcome me. Of waking up alone in the middle of the night fully aroused, but knowing that no relief is forthcoming except by my hand. While wondering if I had imagined how bloody good it had been when you came to me that first time in Bali and I took you under the stars in the night sky."

"It was that good," she added simply. Wishing she was the type that could play games. Wishing she could somehow use his attraction to her, that desperate huskiness of his tone, to her advantage.

But she couldn't. "Okay. Let's get it over with."

"That sounds like you're bracing yourself for battle."

"You don't think the battle's already begun?"

"I guess you will claim I started it?"

"Yes."

"And must I finish the battle too?"

"No. I will. You should know, though, that I intend to win. At any cost."

"All I wanted was a peaceful marriage with a biddable woman," he said, with a put-upon sigh.

Laughter roared out of her, melting away the stress and grief of the past few months, at least for a moment. This was the man she'd fallen for in that lush island paradise. This man who'd laughed with her, who'd teased her. Who'd listened to her talking about her dreams.

He didn't quite laugh with her but his eyes gleamed in the darkness. In the flickering light and shadows of the club, the lines of his face looked astonishingly beautiful. "And the prize for winning?"

"There's a prize?"

"There's always a prize in these things. Shall I tell you

what it is, Princess?" he whispered, his breath hot against her lips, his arrogant nose flaring.

Alex placed her open palms against his chest. His heart thundered under her fingers, the beat steadily rising as she leaned her thighs against the rock-hard cradle of his. Heat. Hardness. Hunger. His maleness was an ocean she wanted to drown in. "What?" she croaked.

"Surrender."

"Never," she declared just as arrogantly, his very words imbuing her blood with challenge.

She pushed her palm up, up until she reached his neck. Sneaking her fingers into the thick hair at the nape of his neck, she tilted her head. His breath drew a hot path down her cheek, the scent of him a trigger her body instantly associated with long, lazy nights and indescribable pleasure.

Her other hand she kept on his abdomen, loving the tight clench and release of those powerful muscles every time she touched him.

"Not unless…"

"Not unless what?"

Slowly, she pressed her lips to his, pressing his head down with her fingers. As if he'd been made for the express purpose of pleasuring her. "Unless I take you down with me."

"Is that what you want?"

"Yes. I want to make you drown. In me. Until you can't tell what's right and wrong anymore. Until…"

Soft lips met hers in a rush of warmth and rollicking hunger. Alex drew a sizzling trail along the seam of that sensuous mouth with her tongue, her breath a labored hiss against his bristly jaw. The remembered taste of him was like a detonation going off inside her body.

She nipped and kissed, licked and played with his mouth, but it wasn't enough.

Nowhere near enough.

She sneaked her tongue into his mouth on the next swipe. Pleasure exploded in sweet rivulets down her body as the taste of him filled her. Whiskey and want—he was all solid and real. And after the roller coaster of the last few months, here was the thing that had anchored her. She devoured him as if the taste of him on her tongue, the solid breadth of him in her hands, the labored rush of his breaths on her skin could fill the emptiness inside of her. As if he was all she needed.

Pressing herself into him, she took his mouth with a feral hunger. She licked and nipped, bit and laved at the pillowy lushness of his lips. Thrust in and out of his mouth in a rhythm she desperately needed to be feeling somewhere else.

His other hand landed on flesh where the slinky black number bared the curve of her hips. Those long fingers she knew so well fluttered over her skin, tender like butterfly wings, and yet leaving a wake of heat in their trail. "Slow down, *cara*. I'm not going anywhere," he whispered against her skin.

The dry humor in those words was a cold slap to her senses. Alex pulled away from him, her breaths choppy, the lack of solid warmth in her hands painfully real.

But for all the silky control of his words, she could see the stamp of desire on his tight features, the sharp hiss of his breath as he wrestled himself back under control, the curse he bit out when he moved.

"I think that's enough of a PDA to announce our marriage, *si*?" she whispered.

He grunted his assent and she laughed. But as they made their way downstairs, the caged passion of his body sliding deliciously against her own, answering the questions thrown their way, Alex wondered how a win could feel so much like a loss.

CHAPTER SIX

AN UNCOMMONLY BRISK September breeze plastered her silk blouse and long skirt against her body as Alex stood waiting on the steps outside the Brunetti villa.

Her temper matched the wind's bite. God, she was surrounded by the most infuriatingly stubborn people on the face of the planet.

The roar of the Lamborghini Aventador had cut short her rapid-fire argument with Greta, who'd refused to even contemplate the idea of apologizing to Vincenzo. As much as it galled Alex to acknowledge it of the woman who had welcomed her with open arms, Greta's actions toward Vincenzo and his mother all those years ago had been thoughtless at best and cruel at worst. Even Massimo had blasted Greta for it.

It didn't matter that at that time, Greta had been doing her best to corral her son, Silvio—an egotistical monster bent on destroying the revered institution that was BFI as well as Massimo and Leo's lives. Neither was Greta willing to understand that Alex's marriage to Vincenzo wasn't a momentary madness that she could simply walk away from right now.

On the other side was Vincenzo, using their intimate, spine-melting kiss at the nightclub, using every detail of their relationship to enable him to continue his siege on BFI. Whatever setback the article in the press had initially caused him, he was using their "fairy-tale-esque romance" to clean up his image.

It was bad enough that Leo's own reputation as BFI's CEO had taken a hit after Vincenzo's sustained attacks for over a year now. And now the news of his marriage to her... Alex could almost see the neat twist.

If Alessandra Giovanni—the adopted daughter of the Brunettis—had fallen head over heels for Vincenzo Cavalli, he couldn't be all that bad, could he?

The press had turned the untamable wolf that was Vincenzo Cavalli into the most romantic man on the planet.

Alex pursed her mouth as the purring engine of the Aventador came to a smooth halt in front of her. Her pulse spiked as Vincenzo stepped out and walked around to her side.

In a V-necked sweater and denim that sinfully molded to those hard thighs, he looked like every sinful temptation she'd ever had. His jet-black hair had a wet sheen from the shower, his freshly shaven jaw all sharp angles. Looking composed was hard when all she wanted to do was press her face against the exposed skin at his throat and absorb some much-needed warmth.

The media had exploded after their kiss and the subsequent reveal of their wedding, but they still hadn't worked out all the logistics of where they would live. She was still finishing up her last contracts, talking to Charlie every day and playing out the social circuit in Milan with Vincenzo by her side.

Not that she didn't welcome the reprieve it gave her. Resisting him was a much easier concept when they parted ways at the end of the night.

Leaning against the Aventador, he looked effortlessly urbane, sophisticated in a raw, powerful way. Not even the most gorgeous male models she'd known could achieve that confidence, that wicked arrogance without a lot of practice.

Here was a man who did not need his ego to be stroked.

Or pandered to, in any way. Who had earned everything he possessed the hard way.

His gaze took her in with such thoroughly possessive leisure that all her animosity for him misted away.

"I thought a chauffeur was picking me up."

He unfolded his hands and stepped forward, a smile tugging at his lips. "Ah…but I wanted a few private minutes with you. I caught your speech at the Women CEOs Summit. It was refreshing and bold."

The genuine admiration in his voice… He took the fight out of her far too easily. She licked her lips and said, "Thanks," in an uptight, frosty voice.

Grinning, he neared her. Not quite caging her against the car. But close enough for the fresh, soapy scent of him to assault her every sense. "I never thought about the perils of marrying a woman who's a powerhouse in her own right. Charity galas, and runway shows and photoshoots… I feel quite the poor neglected husband."

A thick, damp lock of hair fell on his forehead and she pushed at it instinctively. The tips of her breasts grazed his bicep and she felt the soft hiss of his breath. "You're not the poor anything, V," she added. Not in the throaty way she'd intended but more like a whisper.

He stepped back, removing that easy intimacy. And his gaze swept over her in an approving survey that spawned warmth.

For all the years she'd spent with makeup artists, Alex preferred simple, easy looks.

The white sleeveless silk blouse draped around her torso was not loose, not figure hugging, but bared a strip of her belly. The inner layer of the skirt ended several inches above her knees, while the outer sheer silky hem fell all the way to her toes, caressing her legs every time she moved.

She'd added diamond studs at her ears and a thin gold

chain with a tiny pendant for her jewelry. Her unruly hair, she'd subdued into a French braid while it was still wet.

"You look…different," he added finally.

"Bad different?" she asked, over the loud thudding of her heart.

"Enchanting different," came his quick reply, accompanied by a grin that threatened to take her out at the knees. "You look striking on the runway but I like this version of you more."

"The *not strutting in only three triangles of clothing* version?" she said, cocking her eyebrow.

His laughter dug deep grooves at the sides of his mouth. His gray gaze shone like liquid metal. "That too. But it's not just that. You look real. Like the woman I met in Bali that first night."

Warmth crawled up her neck and she stared, tongue-tied.

Seducing her like this was a game to him. Surrender, his prize.

His thumb traced the dark smudges under her eyes that she hadn't been able to cover up as well as her makeup artist. "However, you look tired." Low and tender, his voice snaked itself around her. "Anna told me your calendar looks impossible."

She tilted her chin up, dislodging his fingers from her skin. "Your assistant should keep her opinions to herself."

This time, he came closer, caging her against the car. Fading sunlight caressed the planes of his face, much like she wanted to. "You're pushing yourself too hard. I don't need Anna to point that out to me."

"This is the pace of my life, V. I want to clear out my calendar and be available for any situation with Charlie."

"You can't run away from your grief, *cara*. Nor can you wrap up six months' worth of work in two. You need to take better—"

"I've been taking care of myself for as long as I can remember. No one else did it for me."

He raised his palms in surrender. "I'm showing concern, *bella*. Not condescension."

The fight went out of her. It wasn't as if the latest designer she was modeling for hadn't muttered about Alex's dress for his show needing to be altered because she'd lost weight. She sighed. "I haven't been sleeping well."

"Missing me in bed?"

"It's not my fault you refuse to stay here at the villa. Neither Leo nor Massimo have any objection to it. You can get to know your br—" he went from warmth to frost in a matter of seconds and Alex took a long breath "—the men you hate, a little better."

A smile broke the stiffness of his upper lip. "You really think you're very clever, *si*?"

"I've no idea what you mean."

"You think putting me under the same roof as Massimo and Leonardo will change my mind?"

"I told you… I have easy access to everything from the villa. I have my design room set up the way I need. Why can't you just move into the villa? Or are you afraid of living under the same room as the men you've loathed for most of your life in case you discover you actually like them?

"As for missing you in bed—" she licked her lips and his gaze got hotter, hungrier "—did you see the ad I did for that sex toy company?"

He grunted and flushed slightly. And it was her turn to laugh.

It wasn't easy to pose as a smitten couple to the world, day in, day out.

Charity galas and fundraisers, cocktail parties, being near each other, the intimate looks and touches, the rush of being near him, of feeling the lean length of him at her back and then ending the evenings abruptly, and not in the pleasurable way they could, was taking a toll on her.

It wasn't so much the sex that Alex wanted—which she absolutely did—but the connection that had come with it. Before and after. The intense high of being seen by a person who really mattered to her. Of being wanted for who she was.

She desperately wanted to find that connection again with him—especially amidst the rubble of their relationship right now. She was terrified that Greta might be right—it had been unbelievably good sex and nothing more.

Even when they'd been hidden away from the world, it had been she who'd done the chasing. It had been she who'd been desperate to be with him, she who'd wanted their relationship to deepen.

For a man who rarely betrayed his emotions, he had been a revelation in bed. The more she gave, the more he'd demanded of her. Until she'd given him all she had—her heart and soul. Believed that he'd needed her just as she'd needed him.

For all his renewed commitment to their marriage, she wondered at his self-control. Thought again about the original reason he'd married her.

Had he thought she'd be so much putty in his hands as to betray her family? Or had she simply been something to steal away from Greta?

But now that she was getting to know him a little more, now that she understood what drove his actions, that didn't fit with the other pieces of the puzzle.

For all the incredible arrogance of the man, there was no way he could have thought she'd be an asset to him in any way. Then why?

"*Si.* I saw the magazine spread you were kind enough to send me. You nailed the sexy, confident, contemporary woman perfectly."

"Didn't I?" Alex said, a tingly thrill electrifying her all over.

It had been the most fun she'd had in a while. And of course, sending the spread to Vincenzo—her naked limbs peeking out from under a cloud of white sheets with the pink vibrator lying next to her, had been the most fun part of it all. "Anyway, they sent me one as a complimentary gift. Technology is so marvelous, isn't it? It was brilliantly built—steel cloaked in velvet."

"Is there a point to this story?" His jaw tight, the words were gritted out.

"You said I needed stress relief, remember? So the other night, I couldn't sleep and there it was, in its cute pink package. I unpacked it and got back into bed and…"

"And?" he growled as she paused.

"This was my first time using one, you see and—"

In the blink of a breath, he folded his body against hers, one firm hand pulling her arms above her. His breath feathered over her cheeks, his nose rubbing against the tender skin on the inside of one bicep. "You play dirty, *cara*." He whispered the words against the soft flesh of her arm, just above the elbow. His other hand landed unerringly on the narrow strip of skin her outfit bared. Heat from his fingers seared her. "Am I allowed to? Am I allowed to use all the… weapons at my disposal?"

She leaned into his chest, the sides of her breasts pressed against his hard chest. "You already play dirty, V. You use everything you do with me for your PR. Nothing is real anymore."

"What—?"

She meant to back off and miscalculated, their legs tangling instead. Her hip hit the rock-hard slab of his abdomen, her thigh rubbing against his groin. His reaction was instant.

"Oh…" Alex whispered, incapable of rational thought.

Her mouth was dry. Punch-drunk on need as she settled her body—chest to thighs, against him.

His fingers dug into her hips as he held her like that, his erection rocking into the notch of her sex. "You think I don't miss you in my bed? You think I was not driven to mindless lust when I saw the magazine spread? You think I didn't take myself in my hand while thinking of you like some rabid fan even though you already belong to me?"

Awareness was a cage around them, the slip and slide of their bodies, the settling of his hard muscles and her softer ones into a familiar groove, begging for that instinctive rhythm to begin...

Hands tight around her, he rocked his hips into her. Their combined moans rent the quiet evening air.

Alex shivered, her skin too tight to contain her. "Please, V..."

"Please what, *bella*?" He licked the sensitive skin at the crook of her neck. And she rubbed her thighs together, desperate for friction there. "Shall I make you climax here, against the car in full view of the villa? Do I win this round then?"

Her own fingers pulling at his hair, Alex buried her face in his throat. "Sometimes, I wish I had never met you on that island. I wish..."

His fingers gentled on her back, as if she hadn't just damned their entire relationship. "I would love to give you what you want. What both of us want. But whom shall you hate more tomorrow morning? Me or yourself?"

Alex drew air in as if her lungs were starved. He was right. This was a dangerous game she was playing. One she might very well lose. "Let me go," she whispered, because it wasn't in her to walk away from him.

He released her slowly, a perfect gentleman. Not betraying by the flicker of an eyelid that he had indeed won this round.

* * *

The car pulled away from the villa. For long, silent minutes, Alex lost herself in the spectacular views of the high alpine peaks and the shimmering lake.

His long fingers drew her attention to the steering wheel. The simple but expensive gold band she'd purchased at an exclusive jewelry shop in Bali glinted in the darkness of the interior.

She felt his assessing gaze on her and looked away.

"Do you want to start over and tell me what has you in such a mood?"

"I'm fine."

"No, you're not. As usual, I lost my head when I saw you. Looking like a morsel I wanted to inhale. You were already angry about something."

His perceptiveness didn't surprise her. "This was my only free evening in two weeks. I don't appreciate your personal assistant adding events to my calendar without consulting me first," she said when she finally had a measure of composure. "I need more than—'Important Dinner with Mr. Cavalli—Casual Dress' a few hours before I'm supposed to show up."

"It's easier for Anna to coordinate our mad schedules than constantly talking to your assistant."

Alex didn't miss his obvious affection for the paragon Anna.

The quaint village of Bellagio welcomed them with its narrow, cobblestoned streets and charming alleyways, the Aventador roaring through. "Who's this VIP we're meeting anyway? Another backstabbing board member of BFI who wants more of its profits? Another man who has some kind of vendetta against Leo and Massimo?"

"We're meeting an old friend of mine. Antonio is…he's very dear to me. And despite my many warnings, he and some other friends have arranged a surprise party for us in his house, to celebrate our marriage. I would appreciate it if you can put aside our differences for a few hours and treat him with the respect he deserves."

His gruff request took Alex by surprise. "I'll act as if you were my sun and moon. As if you were the answer to my every romantic fantasy."

"Alessandra, this is important to me." His sigh rattled in the silence. "I wanted to give both Antonio and you a chance to meet outside of what will definitely become a media circus once I take over BFI. I don't want us talking about how you abandoned our marriage on our honeymoon or how you only returned to make a deal with me for your brother's sake. Antonio's a very traditional man."

"Shall we also not talk about how you kept your biggest ambition a secret from me? And how—"

"Antonio knows my background. My goal all these years. All the things I've done."

All the things he'd done…

Suddenly, Alex felt as if she was being given a key to unlock this man. To understand him better. To find some way to stop him. To figure out if her first instinct about their marriage had been right, that there was something to salvage from this mess.

Vincenzo stopped the car near the lakefront. A row of pretty, colorful houses opened up the narrow winding street. When Alex reached for the door, he swung an arm across her torso toward the handle, locking her in place. The corded strength of his forearm pressed between her breasts, sending pulses of awareness jerking through her.

The sun had set during their drive and the interior of the car was faintly lit.

"We have been on display for three whole weeks now, ever since the news broke. I thought a quiet night would do us some good. There's no pressure to be in the spotlight tonight."

"I would like advance notice about these things. Especially if I'm to appear in good humor."

"I asked you for one evening, Alessandra, for an important thing."

"It would be nice if things that were important to me were valued just as equally by you."

"*Cristo!* What the hell's bothering you?"

"There are certain things I can't forgive, Vincenzo. I just can't."

"Yes, *cara*. And we're both constantly testing those certain limits, aren't we?"

"Everything you do with me is for the media—I understand that. Your damned PR team used that kiss at the nightclub to its full extent. To put a romantic spin on the whole thing. Used it to cloud the very real threat you pose to Leo and Massimo."

"This whole charade was *your* plan. Do you think that I forget for one moment that you came back to me for your own damned reasons, however noble they are? That not for a single hour will you forget your ties to that blasted family? You're the one who wanted to show the world that you're settling down into a life of domesticity and stability, *bella*."

"Yes. And it's enough that we're parading ourselves in front of this media circus. That we pretend as if we can't keep our hands off each other. But some things are not for public consumption. Some things are not…"

"What on earth are you talking about?"

"The picture of our wedding. The only one we have. The one I asked that passing local to click. Neither your PR team nor your wonderful assistant asked me for permission before they released that picture to the press."

His disbelief showed in the jerk of his head. "Alessandra—"

"You entered this marriage for God knows what reasons of your own. I have tried to put those behind me. I've convinced myself that what I want doesn't matter anymore. That this is all for Charlie. I have tucked away my foolish hopes.

"But that picture…it's precious to me. That moment was real, at least it was to me. In fact, it was the most real moment of my life, and you used it to manipulate the world.

"You stole it from me."

"You stole it from me."

Alessandra's words echoed inside Vincenzo's head as he made the rounds on the beautiful, moonlit terrace of Antonio's small house and greeted acquaintances and friends he hadn't seen in a long time. Even in the dark of the car's interior, he'd seen the glint of hurt in those beautiful eyes. The catch in her words.

Reminding him that beneath the fiery woman who'd strutted so confidently across the runway, beneath the woman that challenged him at every step, beneath the mantle of responsibility she'd put on for her half brother, his wife was vulnerable.

To him, his actions, his words.

And that very quality he'd wanted to see in her sat uncomfortably in his chest. Weighting him down.

It made him want to banish the hurt from her eyes. Made him want to protect her from anything in the world that could cause her pain. Including him.

Dio santo! If that wasn't messed up, he didn't know what was.

He turned to look at the tall, elegant figure of his wife, standing amidst a group of people, a soft smile playing around her lips. The same lips that had whispered such provocative words in his ear, pushing him to the edge of his control.

She was tallest of the group, and the most beautiful, by a wide margin. And yet when one of the teenagers Vincenzo had known for a while, Marco, approached her and said something, she nodded and laughed. Boxing, they were talking about boxing, he knew.

She handed off her wineglass to someone else, got into position with an animated smile and showed Marco her mean right hook. The toned curve of her arm, the flash of thigh as she pulled the inner skirt up to stretch her legs into a fighting stance, the utter joy in her eyes as she ducked Marco's left fist… She looked incredibly sexy.

He could see the people he worked with reassess their opinion of her. Could sense their shock as they realized there was so much more to Alessandra than her looks.

"She's not what I expected from you," Antonio said, handing Vincenzo a glass of the bubbly champagne that they had been toasted with earlier.

Vincenzo looked at the man who had given him a sense of purpose when he'd been lost. Not just moral support. Antonio had provided seed money when he'd been starting out. He'd helped Vincenzo go from strength to strength. He owed everything he had to the older man. But… Some things, Vincenzo considered private. Off-limits. Even to Antonio.

It was the most real moment of my life.

Suddenly, he understood what Alessandra meant by that, and regret filled him.

He took a sip of his champagne. Laughter and shouts surrounded him as Alessandra's fist gently connected with another youth's angular chin. "What did you expect?"

Antonio shrugged, his weathered face splitting into a smile that didn't really reach his eyes. "An international supermodel, Vincenzo! Parties, and designer dresses and the high life…all sparkle and no substance."

Vincenzo didn't like hearing Alessandra reduced to being some one-dimensional bimbo. "Alessandra's more than just a supermodel. Give her a chance, Antonio."

"All of us fall victim to stereotyping, *si*?" The older man laughed at his own joke. "Hearing that you married is shocking in itself. You never even hinted at wanting to settle down in all these years."

"No, it was never on my mind."

"If I had known, I might have suggested a better alternative," Antonio said, his gray head nodding in another direction. Vincenzo turned and saw his assistant Anna, standing stiffly to one side, a frosty smile fixed in place. What the hell did Antonio mean by that? "You need a strong, steady woman who can stand by you like a rock, Vincenzo. Who knows her place in your life. Not this…frothy creature from some fantasyland."

"She's my wife, Antonio. And I never gave Anna the idea that she meant anything more to me."

"After all, you're a man too," Antonio added with a shrug. His gaze shifted back to Alessandra, who was now talking to Anna. "Ah…so the woman is as irresistible as she looks, then, *si*?"

Vincenzo shrugged. Even with Antonio, he didn't want to admit to the complete truth.

Which was that he had completely lost his mind over Alessandra. Continued to, in fact. Her loyalty to the Brunettis amazed him. Her determination to do right by her half brother resonated deep inside him. Her vulnerability when it came to himself… Shook him. At a level he hadn't thought possible.

"Her Brunetti connection is an unnecessary headache you don't need right now. A distraction from your true purpose," the older man insisted.

"It is a headache. She—" Vincenzo swallowed the word *hates* "—does not like what I intend to do to them. In fact, she's waging a quiet campaign to shift me from my plans, I believe."

The warm glint disappeared from Antonio's dark eyes. "And? Do you think she will succeed?"

Vincenzo frowned at the quiet question. "You know me better than that, Antonio. She's a small part of my life. An indulgence I allow myself." He didn't say she was fast becoming an obsession he craved. When she looked at him with that vulnerability in her eyes, he wanted to promise her the world. He wanted to promise her anything just to make her smile again. "Alessandra is a prize. A worthy wife for a man building an empire. She's the final reward for all the fights I have won and for the ones I'm still waging."

"And yet you watch her with such hunger in your eyes. As if you don't already own her. As if you want…more."

More… Did he want more from Alessandra? More of what?

Vincenzo refused to betray how accurate Antonio's words were. "Maybe you've forgotten what it is to look at a woman you want, Antonio. I do not deny that she's got a hold over me."

"That bothers me. About how powerful her hold is on you. About how much you will forgive her, how much you will forget in order to please her."

"Speak your mind plainly, Antonio."

"I'm not so old that I do not keep up with the news. She set you back a few steps with that leak about who you really are. The financial world is still wondering where you come from, how you've amassed your fortune and with what intentions. You lost the support of two men who were almost in your pocket. Now you have to begin the hunt anew to find other candidates who will stand against the combined might of Leonardo and Massimo Brunetti."

"My PR team has been doing a lot of damage control since then. But it's not Alessandra who leaked that information."

"And you believe her?" The older man's softly spoken words resonated with doubt and disbelief.

"Yes," Vincenzo replied firmly.

"We've worked far too hard, for far too long to bring the Brunettis down. This marriage of yours could derail everything. Worse, it could—"

"I want to build what I have been denied all my life—a standing in society, a home to return to, a dynasty. What will stand in its place when the past is brought to its knees?" Vincenzo demanded, angry and tired and resentful in a way he'd never felt before. "For the first time in my life, I acted selfishly. It is neither a mistake nor a strategic move."

Did Antonio see him as nothing but a device for vengeance? Was there anything left of him that wasn't a weapon to fuel him toward his goal? This restlessness… He realized it had been growing in him for a while. A small crack that threatened to expand into a yawning void every time he visited his mother.

And then he had met Alessandra.

A breath of fresh air. A woman who had filled his days with laughter and warmth reminded him that he was a man who wanted more. A woman who made him think of the future.

"As long as it doesn't distract you from your mission," added Antonio, his expression implacable. That implacability had once been the backbone that had built Vincenzo's confidence sky-high. Antonio's belief had goaded him to the heights of success and through dark nights of self-doubt. And yet now, it felt like a painful echo from the past he couldn't outrun.

"It does not mean that I've forgotten." He ran a hand through his hair, tension swathing his frame. "I cannot, even if I wished it. Every time I see Mama…" He swallowed and looked away. His wound would never heal. Because every time he saw his mother, it was gouged afresh. "Keep your trust in me, Antonio."

The old man gripped Vincenzo's shoulder. "I do. Maybe this is not a bad move. Maybe you can use your wife to move even faster toward your goal."

Everything in Vincenzo rebelled against the idea. "What do you mean?"

"You and Leonardo Brunetti are in a deadlock now for majority on the BFI board, *si*?"

"Si."

"The matriarch, Greta Brunetti, still holds stock in BFI, doesn't she? If your wife is truly important to her, maybe she could be persuaded to jump ship in your favor."

Shock pulsed through Vincenzo. *"I'll be damned before I let you use me against them,"* Alessandra had vowed.

"You want me to persuade Greta Brunetti to betray her own grandsons if she wants Alessandra's happiness?"

"There must be some substance to your wife's devotion to the old woman and that family. Test that connection. See how far you can push them with it.

"Think of it this way, Vincenzo. The faster you win this war, the faster you break up BFI into parts, the sooner you can settle into a blissful wedded life."

Vincenzo couldn't muster a reply. To use Alessandra and her happiness as a bargaining weapon against Greta Brunetti… The very thought filled him with distaste. What kind of a man would he have become then?

"I'd like to go home now, please. If you're done for the night," Alessandra whispered with a polite smile pasted on her mouth the moment Vincenzo reached her.

"That picture of us on the morning of our wedding… leaking it to the press… I never gave a direct, specific instruction to do that." He pressed his fingers to her mouth when she'd have protested. "Hear me out, please, Alessandra.

"And before you shred my team into pieces, they only followed my order—to a T—that they improve my image in the media.

"So, yes, the ultimate responsibility is mine, but it was a thoughtless, general action rather than a deliberate, strategic one to hurt you, or to lessen the significance of that day for you."

Her beautiful brown gaze mirrored her disbelief and hurt.

Vincenzo took her fingers in his and pressed. A harsh exhale left him when she didn't pull away. "I should have realized it was so important to you. I should have—"

"It doesn't matter."

"*Si!* It does matter. What you think of all this, it does matter." He'd been about to say *What you think of me*, but held it back, "I'm beginning to understand how much what I did hurt you. But my intentions for you, for this marriage have always been the same. From the beginning."

She held his gaze, as if she could hold him to his word like that. As if she could see into his heart.

"Just promise me that you won't use me in this battle of yours," she said.

"I won't. I have already said our marriage will stand outside of it. Come now, Princess. Dance with me."

She said nothing. Didn't move.

"It's a beautiful night. And I want to dance with my beautiful wife. I want to show all the men salivating over you that you're mine. Only mine."

Vincenzo waited. For all of Antonio's disapproval, he knew in his heart that she was the one he wanted when he finally reached the end of all this. She was the one who had birthed the future he hadn't even realized could be his.

He left his hand outstretched. Finally, with a soft sigh, she came to him. And everything else ceased to exist for Vincenzo. The crowd around them, the soft music, the moonlight, everything became secondary to the sensation of having Alessandra in his arms.

She was like liquid silk poured over taut, warm limbs, her face hidden in the curve of his shoulder. Her fingers a brand on the nape of his neck. Her breaths a soft whisper against his skin. For long minutes, they just moved to the music, their bodies easily swaying in a matching rhythm.

"You stole it from me."

"Have you forgiven me yet?" he whispered. "For making that picture public."

"You're who you are." The defeat in those words slayed him.

"I...there was something between us on the island, *si*. But I think, in the real world, we've broken that trust. Both of us."

She lifted her head and stared straight into his eyes. And nodded slowly. She pulled away from him and leaned against the balcony. The chitchat around them carried on, but everyone was giving them a wide berth.

She looked around, her gaze thoughtful. "All these people...they worship the ground you walk on."

"That's a bit dramatic."

She shook her head. "I don't think so."

"They have known me for a long time, *si*. When I had nothing to my name, when I was nothing but a boy with big dreams. Even from a young age, I had a way with numbers. The stock market was an easy pattern for me to predict."

"Like Massimo is brilliant with computers," she interjected.

He let it go. "Antonio saw my talent and nurtured it. When I started playing the market, these people trusted me with their savings. When I started my investment firm, they were my first clients. They trusted me to do right by them. Now that I have a million times more, I try to remember them. I try to give it back."

"I'm glad you were not all alone. But it's still not family."

He shrugged.

"She's in love with you, you know."

His head jerked to her. "What the hell are you talking about?"

She wrapped her arms around herself, her wide mouth pinched. "Your assistant, Anna. It's obvious. She thinks... they all think I'm a backstabbing witch who doesn't deserve you."

"What?"

"Were the two of you ever together?"

Vincenzo blew out a breath, looking out at Alessandra and then back toward a small group where Anna stood talking.

Antonio's remark had suddenly made him see Anna's frosty reception toward Alessandra clearly. "A long time ago. Years before I met you. And it was only ever a brief fling that I put a stop to as soon as we started working together."

"And yet she had hopes that it would eventually be rekindled."

He didn't discount the truth of it now he understood. "Then it is my fault for not making myself clear to her. I never even realized until... Alessandra, I never led Anna on."

"I believe you." Said with such simplicity that he stared at her, stunned. "She told me that you have had an architect draw up plans for the Brunetti Villa. That you intend to pull it down and build something else in its place. That you mean to take over BFI by the bicentennial celebrations."

Shock pounded through him. "Anna would never be so unprofessional as to betray my plans."

"How else do you think I know about them? She hates my guts, because she thinks I stole her man, and she wants me to leave you. They couldn't be more shocked if you had suddenly taken up farming, V." Her gaze turned thought-ful. "Apparently, you went full on rogue in this operation by marrying me."

"My life is not a democracy for them to vote on."

A frown tied her brows. "It sure sounds like it is."

"You're my wife, Alessandra. If Anna can't realize how important that is, she will have to be let go. I'm sorry she made you uncomfortable tonight."

"How about you're sorry for all the things you hide from me? How about you're sorry that you ever conceived those plans in the first place?"

"Again, they were in place long before I met you. These people have been in my life for many years while you…"

"While I what, V?"

"While you flit in and out of it. While you run away from me the moment the fantasy falls apart."

"And if I do stay in this marriage? When you take over BFI and break it down into parts, when you raze that villa to the ground and build a new one in its stead, is that where you expect me to live?

"Is that where we're supposed to start our new family? Our new life?"

"Si."

"Leo and Massimo will never give up their home."

"We shall see about that."

"Love cannot grow where there's so much hate, V."

"But I've never asked you for love," he bit out, and she flinched. A wet sheen coated her eyes and Vincenzo wanted to believe it was caused by the suddenly cold breeze. "Is that why you married me, *bella*? Because you fancied your-self in love with me?" Neither could he take the bitter edge out of his words.

It was high time they discussed their expectations. High time he set the record straight that he wasn't going to change his mind about his course of action just because she was in his life. "Was it love that made you run at the first hurdle? That made you abandon our marriage when it had barely started?

"That makes you imagine I should give up things I've set into motion years before I met you?"

He reached for her and set his hands on her shoulders. She stiffened but didn't push him away, those gorgeous brown eyes of hers drilling into him. "Love is for fools who don't realize how it can turn to poison in a minute. It pushed Anna into jeopardizing her position with me.

"It drove my mother into believing falsely sweet promises from a monster and breaking the heart of a simple man who respected her and admired her."

"Antonio?"

"*Si*. And when he demanded Silvio Brunetti do right by her, when he dared take him on, Brunetti crushed Antonio, as if he were an ant. He came for his business, for his family. He ruined everything Antonio had and anyone who dared helped him."

She looked around the empty terrace, her eyes widening. Comprehension twisted her features into horror. "All these people you've collected, you've surrounded yourself with…they are all—"

"They've all been harmed one way or the other by the mighty Brunetti family, *si*."

"By Silvio Brunetti," she amended. "Not by Leo and Massimo." She stepped back from him, her mouth compressed. He'd never seen her look more defeated. "They're all equally invested in the path of destruction they want you to take. Even if you wanted to walk away from it now, they won't let you. That explains their chilly attitude toward me. They think I will turn your head."

"You won't," he reiterated so forcefully that she flinched.

"Well, that's put me in my place," she added with an empty laugh. "But in the end, you'll be the only one who pays the price, V. Not them. You'll be the one who stands on the ashes of your family's happiness, ruining any chance of a relationship with them."

"My family? If you think even for a moment that I will ever consider Leo and Massimo to be my family at the end of all this, that somehow we will become brothers in truth…then you're even more naive than I'd ever thought.

"They are not my family. They were not there for me when I struggled to fill my belly. When I saw Mama become a shadow of herself. When I had no money to pay for treatment for her."

"But you—"

"This is not your fight, *cara*. Let it go."

"And if this fight ends up hurting us, V? If it ruins any chance of happiness that we might have had?"

He stared into her eyes, the answer jolting out of him. Somehow, somewhere along the way, Alessandra had gotten under his skin. Had begun to matter to him more and more.

But only so much. It could only ever be so much that he could give her. Only so much he could feel. He didn't know how to be vulnerable. To remove the very defenses he'd put up for sheer survival.

He couldn't give voice to that yes that whispered in his chest. Couldn't let himself become so caught up in her that he forgot all the years of loneliness and fear and pain. Forgot what he'd set out to do. To prove.

To the world. And to himself.

"Whether my actions hurt you is not in my hands, Alessandra. It's in yours. In the end, we all have to make choices.

"Whether you want this marriage only for Charlie's sake or for yourself, you have to decide. You need to decide how much of this is just a deal and how much is real.

"Because for me, nothing has changed. Not since I slipped that ring on your finger."

The stricken look in her eyes told him she more than got the message. And as much as it bothered him to leave her like that, he walked away.

A strange tension gripped him but he refused to give it a name. He could have used the attraction between them, the constant tug of awareness to nudge her over into acceptance. But Vincenzo needed her to come to him. Needed her to choose him.

Like he wanted nothing else in his life.

He didn't examine the urge, didn't rationalize it. It was just there.

And yet as he joined Antonio and the others—people who had always been on his side, people who looked at him with respect and admiration, people who had looked to him to solve the injustices done them—for the first time in his life he felt as though he didn't fit in with them either.

CHAPTER SEVEN

IT WAS THE last scene Alex had ever imagined she'd come home to when she returned to the Brunetti villa the following Friday evening after an exhausting, weeklong trip to New York to visit Charlie.

Leo, Massimo and Greta were dining al fresco on the terrace, making the most of a beautiful late September evening. But the magnificent view couldn't hold Alex's attention.

Seated by Massimo, his arrogant head jerking up at her as she walked up the last step, was Vincenzo.

His gaze held hers over the length of the terrace, awareness stretching between them, holding her captive. For a few seconds, Alessandra forgot her exhaustion, the fresh grief that had been raked up the past week, the uncertainty of where all this would end.

When she looked at Vincenzo, she forgot everything but him.

"How is your brother, Alessandra?" His question, in a dry tone, pulled Alex out of her reverie.

Alex blinked, feeing heat climb up her cheeks. "He's okay. I wish he cried a little more though, or screamed or something. He's far too self-contained for a seven-year-old boy."

"But then boys are often taught that it's a weakness to cry," Massimo added with a bitterness that made her heart ache.

Alex saw the disbelief in Vincenzo's eyes.

"Our father verbally abused Massimo, unchallenged, for years." This little nugget was supplied by Leonardo.

His jaw tight, Vincenzo stared at both men. Alex held her breath, waiting for him to rip into these men who had enough courage to own up to their torturous childhoods with the man Vincenzo thought had abandoned him.

But Vincenzo remained silent and with it didn't invalidate the pain of the brothers he considered his enemies.

"Charlie told me one of the boys at school has been bullying him," she said, running a hand through her hair. "I reported it to his teacher and she's looking into it. However, I also taught him how to sucker punch the bully if he ever bothered him again."

All three men simultaneously cheered on that suggestion, and the tension broke.

"Come, sit down, *bella*. Unless you're planning on leaving again," Vincenzo drawled, an edge of censure in his tone. He looked up at her, and she had that feeling of being consumed by his gaze. Only it wasn't just desire. It was more. "Soon, you're going to run out of places to hide."

Heat washed over her face, but Alex took the chair he pulled out for her. "I had my mother's affairs to take care of in New York. Her husband's estate is huge. Not to mention the fact that Charlie was missing me. I did text you that I was leaving."

"Ah, yes, so you did. Five minutes before takeoff."

She refused to let him put her in the wrong this time. "What would you have done if I had told you any earlier? You're so busy spinning your webs around people. It's hard enough that I can't even give Charlie a specific date yet as to when he can join me."

"Maybe I would have joined you in going to New York, Alessandra. Did you think of that?"

Alex jerked her gaze to his. "Why?"

"For the simple fact that you're going through a lot in

your life right now and I wanted to be there to support you? For the logical fact that it would have been sensible to present a united front to Charlie's extended family and the lawyers?

"To reassure Charlie himself that I'm just as invested in his well-being as you are? I'm a stranger to him, after all."

Shame streaked bright color across Alex's face, and she struggled to hold his gaze. He was right. It was the whole point of their deal, after all. And yet, all she'd wanted was a reprieve.

From the emotional turmoil he plunged her into with one look, one touch, one kiss.

From the trust he demanded she give him without having earned it.

The more she learned about him, the more complex he turned out to be. This whole thing had never been simply about revenge, or ambition, or wanting power for himself. Not the man who'd helped so many, who had such a strong moral compass.

Her first instinct that he was a man worthy of knowing had been right.

The more she wanted to remain detached, the more she felt lured in. Before, she'd been afraid of the harm he would cause Leo and Massimo and Greta, but now she was beginning to worry about him.

About the bitterness she'd seen in his eyes when he spoke of his mother. About what would be left of him when all this was done. About the crushing emptiness that would come no matter his material success if there was no one to share it with.

She rubbed the pads of her fingers over her tired eyes. "I'm sorry. You were right. I... I didn't think of all those eminently sensible reasons."

He clutched her fingers on the table and squeezed. "You're still fighting this, *bella*."

She nodded and pulled her fingers away. Three gazes watched them with varied levels of interest.

"What finally convinced you to come here to the villa?" she asked him, reaching for a glass of wine.

"I was getting bored of sleeping alone," he said bluntly.

Greta's fork clattered onto the plate.

"I invited him," Leo said into the awkward silence. "Neha reminded me that in all this…you're the one caught in the middle.

"So I will tell you again, Alex, and in front of him, this time.

"Neither Massimo nor I expect you to fight for us. But if you need an out from this marriage, if for any reason you want to be done with it, we'll throw everything we have behind you."

The absolute fury in Vincenzo's eyes in contrast to the stillness that came over him had Alex drawing in a sharp breath.

"Telling my wife that you'll help her walk away from me, in front of me, is surely a fool's play, Leonardo." The very smoothness of his words raised the hairs on her neck. "Like waving a red flag in front of a bull. Especially after all the work poor Alessandra has been putting in to persuade me to rethink your ruin."

Leo didn't even bat an eyelid. "No threat of ruin will make me forget my priorities, Cavalli. You think you had it hard? You didn't have our father filling your head with poison when you barely knew right and wrong. You didn't have to unlearn toxic truths about why your own mother would desert you.

"I had to protect my family, and myself, from him, when I was barely a man. And Alex has been a part of this family for a long time."

Again, Vincenzo stayed silent.

Alex chewed her salad, feeling a spark of hope for the

first time in weeks, while Leo and Massimo started casually chatting about the upcoming bicentennial celebrations of BFI. The preparations were already in full force.

She had told neither Leo nor Massimo about Vincenzo's plans for the villa or BFI. God, she hated being the bearer of bad news. Especially when there was nothing she could do to help them. Fortunately, both of them had been out of town when she'd returned that night, still reeling under the impact of all she'd learned.

"Did you clear your calendar for the celebration, Alex?" Massimo asked. "There will be journalists, of course. But also, a photographer for the family's photoshoot for the feature they're doing on BFI's history."

"I'll sit that one out if you don't mind," she replied.

Vincenzo covered her hand on the table, his gaze filled with a wicked humor. "Of course, she will come. We will both be here to celebrate the success of such a long-standing venerable institution as BFI. Especially on such a momentous day."

If Greta heard the resounding mockery in his words, she didn't let it show. Slowly, she pushed her chair back, and stood. She pressed one hand into Alex's shoulder and then walked away. Without a word.

The stoop of Greta's proud shoulders made a lump settle in Alex's throat. Greta's past actions and Alex's present sat like painful, snarly knots in their relationship. She hadn't realized how much Greta's implacable but quiet presence in her life meant to her. Until Alex had lost it.

Massimo and Leo followed Greta.

The moment it was just them, Alex turned on Vincenzo. To find him frowning, a thoughtful tilt to his mouth.

"What are you doing here at the villa? What new game are you up to?" she demanded.

"Following your dictates," Vincenzo replied silkily, sitting back in his chair.

Alex slammed her wineglass down, hard enough for it to slosh over her fingers. "Please, V. No more games."

"I hate living like a bachelor in hotels when I have a perfectly nice wife here at the villa. I realized you were right all along."

"You mean you realized you can torment Greta in her own home?"

"Asking me to behave as if I finally found my long-lost grandmother is a bit much, even for you, *bella*."

Why had she thought bringing Vincenzo face-to-face with the Brunettis would be a good idea? Already, her head was pounding. "If you think you're going to wear her down into regretting her actions, you'll wait forever. To her, the past is done, V. She had to deal with the consequences of every selfish, vile act Silvio perpetrated, and that has turned her into stone."

"Consequences that became the crumbling foundation of my life."

"I'm not asking you to forgive her."

"*Bene.* Because I hate disappointing you."

"Do you really? Is this all anything other than a game to you?" she demanded.

She'd had enough. It felt as if she was still dreaming, amidst the fitful sleep she'd caught on the flight back to Milan. Wondering if all the pieces would ever come together. Wondering if she would always feel ripped apart by conflicting loyalties.

She pushed away her chair, every inch of her vibrating with an internal fight she couldn't win. "I'm out of here."

"Alessandra—"

"I have to get ready. There's a designer launch in Milan. I have to show my face." Although the thought of being in front of cameras right now made her want to throw up.

Vincenzo followed her down the steps. "I contacted your agent and got you out of it."

Alex stilled. "What? That's… How dare you?"

"Alessandra, you look like you'll collapse if someone blows hard enough."

"And whose fault is that? I just spent an entire week going through my mother's things. Sorting what to keep and what to give away. For Charlie. Her entire life…in boxes, V. Then I came back to this. I know why you can't forgive Greta for what she did to you and your mother. Even I can't. But…have you thought for one minute that I might actually need you? That I might want to lean on you?"

"Of course, yes."

"I'm so foolish. I can't believe I actually thought it would be a good idea for you to be here. You're right. I'm pathetic and—"

His arms enveloped her so tightly that Alex was forced to stop shivering. "Shh…*tesoro*. Shh…breathe, Alessandra."

"Sometimes, I feel so alone. It doesn't matter what I do, or where I run. In the end, I'm always terrifyingly alone."

"Look at me, *bella*. Concentrate on me."

Alex looked up and the panic that had been closing in on her receded. She focused on her reflection in the gray of his eyes. Breathed in until that fresh, crisp scent of him was an anchor in her blood. Let herself drown in the warmth his body gave off.

A tear rolled down her cheek and he held her gently. As if she was the most precious thing in his life. "You're not alone, Alessandra. I'm here. *Mi dispiace…* I'm sorry, you were right. I forget how much you've been through."

In that moment, he was the haven she'd been looking for all her life. He was the prince she'd always wanted. He held her heart in the palm of his hand.

And Alex wanted nothing more than to sink into his strong body. Nothing more than to share the grief that choked her sometimes. Nothing more than to give herself over to him.

But the girl who'd been seen by her own mother as a punishment, the girl who'd always wondered what she'd done wrong, the girl whose heart had been seriously dented over the last few months, reared its head. Bringing rationality along.

She looked up into those magnetic eyes, forcing herself to break the spell. "Why?"

"Why what?"

"Why do you act as if this marriage is so important to you?"

His curse rang around in the garden. "Because it is." He ran a hand through his hair and she realized, even he didn't know why. "It just is." But the conviction she wanted was there. In his gaze. In the set of his mouth.

"Why?" she pushed, instinctively realizing they were standing on the cusp of something vital.

"Because you made me see a future for myself. All my life, I had no plans beyond the destruction of the Brunettis. I came to Bali because I had been so curious about you, about your role within the family. But when I got there, when we met, it… I have never acted like this with a woman before. There's no precedent for my actions."

A burst of air burned her lungs as Alex took in a deep breath. All around her, fragrance filled the air. The sounds and scents of life itself underscoring the hope flickering in her chest.

He was right. She couldn't do justice to anyone this way, sitting on the fence in the middle of everyone. She had to choose. She wanted to choose him. She wanted to bridge this gap between them. She wanted to hope that everything would turn out for the best.

"You really want to spend time with me?"

"I've barely seen you for more than a few hours since the

wedding. Either you're finishing off a contract, or saving *them* from me, or showing up for Charlie on the other side of the world." His thumb traced the dark circles under her eyes. "I would feel quite the neglected husband if I didn't see that you're neglecting yourself too."

She shrugged. But she couldn't conjure the energy to dislodge his hands. No, she didn't want to dislodge them. She was tired of fighting. She wanted to be held. By him. It was an ache in her belly, this want. "We both have busy lifestyles."

"I miss you, *bella*. That's why I moved in here. I miss—" he swallowed, his eyes glinting with desire and awareness, slamming into Alex like a bulldozer "—spending time with you."

She snorted, a lightness filling her despite the emotional roller coaster of the last week. It was hard not to be moved by the raw need in those eyes. "You mean you miss sex?"

"Si." He ran a hand through his hair. "But I miss having sex with *you*."

And just like that, he felled her where she stood with that raw admission, with that naked hunger he made no attempt to hide in his eyes.

Electricity arced between them, and she found herself swaying toward him. Every cell in her begging to give in.

His palm kneaded her hip with gentle pressure, his powerful thighs teasing sinuously against her own. "Stop running away, Alex," he whispered in her ear.

He touched his mouth to the line of her jaw, his breath a caress against her skin. Heart beating a thousand to the minute, Alex leaned into him. Those soft lips drew a lightning path down her cheek until they reached the corner of her mouth. And stilled. A meteor dropping on them couldn't have moved her then.

"Maybe catch up on your sleep first, *bella*.

"Because we have a lot to make up for."

* * *

Vincenzo closed the door of Alessandra's bedroom softly behind him. The gaunt set of her face—*maledizione*, she looked like stretched glass—haunted him as he walked through the long corridor toward the room he had set up as a temporary study.

Lust he understood. She was gorgeous and more than matched his appetite in bed.

But this tenderness when he'd found her fast asleep on top of the bedcovers, still in the sweats and old T-shirt she'd worn this evening, dark shadows under her eyes—this he didn't understand.

He stayed inattentive all through the conference call with Massimo and BFI's CFO, two of the most dynamic board members of BFI, both Leo's recruits.

Frustration raked through him as the call ended. The second man left while Massimo closed his laptop with a hard thud that spoke all too loud.

"You won't find anything against him," Massimo said calmly.

"What?" Vincenzo spat out, his mind all too focused on his wife. And the very real grief he'd glimpsed in her eyes earlier that evening. Grief for her mother that she still refused to share with him.

"You won't find any dirt on Leo. Or me, for that matter."

Vincenzo looked back at the younger man he was unwillingly coming to more than respect. "Look, Massimo—"

"Don't insult my intelligence, Cavalli. You've been like a rabid dog these past few weeks trying to find ammunition against Leo.

"The men who are hungrily following in your wake to oust him…those are the kind of men Leo took on in the first place in his fight to turn BFI around. Who didn't agree with him when he instituted an ethics committee, who didn't want to give up even a small share of their profits to clean up the mess Silvio created.

"But then you already know all this."

Massimo picked up his laptop and crossed the room. "For a man who hates the name Brunetti and everything it stands for, you very much act like one, Cavalli."

The air left his lungs as if he'd been gut punched. "Don't you dare—"

"No? It's a Brunetti trait to destroy the very people who might save us.

"Didn't you realize that in all the research you did on us? Didn't Natalie tell you I almost lost her because of how screwed up I had been? Isn't that what you're doing to Alex?

"Our father—*si*, our *father*," he emphasized when Vincenzo flinched, "drove away two good women who could have turned him away from his destructive path.

"See this through and you're truly his son. More than Leo and I have ever been."

Massimo's words ate through Vincenzo like acid, eating away at his resolution, corroding his certainty.

Destroy the name Brunetti and everything it entailed in this world. That had been his goal for so long. A number of people were counting on him.

But the Brunettis were men he was coming to see as more than honorable. Despite all his aggressive tactics, there had been no attempt at retaliation from either.

In fact, they had invited him into their home, the very home he wanted to ruin.

All the evidence only pointed to the fact that they cared about what he did to Alessandra. Not to them.

He had started on this path to right a multitude of wrongs, yes. But he never wanted to hurt an innocent in the process. He was beginning to feel like a man caught uncomfortably between his past and present. A man caught between his promises and his own selfishness.

And the woman he'd married so impulsively, who'd looked today as if he was breaking her apart, she was caught in the middle of it all with him.

Alex stood inside the huge BFI office that Leonardo occupied, indecision cleaving her in half. She had a decision to make. Vincenzo had been right. And the fact that she'd turned up here meant a part of her had already made it.

But she couldn't just leave things in limbo anymore. Not after she'd learned about Antonio and all the people who'd been harmed by Silvio Brunetti. Not after finally understanding the burden Vincenzo had been living with for so many years, the burden that fueled his need for justice.

Now she knew what fired him. He was still wrong, but God, she couldn't just walk away from him. She couldn't just sit tight while there was still a chance that she could do something to help him heal.

"Did you mean what you said at the villa yesterday?" she asked the question before the vulnerability she felt swallowed it up. Before she second-guessed herself again.

Leo and Massimo turned as one, Milan's skyline behind them a beautiful blend of orange and blue. Shock and concern played on their achingly familiar faces as they took her in.

"Alex? Is everything okay?" Leo asked, coming away from his desk. His tie had been undone, and his jacket discarded. Alex saw the lines of worry that had deepened on his face and felt guilt slam into her yet again. God, he was already worried about Neha and the babies she carried since her blood pressure was too high. Now she...

"I'm sorry. I shouldn't have come."

Massimo moved like lightning, blocking her before she could take two steps away. "No, *bella*. Don't run away."

"Of course I meant every word," Leo said behind her, his words ringing with conviction. He clasped her shoulder and squeezed. "This is not, and never was your battle to fight, Alex. You don't owe us anything."

Alex took a deep breath and turned around. For as long as she'd known him, Leonardo had been fair and honorable, determined to be different from the man who'd sired him.

His gaze swept over hers with concern, and he sighed. "Say what's on your mind, Alex."

"I know you can't forgive Vincenzo for what he's doing. For everything he's already done. But I understand his reasons now. For years, he's been caught up in this, fighting for justice for people who can't demand it for themselves. And while he's laying the blame at the wrong feet, his reasons are…painfully just. I need you guys to believe me that he's not…a monster. I can't…go on with my marriage if you think that. I just can't. You are both too important to me. You're family."

"And nothing will change that, Alex. We already know he's not a monster, *bella*," Massimo interjected, coming to stand by her. "Even if we forget, Natalie reminds us daily. Any man who willingly helps a lost teenager couldn't be one."

"And will you forgive me if I…stay with him?"

Massimo whistled and Leo sent him a glare. "You don't need forgiveness. Alex, this is your life. Your happiness. Whatever choice you make, we'll still love you." Leo sighed. "As long as he doesn't hurt you."

"He won't," Alex said, not knowing where the words came from. Where the trust came from.

But she'd done enough running in her life, lost enough by not staying and fighting. Her mother was never coming back. And she couldn't bear to lose this chance with Vincenzo too.

When she spoke, her words rang with conviction. "He won't hurt me, Leo. He has reasons for his actions. So many of them. He can't see anything else right now. But there's more to him than this revenge. He's a man worth standing by. And I want to try."

Massimo wrapped his arm around her, as if he could sense how tightly stretched she was. "We've been preparing for the worst for a long time, *bella*. Before he stepped into your life."

"And even if he takes everything we have built, we'll rebuild again. He's not going to make us destitute, Alex. I hope you have that much trust in us," Leo added archly, and Alex smiled, despite the tears in her eyes.

How could Vincenzo not see what these men were made of? How could he not see that despite Silvio Brunetti's horrendous actions, these men shared the same code of honor he himself lived by?

"In the big scheme of things, BFI and the villa matter very little. Both Massimo and I have learned that lesson the hard way. Neha and the babies, Natalie…the people who matter the most to us, we will still have them even if Vincenzo takes everything else, *si*?

"So you do what feels right to you. You do whatever your heart wants, Alex, and we're right behind you," Leo finished, reaching for her.

Alex went into his arms and buried her face in the familiar scent of him. This was what family meant. And this was what Vincenzo had never known. This was what she wanted to build with him, for her and for Charlie. And for V.

She was going to take the leap.

CHAPTER EIGHT

VINCENZO OPENED THE door and walked in. For a few seconds, he stood still, disoriented. He had given Alessandra more than a few days to recover. And she had taken to hiding in here, not just from him, but from everyone.

The conservatory was all glass on one side, giving a spectacular view of the lake. It was ablaze with lights and looked like a thunderstorm had raged through it and left utter chaos in its wake.

Boxes and boxes—some closed, the majority open with overflowing fabrics in every imaginable color—lay haphazardly around the vast room.

The surface of a dark mahogany table peeked from under a surfeit of sketchbooks and papers. Vincenzo picked up a book and rifled through hundreds of pages of sketches and designs, from elaborate evening dresses to stylish work shirts and suits. Two state-of-the-art sewing machines sat at a far corner and two mobile racks held dresses and other accessories in varying stages of completion.

A sheaf of papers had different versions of the same logo—a curlicued *A* and *A* wrapped around each other in different sizes. He was about to call out Alex's name when he heard a hiccup from the other end of the vast room.

Slowly, he made his way through the jumbled mess on the floor to the other end of the room, where a partition separated the work area from this second area. Sitting on the floor, with a half-empty wineglass and a bottle of red, was Alessandra. With her back to him.

Vincenzo took a few seconds to breathe through the desire that hit him like a gut punch.

She was wearing a white, wispy lace thing that plunged into a deep V at her back, showing off the toned musculature. Silky smooth, golden skin beckoned him for a touch.

While he watched in bemused fascination, she emptied her wineglass and hiccuped again.

"Alessandra?" He called out softly so as to not spook her.

She turned and threw him a glance over her shoulder, then looked away. In the brilliance of the lights, the tears in her eyes looked like crystals.

The slippery whisper of the silk of her dress made him look down. To sit comfortably, she had pulled fistfuls of fabric away from her long legs. The result was that it was gathered around her upper thighs all but baring every inch of her gorgeous body to his hungry gaze.

Vincenzo went to his knees next to her and gently placed his hand over her bare shoulder. Her skin felt freezing to his touch, though the room was comfortably warm. "Cristo, you're like ice!" He spread his fingers around desperate to warm her up.

"What?" She jerked, as if coming out of a trance. Dislodging his fingers in the process. "Oh, the cold, you mean? Yeah, I'm always cold," she said in a nasal voice that confirmed that she'd been crying.

For a few seconds, he got distracted by a memory from Bali. He had been startled awake from a deep sleep early one morning to find her wound around him. But what had woken him had been her cold feet tucked into the groove between his own ankles.

He had gone back to sleep, a smile on his lips, his heart brimming with a feeling he couldn't define. It had been a perfect morning.

"You know, when we met…it's so silly," she muttered and then laughed at herself. "I used to think it was so utterly

romantic that you were always warm. As if there was a…
volcano inside you. I actually took that as some sort of sign.
That you'd always warm me up. For the rest of our lives.

"Can you believe the depth of my foolishness?"

He slid to the floor with not quite the economy he usually had, her words hitting him hard. The ache in them cutting deep. "It's not foolish, *cara mia*."

She tucked an unruly lock of hair behind her ear, and he
noticed the dangly diamond earrings glittering at her ears,
the drop at the bottom kissing her shoulder every time she
moved. An elegant choker—a matching set with the earrings, glimmered at her neck. Her dress, now that he was
noticing things other than her painfully lovely face, was of a
rich lace and ivory silk material. And it fit her to perfection.

In the beautiful white dress and the expensive jewelry,
she looked like a bride.

She hadn't dressed up like this for their impromptu,
impulsive wedding. He frowned. "Princess, is everything
okay?"

"Hmm?"

He lifted the bottle to his gaze. Half-empty. "I didn't
know you drank."

One bare shoulder rose and fell. "I don't usually, but I
feel like I'm drowning. Tonight, I just want to not care."

He watched in increasing fascination as she took the
wine bottle from him and swallowed a mouthful. A drop
fell on the golden skin of her neck and rolled down into the
valley of her breasts. He cursed under his breath, feeling
the tightness in his trousers.

"You should be wary of me. I'm a mean drunk."

He smiled. "I'll take my chances, *bella*."

Trembling fingers dug through the rumpled mass of her
hair. Her chest rose and fell. She rubbed her nose against her
upper arm. The grief painted on her tight face sent alarm
bells ringing inside his head. He took her hand in his, and

pressed his thumb over her knuckles. In a rhythmic movement, back and forth.

"Talk to me, *cara mia*."

She shook her head.

"Afraid you'll spill your secrets?" he teased, faking a humor he didn't feel.

"I don't want to be responsible tonight."

"Then that is exactly why I should be here, *tesoro*. You can be as dangerous and impulsive as you want. Do your worst, Alex. I won't tell a soul."

The brown of her eyes seemed strangely feverish, and intent. Far too present to be truly drunk. The flimsy silk dress looked like it had been made for her. With her hair falling away from its knot and the dress a rumpled mess around her, she still managed to look delicately feminine. Fiercely sexy.

She licked her lower lip and held his gaze. "And if I want things I shouldn't want?"

His body hardened instantly. "Then we will indulge in that too."

When she leaned sideways suddenly, her breasts rubbed against his bicep. He felt electrocuted. Singed by the press of her soft flesh. Softly whispered words blew warm air over his neck. "And if the wine doesn't do its thing, will you help, V? Will you come inside me and—"

"Tell me about this room," he said loudly, cutting her off.

"Now who's running scared?" she taunted.

"I'll give you anything you want, Alessandra. Even if that is me pounding away inside you so that you can forget the grief I see in your eyes. I will let you use me any way you want, *bella*. But when that's done, when you wake up tomorrow with your body sore in the most delicious way, that grief will still be there. Waiting for you."

She wiped her mouth with the back of her hand. "I hate it when you get all sensible."

He let out a long groan. "I hate it when I have to be sensible when you're offering sex."

He saw her lips twitch at that. And it felt like a victory. A small one but one nonetheless. "This is my design studio. Leo had it built for me. He didn't want me to feel left out."

"Left out?" The mention of Leo's name cooled his ardor considerably.

"He had the old wine cellar transformed into a state-of-the-art tech lab for Massimo. Renovated the skeleton of an old greenhouse for himself. When he found out I was cramming yards of fabric in my bedroom, he had this conservatory remodeled into a design room for me." She ran a hand tenderly over the chaise longue, her voice catching. "I had only been here a year by then and I didn't trust him at all. When I asked him why, he simply said this was my home too and it should feel like that.

"He was maybe twenty. But then he's always been a protector at heart."

Vincenzo swallowed the bitter retort that sprang to his lips. "What do you design here?"

Her shoulders straightened with the deep breath she took, sending one silky strap falling off her shoulder. His fingers itched to trace the smooth expanse of that exposed skin, and follow it up with his mouth. "Evening dresses, mostly. I use vintage clothing and repurpose them to give them a new edge."

"Are you any good at it?"

"I'm brilliant at it," she answered, and he smiled. The few pieces he'd seen on the rack looked astoundingly beautiful even to his untrained eye. "But I… I have a love-hate relationship with it. For a long time, I pursued everything but design. Actually, I mostly hated it."

"Still do?"

A lone tear fell down her cheek. "No. Design is where

my heart is. I just… I hated it because it was associated with her. Alyssa. It was the one thing she gave me."

"Your mother?"

"She was a very talented seamstress. An artist with a glorious vision, to be honest. Designing clothes was the one thing we had in common. She taught me when I was a little girl. All these boxes…they are hers. I wanted to donate the whole lot to charity and wash my hands of it. But… I couldn't help myself."

"She made this dress?" he asked, rubbing the silk between his fingers at the hem.

"I think so. It fits me almost perfectly. The lawyer overseeing their estate handed me the jewelry. I… Apparently, it was supposed to be her wedding gift to me."

"Alessandra—"

"But I didn't even tell her that I got married. I sent a postcard to Charlie from Bali, telling him, which she must have read. After I left you…she got in touch with me through Javier, wrote me a letter that he sent on. She wanted to meet you but I called her and told her we were too busy. I…told her she'd never been a part of my life and that it wasn't suddenly going to change. I was absolutely cruel. And a week later, she was gone. Poof. Just like that."

He took her hand in his and was again struck by how cold she was. Pulling it to his mouth, he blew warmth into it. "You had no way of knowing she'd be in an accident, Princess. Life is…"

"Unfair sometimes, yeah. She cheated on my stepfather. Did you know that? With my real father. Greta's second husband. She took off on holiday after they'd had a fight, met Carlos in Milan, had an affair and then returned to her husband, pregnant with me.

"And somehow, Steve forgave her. Except for the fact that there I was, the symbol of everything she'd done wrong, growing up in front of his eyes. Forever reminding him of his wife's infidelity."

"Was he cruel to you?"

"No." More tears drawing tracks on her cheeks. "Oh no, Steve was an honorable man, in his own way. It was her, you see. My mother never forgave herself for her mistake. I was the punishment for her sin."

He pressed his mouth to the back of her hand, feeling helpless against her pain. "You were only a child."

"There was always a coldness to her when I was growing up. A distance I could never cross. And finally, when I was thirteen, it all came out. The truth about my parentage. And I realized why she could never love me. So I reached out to Carlos and moved to Italy to live with him.

"I refused to live in a situation where I was considered a weakness. A shameful secret. A weapon to be used in any argument."

"I'm sorry, Alex," Vincenzo whispered, the full scope of what he had done only just dawning on him now.

"I will not be a weapon to be used against them," she'd said again and again. *"I'm not a prize."*

"Do you know what's weird? I did so many things in life to enrage her. It wasn't enough to leave her.

"I became closer and closer to Greta. I took up modeling because I knew my mother would not approve. I…refused to even visit her, despite numerous calls from Steve. I thought I was hurting her. But really I only hurt myself."

"You did whatever you had to in order to survive."

She scrubbed at her tears roughly. "She reached out to me again after Charlie was born. I went, not to take her up on the olive branch, but because I was curious about Charlie. I was curious about how she would love this baby, if she did at all.

"And she did. I could see it in her eyes—he was a piece

of her heart. She loved him like she never did me. And it broke my heart all over again.

"I love him so much now, but when he was first born I was so jealous of this small baby, Vincenzo. Can you believe it? This tiny human being had what she'd always denied me. Now she's gone. And Charlie's lost everything too."

"Shh…*tesoro*. Shh…none of this is your fault. Grief and guilt are a poisonous cocktail, *cara*," Vincenzo crooned as she broke into heart-wrenching sobs. He pressed his mouth to her temple and held her in a firm grip, his chest tight with an ache he couldn't name.

Her pain felt like his own, and his guilt that he'd only made it worse… It raked claws through him.

"How horrible does it make me that I don't truly miss her? I only miss what could have been…if we'd patched up our relationship."

He understood her so perfectly at that moment. The tangle of emotions that could choke your breath, a beautiful future slipping through your fingers and the helplessness it brought… His arms tightened around her and he rocked them both gently.

His mind turned to the implicit trust he had seen between Leo and Massimo Brunetti. The ethics they'd strived hard to instill in themselves were becoming clearer as he delved into BFI's operations ever since Silvio had been kicked out—with Greta's help, indeed—and Leo had taken over as CEO.

The bond the brothers shared despite Silvio Brunetti's cruelty toward his own sons… He'd seen the evidence of it with his own eyes.

Slowly, she turned into a languorous weight on his muscles. Sinking his fingers into her thick hair, he whispered sweet nothings in Italian. "You're human, *bella*. Not horrible. *What might have been* taunts us all."

Her fingers dug into his muscles, her mouth open against his shoulder. "You were right, you know."

"About what?" he whispered.

"I'm impulsive. I'm… I run away from hard situations. I take things on for all the wrong reasons. Sometimes, I'm…"

"What, Alessandra?"

"I'm scared, V. So much."

"About what, *bella*?"

She took a bracing breath. "What if I'm not the right person to raise Charlie, V? What if that jealousy I initially bore for him translates into my future actions? What if he can see it in me? What if he ends up believing I don't really love him? What if you were right, and I haven't thought this through completely?

"He's so scared right now. Only seven years old and he's been through so much already. I can't be another person who lets him down."

The fear in her voice cut Vincenzo deeply. With rough movements, he turned her until she was looking into his eyes. With her own puffy from her tears, her hair a ragged mess, she was still the most real thing he'd ever laid eyes on. "Listen to me, Princess! You came storming back into this marriage just for him. Your love for him shines through in every word, every action. Trust me—he knows it.

"You don't know how amazing it is to see your strength, *cara*. You hated asking me for help, yet you did. Fighting me with everything you had. For Charlie. He's incredibly fortunate to have you."

He pressed another kiss into her hair, loving the silky tumble of it. Breathing in the essence of this woman who fought to do the right thing even when she was terrified. "It made me see things in you I've never seen before."

She stilled in his arms, her mouth a warm heat against the hollow of his throat. Her fingers dug into his muscles, but he welcomed the contact. "Like what?"

He shrugged, loath to share his doubts. Doubts she'd created in him.

"I thought of what a ferocious mother you'd be to any children we have," he finally answered.

She moved out of his arms and the loss of her warmth, her softness was acute.

He swallowed the urge to pull her back into his embrace. "You're one of those women around whom families are built. Your loyalty…staggers me. You give back everything you receive a hundredfold."

"And yet you would change the very core of me."

"No," he said with careful emphasis. "I only reminded you that I had a right to your loyalty too."

She looked away and then back, and he noted the resolve in her eyes. He could practically see her emerge from this bout of intense grief, bent but not broken. Ready to take on whatever came next. And that determination aroused him as much as the beautiful dress offering him flashes of long, honey-colored limbs.

"Do you think we made a mistake?"

He didn't need to ask her to clarify. *"No."*

"I don't want to think of…us having children for a long time. Not until things are…settled. With Charlie. With us."

"That's fair," he said softly, swallowing away the instinctive protest.

"Would you forgive me if I did something like that?"

"Like what?"

"If I cheated on you, like my mother did to Steve. If I slept with another—"

"No!" His answer bounced off the walls and the floor, increasing in volume until it was reverberating all around them.

The idea of losing Alessandra—to anything, much less another man… He felt shaken up from the inside. On levels he didn't understand. A few months ago, he'd been unaware of her existence and today—he had no words for all the feelings she evoked in him. Only that she was coming to mean so much more than he could ever have imagined.

Too much.

He took a deep breath. "What is it that you're trying to achieve with these ridiculous questions, *bella*?"

Defiance glared at him from those golden-brown depths. "Establishing boundaries, I suppose."

"That question is moot, Alessandra, because I don't believe you would ever do such a thing to me.

"Strip me bare of every rule I've ever lived by, *si*.

"Drive me crazy with your stunts to protect those two bastards from me, *si*.

"Make me pant after you like a damn dog in heat, *si*," he bit out, with a self-deprecating shake of his head. "But to cheat on me is to cheat on the life we want to build with each other—so, no, *bella*, that's not you."

And in that moment of vulnerability, of giving voice to things he'd never admitted before, even to himself, Vincenzo knew exactly how much she was changing him. Antonio had been right to worry.

From the first day he had met her, she had bowled him over with her beauty, but even more with her generosity, her integrity, her constant attempts to open herself up to others.

Alessandra made him want to be a different man. A better man.

A man who could open himself to the possibility of a relationship with his brothers, a man who gave others the second chance that he'd never been given. A man who could even consider forgiving the woman who had directly ruined his life, who had so thoroughly broken his mother's heart that she'd never recovered from it.

But he couldn't. He didn't know how. His path had been set so long ago that he didn't know how to choose a new one now. He didn't know how to be a man whose every waking thought was not filled with taking everything that had been denied him. How to be the man who had to face all the things he'd already done in the name of revenge.

"I was insanely jealous of Anna. How much she's a part of your past, a part of your present."

He wasn't shocked by the sudden turns their conversation took anymore. Neither did he derive any kind of satisfaction from the revelation. It had been a power trip to learn how much he affected Alex. But that was before. Before he realized that it worked both ways. Before he'd begun to view himself through her eyes. "She's firmly in my past. You're my future."

"I want to trust this so much. And not just for Charlie's sake. I need to believe in this marriage, V, in you.

"I want to stop caring about everything else. About Leo and Massimo, about BFI, about the entire world. I want what you promised me on the island, our life together."

His chest felt like it would burst open, so much emotion filled him. "All you need is to take a step toward me, *bella*, that final step."

"Then why does it feel like defeat?"

He shook his head. "I want your surrender, *bella*. Not your defeat."

Some unnamed emotion glittered in her eyes. Pulling the damned dress away from those legendary legs, she crawled toward him on her knees, flashes of bare golden flesh toying with him.

Her hands on his knees pushed them apart and she moved close, intoxicatingly close. The tips of her breasts brushed against his chest, her flat belly against his. Her fingers directed his hands to her thighs with no hesitation. The silk of her skin under his calloused fingers, the incredible scent of her teasing his nostrils… She was a feast he'd been denied for far too long.

"Alex, *bella*, we don't have to do this tonight, when you're still grieving—"

"No, I need this tonight. I need this now." Her hand moved to his neck, then upward to sink her fingers into his hair. Her warm lips skated over every inch of his face, branding him, staking a claim. "I don't want to think. I just want to feel."

Her breath was a warm benediction against his other cheek. He felt engulfed by her. Every moment, every day, she was beginning to own another piece of him. His breath began to come in harsh pants, as if he was trying to catch up to her. And he had a strangely feverish feeling that he would forever be trying to catch up.

"But sometimes I wonder if you're the devil or an angel," she whispered, the words flickering over his skin as she shifted that gloriously lithe body closer. And closer. Her lips descended toward his, her grip on his hair getting tighter. Until his head was tilted up to look into her eyes.

"All I care is that you're mine." That first press of her mouth against his, after so long, sizzled right through his skin. "Please, V…say you're mine."

Words came and fell away from his mouth as she looked deep into his eyes. He considered and threw away platitudes that had no meaning, lies that would damage the surrender she was giving him. Surrender he wasn't sure he deserved.

And then they came, so easily, slumbering awake from some deep place he didn't even know existed within himself. They burned in his chest, lit a fiery path through his throat as he tried to process the weight of the feeling. Of how unprepared he was for them.

"I'm yours, *bella*. Like I've never been anyone else's."

She came at him like a wild storm then, pushing into him, pressing into him, shaking the very ground he stood on. Her mouth… *Madre di Dio*, in all the wildness, her mouth was a lush escape. A warm invitation to heaven.

"And I'm yours. All of me is yours," she whispered frantically against his mouth, a benediction he hadn't even known he'd been waiting for.

Vincenzo cupped her hips, eager for more of her taste. He growled when she sank her teeth into his lower lip and then swiped that wicked tongue over it. Desire pounded at him, urging him to pull the flimsy dress up and away, until he could reach the hot apex of her sex. Patience was a hard-earned battle as he buried his mouth in her neck. The warm, sweet taste of her skin calmed him even as it aroused him, and he nipped at it with his teeth.

She rocked her hips into him at that, making him uncomfortably hard in his trousers. "I missed you, *bella*. I missed this with you," he whispered, licking the tiny mark on her neck. "But I'll be damned if I do this here, on the floor like an eager schoolboy when I can think of a hundred different ways of torturing you for all the months I've waited."

Her laughter enveloped him. She clung to him as he easily pushed them both off the floor. He was stunned at how much he had missed that laughter of hers too. The open joy she found in the most intimately carnal things he did to her.

"I would have much preferred the floor if for nothing else that it clearly says you can't wait until we get to the bedroom to have me."

"Ah…but I want to take my time with you. You cut our honeymoon disastrously short and there's so many things we still have to discover about each other, *si*?"

She shivered at that and he took her mouth roughly, thrusting his tongue into the warm cavern of her mouth. His muscles burned with the need for more… More contact, more friction, more of her. She and him… It had never been just sex between them.

Antonio had seen it. Had warned him.

And yet, Vincenzo couldn't even imagine controlling this somehow, much less walking away from it.

CHAPTER NINE

"I'M YOURS, BELLA."

Alessandra hugged those words close as Vincenzo deposited her on her bed and devoured her with those penetrating eyes. The luxurious sheets were cold against her skin, a startling contrast to the heat pouring off the man, looking down at her as if she were his downfall and salvation all at the same time. For long, painfully pregnant moments, he did nothing but look at her. Pushing up on her elbows, Alex returned his stare without hesitation.

Like I have been never been anyone else's. Those quiet words resonated around them, explosive in the silence, though she knew they had been given reluctantly.

Her breath hitched in her throat as urgent hands landed on her knees and pushed them indecently apart, making space for himself between her legs. The silk of her dress whispered sinuously against the sheets as those very same hands found her buttocks and pulled her to the edge of the bed. Until his hips kissed her inner thighs. His fingers dug into her bottom as he tilted her up. Until his erection glided against the hottest part of her.

Alex thrust involuntarily, the shape and weight of that hardness making her feverishly delirious for more. Fingers clutching the sheets, she let out a moan when Vincenzo rocked against her, his hips doing that wickedly erotic thing that had made her go crazy that first time.

Hungry gaze holding hers captive, he pushed aside her flimsy thong and traced a finger up and down her wet folds.

Circled the hot place she needed him to touch without quite giving in to her.

"Please, V," she whispered, desperate for the clawing under her skin to subside.

"You mean this is better than your new technological friend?" It sounded like a tease, but the fire in his eyes told her it was anything but. His hands cupped her knees. Bent over her like that, he looked like a warrior intent on plunder.

Alex could barely hold the whimper at the loss of the acute pressure. "You never let me finish the story that night," she murmured now.

"Si?" His tongue licked at her mouth, his flat, hard abdominal muscles gliding temptingly against her wet folds. She slid up and down on the bed, and he rewarded her with a movement of his own.

Alex groaned, her lower belly corkscrewing at the contact.

"Finish it now, Alessandra."

The quiet command sank into her pores. Alex opened her eyes and smiled. "I had an orgasm that night, yes. But it felt empty without your whispered commands in my ear, without your body pushing down on me, without the warmth of your skin against mine... Nothing feels as good as you do, V. Nothing in the entire wide world."

His answering grin, full of wicked charm and self-satisfied arrogance, was so devastatingly gorgeous that she reveled in it.

And then his hand drifted down again, down her belly to that aching place, rubbing the sensitive bundle of nerves with those wickedly clever fingers. His thumb drew erotic circles while he thrust a finger inside her.

"*Cristo*, I've missed this warmth of yours," he said, his gaze devouring every dazed expression in her eyes. "Make those sounds for me, *bella*."

His fingers moved again with a mesmerizing rhythm

that lit up every nerve center in Alex's body. When he bent down and took her mouth in a sensual tangle of a kiss, she clung to him, her body writhing under him, chasing that rhythm.

"Tell me what you need," he asked, like he'd done every time they made love. Every time, he learned her body by making her learn her own. Every time, he pushed her to new discoveries about herself and what she liked. "Tell me what will make this all the sweeter for you, *tesoro*."

"Touch me here," she said, cupping her aching breasts. Just imagining his mouth there had sent her off the edge that night she'd had her empty orgasm.

"Pull the straps down."

Alex raised her hands automatically, every cell in her body attuned to his demands, ready to surrender to his every wish. Slowly, with movements that made those gray eyes darken into something indecently erotic, she hitched each index finger under the straps and flicked them off her shoulders. But the straps didn't fall all the way down and she locked them about her elbows by stretching her hands toward him.

"I want to touch you first," she demanded in a husky voice, knowing that once he got his hands on her flesh, her all too willing flesh, she was going to be cast into a vortex of sensations. Of need and pleasure.

If she wanted to take a little of him, wanted to ensure he was as far gone as she in this, she needed to do it now. She needed to touch, caress, kiss, every inch of him before he took over.

"You haven't tormented me enough, *bella*?" he said, his thumb tracing her collarbone, while the other dipped into her wetness, and out, in a mesmerizing rhythm that threatened to steal her resolve.

Fingers on his wrist, she stilled his hand. "I want to be

more than a participant in this. I want to take something from you too."

He dipped his head in a sudden movement and took her mouth in a rough kiss that mocked his control. "You think I haven't given myself to this...to you?" he whispered against her mouth, his breath melded with her own.

"But whatever you give," she said, pressing her face into his throat, tasting his skin, "it's not..."

He didn't let her finish. As if he knew she was about to say. That whatever he gave, it wasn't enough until she had his heart.

She couldn't bear to look at him, to see the answer in his eyes.

And he... For the first time since she'd known him, Vincenzo didn't meet her gaze. He capitulated. Lost the battle, she knew, instead of the war.

Long lashes hiding the expression in his eyes, he brought her hands to his shirt. "Then do what you will with me, *Princess.*"

Alex blinked away at the hotness that threatened behind her eyes. She was going to live for what she did have.

Him.

This.

She was going to build the family she'd never had. She was going to give it her all, regardless.

She didn't hesitate as she unbuttoned his shirt and pulled it out of his trousers. Almost frantic with the need to touch, she pushed the shirt off his shoulders and ran her hands, palms down, from the tight muscles in his shoulder to his jutting collarbone and then down, tracing the ridges of his chest to the rock-hard muscles of his abdomen.

Up and down, left and right, she zigzagged her hands, her cold hands, over his warm, taut skin. Though he stayed still, she didn't miss the way his breathing became shallow, even harsh, with each path she traced on his skin. Pushing herself up, up, she followed the path her hands traced on his chest and abdomen with her mouth.

He tasted of sweat and salt and something so gloriously masculine that she whimpered. This close to him, each breath he inhaled and exhaled hit the upper curves of her breasts in a tantalizing rhythm that had her nipples tauten, begging for more.

She tested the give of his muscle with her teeth, and an animalistic grunt escaped his mouth when she gently bit his pectorals. She busied her hands with, first his belt, and then the clasp of his trousers. And still she was aware that he was letting her. His control, she had no doubt, was on a short leash tonight. Almost at the end. But then, she had given him her surrender, unconditional surrender, and she had known from the first moment she'd met him, that Vincenzo would gift her with the entire universe in return for that surrender. She shivered now, even as his warm skin somehow diffused its heat into her skin.

All thoughts fled her brain when she pushed his trousers off his hips and instinctively reached for the hardness that she wanted. Again, that guttural grunt, that sharp hiss of an inhale, when she touched the thick length of him.

Steel coated in velvet, he lengthened and hardened further even as she wrapped her fingers around him. As a man, he was just the same, she realized. Smooth words, gorgeous smile, and at the core of him, he was unshakable in his resolve, in his quest toward revenge.

If destruction was what he wanted, then she would give it to him.

She turned her fingers into a fist and moved it up and down that hard length, as she'd done in those first few days when they'd been busy discovering each other's bodies like explorers on some new land. But there had been no challenge between them then.

Only an intrinsic need for each to discover what gave

the other the most pleasure. She rubbed the soft head with her thumb in movements that mimicked the gentle torture he'd rained over her. Head thrown back, eyes closed, that lean, hard chest breathing deep, he groaned out loud.

But she wanted even more. She was determined to wrest the last of his control from him. Until he too stood in the wake of this thing between them, stripped and vulnerable.

"Tell me your deepest fantasy," she coaxed, the very thought of that steely length inside her making her sex ache with want.

"This," he said, his face bathed in moonlight from the French windows. He clasped her jaw, his thumb tracing her lower lip. His other hand tightened in her hair, tugging, raising her face up. "You...like this. All mine."

"Me...doing what?" she demanded, scooting to the edge of the bed. She pulled her legs up and under her, and propped herself up on her elbows, bringing her face to the height of that hard evidence of his arousal. Leaning down, she blew on it.

He tensed. "Do it," he whispered after what felt like an eternity.

"Do what?" she threw back, fluttering her eyelashes at him. "Ask me nicely."

"Take me in your mouth now," he commanded, but there was a desperation to it.

Falling onto her knees, she obeyed.

Another loud groan ripped through the air around them. Digging her nails into his hard thighs for purchase, Alex licked the entire length of him, up and down. A filthy curse came next, filling her with power and arousal, a cocktail that vibrated through her.

Then she took him in her mouth and his fingers plunged into her hair, giving her instructions in a hoarse voice that rumbled right through her.

She had no idea how long he gave her free rein of his

body, but she loved having him like this. Had no sense of time or the world around them as she played with the evidence of what she did to him. For a few minutes, or it could have been hours, he was putty in her hands.

Every thrust and jerk of his hips as she licked the length of him with her hands at the base, every curse gritted out through a tense jaw, every tug of his fingers in her hair urging her to go faster and harder, was music to Alex's ears.

"Enough, *bella*!" he declared, and within moments, Alex was lying back on the bed, her dress rucked up to her hips, and Vincenzo eyeing her as if he meant to consume her.

With her golden-brown hair spread out on pristine white sheets, her eyes glittering in her flushed face, Alessandra was the most beautiful thing Vincenzo had ever seen.

Her bare breasts with those plump brown nipples, the taut flat belly with the white bridal dress rucked up to her waist, and the long, toned legs, the strip of hair covering the wet warmth he desperately wanted to bury himself in… And that mouth, that gloriously pink, pouty mouth that had licked and stroked him right to the edge of heaven…

If she'd asked him for something tonight, he wouldn't deny her. Yet even that warning thought couldn't clear the fog of desire claiming his senses.

But nothing could compare to the expression in her eyes as she looked at him now. As if he were her safe harbor in the midst of a storm. As if he were the only thing that could save her. As if he were as necessary to her as air.

He stepped out of his trousers and filled his hands with her butt cheeks and pulled her close. A light coating of sweat shone on her body. He ran his hands from the sleekly soft skin of her inner thighs to the toned muscle of her midriff, up, up, to the perfect globes of her breasts. Followed that with his mouth, licking and nipping as he went.

Every time, he pulled the skin between his teeth, she jerked and thrust up with her hips. And he got a little harder.

When he finally reached her mouth, he thrust his tongue into hers and she clung to him, panting, sobbing.

And then he began the journey back down, drinking in the silky softness of every inch of her. He pinched the plump nipples between his fingers and tugged, just as he knew she liked.

She bowed off the bed, her body arcing like she'd been hit by lightning. He bent his head and flicked his tongue over one tight bud and teased her. Her hips, her breasts, everything jerked up toward him as if she wanted to burrow into his skin and remain there. He wanted to tell her that she was already there. That she had gotten under the skin of a man whom nothing had ever touched before.

That he didn't know how to dislodge her. That already he was seeing things differently, seeing a future for himself that jarred violently with his present path.

"Please… Vincenzo, please. I need your mouth there," she said, not in supplication though. But with demand, with fierce need. He had loved that about her. She demanded pleasure as fiercely as she gave it. She demanded it as if it were her due.

"With pleasure, *cara mia*," he said, and closed his lips over her sensitive nipples.

Tremors took over her entire body. Holding her lower body tight against his own, he alternated between both breasts, kissing and licking, sucking and blowing air on the wet tips, until they were swollen and glistening in the moonlight. Slowly, he brought her down to the bed and tilted her hips up toward him.

"Keep your eyes open, *bella*," he instructed, wanting her to see what she did to him.

He rubbed himself in her wetness, the erotic glide sending long moans out of their mouths. A shudder racked his entire body when he entered her in a deep thrust that took him home. Alessandra cried out and he stilled inside her, holding her to him.

"Damn it! Did I hurt you—"

"No." Her lithe body stretched under him, as if she wanted to feel him everywhere. "I just…" She locked those beautiful eyes on him, and Vincenzo knew this was the home he'd been chasing for most of his life. "I just forgot how…achy this feels. How thoroughly you fill me up. How well you know what I like."

And then she smiled and raised her hips in an experimental thrust and an arrow of pleasure shot up the base of his spine. But it wasn't just pleasure as he started moving in short, fast thrusts. He had no words for what it felt like when her gaze moved over him, her fingers tracing each feature.

It had felt like home that first time too. It had felt like nothing he'd ever known before. Excitement and arousal, pleasure and warmth, satisfaction and peace—all the things he'd never had in his life, he'd found in her embrace. Only he hadn't seen it then.

And now it was too late.

There was no sense of him when he was inside her— his goal, his ambition, his cause, his revenge— everything disappeared. When she clasped his face in her hands and kissed his mouth. When her hips thrust up in a desperate need to be closer to him. When she was pulling him irrevocably into the fabric of her own life. Her loved ones, her family, her goals, her generous heart.

She made him drown; she pulled the ground away from under him.

"More, please. Everything you have, V," she demanded, her core contracting and releasing him, her thighs slapping against his hips with every damp slide of his body against her.

Every tiny pulse of her body hit him as he pulled out

and then thrust back in again. Every muscle in his body curled against the next, bracing for the surfeit of pleasure.

But he knew Alessandra's surrender did not come without a price.

Even if she didn't ask it, even if she didn't demand her due, Vincenzo knew there would soon be a day when he would not be able to pay it.

How had Alex forgotten how transformative sex was between Vincenzo and her? The magic that seemed to be created when they came together? The rightness of it?

It was what had driven her to marry a man who'd been a complete stranger.

Alex whimpered at the emptiness as he pulled out completely but was rewarded not a moment later, when he climbed up onto the bed, on all fours, a primal need etched onto his stunning features. A drop of sweat dripped from his forehead and plopped onto the swell of her breast and his hungry eyes followed it. As if she were prey, and he meant to consume her.

And then he was back on her again, over her, inside her, around her. His weight on top of hers both a safe haven and a vortex of thrill at the same time.

He yanked her closer and thrust inside her, a deep growl rumbling out of him. Alex cried out at the welcoming hardness, at the incredible friction. She was lifted off the bed, hands on her buttocks pulling her up until she was astride his lap. The bare economy with which he arranged her to his liking, the strength in his lean corded limbs only amplified the thrall he had her under.

Alex wrapped her arms around his damp back, feeling him everywhere inside her in this position. The rub of her breasts against his chest, the intimacy of locking gazes with him deepened her pleasure to an unbearable level.

He was so hard and pulsing inside her, his breath warming every inch of her neck, his scent—a sweaty, masculine combination that filled her very senses. Their mouths locked again in a devastatingly hungry communion that she knew now would never be enough. She held on to him as if she could hold his heart to hers this way. She wanted to stay like that forever, in his arms, surrounded by him, and let time stretch from this moment to the next and the next.

Alex buried her face in his shoulder. Damp, soft, warm, he was an explosive taste on her tongue.

"Look at me, *bella*."

She squeezed her eyes closed tighter, afraid of what he would see in them. Afraid of the wide chasm of need that opened up inside her when he held her like this, when he moved inside her.

"Please, V. Finish me off, won't you? I want to come so desperately I feel like I'll die if I don't," she said, imbuing every inch of want that thrummed through her into her words.

"I won't move inside you while you hide away from me, *bella*," he growled, a vein of tension in his voice. Every inch of him was taut under her fingers. He strummed a line of music on her bare back, his mouth at her temple. "I have become used to seeing myself in your eyes, Alessandra. I have become used to drowning in your gaze."

Her head jerked up at the pure need in those words.

So she let their mouths tangle, their tongues lap at each other, their teeth nip at each other until it was hard to tell where she ended and where he began. His heart was a violent drum against her breast, his body a damp, sleek fortress of demand as he thrust up.

With each grunt of his, Alex moved up and down while need corkscrewed in her belly.

She let the sounds and scents that their bodies created together lead her on and on until no rational thought was possible. Vincenzo murmured, "That's it, Alex. Stay with me."

And then he was pressing her back into the bed, and holding her down with the thrust of his hips. Alex gave herself over to it as he rode her body hard, chasing his pleasure.

Alex opened her mouth against his bicep and dug her teeth in, knowing what he liked. Wanting him lost to this madness like her. "Faster, please, V," she sobbed, her release an ephemeral breath away.

Her legs draped over his shoulders, his pelvis rubbed sinuously against her in exactly the right place every time he thrust.

"Touch yourself, *bella*. Come with me," he commanded, and Alex moved her hand down from his chest to the apex of her thighs.

Eyes wide-open, she held Vincenzo's gaze, and the emotion she saw there pushed her over the edge. "Oh," she whispered, on and on, again and again, into his damp skin as her release flung her open wide.

There was nothing like the magic of her climax when he was inside her, something he made them both work for every time. Nothing like being swept up by the storm of pleasure that drove him toward his own.

Her release continued in short pulses. Vincenzo deepened his thrusts—once, twice, thrice—and fell onto her with a fierce growl. Her name on his lips was a crooning whisper that settled like a blanket of contentment over her naked skin. Alex wrapped her arms around him and held on, as if the physical act somehow guaranteed more than that. As if...

No, she wasn't going there. This was all she needed. She'd chosen this path, she'd chosen him, and she'd stick to it come what may.

He stayed on top of her like that, for long, perfect moments. "You okay?" he asked finally.

Alex turned toward him and smiled. "More than okay," she whispered, and he took her mouth in a rough, snarly kiss that warmed her all the way to her cold toes.

CHAPTER TEN

VINCENZO CAME AWAKE with a start.

Falling asleep anytime before predawn was such an unusual thing for him that he felt disoriented for several minutes after opening his eyes.

Restful sleep had always been impossible for him. For the longest time, he had forced himself to stay awake to keep an eye on his mother, afraid that she might do some irreparable damage to herself if he fell asleep.

Once he had achieved a measure of financial freedom to hire a round-the-clock nurse to ensure his mother's care, it had been too late. His insomnia by then had been entrenched, a by-product of the numerous nights he'd spent through relentless years, building his fortune.

After that, he had a financial empire to rule.

But now, after only a few nights here in the villa, he was so used to the warm, languorous weight of Alessandra's limbs vined around him that sleep came easily. To go to bed without her now seemed like a dreary prospect, even temporarily.

The thought disquieted him enough to rouse him completely. With slow movements, he disengaged her long limbs from his.

He swept a lock of hair away from her face and ran his fingers lightly over those blade-like cheekbones, his heart a strangely weighty thing in his chest. She moaned and rolled and the duvet slipped, offering glimpses of a smooth silky shoulder and the upper curve of a breast.

Instantly, he felt the answering tightness of his own body. *Cristo*, it had been six days since he'd found her in that conservatory, and they'd spent most of those six days burning through the heat between them.

It showed no signs of abating. He had been insatiable, and she'd been there with him every step of the way. Wrenching himself away from the temptation she offered, he pulled on sweatpants and a T-shirt, made his way out of the bedroom.

The long corridors were quiet, the marble cold against his feet. He was not surprised when he arrived at the huge study, the seat of Leonardo's power, the seat from where centuries of the masters of this revered dynasty had used their power.

To this day, Vincenzo still hadn't figured out the older Brunetti, the true heir to all this. Massimo was more open, full of a caustic wit that made even Vincenzo smile. But in Leonardo… He could see shades of himself.

"Imagining yourself here?" came a voice behind him.

He turned to find Greta Brunetti standing just inside the door, her shoulders stiff.

"Imagination is for dreams out of your reach. This chair, this study, this house…it's all within my grasp already. If you must know," he said, surprised at his own rancor spewing into his words, but continuing anyway, "I was wondering what I would wreck first. This study, or the tall towers of BFI."

She paled, and he felt a glimmer of regret. Only a glimmer.

"What do you want, Mr. Cavalli?"

Her formal address raked at something inside him, but he refused to show it. "The time for action is long past for you," he said, leaning against the massive dark oak table and crossing his ankles.

Her claw-like hands folded tightly against her midriff.

"It's never too late to realize one is wrong. Never too late to make amends."

Shock drenched him, stealing away his anger. "Ah…it's your fear of destruction speaking."

"No, it's not. Whatever you're planning, it has little effect on me at this stage in life. But Alessandra, if I could do anything to—"

"She's mine. I won't give her up for anything in this world. She made her choice again not six days ago. She makes the choice to be mine every night," he threw at the old woman shamelessly.

"I know that. I've already lost her respect, and that's worse than anything you can do to me. But I ask you to remember that she's an innocent in all this."

"My mother was an innocent too."

"I did what I thought was right at that time for my family. For years, I put up with my son's antics. Tried to patch up his actions, dealt with the consequences. I had become hardened to everything else—I had no mercy or kindness or even love left in me, because he drained it all away.

"I only did my duty by Leo and Massimo. I…starved them of affection—"

"They had a roof over their heads, food in their bellies, shelter against storms. I had nothing," Vincenzo threw at her, his chest rising and falling.

Not even a childhood. That was the price he had paid for her mercilessness.

He had never been allowed to be a child.

Her chin jerked down, and the old woman looked away for long, painful minutes. He ran a shaking hand through his hair. "I will grant you that your grandsons are not the monsters I thought them."

Alessandra's faith in Leo and Massimo had not been bought with all this wealth or by favors, Vincenzo was learning with each day.

It was a hard pill to swallow: the genuine affection she shared with both men, being here in the seat of the family's power for generations, being the outsider.

But worse was the realization—like a shard of glass stuck in his throat—that that affection, that bond with the Brunetti brothers, should have been his too. To see them over the breakfast table, to understand the easy camaraderie between them, to feel like the outsider when he had just as much right to that bond with them… It was a special kind of torment.

Alessandra's hope that somehow he could cross the divide between them and build that bond with them—now, after everything he'd done to bring them down, after all the bitter hatred he'd nursed for them for over two decades… It was just that—a naive, pathetic hope that he refused to indulge in.

"That was despite my presence in their life," Greta added softly, and Vincenzo turned to her with a frown. "You are under a grand delusion if you think Leo and Massimo had a nurtured upbringing in this home.

"After dealing with Silvio's cruel antics and the fallout for so many years, I had nothing left to give them. They grew up to be honorable men, despite their abusive father and me.

"It was only when I married Alessandra's father, Carlos, that I realized…how many mistakes I had made. How I had let my son and his actions change me into this…bitter woman who had not even a kind word for her grandsons."

Vincenzo refused to indulge the thin thread of sympathy that reverberated within him at the woman's words.

Nothing, nothing could forgive what she'd done to his mother and him. This was all Alessandra's doing. The blasted woman was changing how he saw things, was undoing him at a cellular level.

"*Per piacere*, Vincenzo, do not…hurt Alessandra."

"I'm to believe you care for her that much?"

"*Si*, I do. She gave me a chance to be someone else. To redeem myself. To…find love in my heart again. Please…"

"Promise me you won't use me in this battle of yours?" Alessandra had asked him just before they'd danced at Antonio's party.

And he'd given her his word. And yet, if he could end this war he'd waged all the sooner, all the more cleanly, by using her, if he could avoid the total destruction he'd originally planned, wouldn't she ultimately be grateful to him? Wouldn't she understand why he'd done it?

His thoughts ran away from him like a runaway freight train before he could hold on to one and process it.

If, once he'd pulled apart BFI, he left this house intact instead of bringing it down—this house that she loved so much, this house that had been her safe harbor… If Alessandra and he could build that family of theirs here, if they could have a fresh start in this place where once his dreams had been crushed… Wasn't his revenge still complete?

Wasn't justice served then?

"If she's that important to you, then prove it to me," he said, pushing away the quiet voice of conscience that threatened to take over if he let it.

Her skin whitened to such deathly paleness that Vincenzo felt a twinge of remorse. He had hated this woman so much for so long, and yet she looked like nothing but a husk of the person from his memory, who had with one merciless decision, ruined his childhood, his mother's sanity.

The years in between should have etched that hardness she had showed them that day onto her face and yet, her eyes shone with conviction. With love, he realized, a cold chill taking over his skin.

Love that Alessandra had created in this old woman's bitter heart.

Love and something like the longing that he had glimpsed in Alessandra's eyes when she looked at him.

It was the most terrifying thing he'd ever seen. Because he was beginning to realize he didn't deserve it. It amplified into an urgent drumbeat in his blood—this need to finish what he'd started soon. Before it was too late.

"How?" the old woman asked, pulling him out of his own murky thoughts.

"Ask your grandson to step down as CEO of BFI."

"Leonardo has worked far too hard for far too many years to just give up now."

"Then *make him*."

"It's not—"

"Throw your support behind me at the next board meeting."

The old woman swayed on her feet and reached for the support of the table. "If I back you, Leonardo will lose the controlling majority."

"It is a far better fate than what I had initially decided for them both."

Her eyes held his in a defiant challenge, an almost mirror image of the resolve he spied in his own eyes. A resemblance that he wanted to deny at any cost, and yet it was there. "For two centuries, only a Brunetti sat on that chair." A hint of that Brunetti arrogance crept back into the woman's words, her spine straightening. "It's against tradition—"

"The choices you have are very simple," Vincenzo said with a shrug. Any doubts he might have indulged in washed away at the flash of that Brunetti arrogance in her eyes. "Either keep BFI intact by throwing your support behind me or see all of it torn into pieces like I initially planned.

"With the first choice, you might even save Alessandra some heartache in the process. That's what you came to ask me for, remember? That I don't hurt Alessandra in all this."

"And you would use my affection for her this way?"

"Your words, your actions created the man I am today. You only have yourself to blame."

"This will break her heart. You're truly—"

"My father's son, *si*? So I have been told. You'd better not tell her then." He refused to think of what would happen if Alessandra found out. He refused to let it sway him when he was so close to being done. *Cristo*, he so badly wanted to be done. He wanted that future life with Alessandra to begin right now. "Alessandra has already chosen me. Chosen a future with me," he said, letting the old woman see his victory. "If I take over BFI, this can all be over for her too. She won't feel so caught up between her past and her future."

He left the room without looking back, a sort of desperation filling him to see Alessandra in that bed. To hold her. To reassure himself that she...

He felt dirty. As if he completely deserved the loathing he'd seen in the old woman's eyes.

He reached the bedroom, and only then did air fill his lungs. He stripped fast and got back into the bed. Like clockwork, Alessandra reached for him and burrowed into him. Only then did his heart slow its savage race.

"Did we make a mistake, V?"

Had she asked him that only a few nights ago?

And he realized with a sinking dread that the answer was yes. He had made a mistake. He had involved a woman who deserved far better than him in his life. He had tangled with a woman who deserved to be loved, to be worshipped. Who didn't deserve to be used as currency against the woman she loved.

But as Alex wrapped her long limbs around him, as she pulled him over her sweet temptation of a body, as she took his mouth in a warm kiss, as he lazily thrust into her and built them both up into that delicious frenzy again, Vincenzo didn't even consider for one second if he could give her up to fix the mistake. Release her from his life.

He couldn't. He wouldn't.

Because she was his. Not the prize he'd once so foolishly thought her. But so much more.

His salvation and his sanctuary.

Alessandra was still riding the high of the evening as she walked into the New York penthouse, put away her portfolio, stripped and went into the shower in quick succession. Her skin tingled as she thought of seeing Vincenzo again after four long days apart, of returning the favor he had done her in the one way she knew he would appreciate.

The warm spray from the powerful jet invigorated her as she smiled, anticipation building like a current inside her.

Thank God he'd had Anna tell her, even if it had been a bit dicey, at the last moment to bring her design portfolio with her. That the surprise he'd arranged for her was a dinner meeting with the talented CEO of an up-and-coming couture house with its base in New York City—a meeting Alessandra had been pursuing for more than a month now with no success.

One of the numerous things that Vincenzo arranged in her life, with an incredible arrogance that sometimes stole her breath.

But for all the initial protest that rose up inside her at his high-handedness, Alessandra could never fail to see the intentions—usually good intentions, behind his presumptuous actions. Like this meeting with the trendsetting CEO.

She had only just admitted to herself, and whispered to him that night in her design studio a few weeks ago, that she wanted to launch herself as a designer. That she wanted to launch her own label as Alessandra & Alyssa—a label that would commemorate her mother's artistic vision and the peace that Alex had finally found after all these years.

It had been a painful internal journey but she knew it was the right thing to do—to acknowledge that her mother had loved her, in her own way, to use the talent and vision for design she'd inherited from Alyssa to build her own company.

Neither could she lie to herself anymore. Vincenzo had helped her achieve that peace. For a man who was so ruthless about so many things, he had been insightful and kind when it was her grief they were dealing with.

As soon as he'd understood what she'd wanted, he had set in motion so many meetings for her all across the globe. Using his connections.

Not that Alessandra lacked a network. But his was just bigger and better, she reluctantly admitted to herself.

For example this particular CEO—his couture house had been in the news of late for its ethical practices, for designing couture using recycled vintage wear, and for its fair trading policies with so many third world countries where it sourced the vintage fabrics. It would be the dream of a couture house to launch her first line with. But even with her connections and her agent's clout, Alessandra hadn't been able to acquire a meeting with the man.

No sooner had she revealed her frustration to Vincenzo, there it was in her calendar, a meeting with that CEO.

And it had gone tremendously well, she and the man instantly hitting it off.

At least the nausea that had threatened her all day—she frowned…no, all week, actually—hadn't ruined the evening. Victor Emmanuel had been both excited and amazed by her portfolio, and Alessandra couldn't wait to begin working with such a brilliant visionary. Couldn't wait to see her label launched—a future woven from the threads of the past.

When she had laughingly mentioned Vincenzo twisting his arm to get her the appointment, he had, with a sudden seriousness, admitted that he was the one who owed Vincenzo a favor. Because her husband had been the very man who had helped him raise seed capital in what was a cutthroat industry all those years ago.

Every time Alex thought she knew Vincenzo, that she understood him, he threw a monkey wrench into it.

She toweled her damp hair and pulled a robe on, a strange lethargy gripping her. Barefoot, she walked into the bedroom of the penthouse that challenged the New York City skyline with its magnificence.

They had been here for three weeks now, and Alessandra had discovered she didn't want to return home. God, she wanted to stay here forever, away from Italy and the myriad demands it placed on her husband's time, energy and even loyalty.

It had been a glorious few weeks' respite, and she was loath to see it come to an end.

Since she had made her choice, since she had decided that she couldn't let his war with Leonardo and Massimo break her apart into so many pieces, just as she'd guessed, Vincenzo, in return for that surrender, had been busy placing the world at her feet in return.

And it hadn't been just his support, his encouragement, and the use of his extensive network when it came to launching her new career. He had barely returned from a weeklong conference in Beijing when she had been ready to leave for New York to see Charlie again.

A few hours with him at the most had been what she'd been hoping for. Because, once she had stopped lying to herself, once she'd stopped fighting herself, she had admitted how much she missed him.

How much she missed their talks about their careers, about their futures, their long, lazy nights, where she kept thinking that one more night, one more time would calm the fire that raged between them. But it did not. It was as if a different Vincenzo—charming, contented, that Vincenzo she had first met in Bali—had emerged again since she had thrown her lot in with him.

The only blip, the only thing that marred her near-perfect happiness was his past. He refused to even talk about his mother or his ongoing battle to gain the controlling stock of BFI. As long as Alessandra didn't broach either of those subjects—and she made a conscious effort not to—he was everything she could have ever asked for.

No, he was more than she'd ever expected to have in her life.

A week ago, he had surprised her by joining her on the flight to New York, even though she knew he'd been busy with his own global interests.

He'd been incredibly patient when Charlie had refused to even meet his gaze, reassuring Alex that he knew how to handle the little boy.

He had also made time to spend an entire day with Charlie and her, arranging an impromptu picnic at Central Park, playing the tourist with them. At the end of the day, Charlie had asked Vincenzo when he'd visit again.

"What's important to you is important to me," he'd said simply when she had inquired.

Except the Brunettis.

Even a single mention of either Greta, or Leo or Massimo, and instantly, he transformed into a man Alex didn't understand. A man that she was increasingly afraid for. How long could a person sustain such hatred, such anger and not be changed by it? When it was finally over, what would be left for her?

Alex sighed and poured out a glass of water when the private elevator pinged behind her. Like a teenage girl, her heart beat faster, her skin prickled with anticipation as footsteps echoed down the sitting room and then into the bedroom where she stood by the French doors.

She hadn't seen him in four days. A meager four days, and yet it felt like a lifetime. "Hey," she said, leaning her wobbling knees against the cold glass, her throat already parched again.

He stood still, framed by the rounded archway and suddenly the distance between them felt like a chasm. A chasm he was creating between them.

"What's wrong?" she asked, knowing that she was overreacting and yet unable to stop the thread of fear unspooling in her belly.

"You said you wouldn't interfere in this anymore. You said you'd chosen your path, that you chose me."

"I did."

"Then what do you call all the maneuverings you've set into motion behind my back? I can't leave you alone for a few days? *Cristo*, no wonder Antonio thinks I'm whipped."

"What maneuverings? What are you talking about?" She had never seen him so angry and his anger brought out hers. Suddenly, the magic she'd found in the city with him seemed to evaporate right in front of her eyes. "Also, I'd appreciate it if you didn't discuss our marriage with that bitter old man."

His eyes narrowed. "That bitter old man is the only father figure I've ever had. That bitter old man is the only reason I stand before you as a successful businessman instead of a criminal languishing behind bars."

As quickly as it came, her anger got swept away. She reached him and clasped his jaw in her hands. He hadn't shaved in a while, and the stubble was a raspy purr against her palm. Dark smudges cradled his eyes. And all she wanted was to kiss away the bitterness from those proud features. "I forget how hard you've worked to get to this place."

He stiffened. "Do not pity me, Alessandra."

She smiled, her chest swimming with a most peculiar

cocktail of emotions. "Antonio deserves my respect if nothing else. I'm sorry for speaking of him in such a manner. But—" she chose her words carefully "—he's determined to tether you to the past so tightly, V…" She pressed her mouth against his, desperate for a taste of him. Every word Antonio said to him, every meeting pulled Vincenzo away from the possibility of the future they could share. From finally releasing all the bitterness and anger he'd nursed for so long. From her. "And it terrifies the hell out of me."

That he didn't offer her words of reassurance made her belly swoop. Fear coated her skin with a cold chill and she started shivering.

There was change on the horizon—good and bad—so many chances that she could be split open and everything in her urged to run away again.

Instead, she embraced the fear and ache. She tightened her arms around him and let the vulnerability wash over her. Drown her. The lazy flick of his tongue against hers, the solid feel of him in her arms, the scent of him in her blood anchored her amidst her own fears. Rooted her.

Could the very man who might break her also give her strength to stay strong?

She'd have laughed at the question if it wasn't her heart in the balance.

His hands untangled hers from him. "You told Leonardo and Massimo about Antonio, about all the others."

"I didn't think it was a secret."

"I was a fool to believe that you would…" He moved away, his face set in tense lines, his mouth pinched.

As if she had truly betrayed him.

Suddenly, she felt as if she'd been given a painful insight into his thoughts.

Was that what Vincenzo expected of her? That she would betray him, abandon him at some point? That she would simply choose to walk away from all this?

But instead of feeling anger that he should trust her so little, Alex realized something else. This wasn't about his trust in her, this was about his own inability to trust. These were the scars left by a painful childhood where he hadn't had anyone to depend on. Anyone in his corner.

Her tone softened. "What Antonio wants for you is not healthy. So of course he'll paint this as some kind of deception on my part."

"I'm not discussing this with you."

"So don't," she said, suddenly angry herself. "We will add it to the list of things I'm not allowed to mention if I want to keep the delicate boat of our marriage from capsizing."

"What the hell are you talking about?"

"I'm not allowed to even ask you about your mother. I'm not allowed to be a part of Leo's and Massimo's lives, men I consider family. And I've made my peace with all that. To be with you.

"I did them one small favor in return for the hundreds they've bestowed on me. I'm tired of you constantly questioning my loyalty."

He sat down on the bed, his head in his hands, a deep sigh rolling out of him. He looked as though he had the weight of the world on his shoulders. And maybe he had carried it all this time. But things were different now. Changing.

And Alex was damned if she'd let him shoulder this alone anymore.

"Give me a chance to explain, V."

"Why did you tell them?"

"Because they deserved to know that their father's actions still had serious consequences, such far-reaching potential for destruction. Because I wanted to show you that you don't have to carry this burden alone. The burden of righting all the wrongs Silvio did, of bringing justice to those who can't fight for themselves."

He pulled her to him then, with a half-swallowed growl that sounded like a feral animal fighting for its last breath, and her heart thudded painfully in her breast. His face buried in her chest, his arms clung around her waist.

She sank her fingers into his crisp hair. "Leo's about to become a father to two children. Imagine you and I having a child and someone out there wishing our family so much ill will as these people do…" She shuddered and his arms tightened around her.

"How is it that you keep unraveling me?" he asked.

She looked down and their eyes held. Fused with a connection that they hadn't been able to deny from that first moment. The connection he wanted but not the force of emotion that strengthened it. The compromise and change it constantly asked of him, even the sacrifice it sometimes demanded.

"I've already decided not to demolish the villa," he said, and the small flicker of hope turned into a full-blown flame in her body. "But—"

She didn't want to hear any more. Pressing her finger to his mouth, she shimmied out of the flimsy robe and stood naked in front of him. Their kiss was a conflagration of desire and hope and such emotion that her heart stuttered in her chest.

His mouth was hard, rough; his kiss desperate, intense, a hard taking instead of giving. A demand for everything she could give.

She could sense it in the hunger in his eyes. In the tense jut of his muscles. But this wasn't pure lust. This was him reaching out to her when the ground was shifting beneath him. He palmed her breasts, pinched her nipples as she pulled his shirt out of his trousers with a fervent need. Tugged the zipper down and sneaked her hand inside.

His hips thrust against her hand as she molded the hard length of him. "I want to be inside you, now, *bella*."

"Yes, please," she whispered back. "Now."

Their mouths clung to each other as he shucked off the rest of his clothes.

A soft moan left her mouth as her body settled against his—breast to chest, thigh to thigh, his abdominal muscles a hard slab of heat against hers. Wrapping her legs around him, she threw her head back and moaned.

And then he was inside her, her back against the wall, her front a delicious slide against all his muscles. But he didn't move inside her. Just held her like that, where she could feel him all over her body. His heart thudding against hers.

"We will live in that house, *bella*. You, me, our family. That's the only way I won't ruin it."

"But—"

"My wedding gift to you, *cara mia*. It's your choice now."

But he didn't wait for her answer. He started moving and her eyes rolled back.

Another searing kiss that swallowed not only her protest but her very breath. But she had no real protest anyway. She would take the little he gave her. He had changed for her. Because of her.

One corded arm rested near her head as he pulled out with a grunt and thrust back in. His teeth in the juncture of her neck kept that small edge to the waves of sensation building inside her, amplifying their sweetness in contrast.

With each upward jerk of his hips, she was pushed up and against the wall. With each wicked twist of his hips, sensation swelled and swirled downward. His face was savage in his utter lack of control. But even in the wake of such hunger, he didn't forget about her. Every upward thrust rubbed her in just the right place. When he tugged her nipple into his mouth, Alex fragmented. And he followed.

Alex held him as he released into her with a feral growl.

The words rose to her lips, desperate to be set free. The emotion in her chest taking the space of everything else. Rumbling like a volcano about to explode.

Instead, Alex buried her own teeth in the taut curve of his shoulder and swallowed away the words. Words never meant much to her anyway.

He'd shown her in actions that he cared about her. Which gave her hope. And hope was more than enough right now.

It was a long time later, tucked into the crook of his arm, his body a warm embrace, that Alex said, "What did Leo and Massimo do that angered Antonio so much? You never told me."

She'd expected him to shut her down; instead he only sighed. The darkness helped, she knew. And it wasn't just that. She'd seen something in him earlier. A shift. A change. A vulnerability that made her throat ache. And everything in her wanted to embrace that hope. Cling to it like she'd never done anything else before.

His fingers spread over her throat, his words a harsh whisper in the silence. "They offered financial reparation to the families of those that were cheated, crushed by their father. Training, jobs, even stock options in BFI."

Alex's heart lightened. Her trust in them was once again totally vindicated. She tempered her joy, sensing the tension in his powerful body. "But this is good, isn't it?"

"Is it? They're buying forgiveness, *cara*, don't you see?" But there was no heat in his tone. Resignation. Even acceptance maybe, she thought with more hope burgeoning inside her chest. "Which is why Antonio refused to even touch anything they offered."

"They don't need forgiveness. They didn't even need to redress Silvio's sins. But they've done it because they have a strong sense of right and wrong." She held his gaze in the darkness, saw the flicker of anger tamp down. He looked away, but Alex caught his expression before that. And suddenly she got it. "You're shocked that they're not the monsters you believed them to be for so long. That they're truly honorable men. Good men. It's not too late, V. If you just stretch your—"

"Not this again, Alessandra," he cut in harshly.

"Didn't this whole thing start as helping those who couldn't help themselves? To right the wrongs that Silvio Brunetti perpetrated? Or does it matter more that you have to be their savior than that they be saved at all?"

Vincenzo stilled, Alessandra's words piercing him like a thousand little cuts, stripping away the anger and bitterness he'd nursed for so many years. He wanted to yell at her to stop, to leave him be. To cease digging into him. Because if she stripped him bare of his need for revenge, his thirst for justice, if she took away this fight that had consumed his adult life, what would she find?

If he gave up his quest to take over BFI, what was left in him? Of him?

He'd meticulously planned and executed each and every move, and there was no way back from that. No way out from the hole he'd buried his heart in.

If he stopped now, how could he face the kind of man he'd become? How could he come back from that? How could he open himself up, make himself completely vulnerable at this late stage?

Because that anger, and bitterness, his ambition and his quest for revenge, he was fast realizing were his armor. Armor against hope and vulnerability.

Armor against the crippling knowledge that he had become a man who didn't deserve the woman lying next to him.

Armor against turning into a man who desperately needed love but didn't know how to give or receive it.

CHAPTER ELEVEN

ALEX STOOD IN front of the marble vanity a few days after they'd arrived back from New York and stared at her naked body in the steam fogged mirror. Something was different. Strange. She ran her fingers over her belly, and then up toward her breasts and cupped them. They felt achy and heavy, just as her entire body did.

Was all the stress of the past few months finally catching up with her? Or was it something else entirely?

No. It couldn't be. She had been on the pill the entire time—even before she'd met Vincenzo in Bali. After those first few nights together, after they'd been married, they'd stopped using condoms.

She wished she could talk to someone. But Greta was gone. As were the rest of them. All of them. This villa was their home now. Hers and Vincenzo's.

And it would be Charlie's, once they'd won custody of him.

And, she was suddenly quite sure, it would be this baby's too.

She kept her palm on her belly, waiting for panic to set in. For the mother of all freak-outs.

It didn't come.

Instead, total calm filled her. Even as she was aware that, right at this moment, Vincenzo and Leo and Massimo and Greta were all at the BFI towers in Milan for an emergency board meeting that Vincenzo had called.

He was almost there at the finish line, she knew.

There would be a vote of no confidence against Leo, and she also knew that Vincenzo had control of the majority. That he would be voted CEO of Brunetti Finances Inc. any minute now.

For all that she hated to see Greta and Leo and Massimo leave this villa, this war Vincenzo had waged for so long would finally be done with now. And they didn't hate her, or him.

Vincenzo would have achieved his goal. He would be finished. And their life could begin. Once they were a family, once he had everything he wanted—Charlie and her and this baby, maybe he would even finally open himself up to understanding what the Brunettis meant to her.

If Leo and Massimo could let his actions go, couldn't Vincenzo be convinced to let the past go? If he could do that, he would be free. His heart would be free.

Alex smiled at her reflection. Anything was possible. And that hope was a powerful thing inside her.

Vincenzo went in search of his wife upstairs in the villa, a sense of inexplicable dread descending on him.

All of Milan's financial society was downstairs and out in the gardens, celebrating his victory. Lauding him. Courting his favor. Already catering to him.

He had soundly defeated Leonardo at the vote of no confidence. But of course, he would have enjoyed it so much more if Alex hadn't disappeared after barely showing her face. Both when he'd returned from the board meeting earlier and tonight at the party.

Any irritation he felt died down as he walked into the terrace and found her looking out at the garden and the lake. The magnificent view did nothing to dim her beauty.

She turned and he drank her in. The soft pink evening gown draped over her curves, highlighting the lithe body.

Her beautiful hair flew in the breeze, the diamond choker he'd bought her yesterday glittering at her neck.

And yet, one look at her pinched face told him that for all her standing by him as the perfect wife, she was less than happy.

No, she was miserable.

But it wasn't just physical exhaustion. The vitality that had struck him like lightning on their first meeting, the joy he'd seen on the day of their impromptu wedding was nowhere to be seen.

Guilt nagged at him like a persistently sharp shard of glass stuck in his skin. He hated having to admit that he was responsible for that haunted look in her eyes. For the first time in his life, he had an emotional obligation to another person and he was fast failing in keeping it.

"Are you happy now?" she asked.

He shrugged, wary of the bite to her tone. "Alessandra, I want to celebrate tonight. I want to take you to bed, *bella*. Not have a down-and-dirty fight. Not again."

She nodded, and it was as if there was a brittle wall around her. "I wanted to celebrate your victory with you tonight too. I even thought of it as freedom, you know. Freedom from the shackles you've bound yourself with. Freedom from the past.

"So that you could be mine. Only mine."

"I am yours, *bella*. I've told you that before."

"Only under your conditions, V. I see that now. And still, I was happy. For you. I wanted to go to bed with you, to be held by you while I told you the most glorious news that I've been dying to share all day. I wanted to…" A silent tear rolled down her cheek. "I wanted so much. Everything. It was all in my grasp."

He walked to her, that sense of dread building inside his chest, choking off his breath. "Alessandra, you knew this was going to happen, *bella*."

"I knew it. I begged Leo and Massimo to forgive you. I told them about your mother, about how much you've been through. I made my peace with the fact that you're who you are and that despite it all I… I loved you. So much, V. I love you more than anything else in the world. And that's why this hurts so much." She rubbed a hand over her chest and gasped for a breath. "It feels like my heart is breaking all over again."

Her words were like punches coming at him, stealing his breath. She loved him. *Cristo*, she loved him. It rang through his body like a peal of painful truth. Like the ground was shifting beneath him and he didn't know what to grasp for an anchor.

"Alessandra—"

She jerked away from him. "I always thought I would be able to save Leo and Massimo and Greta from you. I thought… But they didn't need saving. Even after you took the CEO position from Leonardo, even after you took this house, their home from them, they're fine. You're the one who's lost everything that matters. You're the one who needs saving."

He felt as if she'd slapped him. "I don't need saving."

She went on, as if he hadn't spoken. "But that's the most important thing I've learned in the last few months.

"No one else can save us, can they? However much I want to, I can't save you. From yourself of all things. We have to do it ourselves. We have to want to be saved. The only hope is that someone we love, who loves us, will stand by us while we do it.

"Someone who believes in us even when we don't. When we're so blinded by fear that…we can't see a way forward."

She clasped his cheek, tears pouring down her own. "You did that for me. You made me realize I should stay and fight. You made me…" She buried her face in his throat, and her tears drenched him. Seared his bare skin. The weight of her love for him burned him.

He wanted to pull her close and hold her. But he couldn't. Not when he himself felt as if he were drowning. "Alessandra, just tell me what's happened. Tell me—"

"You know, you were right when you said I didn't understand the magnitude of the consequences Greta wreaked on you that day. I didn't truly comprehend the depth of pain you must have felt every time you saw her. To have all this and not even be able to tell your mother that…"

"Alessandra! You knew all this when you made your choice, *bella*. What has changed?"

She tilted her head up, her gaze crystal clear. Her palm went to her belly and she held it there. "Discovering that I'm pregnant."

Another punch. Another blinding hit. Vincenzo couldn't speak for several seconds. His gaze went to her hand on her belly and to her eyes that glowed with conviction. "You're… pregnant?" He pushed his hand through his hair. "When—"

"Yeah. Can you believe it? I was all set to freak out. But when I saw the test come back positive… I was actually giddy. You and I created this life. I thought this was the universe's way of giving me what I wanted. A family. A child to love created with the man I adore. I had everything I wanted."

"Alex, if this is good news, why are you crying?"

"I was overjoyed. I decided magnanimously that I would forgive Greta for what she'd done to you. I…called her. I could tell something was seriously wrong and I made her tell me how you threatened her and that my happiness was the price she had to pay. Her love for me and my love for you was your currency. Do you even realize how wrong that is? Do you—?"

"Alessandra, listen to me. Today's win at BFI—"

"No! I've listened to you enough. I can't do it anymore,

V. You know why?" She wiped her cheeks angrily. "Because the last shred of hope I had that we could salvage this marriage is gone. Whatever you say now, you can't bring it back." Fury shone in her beautiful eyes, radiated from her body.

"You promised me you'd never use me against them. You said you'd keep me out of this infernal war you've been waging and you broke your word. You used Leo's and Massimo's guilt for what other people did to you to drive them out of here.

"You think love is a weakness to be exploited… You will never be released from this poison. You will never open yourself to love. It's too late. The poison has already festered inside you for far too long.

"And while that might have been okay for me, it's not okay for this child. It's not okay for Charlie."

"So you're giving up on us again?"

"No, I'm refusing to accept anything less than what I deserve. I deserve to be with a man who will at least acknowledge that love is important. This child and Charlie deserve to grow up with a father who has the capacity to love them."

He reared back, stung. "I will love our child."

"Will you? Will you tell him or her about what you did to your brothers? Will you speak about the cousins it has? What is the legacy you're creating for this child, V? One of love or one of hatred and revenge?"

"Don't do this, Alessandra," he said, and a part of Alex melted at the desperation she heard in his voice.

She was the one breaking apart and he looked equally ravaged. "So you're ready to destroy everything you wanted? You're giving up on Charlie too?"

"No, I'm not. I will never give up on Charlie. And I will gain custody of him because you will help me do that, V. This relationship is over between us but not in the eyes of the world. Not until I have Charlie, safe with me. You owe me this. I'm hoping you have enough honor left in your body to see that promise through at least.

"As for raising him alone, I do have a family. Leo and Massimo will support me if I need help. Charlie already has a family that will love him, through me."

"And this child? Our child?"

"I will love our child too. Fiercely. You made me see that.

"I will take on anyone and anything in the world to protect our baby. Including you. But then, you're not the kind of man that would separate a mother from her child, are you? I won't lose sleep over that worry, at least."

"You're walking out on me and yet you still have such faith in me, *bella*?"

"I do. Because you're only punishing yourself, V. I see you watch Leo and Massimo with such an ache in your eyes. You can't understand the depth of Greta's love for me. Your support network for close to two decades has been people who were invested in seeing you destroy the Brunettis.

"You have made an island of yourself.

"But I can't bear to see you in pain. I can't bear to see the loneliness in your eyes, the need for connection. I refuse to stand here and watch it eat away at you, month after month, year after year. I refuse to let the corrosive shadow of your grief and guilt consume me and two more innocent lives.

"You wanted this empire, V. Well, you got it. But you haven't got me."

Anger raged in his eyes, and a stillness came over him. "At least don't lie to me that you love me, *bella*."

"I do love you. With all my heart. I truly understand what it means to love someone so much that all you want is their happiness. Their well-being. But it's not a weakness, V. Despite all the pain in my heart, I can't call it that."

And with that, she walked away from him, head held high. Out of his life.

Leaving him standing empty-handed on the grounds of the very empire he'd built.

Alessandra's words haunted Vincenzo as he walked around the hallowed halls of his ancestors, with a bottle of Leonardo's fine Scotch hanging from his fingers.

For the first time in his life he was filthy drunk, his self-control shot to hell. Apparently, there were a lot of those happening currently—these first times in his life.

He walked from room to room—he couldn't bear to be in the bedroom he had shared with her for more than a few minutes. He walked from the vast kitchen that had rung with laughter only last week when Natalie's younger brother had visited and Neha had screamed that the babies were playing soccer in her belly to the conservatory, where every piece of silk reminded him of his wife's skin; to the lounge that housed the ancient piano; to the arched hallway with portraits of his ancestors hanging there, looking down upon him with, it seemed, approval.

All my life, our father constantly told me that I wasn't good enough to belong with them. That I would never be good enough. But then it took Natalie to make me see that it was okay to not belong with those monsters.

Massimo had told him that during one of their midnight chats weeks ago, those long nights where more than once he'd found himself wandering the villa and run into his younger brother doing the same thing.

Just thinking of the brilliant tech genius as his younger brother, as the man who had Natalie's hard-won loyalty and love, sat like a boulder in Vincenzo's throat, jammed in there to force him to acknowledge the connection, the affection he had developed for the irreverent genius, despite himself.

What did it say that when Vincenzo looked at those same faces of Brunetti ancestors, he saw their approval? Was he truly Silvio Brunetti's legacy then—a legacy of cruelty and hatred and destruction?

He had hated this family for so long. He had used that hatred to propel himself to incredible heights. He'd thought there would be victory once he had achieved his ambition, his revenge.

Suddenly, the consuming force of his life was gone and he felt as empty as this damned house.

He even walked to the state-of-the-art tech lab that had belonged to Massimo. The underground lab that had once been a wine cellar, Alessandra had told him with a twinkle in her eyes.

She'd been happy here and he had taken it away.

He punched in the entry password and walked around the now-empty lab. Then he made the trek to the greenhouse that Leonardo had renovated for himself.

The greenhouse, he'd learned, had once belonged to Leonardo's mother. Silvio Brunetti's first wife—a woman who had run away in the dark of the night, leaving her five-year-old son with the monster, the very monster she had run from.

The damp air inside the greenhouse was a warm blast against his chilled skin as he walked around, touching the parts here and there, imagining Leonardo and his very pregnant wife, Neha, in here, making plans for their children.

And now because of him, this was empty too.

Leonardo had given up ownership of this house, a real estate asset, two centuries of legacy that should have gone to his children, to Vincenzo far too easily.

He slammed the door of the greenhouse behind him and walked up the pathway back to the house. He had no idea how many times he'd made that trip recently—a sort of pilgrimage from the villa to the laboratory to the greenhouse to the conservatory, and then back around again.

Everywhere he looked he saw Alessandra laughing, crying, kissing him, teasing Massimo, hugging Leonardo.

He felt like a forlorn ghost, a cursed specter, haunting these halls, the very hallowed halls he had once wanted to belong to. He had everything he had ever wanted.

And yet he had lost the one thing he desperately needed. The one thing he couldn't live without—Alessandra's love, her laughter, her smiles, her kisses, her tears, her joyful presence.

He hated admitting it, but there it was.

All his life he had been alone, so he shouldn't have minded this so much. But this loneliness was different. This was deeper, harder, felt in a place he hadn't known existed within him. Felt by a different man. A man who should've stopped long ago, but hadn't because then he'd have had to face what he'd become. How empty he was inside.

And he stood in that place of emptiness now anyway.

The sound of footsteps had him prowling into the lounge, his heart thudding so hard in his chest that its beat roared in his ears. Hope oozed out of his every pore, coating him with a layer of desperation so thick and rabid that he couldn't shake it off. It was unlike anything he'd ever felt, almost felling him to his knees.

The moon outside painted two dark silhouettes through the open archway. He blinked as the crystal chandelier overhead burst into life, throwing dazzlingly painful light over the room. The black-and-white-checkered marble swam in front of his eyes, and he instinctively reached for the grand piano to steady himself.

He looked up then and cursed out loud.

Massimo burst out laughing. Leonardo remained serious, but there was a twitch to his mouth that Vincenzo wanted to rip off with his bare hands.

"What the hell do you two want?" he demanded, straightening.

"We came to check on you," Massimo said. He took in Vincenzo's disheveled state with a distinctly obvious grin. "I have to admit, Leo. I'd hoped to find him like this. This almost makes up for everything he did to us. Almost."

Vincenzo let out another curse. "Get out! Get out of my house!"

Leonardo reached him, a sneer curling his mouth into a twist. And finally, Vincenzo could no longer deny the resemblance between himself and this man… This man who he had no doubt now would have made a spectacular older brother. A role model. A protector. "My wife is about to give birth any moment! To twins, you ungrateful bastard! And here I am in the middle of the night, checking up on you because she asked us to."

Massimo laughed again, and both he and Leo cursed him soundly. "Our older brother, as you can tell, is quite nervous. Everything is out of his control with Neha and the babies and it's driving him crazy. And he's driving her crazy." Leo growled. "Which is why she begged me to take him on this midnight run," Massimo finished. "I left Natalie behind because if she's here, she won't let Leo beat some sense into you."

Vincenzo rubbed his head, trying to figure out the puzzle of what they meant, who they were talking about. Even the threat of Leo's fists couldn't distract him from trying to figure it out. "Wait, who asked you to check up on me? You're not talking about Neha, are you?"

"Your bloody wife, who else?" Leo roared. "The woman whose heart you so thoroughly broke. The woman you don't deserve."

"She walked out on me," Vincenzo offered in a lame, pathetic voice. "And you're right. I don't deserve her. Still she gave me a chance to redeem myself. And I destroyed that chance. I…drove her away. I…killed whatever she felt for me with my own hands."

Whatever he'd been about to say died on Massimo's shocked lips.

His knees finally gave out, and Vincenzo slid to the floor. He buried his head in his hands. *Cristo*, what had he done? What was this cursed villa, the blasted company, even this world, to him, without her? He looked up, fear unlike anything he'd ever known clamping his belly tight. "I…I won everything and lost everything all in one fell swoop."

Both men knelt on either side of him. And he felt shame and vulnerability and something else lodge in his throat, cutting off his breath. "Why are you here after I drove you out of your own home?"

"We can't imagine what you've endured for so long. What it feels like to see your mother and not have her see you in return. But actions can be rectified, V," Massimo said kindly, using the abbreviation only *she* used for him. "You can still prove that Alex's faith in you was not misplaced."

"And because we've each been here," Leo added. "In this place of destruction. Standing on a pile of ashes that we created with our own actions. Not our father's actions, Vincenzo." It was the first time Leo had said his name. "Not Greta's. Ours. You're the one who's letting the woman who loves you go."

Vincenzo pushed himself off the floor.

"Go to her, but only if you think you can do right by her. Only if…" Leo's tone edged into that warning zone again.

"Alex deserves the best a man can give," Vincenzo added, and both men nodded.

"We have to want to be saved. The only hope is that someone we love, who loves us, will stand by us while we do it."

She'd been right. So right. Vincenzo hoped with every

cell in him that she would still stand by him. That he was worthy of that.

"Now, I would suggest a grand gesture of some sort," Massimo added, clapping him on the back.

Vincenzo rubbed his eyes and stared at the two men whose forgiveness he still needed to beg. But not yet. Not now. "*Cristo*, if this is the kind of psychobabble that Alessandra thinks I miss out on by not being one of you, then I shall gladly tell her how wrong she is. I…don't need a couple of Brunetti bastards to tell me I messed up. Royally."

"Ha! We came to tell you that you chose a woman who will forgive you almost anything. If you grovel hard enough, V."

Leo stood up. "Massimo has enough experience with that if you want some guidance."

Vincenzo looked at them. "This is not easy for me. I've never asked anyone for anything in my entire life. I have never—" He stopped and swallowed. "Whatever I have to say, she deserves to hear it first."

CHAPTER TWELVE

IT WAS PANIC.

It was sheer, unadulterated panic that sat like a boulder in his chest, that crawled up his throat like nausea at regular intervals, which had made him lose his head. Which had made him chase her halfway around the world—the wrong way.

Of course, she hadn't been in New York. Nor in Milan. Nor in Beijing sourcing fabric.

She was at the place where it had all started. Where, by some stroke of fate, he'd tangled with the woman who would end up becoming his saving grace.

The lush greenery surrounding the small village of Ubud hit Vincenzo with an onslaught of memories as he walked through the villa they had stayed in the last time to the private beach area behind it.

He found her sitting on the massive deck, a glass of water on the table next to her and a paperback on her stomach.

She was sleeping. But not peacefully. Even from the length of the deck, he could see her eyelids fluttering. Her body tensing up.

Guilt raked its fingers through him.

He made his way to her softly, loath to disturb her rest. He was about to sit down when she startled awake.

Her golden-brown eyes found him, only half-awake.

"Hello, Princess."

"V…?"

She rubbed her eyes, an innocent action that made his

chest ache. When she realized he wasn't a figment of her imagination, she sat up. And her mouth took on the stiff slant he hated.

"You ran away again, *bella*," he said, finding that his voice was scratchy. As if he hadn't used it in months.

"But I told you I was leaving this time," she said in a low voice. Her chin lifted. "What are you doing here, V? I already told you the hearing for Charlie's custody is in New York in two weeks."

"I thought I would accompany you there."

"I appreciate the consideration but I don't need it." The silence bore down upon them. He saw her swallow, as if she was bracing herself. "This polite courtesy needn't be extended when it's just the two of us. Hopefully, it will all be over soon. I'll get custody of Charlie and we don't need to see each other again."

"*Cristo*, Alex! Don't talk to me as if I'm a stranger."

"I'm not. I just… I need to be strong. I can't keep seeing you and stay sane."

He nodded, that strange fear swallowing away the one thing he needed to say. Instead he said, "How are you feeling?"

"Good. I… I have morning sickness, except it's all the time. Like morning, noon and night. I…but apparently, it's normal. For some people."

"Alessandra—"

"But I'm lonely, you know." She rubbed her chest as if she could dislodge that ache. "I miss Greta and Leo and Massimo. And Natalie. And Neha and the babies. Did you know she had the babies?"

"*Si,*" he said, smiling despite the pain in his throat. "They are…healthy and thriving. They are naming them Maya and Matteo. The girl child is especially beautiful, just like her mother—"

"Wait, you went to see them?"

"*Si*. I… I asked Leo if I could and he said yes."

Her eyes widened. "Oh." She looked away, but not before he saw the flash of hope. But when she looked back at him, her eyes were full of a wariness that was like a knife to his chest. "Why?"

He considered answers and discarded them, incredibly nervous for the first time in his life. "I went because I… I knew you would appreciate hearing firsthand how they're doing. But I also went—" he swallowed "—because that bastard Massimo told me he was going to be the fun uncle they adored and I couldn't have that." The words kept coming like a torrent, unchecked. Unabashed. "But then I also thought of what you said. How they're my niece and nephew and how they'd be our child's cousins and I realized that I wanted all that for our child.

"I don't want our child to grow up all alone. Like I did.

"I want him or her to be part of a big family. A clan. A dynasty."

Tears poured out of his beautiful wife's eyes. A sound, like the combination of a sob and a moan, came hurtling out of her mouth. Vincenzo went to his knees in front of her. And buried his face in her belly. "*Ti amo*, Alessandra. With all my heart. Without you, there's nothing in my world, *cara*."

"V, if this is a game again—"

"It is not, *bella*. I don't think it ever was a game to me. You felled me from the first moment I met you, Princess. I just didn't realize exactly what that meant to me all this time."

He raised his head, his breath suspended at the love he saw blazing in her eyes. It was almost unbearable, the strength and depth of emotion she clearly felt for him. It shook him to his core that there might come a day when she wouldn't look at him like that. That she might leave again, another day.

But he couldn't think like that. He couldn't doubt her love or his. He couldn't keep looking at his past actions and ruin his future.

"If I tell you something, will you believe me?"

She nodded warily.

"I never used Greta's vote against Leo at the last board meeting." He pressed his palm against her mouth. "I know that that's not much solace. I'd already threatened to use her love for you, your happiness against them, and that itself was unforgivable.

"But that same day, I also talked to Antonio, and something he said made me realize it was he who leaked my relationship to the Brunettis to the press all those months ago. He made a calculated risk that I would be able to recover any lost ground, but his primary goal was for me to leave you and carry on with my plans for vengeance, regardless of how much it would hurt me.

"And I realized how much hatred he has in him. In him, I saw my future, *bella*, the companionship of loneliness and hatred instead of family and love. I had already begun questioning everything I had done against my own brothers.

"But to turn away from my path completely, it terrified me. It meant I had to face what sort of a man I had become. It meant…facing the fact that I'm not worthy of you."

"But I never wanted some perfect man, V. I wanted you. I loved you despite everything you'd done."

"Forgive me, *bella*, for not seeing that before. Do you know, I wake up in the middle of the night with the most horrible nightmare now?"

She frowned. "What do you dream of?"

"That I didn't follow you here that first time. That for some reason or the other, I changed my mind about coming to Bali. That I never met you until I had already ruined everything. My own future with both my hands. That I never got the chance for you to love me.

"And I wake up, thrashing, the sheets cold around me. My chest the coldest of all.

"I reach for you and you're not there.

"You saved me, *bella*. From myself.

"And I will love you all my life for it."

She was sobbing again, as if her heart was breaking, and Vincenzo folded her into his arms. He settled into the lounger with her in his lap, crooning to her, kissing her temple. Rocking her. Cursing himself for causing her this much pain.

"Every night I went to bed, hoping that you'd come the next day. Walking away from you was like ripping out my own heart and I couldn't do it again, V."

"Shh...*tesoro*. You will never have to leave me again. Never, bella. Never will I doubt your love for me. Never will I make you doubt mine for you."

She kissed him, and Vincenzo felt as if he was born again. He became a different man in her kiss, in her embrace. "When you're ready, we will fly to New York and see Charlie. And then we'll take him back to the villa, to meet the rest of our family."

"Really?" she said, looking at him like he was a hero.

And for the first time in his life, Vincenzo felt as if he was, if not exactly a hero, at least not a villain.

"I have tried to return the villa to Leo and Massimo. In fact, I begged them to take it back, to come back home, and I think Massimo in particular enjoyed it. He kept urging Leo to torment me a little more, and Natalie kept yelling at him to leave me alone.

"After all these years, she still has faith in me. She threw herself behind me without a moment's thought." He looked away.

Fingers in his hair, Alex tugged his head back around until he looked into her eyes. "Because she loves you, V. Don't you get it? She's already seen you at your worst and she still loves you. That kind of love…it doesn't go away overnight."

He kissed her deep and hard. "I'm finally beginning to understand that, Princess."

"What happened then?"

"Leonardo won't take it back. He's having another villa built to his own design and he wants to live there with Neha and the babies and her mother. And Massimo and Natalie said the Brunetti villa is too big for them."

"What about BFI?"

He swallowed, shame filling up his throat. "Leo… doesn't want the CEO chair back either. He said that he's carried the mantle of the Brunetti legacy, of BFI's weight, for too many years. He'll still work for the company, with me, but not as the CEO. I asked Massimo if he wanted it, and he backed away as if it was the very devil. He said he was happier running BCS, that the bureaucratic nonsense wasn't for him and keeping the jackals on the board happy should be punishment enough for me."

"Are you okay with that?" she asked him perceptively.

Vincenzo shrugged. "Only if you are, *bella*. I never want you to think that BFI or the villa or anything else is more important to me than you are."

"I won't, V. I never thought you were power hungry even before, and I don't now."

"So the villa is ours, but only if you want it. Only if you'll be happy living there."

"And Greta? Can I ask her to live with us, V?"

"Is this another test, *bella*? Have I crushed your faith in me so badly?"

She cupped his cheek. "No, not at all. You know when I pushed her to tell me what you'd threatened to do, she… she broke down into tears. She…said she'd hated having to tell me what you did. She said, for all the wrongs you'd done me, she was sure you did love me. In your own Brunetti way, she added. As if that pigheaded stubbornness was something to be proud of."

He smiled as Alex pulled him close and kissed him. "You both need time to heal, V. And it's a damn big villa. We can even have your mother and her nurses live with us. In fact, I insist on it."

Vincenzo swallowed the tears that clogged his throat and looked into the eyes of the woman who'd given him everything. "It's not always easy to have her around."

She shrugged. "But family is never easy, right? I have always wanted a big family, and you and me and Charlie and this baby and Greta and your mother…this is our big family, V. This is everything I always wanted."

"You're my heart and soul, Princess, and my happiness lies wherever you are. With this baby. With Charlie. So, yes to everything, *bella*. To a life full of laughter and joy."

"Yes, please," she whispered against his mouth, and he felt as if his heart would burst out of his chest. For there was a strange giddy quality to it he had never known before. Love.

EPILOGUE

Eight months later

ALEX PRESSED HERSELF back with a deep moan as strong hands descended on her hips. As rock-hard thighs cradled hers. As the hardness she ached for nestled enticingly into her buttocks.

Vincenzo nuzzled into her neck, and she happily threw her head back, more than greedy for her husband's caresses after a busy three months.

"I've missed you, Princess," he murmured, his lips and teeth and tongue wreaking havoc on the sensitive spot on her neck, sending live wires of sensation straight to her sex.

"I've missed you too," Alex whispered, pressing her fingers onto his. And then pulling them up until his hands cradled her breasts. He immediately obliged, rolling her already tightening nipples into harder peaks with his clever fingers.

"Think we have a few minutes before we have to rescue Greta from down there?"

Alex looked down at the front lawn, where Charlie was running around in circles, Vincenzo's mother kept darting looks at the little baby boy in the stroller, calling him Vincenzo, and Greta was very efficiently keeping an eye on the whole lot of them. "Greta doesn't need to be rescued at all. She soothes your fractious son, Luca, and your mother all at the same time with one magic word uttered in that commanding voice of hers. They both respond to her so well, V. It's really something to watch."

He didn't say it, but Alex felt the slight tension in his body when his mother ventured closer to their son's stroller. And his exhale of relief when she simply bent to pick up the pacifier their son had spat out and plonked it back into his mouth with a tenderness that made Alex's throat ache.

She turned around, determined to distract him. The kiss she took from him—a heated tangle of teeth and tongues—was nowhere near enough. The last eight months had been laughter and joy and pain and sometimes plain awkwardness as her reticent husband learned to embrace all the things that came with being part of a large family.

But not a day went by when he didn't let her know how much he loved her. Not a day went by when he didn't show how much their sons, Luca and Charlie, and Leo and Massimo meant to him.

How wrong she'd been to think him a frog. No, her husband was indeed a prince among men. For he had learned how to love when he'd never really known it for most of his life.

Keeping her arms around his neck, she kissed his jaw. "You don't have to worry about her, V. Greta and I took alternating turns watching her, not forgetting her nurse is always there too."

He nodded, his brow relaxing. "I just…it's a habit, that's all, *bella*."

"I know," Alex said, rubbing her nose against his. "How did your lunch with Antonio go? Is he coming around yet?"

Vincenzo shrugged. "I don't know. But I will not just abandon him, in spite of what he did."

"Of course you won't. Maybe you should invite him to lunch here next time. Don't you think he should meet the little monster that is your son?"

"Ah…so he's my son when he's a monster and yours

when he sleeps like an angel?" Amazement spiraled through Vincenzo. He knew that Antonio's intensity still made Alex a bit wary. But she was willing to try again for his sake. "You won't mind?"

"He's a part of your life, V. He was there for you before me. And like you said, he's an old man, settled in his bitterness. We can't expect him to come around just like that."

Vincenzo took her mouth in a hard kiss that still left him hungry. "*Ti amo, bella.* More and more every day." When he reached for the zipper on her dress, she slipped out of his embrace.

"I need you, Princess. Desperately," he said, unbuttoning his shirt.

"But we have only a few minutes before Leo and Neha and the babies and Massimo and Natalie descend upon us."

He caught her and stole another kiss. "I'm sure I can satisfy you in a few minutes, *bella.*"

Alex shook her head, all the while running her greedy palms over his hard, lean chest. "Ah…but I don't want quick satisfaction. I want a whole night of indulgence, V. I want…everything tonight."

Vincenzo groaned but nodded, anticipation building inside of him already. When she'd have run away, he caught her, lifted her in his arms and brought her to the chaise that looked over the window and settled on it with her in her arms.

"Then let me just hold you, *bella.* Before the boys or my mother or your stepmother or someone else demands your attention. Just let me have you for myself, *si?*"

She nodded and burrowed into him and only then did his heartbeat settle into a steady pace.

And Vincenzo sat there like that, with the woman he adored more and more each day, in his arms, his life sweeter and richer than anything he could have ever imagined.

* * * * *

COMING SOON!

We really hope you enjoyed reading this book.
If you're looking for more romance, be sure to
head to the shops when new books are
available on

Thursday 26th June

To see which titles are coming soon, please visit

millsandboon.co.uk/nextmonth

MILLS & BOON

Coming next month

REVELATIONS OF HIS RUNAWAY BRIDE
Kali Anthony

'This marriage is a sham.'

In some ways, he agreed with her. Yet here he stood, with a gold wedding band prickling on his finger. Thea still held her rings. He needed her to put them on. If she did, he'd won—for tonight.

'You're asking me to return you to the tender care of your father?' A man Christo suspected didn't have a sentimental, loving bone in his body.

Thea grabbed the back of a spindly chair, clutching it till her fingers blanched. 'I'm asking you to let me go.'

'No.'

Christo had heard whispers about Tito Lambros. He was reported to be cruel and vindictive. The bitter burn of loathing coursed like poison through his veins. That his father's negligence had allowed such a man to hold Christo's future in his hands…

There was a great deal he needed to learn about Thea's family—some of which he might be able to use. But that could wait. Now it was time to give her something to cling to. *Hope.*

'You'll come with me as my wife and we'll discuss the situation in which we find ourselves. That's my promise. But we're leaving now.'

She looked down at her clothes and back at him. Her liquid amber eyes glowed in the soft lights. 'I can't go dressed like this!'

No more delays. She glanced at the door again. He didn't want a scene. Her tantrums could occur at his home, where any witnesses would be paid to hold their silence.

'You look perfect,' he said, waving his hand in her direction. 'It shows a flair for the dramatic—which you've proved to have in abundance tonight. Our exit will be unforgettable.'

She seemed to compose herself. Thrust her chin high, all glorious defiance. 'But my hat... I told everyone about it. I can't disappoint them.'

'Life's full of disappointments. Tell them it wouldn't fit over your magnificent hair.'

Thea's lips twitched in a barely suppressed sneer, her eyes narrow and glacial. The look she threw him would have slayed a mere mortal. Luckily for the most part he felt barely human.

'Rings,' he said.

She jammed them carelessly on her finger. *Victory.* He held out the crook of his arm and she hesitated before slipping hers through it. All stiff and severe. But her body still fitted into his in a way which enticed him. Caused his heart to thrum, his blood to roar. Strange. Intoxicating. All Thea.

'Now, smile,' he said.

She plastered on a mocking grimace.

He leaned down and whispered in her ear. 'Like you mean it, *koukla mou.*'

'I'll smile when you say *that* like you mean it, Christo.'

And he laughed.

This second laugh was more practised. More familiar—like an old memory. But the warmth growing in his chest was real. Beyond all expectations, he was enjoying her. For his sanity, perhaps a little too much...

Continue reading
REVELATIONS OF HIS RUNAWAY BRIDE
Kali Anthony

Available next month
www.millsandboon.co.uk

LET'S TALK
Romance

For exclusive extracts, competitions
and special offers, find us online:

 facebook.com/millsandboon

🐦 @MillsandBoon

📷 @MillsandBoonUK

Get in touch on 01413 063232

For all the latest titles coming soon, visit
millsandboon.co.uk/nextmonth

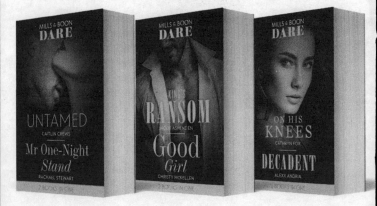